A sound of

Desperation.

The m [...]
grou [...]
and felt [...]
moonli [...]
mouth.

A twig broke beneath his shoe. The man's head snapped up and he sprang to his feet and rushed toward him. Nicholas saw the flash of a knife. He pushed the man away and felt the knife slice his arm.

Get to Olivia, make sure she's all right.

By Jaime Rush

TOUCHING DARKNESS
OUT OF THE DARKNESS
A PERFECT DARKNESS

Coming Soon

BURNING DARKNESS

JAIME RUSH

TOUCHING DARKNESS

AVON

An Imprint of HarperCollinsPublishers

AVON BOOKS
An Imprint of HarperCollins*Publishers*
10 East 53rd Street
New York, New York 10022-5299

Copyright © 2010 by Tina Wainscott
Burning Darkness copyright © 2011 by Tina Wainscott
ISBN 978-0-06-169037-2
www.avonromance.com

First Avon Books paperback printing: May 2010

Avon Trademark Reg. U.S. Pat. Off. and in Other Countries, Marca Registrada, Hecho en U.S.A.
HarperCollins® is a registered trademark of HarperCollins Publishers.

Printed in the U.S.A.

10 9 8 7 6 5 4 3 2 1

With love to my mom and dad,
Christine and Steve Ritter.
To all of the people who make
my North Carolina home special, including
John and Nanine; Mary Pat and Bill;
Herb and Gloria; Nancy and Bob;
Steve and Ann Marie;
Karen, Curtis, and family;
Mickey, Dina, Clare, and Grant;
Dave and Priscilla, Jayne and Mike;
Kay and Steve; Peg and Bill;
and Maureen and all my friends
in the workout class.

To My Readers:

If you've read my previous books, welcome back to the Offspring series! If you're picking up one of my books for the first time, this is the third book in the pulse-pounding series that started with A Perfect Darkness *and continued with* Out of the Darkness. *Fear not! You'll get caught right up with what's going on, like jumping on a moving train. And I predict that you'll want to go back and read the first two books so you can experience all the excitement you've missed.*

Cheers,
Jaime Rush

CHAPTER 1

Nicholas Braden was either about to learn a terrible truth or be killed. He rode on the back of a motorcycle through an area of Baltimore the likes of which he'd seen on *Cops*. The only certainty was that he had made a mondo mistake. He'd soon find out if that was trusting the man driving the bike and his comrades, known to him as the Rogues.

They didn't trust him.

Nicholas was the baton in a relay. He had gone to the designated place and met a gang-banger-type guy named Taze, who took him on a beat-up motorcycle to another guy on a bike. After a decoy handoff, the second guy delivered him to Rand Brandenburg.

Nicholas braced himself on the back of Rand's motorcycle seat as they drove to a dead area, with abandoned buildings and roads pocked with potholes, that gave him the creeps. They approached a building begging for demolition. Windows had been smashed out, leaving wicked shards of glass to catch the sunlight.

Nicholas got off the bike the moment Rand pulled behind a crumbling, concrete square that had once held garbage containers. He scrubbed his fingers through his thick, dark hair after removing the helmet and tapped his cross pendant twice, something he did whenever he embarked on a risky adventure.

Rand kicked down the stand while he kept an eye on Nicholas. Rand was solidly built, with dark blond hair and a silver bar through his eyebrow. Nicholas was pretty sure the lump under the back of his shirt was a gun, and that gave him a hell of a lot more than the creeps.

A car pulled up nearby, and a tall, lean, redhead got out and walked over. He knew her, too: Zoe Stoker. He'd been told these people were his enemies. Maybe they were, but his gut told him they weren't.

Rand nodded toward the entrance of the building. Nicholas's chest tightened the way it did when he was about to sink into the depths of a dark underwater cave with only a rope and an air line to link him with the world. No one knew he was here, though. There would be no one to send help if he signaled.

He followed Rand into the first apartment, Zoe behind him. The place was trashed, a dinged-up dining table the only piece of whole furniture left. The smell of mildew and urine permeated the debris on the floor.

Nicholas took only a few steps in before turning to face them. "Is all this really necessary?"

"Afraid so." Rand stepped closer. "The last time we tried to contact you, we nearly got our heads blown off. Call us a little paranoid, but it keeps us alive."

Nicholas's brows furrowed. "The shootout at my house. That was the second thing that got me thinking. Made me suspicious. Darkwell, Director for Science and Technology at the CIA, is my temporary boss. He told me to tell the police I had no idea why someone used my house, which is true. He said you guys—the Rogues, he calls you—were going to kill me. But he never gave me a good reason why."

"Because he wants you to fear us. And he sure as hell doesn't want us to tell you what's really going on or get you suspicious."

The shootout had happened a week and a half ago, and Nicholas still couldn't physically check his house to see what kind of damage it had sustained. Darkwell told him it was too dangerous; the Rogues could be watching. He promised to restore anything that had been damaged, but Nicholas had a lot of salvage items that couldn't be replaced. He had other ways to see his place, though, and it looked as though it had been cleaned up.

"What's really going on?" Nicholas asked.

Rand said, "You wanted to meet with us. Tell us what you know."

They had him there. He wanted answers; he would have to give some first. "A month ago, I was contracted by Darkwell to use my skills in a classified program called DARK MATTER. I've got an uncanny ability to find things."

Zoe tilted her head. "And you found out that your *skill* is actually a psychic ability."

"Yeah." That had blown his mind. "And that I inherited it from my father." Robert Braden, a man he had no memory of. Nicholas tested the strength of the table and leaned against it. "Darkwell promised to teach me to develop my skills so I could help locate hostages. I liked that idea."

He'd never found a live person before, only weathered remains for Bone Finders, an organization of volunteers who pooled their varied skills to give closure to families of missing persons.

The satisfaction he'd gotten from participating in those searches had instilled a desire to find live missing people, like abducted children. The possibility filled him with a deep sense of purpose. The one time he'd tried, though, he had nearly fallen into an abyss that kept him from doing the find.

The more emotions tied to the missing article, the more of a toll it took on him. Finding lost ships or equipment was simple. Finding a child's bones sucked out his energy for a week, though it was worth it. At the promise of learning to overcome that, Nicholas had signed on with Darkwell, getting a bonus for residing at the old psychiatric hospital where the program was being conducted.

"Plus he offered me a wad of money to do it, enough so when I'm done with my contract, I can start my own business. He taught me how to psychically see distant places—remote-view—explaining that it was an extension of my location skill. But before I can find any hostages, I'm ordered to find these bad-ass Rogues—all of you."

They were definitely badasses.

"You're supposed to be terrorists, but you seem like ordinary Americans like me." In the surveillance and driver's license pictures he'd seen of them, they looked like normal twentysomethings. "He told me he wanted to question you. Then you guys break into the hospital and"—he rubbed his hand over his face—"that was some hairy shit, but what bothered me as much as anything *you* did was seeing one of *our* guards holding two women at gunpoint. I knew he would have killed them."

It was more than hairy shit. It was everything he'd imagined his father going through in the final moments of his life.

"When it was over, Darkwell told me it was an unprovoked attack, but I overheard him talking about a prisoner being rescued. I had no idea there *were* prisoners. Darkwell denied it when I asked him. I knew he was lying. That was the first thing that had me suspicious. I haven't been comfortable since, but I've got another month on my contract." Nicholas hated lies. Black lies, white lies, it didn't matter; a lie was a lie. He also hated breaking obligations.

Rand stood rigid. "Two of us were being held at the asylum. Darkwell was using us as guinea pigs, shooting us up with drugs to see if they would boost our abilities."

A chill trickled down his spine. A nurse had taken his blood when he'd started, ostensibly to check his health. Taken, though. Nicholas had watched the blood going into the syringe; nothing had gone into his body.

What Rand said seemed too horrific to be true, but

Nicholas wasn't about to discount it. "Earlier this week, I was told to find the women again." One of those women was Eric Aruda's sister, Petra. By focusing on her, he could not only find her, but remote-view her. She usually sensed him and kicked him out. This time she'd talked to him:

"Whoever you are, you're on the wrong side! Darkwell is lying to you. You lost your mom or dad when you were young. Twenty years ago he or she was working for the government or part of some program that no one can tell you anything about. Your parent died because of that program, and now you're working for the man behind it. He only wants to use you. All we want is the truth. Don't you want to know why you have the psychic abilities you do? Don't you want to be on the right side?"

Being on the right side was important to him.

"When Petra told me I was on the wrong side, it jibed with my suspicions. Then this guy, Cheveyo, gets into my head, and even as freaky as some of this stuff is, that was mind blowing." Wicked wild. Like thoughts in his head, but not *his* thoughts.

In a psychic conversation, Cheveyo confirmed what Petra had told him: Darkwell was trouble. Cheveyo's father had worked with Nicholas's father and was also dead. Cheveyo explained he was not part of the Rogues but was acting as a go-between because he had the ability to communicate psychically. "Petra said something about the classified program my dad worked in twenty years ago. That he died because of it."

Zoe nodded. "Darkwell created a program that put people with psychic abilities to work finding hostages and terrorists."

"Darkwell mentioned the program but never said he'd created it."

Rand said, "It was his baby. He gave the subjects—our parents—something called the Booster, which enhanced their abilities . . . but messed up their heads. Ask your mother about it. Your dad probably started acting erratic, maybe got really, uh, let's just say he got pretty randy. Their mental states deteriorated, and one of the participants went on a shooting spree at the facility."

His dad . . . His dad and three others had died that day. The blood drained from Nicholas's face. He had spent his whole life imagining what his dad had gone through.

Rand continued. "The program got shut down. Within a year, all the participants were dead. We're the offspring of those participants. In fact, that's what they call us: Offspring. We inherited our parents' psychic abilities and the Booster. That's what made us so powerful. And that's why Darkwell wants us. What we want is the truth. About the program and the Booster."

Rand crossed his arms in front of his chest. "How many of you are working in the DARK MATTER program? We met with Jerryl Evrard, who pretended to be interested in what we had to say, then nearly took out Zoe."

Hell. "What did he do?"

Instead of looking more vulnerable at the memory, she straightened her shoulders in a defiant gesture. "Grabbed me, put a gun to my head, then jumped into the water with me."

"Jerryl." Nicholas shook his head. "He's a Marine. All he ever talks about is serving his country and killing people, like both are a privilege and pleasure. There are three of us. Fonda's the third, and she's tight with Jerryl. Little thing, but fierce."

Zoe leaned against the wall so she could face Nicholas. "What is Jerryl's psychic ability?"

"He remote-views, but I think he can do more than that. He and Darkwell spend a lot more time together than they do with me. They're coconspirators, both with that killer gleam in their eyes."

"Jerryl can mind-control."

Nicholas's eyebrows furrowed. "As in, getting into someone's head and making them do something against their will?"

Rand's expression hardened. "Exactly."

"And I thought this Cheveyo guy getting into my head was freaky enough."

Zoe narrowed her eyes. "Were you the one who found me in Key West?"

"That was me."

"Darkwell sent an assassin after me. And he's come after Rand and me twice."

"In an apartment in Baltimore. The two of you were, uh . . ." Nicholas's cheeks warmed. He'd been ordered to find Rand and had caught them in flagrante.

"Yeah," Rand said. "Talk about killing the afterglow."

Nicholas rubbed his mouth. "I'm sorry. I didn't know."

Zoe checked her watch. "And the thing at your house, that was a setup. Darkwell knew we were going to contact you—contact, not kill—and he put one of his thugs in there to pose as you. The goal was to take all of us out, no questions first."

Nicholas massaged his temples and closed his eyes for a second. It sounded crazy and paranoid and so government-conspiracies-and-spies and stuff. Yet he sensed the truth in it. "This confirms the bad feeling I've had about this for a while now." He looked at them. "This . . . Booster stuff in us . . ."

Rand said, "We don't know what it is. Our parents were told it was some kind of nutritional cocktail, but it was obviously more than that. And it's a good bet it could make *us* crazy, too."

Crazy? Like having nightmares about being burned to death? Like feeling outrageous fear at the sight of a fireplace or a candle? "Why is Darkwell out to kill you?"

Rand stuffed the tips of his fingers into his front jeans pockets. "He would have approached us the same way he did you, but we got suspicious and started digging. No way would we work for the dude who caused our parents to die. He can't take the chance that we'll expose him."

"Is that what you want to do?"

A shadow crossed Zoe's face. "We want to shut him down. He's hurt a lot of people, and he's going to keep on hurting them. Some will be terrorists. Others will just be people in his way. Like us."

Terrorists. That's what Darkwell said he'd be helping to find. Nicholas knew some of it wasn't pretty, some of it was classified, but he liked helping his country. Finally, after seeing all those news reports about bombings, 9/11, he could do something. So far he'd been mostly working on his ability to find living people. He'd been using that ability to find the Rogues.

Rand asked, "Where did Darkwell move the operation?"

Nicholas met their gazes. "Not until I understand more about what's going on. You're not going to storm the place, are you? Innocent people work there. How do I know you *are* the good guys?"

Zoe pushed away from the wall. "Find out for yourself. Ask about your dad, what he was doing before he died. Talk to Jerryl and find out what he's up to. Ask questions about what's really going on there. You already know Darkwell's not being straight with you. You decide who the good guys are. But be careful. Darkwell kills curious cats."

Rand handed him a cell phone. "We'll be in touch. It's set to vibrate. We'll call once, disconnect, then call back in thirty minutes. That'll give you time to get someplace where you can talk."

That was it? They weren't going to interrogate him? Try to force him to give up the new location?

Rand crossed his arms in front of his chest. "There's something you need to know. If you stay on Darkwell's side, you may not get out alive."

The seriousness in Rand's eyes made Nicholas's throat tighten. "You'd kill me?"

Rand nodded. "If you're the enemy, and you help him find us or set us up, we'll have to. Or you may get hit in the cross fire. This is a war between Darkwell and us. And like any war, people are going to get killed. We're going to make damned sure it's not one of us."

Zoe said, "But if you join us, you'll be a target like we are."

Either option sucked. He felt as though he were straddling an alligator.

Zoe walked toward the hallway. "We'd better get you back to your car. If Jerryl remote-views and sees you with us, you're toast. Unless you're a setup."

"I'm not." Nicholas met their hard glares. "Either you or Darkwell is lying. I'm going to find out which one." He shoved the phone into his pocket and followed Rand out of the building.

CHAPTER 2

Nicholas returned to the Darkwell family estate in Potomac, Maryland, his head buzzing with what Zoe and Rand had told him. It had been strange seeing faces that matched the pictures of people he'd been targeting, especially since they hadn't looked or acted like terrorists.

More importantly: Darkwell had lied about their intentions. If they'd gone to his house to kill him, why had they not taken him out today?

From the beginning, Darkwell hadn't lived up to his side of the agreement, making excuses and empty promises. Dishonesty was usually a deal breaker, but Nicholas understood that the government had secrets it couldn't share with the general public. This program was one of those secrets. But now . . . now he knew he was being lied to personally. He'd walk, screw the money, forget that he always saw a job through to the best of his ability. Before he could do that, though, he had to find out the truth. This went beyond him; it involved his father.

He waited until the armed guard opened the gate. The mansion was a hell of a lot better than that creepy hospital where the program had started. He parked his Nissan Frontier in the small parking area. The house was two stories, painted white, with columns flanking the grand entrance. Mahogany paneling and trim, a winding staircase, leather accents, marble floors, the smell of old wood and older money. He'd take his place in the Eastport section of Annapolis any day—three bedrooms, two bathrooms, and a nice little yard where he could work up a sweat mowing and trimming bushes.

He sprinted up the stairs that split midfloor to head to the right wing and the left wing, where the offices and his suite of rooms were. He spotted Olivia, Darkwell's assistant, in the hallway. Whenever he saw her, he felt an odd ping in his chest. She spent most of her days at CIA headquarters and the evenings here.

Her face, a perfect oval framed by long, brown hair, transformed into a smile when she saw him. She tamped it down, though, which he suspected had something to do with Darkwell's glower when he'd spotted them talking in the hallway the other day.

A spark ignited when she'd come to his room at the asylum with employment papers to sign. She'd perched on his small desk and told him a joke about two rabbits and a fox. Then Darkwell walked by, and she'd dropped to her feet, the enchanting smile and glow in her incredible hazel green eyes gone. Later, he told Nicholas there was a rule prohibiting staff/contractor relations.

Since then, the few times he and Olivia had been alone together, she'd dropped a flirty line but quickly retreated. It was clear by the fire in her eyes she hadn't wanted to, and he hadn't wanted her to, either.

Nicholas paused a few feet from her. "Can we talk? Alone?"

She ran her finger down the sensual spiral of one silver earring. "I, uh . . . maybe that's not such a good idea considering the rule that staff and contractors shouldn't be, uh, socializing."

"This is about work."

"Oh. Of course." Her face flushed in that sweet way that told him she had been sheltered as far as men were concerned, which intrigued him even more.

He leaned close, inhaling the faint scent of perfume that reminded him of cotton candy. His eyes held hers. "I'd love to *socialize* with you, but I don't want you to get into trouble."

Her mouth opened for a second before the word, "Oh," emerged.

"Where can we talk?"

She turned. "Come this way."

They passed Jerryl Evrard's room, where he and Fonda were noisily going at it, as usual. Hadn't Rand said the Booster made the subjects randy? Olivia's face flushed again as she looked everywhere but at him. Oh, yeah, he'd love to make her moan and cry out. He'd entertained the thought of hooking up during his time here if Olivia didn't want anything more than that herself. Getting involved in anything long-term was, unfortunately, out of the question. He'd dismissed the fling idea after her reaction to Darkwell. That didn't mean he couldn't fantasize about running his fingers through her hair, tugging it back to expose her neck . . .

He shook off the thought before he grew a full-bore hard-on.

At the end of the hallway, they walked into one of the rooms where he and Jerryl undertook their missions. The balcony had been enclosed as a sunroom, but Darkwell had installed a heavy curtain to block out all light. She pulled it open, and he was still looking at the way the sun burnished her hair with auburn highlights when she turned around, a look of both curiosity and anticipation on her face.

She was dressed much less conservatively than she did during the week, wearing tight yellow pants and a black shirt. It was unbuttoned just low enough to show the creamy skin of her collarbone and the edge of a red bra. In comparison, he felt slovenly in his centuries-old black T-shirt and black workout pants.

He placed his hand against the warm curved glass that

overlooked the courtyard and what he called the east wing, where Olivia stayed. "Darkwell signed me on to DARK MATTER with the promise that I would be locating hostages. So far all I've been doing is finding the Rogues. What do you know about them?"

A shadow crossed her face. "He hasn't told me much about them, either. I . . . I took care of one of them when he was at the asylum. I remember thinking he must have done something pretty bad to be there. You saw what the Rogues did when they broke in. They're ruthless."

He didn't even know he was going to reach out and touch the faint scar on the side of her temple where Eric Aruda, the most dangerous Rogue, had coldcocked her two weeks ago. Her eyes widened at the touch.

"He could have killed you."

"I know." Her voice quivered, and the shadow of violence still haunted her eyes. "Look what he did to one of our men."

His fury returned at the memory of blood running down her cheek, her stark fear. He wanted to teach Eric Aruda a lesson about assaulting innocent women, especially sweet, delicate, soft Olivia. His thumb rubbed her temple in slow circles. Her pupils dilated, and her mouth slackened. His eyes felt heavy as he looked at her mouth, pink and glistening, ready to be kissed.

What are you doing?

He dropped his hand. "No, I mean, he could have killed you. Easily. But he only knocked you out. They broke in to rescue their friends, not attack. Our guy was holding Eric's sister at gunpoint." Then he realized what she'd said. "So there *were* prisoners."

Now her face paled. "I wasn't supposed to tell anyone."

"I overheard Darkwell talking about prisoners right after it happened though he denied it when I asked. You only confirmed it. I don't like being lied to."

"We have to trust he's doing the right thing. He has his way, but he's a good man."

Nicholas narrowed his eyes. "You're not . . . involved with him, are you?" He did seem territorial about Olivia, and she acted reverential and obedient toward him.

A bark of laughter erupted from her mouth. "No. God, no. He's just . . . been my boss for a long time." She tilted her head. "Please don't let him know I told you about the prisoners."

He moved closer, his voice lowering. "Only if you"— *kiss me.* He cleared his throat—"tell me what's really going on here."

"I'm strictly administrative. All I know is Darkwell brought in three people with special skills to break up terrorist cells. You obviously have some kind of skill." She paused, as though to let him add what that skill was. When he didn't say, she continued. "The Rogues are one of those cells. They're trying to sabotage the program."

"Why?"

"I don't know."

"Why were they going to kill me?"

"Darkwell has your best interest in mind. If he thinks they're a danger to you, I'd believe him."

She definitely believed in the man. Maybe a little too much.

A man's voice stopped them both. "If you want answers, ask me."

They both jerked around to find Darkwell standing in the doorway. He'd opened the door so quietly, they hadn't heard him. His winged eyebrows gave him a menacing look when he narrowed his large, dark brown eyes.

Nicholas walked up to him, face-to-face. He had to be careful what he said so as not to give away that he'd talked to the Rogues. "Fine, answer my questions."

Darkwell gave Olivia a look, and she left. Only when she'd gone did he say, "Why were the Rogues out to kill you? Simply because you're on the good side. Having strong psychic abilities themselves, they found out about my program. They're antigovernment terrorists who want to impede our progress. You've been a tremendous help with stopping them. I know that's not what you signed on for, but you will be doing what you want soon. In fact, I'm getting information today on a contractor, father of four from Alabama, who's gone missing in Afghanistan. This is our first official chance to show everyone what we can do." The carrot. And then the sense of obligation. "I've invested a lot of my time and energy to enhance your skills."

"I don't like being kept in the dark, not when what I'm doing could cause someone to die. What's Jerryl doing, besides Fonda?"

Darkwell's mouth tilted up in a sardonic smile, his moustache stretching with it. "I'm not pleased with their association, but I'm less pleased about anything that might start between you and Olivia."

Nicholas hoped Darkwell hadn't heard their conversation about the prisoners. "You have nothing to worry about. She's made the policy clear, and I respect that."

"But you have doubts about my intentions."

"I overheard you talking about prisoners, but when I asked, you denied it."

"I thought it might make you uncomfortable, and, frankly, it didn't concern you. Either way, that's no longer a problem." His voice thickened on those words. "I'm going to ask you to trust me a little longer. For now, focus on the missing man."

Nicholas leaned against the back of a chair. "When you first approached me, you said you'd been impressed with my father's location skills."

"Yes, he was very talented."

"What was he doing when he died?"

"Why all these questions, Nicholas?"

Darkwell's eyes were as dark as the underwater caves Nicholas explored in his free time. And potentially just as dangerous.

"The more I get to know my skills, the more I want to know about his."

"He would be very proud of you." With two pats on Nicholas's shoulder, Darkwell turned and left.

He hadn't answered the question, and Nicholas intuitively knew not to press.

Darkwell kills curious cats.

According to the Rogues, Darkwell sent an assassin after Zoe Stoker. If that had succeeded, Nicholas would have indirectly been responsible for her death. The thought crackled like electricity in his chest.

He headed back down the hall, spotting Darkwell talking to Jerryl through a crack in the door. Nicholas strained to hear what they were saying, but Darkwell moved away and went into Olivia's office. A minute later, he emerged with a folder and headed to the end of the hall. Jerryl walked out of his room and toward the same mission room Darkwell had gone into.

Nicholas loitered, hoping to catch Olivia and apologize for getting her into trouble. She, however, didn't meet his gaze when she exited a minute later and strode around the corner.

Nicholas tried to look as though he were waiting for his assignment, bored even, as he meandered toward the end of the hall. Robbins, Darkwell's lead man, was focused on something on his desk and didn't even look up as Nicholas passed. The mission room door was closed, posted with the sign SESSION IN PROGRESS. He leaned closer and tried to hear what they were saying.

"Comfortable?" Darkwell asked. "Good. Now, find Eric Aruda. Get into his head and quickly dispatch anyone in his vicinity. We want him to take out his comrades."

"Gladly."

Get into his head? Take out his comrades? The thought of Jerryl mind-controlling someone shot alarm through him. Zoe and Rand had been right about that, too.

Olivia came around the corner, and their gazes locked for a second before she went into her office. Damn, why did his chest have to tighten at the sight of her? He focused on the room again. Silence, while Jerryl did whatever he was doing.

A few minutes later, "Can't get in, sir. He must be in their hideout."

Darkwell said the Rogues had a psychic shield over their hideout. Now Nicholas was glad. The door opened sooner than he'd anticipated, and Darkwell stepped out and closed the door behind him.

"What are you doing out here?" he nearly barked.

Nicholas was good at remaining calm in stressful situations. It had saved his life during his diving expeditions. "Waiting for you to get me started on something. I'm bored."

Darkwell narrowed his eyes. "You didn't seem so sure a few minutes ago."

"Just frustrated."

He held up a manila folder. "Then this should make you happy." He nodded for Nicholas to follow him into the mission room opposite and closed the door behind them. "I have information on the hostage."

For the next half hour, Nicholas studied the data. Darkwell had even thrown in pictures of his children, a move so blatantly manipulative it rankled. Had the man forgotten that if Nicholas became emotionally involved in the case, he couldn't connect?

Darkwell checked back with him. "What do you think?"

Nicholas set the pictures and notes aside. "I'll give it my best shot."

"I know you will." Darkwell sat at the desk next to the recliner where Nicholas would undertake his mission and clicked on the tape recorder.

At least he wasn't tracking down someone who would then be targeted. Or would he? He didn't know anymore. He glanced at the man's picture, a typical American-looking guy. Not a Rogue; too old.

Darkwell plunged the room into near darkness. Nicholas was too self-conscious about the process to do it any other way. He visualized the man's face, focusing so hard, his body seemed to disappear. He felt weightless, floating in the darkness like he did in the water.

He knew the moment he connected to his target by the *whoosh* in his stomach, as though he were gliding through the ether. He saw flashes of images, and his body twitched with each one. The swirling colors took the shape of a map. In large words: Afghanistan. Then closer, city names coming into focus. Kabul. Closer still. Just outside Kabul.

That had been as far as he could go before, getting a location on the map in his mind. Now he saw the city: ruined buildings, dust everywhere, a house still standing. Like a ghost, he drifted through the open door, then through a wall to a room in the back of the house.

His target. He couldn't get too personal, couldn't think of his kids or even what the man was enduring. Any emotional tie brought that black mass . . . the abyss. He took in the man tied to a chair, looking more haggard than in his picture. Two other men were in the room. One man walked closer to the target, blocking the view. The man screamed.

Nicholas lurched out of the mission, sucking in deep breaths. "I found him."

Olivia walked into the huge kitchen, finding it deserted. Perfect. Given the nature of the program, the staff was limited to the essentials, which included a housekeeper but not a cook. The residents had use of the stocked kitchen. She pushed away the reprimand she'd just gotten and pulled out the cakes sitting on racks to cool. She'd played it safe, choosing chocolate.

"Story of your life, Olivia," she muttered as she began to make icing between the layers. A grin spread down to her stomach as she carved the cake.

She rolled out a sheet of blue fondant and draped it over the cake, which was shaped like a pyramid. She trimmed, then went to work applying the thinner pieces of fondant that were cut into abstract, colorful shapes.

If she'd had some fireworks, or platforms and motors, she could have done something more spectacular. Explosions always made a cake special.

When she was done, she heated water for a cup of vanilla instant coffee, scooping the powder out of the square tin and dumping it in a mug with a rear view of several cowboys sitting on a fence: *Nothin' like starting the morning with buns and coffee.*

She'd taken her first sip when she heard a sound behind her. She turned to find Gerard Darkwell looking at her cake with disapproval. Because she knew the piping, color balance, and lettering were perfect, it wasn't the cake that had piqued his ire.

"Not cozy with Braden, huh?" he said, his voice like a growl.

"It's a birthday cake. There are no hearts, just, 'Happy Birthday, Nicholas!' I thought we'd get everyone together tomorrow and celebrate."

He inspected the cake. "So, you'd make a cake for the other two on their birthdays as well?"

"Of course." Though she didn't know either of them as well as Nicholas, and that wasn't saying much. But she sensed he was a good person, and anyone who spent hours in grueling searches to find the remains of missing people . . . that told her enough about him.

"It's a well-crafted cake," he said, inspecting it. "You spent a lot of time on it."

It was a compliment, and yet, she recognized the slippery quality of his voice. "Thank you."

He picked up the cake stand and dumped it over, crushing the pyramid. Crumbs scattered on the white countertop.

She couldn't breathe. "What . . . why . . . ?"

"This cake tells me you're way too invested in Braden. It will tell him the same. I've seen the way he looks at you. He'll think it's sweet. Then he'll take you to bed. It's my job to keep you from making that mistake. I've guided you, protected you, raised you on my own, and brought you into the most exciting career of your life. I'm not going to let you violate my rules and get involved with a man who brings nothing to the Darkwell legacy. Remember the last time you thought you were in love."

He'd said those last words with a sneer, but they pierced her chest. She pushed them away and stared at the ruined cake.

She was eleven years old again, when she'd painstakingly made a house out of cookies and icing when she was supposed to be reading a boring biography about George Washington. Her father had tossed her house into the garbage, set the book in front of her, and left. He never yelled. His message always got through without volume.

Words clawed up her throat: *Exciting career? Being your secretary? I wanted to go overseas, see the world, but you kept me here, safe and sound. I don't want to be your little girl forever. I never wanted a career in the CIA in the first place, but you denigrated what brought me passion and joy.*

"You'll look back on this and see I was right." He turned before she could utter any of her words.

You'd never say them anyway. She'd been taught to respect her elders, especially her father. Still, she swallowed those bitter words and hated herself for doing so.

Good girls get love. Her father only showed affection when she obeyed. It was earned, the same way her self-worth was. When she didn't go along cheerfully with what he wanted, the punishment was worse than his anger—she was dismissed.

Hiding that she was his daughter was yet another one of those things she'd had to agree to. He didn't want her to be treated any differently, good or bad, because of her name, so she was known as Olivia Damarest, her middle name. She had another name, too. She smiled, feeling smug at the one secret she'd been able to keep from him.

She turned to face the mess of a cake, feeling as torn as she had that day when she was eleven. The worst part? He was right. She *had* invested a lot into this cake. The joy she'd felt in making it, well, only part of that was because of the artistic process. Most of it was imagining the delight on Nicholas's face when she walked in singing "Happy Birthday." Because she cared. Because she cared a little too much.

CHAPTER 3

Heat and pain tore down Nicholas's throat as he tried to breathe. Roaring flames surrounded him, licking at his skin like a dragon tasting his dinner. He couldn't see beyond those flames and the thick, dark smoke that trapped him in his bed. His eyes burned. His skin blistered. *Where's the door? I can't remember.* It didn't matter. He would have to run through a wall of fire to get to it, and he knew more flames waited on the other side. Was there a window in the room? His brain was frying. He couldn't remember.

Then a sound. His cell phone. He gasped one last breath as he reached for it on the nightstand. It wasn't warm. But . . . how? He blinked, confused, looking at the display. His mother's number. Sweat dripped into his eyes, burning them. Then he looked around and saw . . .

The room at the estate. No flames. No smoke. Only a nightmare. *The* nightmare.

He pressed the TALK button, and grunted, "Good morning."

His mother, Lilah, began her annual rendition of "Happy Birthday." He tried to stop her, but she forged on. The woman couldn't sing worth a damn, but she sure loved trying.

He waited until she finished, mopping his face with a towel from the bathroom. "Thanks, Mom."

"Big twenty-three. What are you going to do for your birthday? Something special, I hope."

"I don't know. I may go to one of the parks nearby, get lost for a while."

"Like you could ever get lost." She sighed. "But you were my little boy lost, wandering in the woods for hours, giving me a heart attack when I couldn't find you anywhere."

"That's what happens when you live out in the boonies."

Her voice became contrite. "It was your dad's idea, buying a hundred acres in the forest and living off the land. He didn't think about how his two kids would handle being home-schooled and not being around other children. After we lost him, it was my fault. I couldn't sell our dream house."

That was how she always put it, "lost your dad." She couldn't say the word *died*. He was two when his dad was killed. He'd heard her say that phrase so many times, he thought his dad *was* lost. And Nicholas was going to find him. He knew his dad had explored the forest surrounding their home, so that was where he looked for him. Of course, he never found him, but he did find evidence of him. On a tree, their names carved into the trunk. A shrine of rocks, each marked to represent a member of their family. Nicholas kept looking for traces of his father. He found them by doing the things he had loved: climbing trees, camping out, cave diving.

"Nicky, I'm sorry I made you two live out there for so long. Too long. Is that why you've never felt close to me? Or anyone? You told me once that you'd rather be in the middle of a forest tracking down bones, or 150 feet down in the ocean looking for shipwrecks than to be around other people."

"I think it's just the way I am, Mom."

He wasn't going to tell her that maybe it was because she kept telling him and Jennessy, his sister, not to love too deeply, because when you lost, and you would, it would hurt so much more. He and Jennessy had become self-sufficient children, used to spending lots of time alone, and he wasn't sure either could change that.

Jennessy. She was an Offspring, too.

"Did you have the fire nightmare?"

"I haven't had one of those in years." This was the only kind of lie he could abide, one that kept her from being afraid. When he died, his distance would make his loss a little easier to bear.

Even before he knew what a funeral was, he'd always gone from the horror of the fire to the service. His mother and sister lost in grief, his casket. Other people crying. His sister was about the age she was now. So was his mother.

It wasn't just a nightmare that tore through his dreams on a regular basis, and in particular, on his birthday. He knew it would come true. Just as it did for his father.

"Are you fibbing?" she asked. "Trying not to get me worried?"

"Wouldn't I remember the nightmare if I had it?" Evasive. "Dad had them all the time, right?"

His were nightmares of being shot, of someone coming into the building he was in and shooting at everyone in the vicinity.

"About once a month. When you started getting recurring nightmares about burning . . ."

"But I'm not." He remembered her reaction when he'd had the nightmare the first several times. She'd held him in stiff arms, and screamed, "Stop having those nightmares. Your daddy had them, and they came true! I couldn't stand losing you, so stop them!"

He couldn't stop them, but he did stop telling her about them. "How is your eye?" he asked, partly to change the subject.

"Cataract surgery is set for just over two weeks from now. Doc says it's no big deal. I'll wear a patch for a week, and it'll be over. My friend Velma is going to take me to the doctor, and Jennessy is coming back for the week and take care of me."

She was having eye surgery. He shuddered, and dark tension coiled inside him. At the funeral, his mother wore an eye patch. He was going to die in three weeks.

Lilah's voice sounded strained, devoid of the chipper tone she'd had earlier. "Are you still afraid of fire?"

"Not much." Another lie. It had gotten worse. Even candles, bonfires, fireplaces . . . they clogged his throat with the memory of choking on smoke. He couldn't even watch the news when they were reporting fires.

"Have you heard from Jenn yet? I have no idea where she even is."

He walked to the French doors. "Probably taking photos in Africa or slogging across the Amazon." He rarely heard from her, though if she was near a phone, she always called him on his birthday. What should he tell her about this Offspring business? Nothing yet, but he would find out if anyone had tried contacting her. "Mom, can I ask you something about Dad?"

"Of course. Do you find yourself thinking about him on your birthday?" The wistfulness in her voice was much better than the grief that once saturated it.

"Sometimes. You said I got my skill at locating things from him. Was he always good at that?"

"For as long as I knew him. We never had lost keys or anything else when he was around."

He leaned against the mullioned glass, watching the fog float through the channels in the maze like lost ghosts. The hedges, trimmed into neat walls, were probably fifteen feet tall. He wondered if his dad felt complete when he'd found something that was missing or if, like Nicholas, he still felt a little empty "Did he go into a trance when he was trying to find something?"

"Yeah. It was weird. I thought he was having a seizure, and his eyes went black. But it was a real gift, he had."

Weird. He remembered the first time he discovered his "gift." He was fourteen, down at a lake where the kids were splashing and swimming. They'd moved to town by then, but he was having a hard time relating. He'd wanted to relate to Suzie, though, in the worst way. She'd started hollering that she'd lost her ring. It had been given to her by her grandmother, who was now dead. She was devastated, inconsolable.

The next day Nicholas returned to the lake, determined to be her hero and find the ring. He felt it in his gut, that need, as though she were incomplete without it, and he could complete her by finding it. That need seemed to wake up his ability. He saw the flashes, the ring in the mud, the murky water, then his eyes snapped open and he looked right at a spot that seemed no different from any other spot. He dove in, scrabbling around in the mud before his fingers touched the smooth gold.

When he presented it to her, she hugged him, kissed him, his first kiss. He wanted to do that again for her. He wanted another kiss. Did she have anything else she wanted him to find? She mentioned a pink sweater, her favorite. He made the mistake of going into his trance in front of her. He had no idea that his eyes went black, that his body twitched as the images flashed into his head. She was horrified, accusing him of being possessed by the devil like someone in a movie she'd seen. He didn't think she'd told anyone about it, but she'd clearly indicated to her friends that he was strange, someone to keep as only a distant friend.

After that, he'd never done it in front of someone else.

"Did Dad have any other extraordinary skills?"

"Not that I know of. Other than being smart and kind and honest, and, oh, so much more."

"What was he doing when he died?"

"Working in a classified government project. He couldn't tell me what it was about, and being in the Army, I understood that."

"Was a man named Darkwell in charge?"

"Gosh, I don't remember. Name sounds familiar."

In the distance, a gardener was desecrating a bush by cutting it into the shape of a bear.

"Before he died, did anything change in his behavior?"

"He had trouble sleeping, forgetting things, blanking out. He said he was just stressed. He was excited about the project, though, and the money was phenomenal. I told him it wasn't worth it if it was stressing him that much. And there was something else, but I can't talk to you about that."

"Tell me. I'm a big boy."

She giggled. "He got real . . . amorous."

He took a breath. "Did he mention any medicines or vitamins he was taking?"

"No, he—wait, he did say they were getting some nutritional drink. He thought that's why he had so much, er, energy."

Just like the Rogues had said. He wanted to tell her that was why his dad had started acting strange but didn't want to scare her. The thought of something in his body that had changed him would freak her out. It was certainly freaking him out.

"You know, Nicky, I think Darkwell *was* the name of Bobby's boss. He worked for the CIA. I thought it was pretty special that the CIA wanted him. They made arrangements to transfer him over and all. He was only twenty, in the Army for two years, when he was tapped for the program."

He was in the program for three years. Nicholas was contracted for two months, but he could see how the money and the opportunity to help his country in an exciting way could lure a man to stay longer.

Darkwell had told him he'd met Robert Braden through a mutual friend. He'd never said anything about Robert working for him. Another lie.

"Thanks for the call, Mom."

"When am I going to see you?"

"I'll come by after the surgery to check on you and see Jennessy." But maybe it was better if he didn't see them before he died.

"That would be great. You have a wonderful day, sweetheart. I hope this is a special year."

"Me, too."

He hung up, his thoughts as dark as the corners of the maze. His mother had confirmed what the Rogues had told him. Whatever he'd ended up being in the middle of . . . he had a feeling it was going to end his life.

CHAPTER 4

Olivia stood at the French doors in one of the mission rooms at the end of the hallway, watching Nicholas on his balcony. He wore only athletic shorts on a long, lean body. She'd seen him running through the grounds both early in the morning and sometimes late at night. He had a runner's body, muscular but not bulky, and whenever she'd glimpsed him (okay, she'd out and out gawked for as long as he was in view), she'd fantasized about running her hands over those muscles.

Hm. Curious. He tied a bandana around his head to cover his eyes. Talk about erotic connotations. He walked to the stone railing and threw what looked like a small red ball. It sailed through the air and landed somewhere in the southwest quadrant of the maze. The maze was designed by a puzzle maker and was one of the most difficult in the world, something her grandfather had told everyone with pride.

But Nicholas was the most puzzling of anything she'd ever encountered (and she had gotten lost in that damned maze many times, so that was saying something). With the blindfold still on, he braced his hands on the balcony and launched himself over, dropping to the ground with the grace of a cat. He ran straight to the maze's entrance and disappeared from view.

She felt someone walk into the room but was too entranced to turn and see who it was. Nicholas's shock of dark hair appeared momentarily around a bend, then disappeared again. She glanced over to see who now stood beside her: Jerryl, who was also watching. His ultrashort hair and feral eyes fit his military bearing and attitude, but he seemed to have something to prove.

She turned back to the maze in time to see Nicholas emerge, racing toward the building, blindly but unerringly pulling himself up the molding and climbing back onto his balcony. He held the ball in his hand, which he dropped as he stripped off the blindfold.

"Damned show-off," Jerryl muttered.

"Is it showing off if he doesn't know anyone's watching?"

Jerryl only grunted as he turned to leave. Her mouth twitched in a smile.

She knew Nicholas was scheduled to start working at ten, and it was now nine. She went downstairs and used the kitchen phone to call his room. She hated to admit it, but her father was right; she felt a hitch in her breath when he answered.

"Good morning, it's Olivia. Could you meet me in the kitchen in about fifteen minutes?"

After a pause, he said, "Sure. Be right there."

She felt that hitch again when he walked into the kitchen twelve minutes later, wearing a Polo-style shirt that stretched across his wide chest. His dark brown hair was damp and combed into submission. Usually, it looked delightfully mussed. With his soulful brown eyes and slight pout to his mouth, he reminded her of pictures she'd seen of Elvis in his youth. The smell of soap filled her senses.

"Hey, what's up?"

She lifted a finger to indicate he wait and slipped behind the tall metal shelves. She lit two candles on the small pyramid of cake she'd managed to salvage and walked around the corner. "Happy birthday to you . . ." She didn't go on because she couldn't sing worth a damn and wasn't going to embarrass herself or put him through the agony.

A mixture of surprise and alarm froze his expression. In fact, his whole body stiffened, though a small tremor moved across the muscles of his arms.

"Oh, jeez, you're not a diabetic, are you?"

When she neared, he lurched forward and blew out the candles with a burst of breath. "One of the candles looked like it was about to fall over," he said with a wave of his hand in answer to her questioning look. He released a breath. "No, I'm not diabetic. How did you know it was my birthday?"

"I manage the staff records."

He gave her a smile. "That was really sweet of you."

She set the dark blue cake on the small table the staff used to take their meals. She'd already placed two plates and forks there. "I thought we'd have a piece before you started work." Okay, she didn't want Gerard to see it.

Nicholas sat down, and she handed him a knife to cut it. He did the honors and gave her a slice first. She waited for him to take a bite, and his smile filled her with something close to giddiness.

"Wow. This is the moistest cake I've ever had. Did you make this from scratch?"

She nodded, pride glowing inside her. "I love to bake. I'm a Food Network addict, especially the baking *Challenge* shows. I have this idea . . ." Was she really going to tell him that?

"What?"

She waved it away. "Nothing. It's silly."

"Good." And he waited.

She loved that he was interested, giving her his whole attention, and she hated that she'd now have to tell him. "It's just an idle daydream, you know, because I'm committed to an illustrious career with the CIA, working for my country and all that, but I muse about how fun it would be to have my own business."

He glanced at the cake. "A bakery?"

A grin exploded on her face. " 'Dangerous Cakes.' Not just ordinary, boring cakes but *big, tall,* cakes, with moving parts and pyrotechnics, and . . ." Her enthusiasm was running away on her. "See, silly."

"You don't think so." His smile wasn't patronizing. The way he was looking at her, she'd swear he was absorbing her zest for the idea, or at least enjoying it.

"Well, it is, because I already have a career."

"I don't mean to degrade what you do, but how illustrious can being an assistant be? Even to a director?"

"There are possibilities for advancement." That's what her father had been telling her. So far, she saw only the leash that kept her working with him.

"I don't see that spark when you're talking about the CIA. I saw it when you talked about Dangerous Cakes. Livvie, life is short." His expression shadowed on those words. "It can be over in an instant. Grab it now and suck every bit of juice out of it."

Those words shimmered through her in ways she couldn't even decipher, but her body involuntarily moved closer to his. "I like that. Maybe I'll write it down and tape it to my bathroom mirror. I like the sucking part best."

His eyebrow went up, clearly taking her words for something much more erotic than she'd meant. Or had she?

She tilted her head. "Say it again, so I'll remember it. Grab it now and suck the juice right out of it?"

He cleared his throat, his fingers tight on his fork. "We'd better finish our cake before . . ."

"Before?" Before he tore off her clothes? Kissed her? He was looking at her mouth, making it tingle so that she had to run her tongue over it.

He wrenched his gaze away. "Before I have to report for work."

Work. Father. Rules. Damn.

They ate in companionable silence, catching each other's gaze and smiling. *Okay, a little harmless flirting.*

He took a bite, sliding his fork out of his mouth and rolling his eyes. "This is outrageous. Where did you learn to bake a cake like this, those cooking shows?"

His compliment filled her with champagne bubbles, not so much the words but the passion behind them. "I spent a summer in France in my junior year of high school. I was there to study the language, but I took a pastry cooking class and got hooked."

He took her in with those chocolate Grenache eyes. "'Dangerous Cakes.' Yes, very dangerous."

Did he mean the cake? She wanted to think he also meant her. She remembered what he'd said yesterday, about wanting to socialize with her. She wanted to "socialize" with him, too.

She ran her finger through the cream icing and stuck it in her mouth. He watched the move, his throat convulsing in a hard swallow. Yeah, he could have meant her. The fact that she had an effect on him sent a supercharged thrill through her.

Once again, it seemed an effort to pull his gaze from her and back to his cake.

That's when she realized he'd called her Livvie. She'd gotten totally distracted by the sucking part. "No one's ever called me Livvie before."

"Really? You look much more like a Livvie than an Olivia. Does it offend you?"

"I think I like it." Livvie, fun, light, the kind of girl who flirted. Her smile faded. "Just don't call me that in front of Darkwell."

He feigned a shocked look. "Heavens, no!"

She laughed, loving the sound of her own laughter and the way it tickled through her. He chuckled, a soft, deep sound that did more than tickle. No one had plugged into her body the way Nicholas had, bringing it to life the way the family's fake Christmas tree came to life once it was dragged out of deep, dark storage.

He took a last bite and set his fork on the plate. She stood, leaning forward to take his plate just as he got to his feet. Their noses brushed, and she stepped back, nearly losing the plate she was holding. The fork, however, went flying to the floor.

He started to reach for it, but she said, "I'll get it."

When she stood, she was inches from him. She had to look up at him, since he was probably eight inches taller than she. His gaze flicked to her mouth, before returning to her eyes. She swallowed hard, fighting the urge to lean closer, knowing his mouth would taste like sugar and butter and everything else she'd put into that cake, including feelings she shouldn't be having.

If her father came in right then, he'd see that she'd gone against his wishes. Hell, he'd see much more than that. She felt all of that delicious excitement evaporate. Flirting with Nicholas was just a tease, but it wasn't a harmless flirtation.

"You'd better get upstairs," she said on a rush of words, grabbing her plate and backing away. "You know how Darkwell gets."

She was in such a habit of referring to him as someone other than her father, she now called him Gerard or, to the others, Darkwell. When she set the plates in the sink, she turned to find Nicholas standing next to her.

"I hope I didn't get you into trouble yesterday."

She shrugged. "I violated the rules."

He tilted his head. "Do you often do that? Break the rules?"

"No. Never." She met his gaze. "Well, not usually."

He leaned closer. "I don't like rules. They're too restrictive. Confining."

Fever flashed into her cheeks. "Rules are good." She didn't sound the least bit convincing. "They're what set us apart from animals."

His voice grew soft, and his heated gaze swallowed her up. "Sometimes it's not bad to be like animals. Their lives are pretty simple. Eat. Sleep. Survive." And after a beat, "Procreate."

"But we need rules. We need . . ."

His mouth touched hers, jumping her heartbeat right into her throat.

Her lips were moving, trying to form the rest of the sentence she'd now forgotten. Then she was sliding against his mouth, and she couldn't breathe, and she didn't even care. He captured her mouth in his, and his hand curled around the back of her neck and pulled her closer.

A sound of surrender escaped her throat. He took that as an invitation to deepen the kiss, teasing her lips apart and running his tongue across their surface. Her eyes drifted shut, swept into sensations that started at her mouth and spread through her entire body. Her hand involuntarily came up and connected with his arm. Her fingers curled around his biceps, tensing on the hard muscle beneath his shirt.

"I need . . ." she whispered.

"To follow the rules?"

"For you to keep kissing me."

His tongue dipped into her mouth, once, twice, then invaded completely, and she fully engaged him back. How long had it been since she'd kissed someone like this and enjoyed it? *I'm not just enjoying. I'm lost, sinking, senseless.*

He tasted even sweeter and better than just the cake. Her tongue came alive, as though it had a mind of its own, toying with his, tracing the edge of his teeth and the ridges on the roof of his mouth. His kiss was as deep and slow and sensual as he seemed to be, as he would be if he made love to her.

He is making love to you.

That thought filled her heart with sunshine. He finished

the kiss, withdrawing his tongue but touching his lips to hers again and once more, as though he couldn't bear to part.

With his hand still around her neck, he leaned his forehead against hers. "You were saying . . . about the rules."

She opened her eyes, hazy and heavy. Her voice was weak. "Rules are good."

He laughed softly. "If you say so." He stepped back, and she saw that his eyes were also filled with a sensual haze.

"For you, too. If Darkwell caught us . . ." The thought cleared away the fuzz in her brain. "You could lose your contract."

"Would he fire you?"

"Worse." *You said too much.*

He nodded, taking another step back, the haze clearing from his eyes. "I respect that you respect the rules." He pinned her with his gaze. "But you're not just worried about getting reprimanded. I see fear at the thought of being caught. What kind of hold does that man have over you?"

She squeezed her eyes shut, not wanting to break another rule and not wanting Nicholas to think she was screwing her boss, either. "It's not what you think. But I can't say."

"He's not your lover. That's what you're saying. Because that would be . . ."

"Sick. I mean, inappropriate." Damn, she had a hard time following the rules where Nicholas was concerned.

"Why would it be sick? Because he's older? No, he acts more like a father . . ." His eyes widened. "He *is* your father, isn't he?" When her flushed face gave away her answer, he smiled in a relieved way. "That explains a lot. You don't look like him, though."

"I look like my mother, at least that's what I'm told."

"You've never seen her?"

She shook her head. "She left us when I was a baby. He destroyed all of her pictures. Anyway . . ." She pushed past that. "Darkwell—my father—doesn't want anyone to know. He wants to keep it professional."

He shook his head. "I understand now. But I'll tell you this, Livvie: That rule about socializing isn't so much to preserve the integrity of the program. It's to keep you in line, to keep you from getting involved with the wrong kind of guy. And make no mistake, I am the wrong kind of guy for you."

She tilted her head. "And what makes you think that?"

"Besides who your father is? Besides the rules and the fact that you follow them?"

She was curious. "Yeah. Besides all that."

"When I finish what I'm doing here, I'm gone."

"Well, not forever."

That shadow filled his eyes again. "Yeah, forever." He rubbed the back of his fingers against her cheek. "Thanks for the cake. That was special." His voice lowered. "So was the kiss." He headed out of the kitchen, and she called out, "Have a good birthday, Nicholas."

She quickly cleaned any evidence of the cake. Thank God her father hadn't caught her.

She put her fingers to her mouth. She wanted more of that. Of him. No matter that he wasn't going to be around long. That he'd backed down out of respect for her obedience, well, that made him more appealing. If not for that, they'd still be in the kitchen kissing.

Obedient little Olivia, and look where it's gotten you: alone and in a job that doesn't fulfill you. Nicholas had a point. How could fraternizing with the contractors compromise the program? She didn't know anything. In fact, Nicholas knew more than she did.

She felt pressure in her chest and reached for the pendant hidden beneath her shirt. Her fingers caressed the ridges of the Darkwell family crest, an eagle in profile. She had been required to wear this pendant every day since she was a young girl. Though her father was a man of logic, he'd told her it would protect her. She now took that to mean in a general way and not a superstitious way.

Well, it sure hadn't protected her from falling for Nicholas. She sighed, turning to leave the kitchen after one more inspection. She had fallen for him, hadn't she? Once again falling for a guy who didn't meet her father's standards. The last time . . .

She put her hand on her heart, feeling the ache even now. *What am I going to do this time?*

CHAPTER 5

Nicholas headed downstairs for lunch but paused at the sight of Olivia standing in front of one of the paintings of glowering men. He remained at the corner of the grand dining room, taking her in, remembering how sweet she was, how even more delicious her mouth was than the cake she'd made for him. Though he hadn't made a sound, she turned, and her dour expression transformed to a smile as it usually did when she saw him.

He stepped up beside her but looked at the portrait of a man decked out with all kinds of stars and ornamentation. In a near whisper, he said, "So, all these people are your family."

She did a quick glance to make sure no one was around. "That's my grandfather." She pointed to a portrait of another man, her face going pale, her mouth tightening. "And that is—was my uncle Leon. He died two and a half weeks ago of a heart attack." Her face paled and her mouth tightened.

"I'm sorry. You must have been close to him."

"No one in the family is close, not emotionally. Loyal, traditional, but not loving." She looked at him in surprise. "I don't know why I even said that. It's sad, tragic, but I think his death was harder because he was only two years older than my father. I guess it made me think about . . ."

She shook her head, unable to even voice words about her father's death.

She pointed to a crest emblazoned in brass with an eagle at the center. "That's our family crest." She twirled her finger: *big deal.* "This estate has been in the family for three generations. I never lived here, thank goodness, but we came here for special occasions. My grandfather recently moved into a smaller house closer to the city. This place was empty, and on the market, until Darkwell realized we could move the program here. Now he can do his work at Langley but spend as much time here as he can."

She went on to describe some of the other men, majors, generals, senators, as though she'd memorized them from childhood. Heck, she probably had.

Stuck in a dark alcove was another portrait. He stopped, this one more intriguing than the rest. "Who's this guy? And what did he do to piss off the family?"

She laughed, though it came out nervous. "That's Uncle Gus, the middle brother. And you're right, he did piss off the family. When he was nineteen, he married a woman much older than he was. She'd been married when they began their affair, an affair that broke up her marriage. But worse than that was that she was a buyer for a clothing store, and her job took her out of town a lot. Gus was so in love with her, he quit military school and traveled with her. My grandfather bribed, threatened, but nothing would dissuade Gus."

Her expression was solemn as she spoke. "They had a daughter a few years later and settled down. She was just a little older than I. We both went to a private school here in Potomac." She glanced at him. "Very exclusive. They teach you how to be a snob on every level. Audrey wasn't a snob, though, and we were very close, kind of two against the world. We both loved the equestrian program, until I fell off and sprained an ankle. My father wouldn't let me participate after that."

"That seems unfair. It was only one accident."

She shrugged. "He wanted to protect me." But she still didn't look pleased about it. "Gus and his family weren't invited to family gatherings . . . the shame of it all, you see. But he was so happy. You could see the glow in their faces when they were together. They were so in love."

She let out a soft sigh. "And then he died, a lung aneurysm. Like you said earlier, it was over in an instant. And his wife, Carol, was destitute. They'd been living in a house in the family trust, so she had no claim to it. I can remember the day she came to see my grandfather, begging him to let her and Audrey stay; she was his granddaughter, for God's sake. But he didn't see her as family. My grandfather and his two sons ordered them to leave."

The pain of the memory was etched in her face, and he saw something else, too: fear. "They left in tears. I told Audrey I'd sneak them into my bedroom. It sounds ridiculous now, but I wanted to help them. In the end, I couldn't do a thing."

"Where are they now?" Nicholas's mind was already working.

"The last address I could find was in California. I wrote a letter but never got a response."

"Do you want to find them?"

She looked at him. "In a way, yes. But it would open a can of worms with my family."

He nodded to the portrait. "I'm surprised they didn't hang it in the bathroom."

She didn't laugh this time.

"You're afraid of that happening to you, aren't you?" he asked.

"I don't have a portrait they could hang in the bathroom."

"That's not what I meant. You're afraid to be ostracized. I don't think your loyalty is as much out of love as it is out of fear."

"That's ridiculous."

It all made sense now. Her mother had abandoned her.

Olivia probably thought if she disobeyed, her father might abandon her, too.

"That's his job as a father, you know," he said in a low voice. "Raising and loving you wasn't doing you a favor."

She turned from the portrait. "I don't want to talk about this anymore."

"Do you want me to find Audrey and Carol? I can do that."

She looked at him, her head tilted. "How?"

"Let's just say I'm good at finding people."

"Is that your special skill?"

He gave her an impish smile. "We're not supposed to talk about our skills to the staff. You wouldn't want me to break the rules, would you?"

She seemed surprised by that revelation. "You don't care about the rules."

"But you do. I'm good at finding things. Do you want me to put my skill to use for you?" It was that need rising in him again, to complete someone by finding something that was missing.

Her eyes filled with both hope and conflict. "Yes. No. I don't know, let me think about it." Her expression changed to a slightly sheepish one. "I saw you this morning, throwing that ball into the maze, jumping off the balcony and finding it, climbing as agile as a monkey back up to your room."

"I climbed a lot of trees when I was a kid. We lived on a hundred acres of woods. There wasn't a tree I couldn't climb."

She was regarding him with curiosity now. "You found the ball, *and* you found your way out of that maze within seconds. No one does that. The smart ones eventually find their way out after, like, two hours. Tops. How can you do that? Is that your skill, too?"

He touched her chin and let his finger slide down the front of her throat until it reached the sweet hollow at the base of her neck. "That's just one of my skills, Livvie. But if we're following the rules, the only one I can share with you is finding your cousin. Let me know if I can assist in that."

She sucked in a breath at his touch and his implication, and her shoulders slackened when he lifted his finger away. "You're an evil man, Nicholas Braden."

He gave her a devilish smile. "Indeed I am." He started to walk away, a fine exit if he didn't say so himself, but she grabbed his arm to stop him.

After glancing around to make sure no one—her father—was around, she pulled him down a hall to a part of the mansion he'd never been in before. She led the way to a sunroom that was decked out in flowers, imprinted on the fabric of the sofas and chairs, and even on the wallpaper.

"My grandmother decorated this room," she said. "Try not to gag." She closed the door and walked right up to him. "I've decided to have an affair with you. *Affair,* is that the right word? Does that apply to assignations between people who are not married to each other?"

Affair . . . assignation . . . the mere words brought his body to life, especially when faced with a flushed Livvie standing so close their bodies nearly touched. "You've decided this . . . just now?"

"Yes. No. Sort of."

"What about the rules?"

"They're still in place, I'm afraid, but it seems you're game to flout them, and so am I. Life is short, and I want to grab it and suck all the juice out of it."

She might as well have put her mouth on him with those words, the way his body reacted. She wrapped her arms around his neck, snugged her body against his, and kissed him crazy. She was devilish, too, rocking her body ever so slightly, and she sure as hell couldn't have missed his erection. He took what she offered, plunging in, running his hands down her backside, the indent of her lower back, and sliding over the curve of her ass. Every bit as fantastic as he'd imagined.

She was hungry, no starved, it seemed. She moaned softly at his touch, pressing even closer.

She was too hungry, and he remembered her innocence, and the reason behind that innocence. As much as desire engulfed him, he could not, would not, hurt her. He pulled back, bracing her face, slowing the kisses and nearly losing it again at the sight of her eyes drenched in the same desire.

"Livvie, do you know what having an affair means? It means temporary. It means that at the end we both walk away, and no one's hurt. Can you do that?"

She nodded, leaning forward to kiss him again, and, he was sure, not really hearing his words.

"Livvie," he said against her mouth, "wait. I want to make sure you know what we're doing here."

She finally stepped back, hands on her hips. "Well, we would be kissing if you'd stop talking. I'm throwing caution to the winds, and now you're the one who's being careful."

"I have rules of my own. I want to make sure you know that when my assignment is over in a short time, you will be perfectly okay that I walk out of here and never see you again."

"Why never? We can call, write. Visit."

That's what he was afraid of. "Never."

She pushed out her lower lip in contrast to her words. "Okay, fine. Never. I'm talking about an affair, not marriage. And if you want to cut all ties, then we'll cut all ties."

He tipped her chin up. "You're young. Too young."

"Too young for what? I'm only three years younger than you."

"Twenty is young, sweetheart. Have you ever been in love before?"

"Plenty of times." She paused. "Okay, once, when I was sixteen."

"Just once?"

"I haven't met anyone I wanted to feel that way about. Until you."

He felt a punch in his chest. "Tell me about him." It was a test. He wanted to know how she let go of someone she'd been in love with. Because he already knew if they took this further, it was going to go deeper than any of the shallow "affairs" he'd had. He saw it in her eyes, felt it in his gut. He was willing to endure the pain of the loss, but he wasn't willing to put her through it.

She shifted her gaze away. "I don't want to."

"I need to know you can handle this. The last and only time you were in love was four years ago. That doesn't reassure me."

"Fine. His name was Liam. He was the gardener's son, and one summer he helped out at our estate. He was sweet and devastatingly good-looking and tan and he kissed . . . well, almost as well as you do. He was my first kiss, the first boy I ever let touch me."

He didn't like the thought of her being in love with anyone, and especially anyone touching her, a bad omen for him. "I'll bet your father loved that."

"You'd bet right. He got wind of the relationship and told me to end it. No daughter of a Darkwell was going to date a gardener's son. I hate conflict, and I knew it was pointless to argue, so I acquiesced. But being a teenager, and feeling the first bite of rebellion, we merely took the relationship underground. Unfortunately, my father forced the truth out of me one stormy afternoon. Then he went down to the shed where Liam and his father were waiting out the storm."

Her eyes glazed as she sank back to that distant day. "When he returned, he told me he'd fired the gardener. A man had lost his job because of me." Her expression darkened. "But that wasn't the worst of it. Though my father told them to leave after the storm, the gardener packed his things, and they left right then. He lost control of the car and went off the road into the river. They both . . . drowned." She looked at him, hurt and anger in her eyes. "There, are you happy?"

No, he wasn't happy at all. He pulled her against him, rubbing her back. "I'm sorry. But I had to know."

She looked up at him. "Know what?"

"Whether you could handle taking this a step further and not be hurt when I leave. I don't think you can. And I can't risk hurting you even though I want to make love to you so bad my body aches with it."

She stepped back, obviously hurt by his rejection. "You must think an awful lot of yourself to assume I won't get over you when you're gone."

All this time he'd thought her placid, compliant. Her feistiness pulled at him. He put his hand against her cheek. "I know enough about you to know you could never love lightly. And maybe I'm afraid I won't get over you."

She was beautiful, delicious, like one of those fancy desserts in the bakery case that he knew would crack to pieces after the first bite no matter how careful he was.

She crossed her arms over her chest. "Why do you have to leave? At least tell me that. You make it sound as though you're leaving the planet when you finish your assignment. I know you're not married, or at least no wife showed up on the background check. Is my father sending you overseas? To some volatile place?"

"No, nothing like that."

"I know you did salvage work before you came here, and that was dangerous. I read in your dossier that once you were a hundred feet below the surface looking for the remains of a shipwreck, and your air tank malfunctioned. You dive in caves for *fun*." She shuddered at that. "You'll go back to doing that when you're done here?"

"I'm hoping to start my own business where I can take the assignments I want." *Was* hoping.

"Like what? Treasure?"

"Things that have historical or sentimental value. Shipwrecks, but for museums. Lost jewelry, family heirlooms . . . family." He gave her a pointed look.

"And bones," she said, changing the subject.

"Yeah, I'd like to help Bone Finders without having to beg for time off."

"So you might die on some salvage mission. Or you might not. Does that mean you can't get involved with someone?"

It seemed overly dramatic to tell her he was going to die, even if he made up some logical and believable reason, like a fatal disease. "I'm just not the kind of guy who can be in a relationship, that's all. I date women who aren't interested in anything long-term and who won't be hurt when I go off on some mission and don't call or write or visit or promise to think about them every second. I'm one of those jerks who can't commit. And you, Livvie, are a woman who deserves a man who makes love to her every night and fixes her breakfast in the morning and talks about his day while cleaning up after dinner."

It was a nice picture, but she wasn't smiling. "You're not telling me the truth, Nicholas."

"That is true. And what is even truer is that I will not hurt you." He turned and walked out of the room, the hardest thing he'd had to do in a long time. And that was saying a lot.

CHAPTER 6

Monday morning, Nicholas walked to the French doors that led out to his balcony. Jerryl approached Darkwell, who was standing in front of the maze's entrance. Nicholas had seen the two of them out there before, talking, laughing . . . bonding. Jerryl was definitely the golden boy of the program. Nicholas had no idea what Fonda's skills were. He'd never been friendly with either her or Jerryl.

Nicholas stepped into the hallway. Olivia's door was open, but she wasn't at her desk. Graceful sculptures sat on the shelves of her credenza, and classical music wafted out. What a dichotomy she was, subdued on the outside, feisty with him. It drove him crazy, that he could have her, and yet, he couldn't.

The dark bronze doorknob on Darkwell's office door softly reflected the light. Like a mysterious object in the bottom of the ocean, it called to him. His fingers wrapped around the cool metal. He held his breath and turned the knob.

He glanced in both directions and stepped inside. The pressure in his chest warned him to back away. He realized what had always bothered him about the man: the sense of darkness he glimpsed in his eyes.

A quick in and out, find something that would either corroborate what the Rogues had told him or negate it. He pulled open a drawer and started riffling through the folder tabs. Nothing. He opened another drawer and in the back was a section of red folders with dates from the eighties and initials on the tabs. He grabbed one and opened it. At the top of the sheet on the left was a name scribbled in writing he recognized as Darkwell's: Francesca Vanderwyck.

Lucas Vanderwyck was one of the Rogues Nicholas had been tasked to find early on. He'd been shot during the assault at the hospital. Francesca had to be his mother. Then Nicholas's dad would be there, too, if he was part of the program. He found the folder—and heard a sound at the door.

Olivia stood there, her face a mask of disbelief. "What are you doing?"

He pulled out the folder and closed the drawer. "Trying to get the answers Darkwell won't give me."

She eyed the folder in his hand. "I can't let you take that."

He walked to the door. "This is about my father." And whatever substance Nicholas might have inherited from him.

"You can't just steal something from his office! That's classified information. If he finds out . . ."

"What? Will he kill me?" He'd seen Darkwell's anger. Not loud, but a sinister calm. "I'll make copies and get it back to you."

"I thought you had integrity." She glanced down the hall. Voices drifted from the vicinity of the stairs: Darkwell and Jerryl.

While he was looking in that direction, she snatched the folder and ran to the drawer. He reached her as she stuffed it back into the drawer.

"Get out of here, Nicholas, before he comes."

He made a grab for the drawer handle, but she blocked him in a move so fast it surprised him. No time for more than that. Damn her. Was she trying to protect that data or him? He and Olivia walked out just as Darkwell and Jerryl came around the corner.

Darkwell's gaze narrowed. Of course, he thought they were socializing again. He gave her a withering look as he went into his office, closing the door soundly. Olivia closed her door the same way. Like father, like . . .

No, she was nothing like her father.

Jerryl eyed Nicholas. Why had they come back inside so quickly? Had Jerryl remote-viewed Nicholas in Darkwell's office? The air thickened with a dark tension.

Jerryl rubbed his palm over hair barely longer than a five o'clock shadow as he walked over to Nicholas. "Gerard said you were asking about my skills. Any particular reason?"

"Just curious." *It's* Gerard *now, is it?*

"This is important shit we're doing here, Braden. There's stuff we have no business knowing. Our job is not to question but to act. And if that means killing, we kill."

"I joined DARK MATTER to save people, not target them for killing." He'd seen the result of killing: smashed bones, dismembered skeletons, and shattered families. His own family, too.

Jerryl sneered. "You can keep your hands and your conscience all squeaky-clean while I take out our enemy."

"How are you going to do that? Remote-view them to death?"

His laugh was more of a rumble as he backed toward his door. "Yeah, that's what I'm going to do. And I'll do the same to anyone who threatens the program."

Sam Robbins paused outside his boss's door and listened. He could barely hear through the thick wood, but what he could hear made the hairs on the back of his neck stand up. Darkwell was making arrangements to transfer Sayre Andrus out of prison. In rare instances, CIA could transfer prisoners who had specific value to the government into their custody.

Andrus was an Offspring Darkwell had recently discovered. Sam had read some of Andrus's file. The prison warden would probably be happy to see his troublesome prisoner go. Several accusations had been filed, ranging from "voodoo spells" to unexplained deaths, none proven.

The door opened, and Darkwell stopped at the sight of Sam.

Darkwell's voice was terse. "Come in."

Sam walked in and closed the door. "You're trying to get Andrus out of prison? He *murdered* a woman."

Darkwell sat at his massive desk. "The evidence was circumstantial at best. Besides, that has nothing to do with what I want him for. If he *has* murdered someone, at least he's not squeamish."

Sam couldn't get past that statement. "You know that Andrus is a cold-blooded psychopath."

"Yes, I do." Darkwell's black eyes glittered. "But he'll be *our* psychopath."

The truth hit Sam like a wave of ice-cold water: He'd been working for a psychopath all along. Instinct said to play along. "I suppose you have a point. But I thought Andrus wasn't interested."

"I must have piqued his interest. He called to set up another meeting. He wants out of prison. I just got off the phone with a judge I know in Florida to find out what the process entails. I need permission from the court, and a judge authorizes the release. Should be easy enough. Andrus will work here with us for four months, and I'll let him think it could go on longer. He'll have to go back, of course. I'll blame it on red tape, regulations, whatever. If he escapes, or if word gets out to the public that he's been released, it'll create a media frenzy."

Sam approached the desk. "Does the director know?"

"I'm not involving him unless and until I have to. He's very impressed with the information I've already given him. We just got word that the information Jerryl gave us last week led to the capture of a terrorist cell hiding out in London. If I need to approach him, I don't think it'll be a problem."

Sam rubbed his balding head, nervous at the thought of that man here on the grounds. "Will he be kept secure?"

"Of course. He'll have a guard posted to him at all times."

"What is he capable of?"

"You know his heritage. There are several possibilities." Darkwell smiled with satisfaction. "I'm going to give him a test assignment. Andrus is going to be the turning point in DARK MATTER. He's going to get rid of the Rogues. That should make you happy." His smile faded when he didn't see agreement on Sam's face. "Was there anything else?"

Sam shook his head and returned to his office. Twenty-five years ago, he had been an idealistic CIA agent drawn into Darkwell's vision of changing the world. Then things got ugly when he started giving the program's participants something that enhanced their abilities but not telling them—or even him—what it was. They started showing signs of mental breakdown, but all Darkwell could see were their achievements. When Jack Stoker had gone on his shooting spree, the program was closed down and obliterated from all records.

Then, several months ago, a CIA agent involved in the first program had contacted Darkwell with a concern: One of the subject's grown daughters was showing signs of the same psychic abilities as her father. Would she also succumb to mental illness?

Darkwell saw only the possibility of the subjects' offspring inheriting those enhanced abilities. A search for the offspring revealed that they had. He revived the program and hid it under a cover program, even using his own money to fund some of the expenses. He'd dragged Sam back under his control.

Four of their own had died, several injured. Offspring

had been killed, too. Lucas Vanderwyck and Eric Aruda were probably dead.

It was all going to go bad, and Sam wasn't going to get buried under the fallout this time. He remembered Darkwell's subtle warning when Sam had wanted out before. Darkwell would no doubt eliminate him to protect his program. The man had had his own brother killed, for God's sake, when he'd threatened to expose the true nature of the program to the director.

He searched his computer for any relevant files and printed them. Sensitive, but not enough to hold over Darkwell's head should anything suspicious happen to him.

Sam saw Darkwell head down the hallway toward the winding stairs, then watched his superior pull away in his black Mercedes. He returned to the hall and tried Darkwell's door. It was locked.

Olivia, Darkwell's assistant, stepped out of her office, startling him. "He's gone for the day."

"I gave him a file earlier and realized it contained the wrong papers. You know how he gets when we make a mistake."

She nodded knowingly. "Hold on, I'll get the key." She returned a minute later and unlocked the door. "Go ahead."

He grabbed up the file he'd just given to Darkwell. "Let me get the other file. I'll be right back."

Unfortunately, she was waiting near the door when he returned. He set the same file on the desk, reached around the doorknob, and made the appropriate motion. "I locked it. Thanks. You saved me a browbeating."

She smiled as she pulled the door closed. "No problem."

Sweet girl. She had no idea what her father was. She idolized him, always had, so it was no use warning her.

Two hours later, he walked the long, paneled hallway to see who was around. One guard always wandered the interior in addition to the two patrolling the grounds. He doubted the inside guard knew he had no business in Darkwell's office, but he couldn't be sure enough to risk his life.

His heart thudded as he turned the knob and slipped inside. The computer would be password protected. His only hope was to find something in the physical files. After checking several drawers, he found the notes on BLUE EYES, the original program.

He turned on the copier and started with the first file. He was halfway through when he heard a noise. Adrenaline shot through him. If Darkwell found him, he'd be killed.

He shut off the copier and cracked open the door. He heard the echo of conversation in the grand foyer, one man's voice getting louder as he ascended the stairs. The office offered no place to hide. If he didn't lock the door, and that *was* Darkwell, he'd be suspicious, especially with Sam loitering in the hallway. Reluctantly, he turned the lock, the file containing his copies tucked beneath his arm, and closed the door.

He headed toward his office, fighting the urge to look back.

"Robbins, what are you doing here so late?"

Cringing, he turned to face Darkwell.

"Just heading home." He pressed the folder closer to his body as Darkwell's gaze fell on it.

"What are you working on?"

The blood drained from Sam's face. "Different ways to look at the statistical data."

"Really? Let me have a look." He reached for the folder.

Sam swallowed hard, trying to find some excuse to refuse. That would only pique his suspicions. His trembling hand dropped the folder, spilling the papers on the floor. He knelt and pulled the papers together. "They're all out of order. I'd better get them sorted."

Another sound caught Darkwell's attention. His eyes narrowed at Olivia and Nicholas Braden walking down the hallway in a serious discussion. "We'll talk later." He walked up to the two. "Olivia, can we speak in private, please?"

Sam shoved the papers in the folder and headed down the stairs, afraid his wobbly legs would give out and send him tumbling.

All he had to do was send Darkwell a copy of a couple papers and tell him he'd gotten everything. He would get them to his attorney. Then he would make arrangements to disappear. He'd always wanted to go to Croatia.

CHAPTER 7

That evening, Nicholas set a cheese sandwich in a butter-coated pan. He didn't like eating in the cavernous kitchen, and the dining room was even less welcoming. Most of the time, he ate in his room. His gaze went to the small table where he and Olivia had shared the cake she'd made for his birthday. Damn, that had been sweet. Her proposition had been something else—and infinitely hard to refuse. He could almost forgive her for keeping him from that folder. She was following the rules. *She* had integrity.

As though he'd summoned her, he heard her voice at the entrance. "Mm, something smells—" Her expression darkened when she saw him. Though he had never personally betrayed a woman, he so clearly saw the pain of betrayal on her face. She continued to walk over, her mouth in a tight line. He liked that mouth much better when it was soft, pliant.

"I can't believe you were snooping through his files!" she said in a harsh whisper.

Her personal investment in what he'd done told him she was way too emotionally involved with him. He'd made the right decision. Though perhaps that involvement had kept her from telling Darkwell.

"Darkwell invited me to ask questions the other day, then didn't answer them. The folder I had in my hand had my father's name on it. He worked with Darkwell twenty-four years ago on a program that sounds a lot like this one. Darkwell never mentioned that they'd worked together. In fact, he lied about how he'd come to know him. Why?"

She shrugged. "I know there was a program he had some success with, but that's about it."

He believed her. "My father was killed while he was in that program. Someone came in and shot up the place."

Her hand touched his arm. "I'm so sorry."

He had the strange urge to console the grief she felt for him. "I don't really remember him."

"That doesn't make it any less painful."

He nodded in agreement, seeing a deeper knowledge of that on her face and remembering she'd lost her mother. Lost. The need rose up in him, but he squelched it.

She let her hand drop. "Your father's death . . . I'm sure it was just being in the wrong place at the wrong time."

He leaned against the counter. "Maybe. Maybe not. I have a right to know what my father did with Darkwell because it affects me in ways I can't explain to you. But aside from that, this is about my father, a man I never got to know. Wouldn't you want to know everything you could about your mother? What traits you'd inherited?"

"That's cruel, comparing my situation with yours. *Using* what I told you against me! My mother's records aren't classified."

He leaned closer. "But wouldn't you do whatever you could to find out? Wouldn't you, in fact, try even harder if they were classified?"

Despite the situation, he found her reddened cheeks charming. She turned away and snatched a prepackaged sandwich from the enormous fridge.

He plucked it from her hand, eyeing the wilted lettuce. "This thing's past due, and it probably wasn't good when it was fresh. Sit." He tilted the pan and turned the sandwich onto the plate. "Have a grilled cheese sandwich." So much

for distancing himself from her. Now he was feeding her!
He started another sandwich.

"You betray my trust, and now you want to make me
dinner? I don't think so."

But she was eyeing the sandwich, perfectly golden on
top, three different cheeses oozing out between the slices
of bread.

He lowered his voice. "You know you want it." Her gaze
flicked to him, obviously picking up the sexual connota-
tion. Which was really not a good idea. "You can hate me,
but eat. You look hungry."

She leaned against the counter. "I did forget to have
lunch."

He fired up the gas stove and took the pan he'd just used.
"Eat. It doesn't mean anything."

She took the sandwich and tore a big bite out of it, rolling her eyes. After swallowing, she said, "I haven't had
one of these in years. Sometimes I'd bribe the nanny into
making me one."

Nanny? Well, of course, now that he knew she came
from Darkwell money.

"This doesn't mean I've forgiven you," she said, nodding
toward the sandwich she was devouring.

"It's probably better if you don't." After starting to grill
another sandwich, he pulled out the blender and dumped
in the ingredients he'd set aside earlier: pistachio pudding
mix, peppermint extract, milk, an egg, and a scoop of spirulina, which turned everything green when he blended it.

"What are you making?" she asked.

"A protein shake. I have one every day."

She wrinkled her nose as he poured the green mixture
into a glass.

He held up the blender container. "Want some?"

"No, I'll stick to the sandwich, thanks."

"Just keep remembering the terrible guy who forced you
to eat it. I'm pushy, too."

Her mouth twisted in a wry grin. "You're not pushy

enough." She quickly changed the subject. "What's the green stuff?"

"Spirulina. It's the cyanobacterium that gives stagnant ponds the green color."

"Oh, yum."

He took a swig of the shake. "Did you know that in India, it's considered healthy to drink your own urine? One of the guys I worked with is a bodybuilder, and he swears by it. He's failed to convince me."

"Oh, now that's just yuck." She narrowed her eyes at him. "You're just trying to distract me from being angry at you." She nodded to the sandwich. "Maybe soften me up so I won't tell Darkwell."

He grabbed another plate and flipped his sandwich onto it. "So you didn't?"

"No, but don't go in there again. If he knows you're snooping, he'll fire you. I won't cover for you next time."

Nicholas lowered his voice. "Would he do more than fire me?"

"My father can be hard. Dogmatic. Tough. He's fought in wars, and, though I don't like to think about it, I'm sure he's killed people. But he's a good man. He loves his country. I trust that what he's doing here is for the good. I hope you will, too."

His mouth opened to say *no way in hell* but held his words. Sometimes neither a lie nor the truth worked.

He finished his sandwich as she popped the last bite of hers into her mouth and licked the butter off her fingers like a child. Oh, but she wasn't a child. As he looked at her mouth, which he was doing too much, he couldn't help but remember how soft her lips were, how adventurous her tongue.

She took the plates and set them in the sink, where the kitchen fairies would come and clean them, or at least it seemed that way.

"Thanks for the sandwich," she said, as they walked out of the kitchen.

"Thanks for not saying anything."

Did Darkwell kill curious mice? At this point, Nicholas didn't care about losing the job. The question was, would he die because of leaving or staying?

They turned the corner to the hallway where his suite and the offices were. Sam Robbins was picking up some papers on the floor, looking more uptight than he usually did. No wonder, with Darkwell hovering over him.

That eagle-eyed gaze turned toward them. At that moment the cell phone the Rogues had given him vibrated in his pocket. His chest tightened. Time to make a decision. He had thirty minutes.

Darkwell stalked toward him and Olivia. For a disconcerting moment, Nicholas thought he might know about the phone. His gaze riveted on Olivia, and he forced the polite phrasing: "Olivia, can we speak in private, please?"

Without a glance back at Nicholas, she followed. The man had her under his thumb, no doubt. He thought about poor Uncle Gus.

Sam Robbins hurried down the stairs like the White Rabbit in *Alice in Wonderland*.

Nicholas exited the house, needing a drive for the fresh air as much as the real reason for his escape. He headed down a road, the cool night air blowing through the vehicle, and feeling, for the first time since his meeting with the Rogues, able to really breathe.

Twenty minutes later he pulled off to the side of the road and waited for their second call. He answered on the first ring.

Rand said, "You were able to sniff around?"

"Enough to think you're on to something. And that I don't want to be part of the program anymore."

"You need to be very careful. If Darkwell suspects, you may be taken out. You'll have to play along until we can get together and talk."

"When will that be?"

"After you've proven you're not setting us up."

He understood, but it still irritated him. "What do I need to do?"

"You're the master locator. Give us Sam Robbins's home address."

That took Nicholas back. "What do you want with him?"

"We just want to talk. He knows a lot about the program, then and now, and I think he'd be willing to part with that information."

Nicholas's voice lowered. "If I give it to you . . . I don't want him hurt. I won't be part of your violence."

"He won't be touched. When Lucas and I were prisoners, he was the only person who was nice to us." Rand let out a soft breath. "And I understand your antiviolence stand, but you are going to find yourself in a kill-or-be-killed situation one of these days. You'd better be ready."

He'd felt a dark foreboding for several days now, and Rand's words weren't helping.

"I'll work on Robbins's address. Give me a few minutes. He left a half hour ago, so I'll try to do a locate on him."

Nicholas disconnected and sat back in his seat. He brought an image of Robbins to mind. He hoped to hell Rand was telling the truth. He wanted nothing to do with killing anyone. Even Darkwell.

He saw Robbins in his home running papers through a fax machine to make copies. He looked anxious, a large stain beneath the armpits of his dress shirt, his brow shiny.

The man always seemed nervous and not particularly happy. Now he looked even worse.

Nicholas moved back, hovering over the house and the surrounding neighborhood. He moved higher and the word came to mind: Alexandria, Virginia. Then Robbins's house number. The street name. He came out of the trance and jotted it down, his hand weak, eyes heavy.

He sat in the seat for several more minutes, reorienting himself as he always did.

The phone rang, and he answered with, "I have an address. I'll give it to you on one condition: You tell me when you're going to talk to him. I want to remote-view, see what's going on."

"Deal."

Nicholas tapped his cross pendant twice and gave them the address.

A harsh male voice said, "If this is a trap, know that we're coming for you."

Nicholas asked, "Who is this?"

"Eric Aruda."

The guy who'd coldcocked Olivia.

Rand said, "We'll be in touch. And remember what I said: Be careful."

Yes, he would have to be very careful. He was now Darkwell's enemy. And he knew how the enemy was treated.

CHAPTER 8

Late the next day, Nicholas stepped out of his room but stopped at the sight of the man going into Darkwell's office. Olivia was in the hallway, watching the man with curiosity. She gave Nicholas a nod as she was about to head to her office, but he put his hand on her arm to stop her.

"That man." He couldn't believe he was there. His mind swam with possibilities, none of them good. "The man who just went into Darkwell's office."

"You're going to ask who he is, and I don't know."

"His name is Pope, I know that much." He felt a tightness in his chest. "Does he work with Darkwell?"

She hesitated, obviously weighing how much to tell him. Finally, she stepped closer and lowered her voice. "My father called him when the Rogues broke into the asylum. All he told me was that he wasn't officially CIA and that he cleans up messes to preserve the classified nature of projects. I saw him at the asylum once but never before that. How do you know him?"

She'd given him information, so he'd reciprocate. "I've done salvage work for the FBI, classified recovery missions as a contractor. At least I thought it was the FBI. Top secret experimental stuff, and even though I saw the pieces, I couldn't tell you what they were. Pope was the one—the only one—who approached me, supervised my search, and paid me. In cash. I only know him as Pope."

"Me, too." She glanced at the door. "He's very odd."

He was more than odd, but Nicholas couldn't really explain how. Beyond his looks, which were unusual enough. He was at least six-foot-five, with a muscular body and light skin. His slick, shaved head set off dramatic features and eyes an unusual shade of violet-blue.

Pope had approached him months before Darkwell had. If they worked together, why not tell him? Both had hired him for his skills, though Pope hadn't said a thing about thinking they were psychic. Pope, like Darkwell, had required Nicholas to sign a sheaf of papers swearing him to secrecy, so Nicholas couldn't even ask Darkwell about his connection with Pope. It was baffling. Disturbing.

He was staring at the door but shifted his gaze to Olivia, because he couldn't not look at her. He was tongue-tied. They were beyond small talk, and it would come off as phony anyway.

"Don't you want to know what they're talking about?" he asked.

"Yes. But it's none of our business."

"It is my business. This whole project—"

The door opened, and Pope walked out, Darkwell not far behind him. Nicholas would find out now. Pope would say something to him.

But he didn't. Pope gave him a look that shimmered through him, piercing him with those eyes, stilling his tongue. Nicholas could only watch him walk down the hall and disappear around the corner.

He turned to find Darkwell glowering again and realized he'd been alone with Olivia in the hallway. They certainly didn't look flirtatious, so hopefully Olivia wouldn't get in trouble. Darkwell gave no indication that he expected Nicholas to know Pope.

Nicholas, for his part, was more confused than ever.

* * *

Two nights later, Nicholas was trying to watch a *Lost* rerun in his room. Of course, the "lost" aspect of the series drew him, but his mind was on Olivia tonight. She'd obviously been avoiding him, as he hadn't seen her since their encounter in the hallway. Which was good, he reminded himself. Very good. Now, if they could just avoid each other until he left . . .

His phone vibrated. Twenty-nine minutes later, he closed himself in the bathroom and turned on the water to mask his conversation.

Anyone can hear anything around here, a warning voice whispered in his head.

"Tonight's the night," a male voice said. Probably Rand.

"Be careful. I overheard Jerryl and Darkwell talking about Robbins. I don't know what's going on there. Robbins has been nervous as a rabbit hiding in a wolf's den."

"Thanks for the heads-up," Rand said. "We'll be in touch once we've talked to him."

Nicholas flopped back on the bed and turned off the television. He kept Robbins's face in mind. He would keep checking on him.

At first he saw Robbins sitting at a bar sipping a whiskey. Thirty minutes later, the scene was much different: a scared Robbins hunched in the back of a car, flanked by Rand and Lucas Vanderwyck. Nicholas focused harder, trying to hear what was happening. He could barely make out the muffled words.

Rand was asking Robbins, "What's the purpose of DARK MATTER?"

"Political assassination."

The shock of that nearly spun Nicholas out of the mission. He lost the connection but didn't come completely out. *Hold on.*

The scene in the back of the car came through again, Robbins saying, "I don't like what Darkwell's become, what he's doing."

"Will you help us?" Zoe asked.

"Take me back to my house, and I'll make you copies of the papers. What I can tell you is that Darkwell is gunning for you, and he's getting desperate. He's working on bringing another Offspring aboard, and he's the reason I'm finally leaving. The last straw. He's evil, he's powerful, and there's something you need to know about him."

There was an exchange between Rand and Lucas that Nicholas couldn't hear clearly. The gunshot and splatter of blood coming from Robbins's chest launched Nicholas out of his session with a gasp.

No! He couldn't breathe. *My God, they killed him.* He clutched his chest. It felt as though someone had smashed his rib cage. *I couldn't have been that wrong about them.* With a shaky hand, he punched the CALL button on the cell phone to dial the number from which Rand had called him. No one answered.

He went into the bathroom and turned on the water. *Damn them!* They'd lied to him. He kept calling until one of the women answered in a breathless voice.

"Who is this?" he asked.

"Amy Shane." One of the Rogues. "Nicholas—"

"You weren't supposed to kill him!" He cleared the emotion from his voice. "I remote-viewed you to see what was going on. You lied—"

"Lucas never meant to kill Robbins! Someone got into his head. He just blanked out. He has no memory of shooting Robbins, and he's torn up over it. How do we know it wasn't you?"

"Because I can't get into someone's head and because I'm not a murderer."

In a calm, low voice, she said, "Somebody did and somebody is. If you had anything to do with this . . ."

He hung up on her. Dammit, he didn't know what to believe. He sank to the bed, his head pounding. A man was dead, and he was responsible. What had Robbins said? That DARK MATTER was about political assassination. That

Darkwell was bringing in another Offspring. A dangerous Offspring.

The sound of three sharp knocks on his door jarred him. With one hand to his chest, which was so tight it ached, he stumbled to the door.

Jerryl stood there, his arms crossed over his ripped bare chest. He was going to step into the room, but Nicholas remained in his way. Jerryl leaned to the right and looked behind Nicholas. "Thought I heard you talking to someone."

"Television." He could barely push out words. "What do you want?"

"I know what you're up to, Braden."

Fear spiked in his chest, and he fought to keep it from his expression. "Meaning?"

"Were you remote-viewing just now?"

Nicholas didn't like the look in his predatory eyes. As if he knew. "You think I do that in my spare time for fun?"

Jerryl stared at him, studying him as though he were a squirming insect stuck through with a pin. "Could be lots of reasons you'd do it."

Nicholas kept his expression passive. "None that I can think of. I was about ready to hit it, so . . . 'Night," he added to sound normal.

He closed the door and locked it, remaining there for a minute. No sound of retreating footsteps. Just when he thought he must have missed them, he heard Jerryl finally return to his room.

He was on to Nicholas. Which meant he'd been in that car, too. What had Amy accused Nicholas of? Getting into Lucas's head. He'd denied it without even realizing what he was saying.

Then he remembered what he'd overheard when Jerryl was about to go on a mission. *Now, find Eric Aruda. Get into his head and quickly dispatch anyone in his vicinity. We want him to take out his comrades.*

His legs went weak, and he stumbled to the bed. Hell. Jerryl *could* mind-control. And if he could do it to the Rogues, he could do it to Nicholas, too.

Gerard Darkwell was backing up his computer files in the study of his home when his cell phone rang. The number on the screen indicated Jerryl. Either trouble or news. His chest tightened as he engaged the call.

"Sir, it's Jerryl." His voice sounded rushed, excited. "I've been checking on Robbins, as you asked."

Robbins's usual reticence had turned to caginess in recent days, sending up Gerard's antenna. He'd had a feeling Robbins would eventually outlive his usefulness and become a problem.

Jerryl went on. "Robbins is with the Rogues."

"*What?*"

"I think they nabbed him. He looks scared. I saw Rand and Amy Shane, then I lost the connection."

"All the Rogues would have to do is poke Robbins, and he'll spill everything. Get into Eric's head and take him out."

"I zeroed in on him next, and he's not in the same car."

"Try to get into someone else's head. I'll work on another angle." He disconnected and put in a call to the warden at Gainesville Correctional Institution. "I need to talk to inmate Sayre Andrus. It's urgent government business."

"Hold for a moment, sir."

Several agonizing minutes went by. Finally, that Southern drawl and childlike insouciance. "Howdy ho, what can I do for you, *sir*?"

Andrus intended no respect with his address. Gerard didn't care at the moment.

"Remember I told you I'd be giving you a test assignment? I've got one. Stay on the line and do it now. You get to take out a CIA agent, if that makes you feel any better."

"Sounds yummy. Gimme his name."

"Sam Robbins. You told me you can possess someone

when he's asleep, but also when he's stressed or in a fearful state. That's where Robbins is now."

"I need to get into your head."

Gerard twitched in alarm. "My head?"

"I need a touchstone, something that connects me to that person. That's you. You're gonna have to open that steel-trap mind of yours. Little pig, little pig, let me come in." After a pause, he said, "How bad you want this guy?"

Gerard had been taught long ago how to shield his mind from probing psychic vibes. Back when rumors of the Soviets psychic programs had spurred the U.S. government to do the same, top personnel had been trained to block their minds. Gerard didn't want to let Andrus in—he had apparently already tried to get into his mind—but he had to stop Robbins.

"All right."

"Put a picture of the son of a bitch in your head and hold it."

Gerard closed his eyes. An icy feeling touched the back of his neck, right under the base of his skull. He held the image of Robbins while a cold probe poked through his brain.

What if he . . . ?

He stopped the thought. *Can't let him sense my fear.*

The feeling disappeared. Gerard felt relief for a second before launching into waiting mode. He hated waiting. Dammit, if only he'd been blessed with a psychic ability, he could take care of this himself. He hated depending on others. He hated the envy he felt every time he watched one of his subjects slip into the ether, a place unknowable to him.

Gerard suspected Andrus's skills, based on his heritage, could include dream interception. He had confirmed that in their discussions. It explained why the guards and other prisoners thought Andrus practiced black magic and could get into their dreams. And why one prisoner, after threatening Andrus, had hanged himself.

Andrus was going to be the key to finally destroying the Rogues. Once everything was in place, he had a plan to take care of all of them at once.

His cell phone rang. Jerryl.

"What happened?" he answered. No patience for a greeting.

"Holy shit . . . sir. You're not going to believe this. Lucas was there. I thought he was dead."

"Lucas? Are you sure?" How had he survived? He'd been at death's door when his comrades had rescued him. Getting the last injection of the Booster should have done him in. Then he'd gotten shot in the chest when they'd rescued Rand two weeks ago. Even if he could have gotten medical treatment, which was doubtful, no way could he be out and about so soon.

"I'm positive, sir. But that's not the incredible part. Lucas shot him."

"Shot Robbins?"

"Which doesn't make sense because Robbins was about to tell them about an Offspring, whatever that is. Why kill him before he'd told them everything?"

Gerard smiled. Andrus. Had to be.

"There's more. I sensed someone else remote-viewing. I immediately went next door. Nicholas denied it, but I saw a speck of alarm in his eyes when I accused him."

"Good job."

Someone was calling his name. Andrus on the main phone line. Gerard signed off with Jerryl and said to Andrus, "Nice work."

"How did you know—?"

"Now that you've proven yourself, I'll begin the paperwork to transfer you. But I imagine you have a question for me."

"Bet your ass I do."

Gerard sat back and began to spin a story.

CHAPTER 9

Olivia's official duties at the CIA took up much of her time in the last few days, which was perfect considering it didn't give her much of a chance to see Nicholas. She spent Friday morning at Langley taking care of her administrative tasks. Like her father, she had to cram in her regular duties on top of DARK MATTER's. It was an unofficial program, so she wasn't supposed to mention it to anyone. Unofficial, or as he'd explained, he was expanding on an official program because the CIA wouldn't give him the resources he needed. Before Nicholas's probing, she hadn't thought to question it herself. Now it seemed a bit odd. Why couldn't the director at least know about the program?

"Hi, Olivia," a woman called out from down the hall. "We've got to get together for a drink again. Call me." She disappeared into one of the rooms.

She and Theresa had gone out once, but all the woman was interested in was her career. Olivia felt no connection to her or any of the women she'd met at work. She had no girlfriends to confide in, but she hoped that would soon change. She was new to the "yoga class" she attended, but the mix of strong, interesting women there spurred her need for female friendship.

Walking down the hall, she passed an office with an open door and nearly ran into someone in front of her when she did a double take. The man sitting in the office was Harry Peterson. He'd worked at the asylum and had taken a bullet to the hip when the Rogues had broken in to rescue Rand Brandenburg.

"Harry?"

He looked up from the paperwork on the desk and gave her a polite smile. "Olivia, right?"

He wasn't sure what her name was? She sank down on the plastic chair in front of his desk, dumbfounded. When the Rogues broke Lucas out, Harry had implored her to hide the unused syringe so her father would think Lucas had gotten whatever it contained. She'd covered for Harry because he was a good guy, and she knew he'd get into big trouble. Now he hardly knew her.

"How are you? I tried to visit you at the hospital, but none in the area had any record of you being there. I thought you'd be out for a while."

He gave her a curious smile. "Hospital?"

She lowered her voice and leaned closer. "You were shot in the hip."

"You must have me mistaken for someone else. I was never shot."

For a moment she questioned her sanity, of all damned things. But he *was* Harry Peterson. He *had* been shot.

"It was only two and a half weeks ago. I don't think I'll ever forget seeing you lying on the floor, blood oozing onto the linoleum . . ." Her stomach lurched at the memory. She still felt the fear and anger that had bombarded her.

He rose to his feet, agitation crossing his face. "I wasn't shot."

She stood, too. "I put pressure on the bullet wound to staunch the bleeding."

"What are you talking about?"

"At the asylum, where we worked together."

His chuckle was uneasy. "You've made a mistake. I would have remembered working with you. Now, if you'll excuse me, I've got to finish this report."

She was still mulling it over when she returned to the estate later that afternoon, but it was giving her a headache. She had better things to think about.

Darkwell's door opened, and he peered out. "Tell the contractors to come here in five minutes. I have an announcement."

She knocked on Nicholas's door first. He answered, and darned if she didn't feel that hiccup in her heartbeat. His dark hair was mussed, as though he'd been working on a difficult problem. Or, taking in the rest of him, as though a difficult problem had been taking on him. His eyes were bloodshot, brow furrowed. Something was heavy in his heart, something that had obviously kept him up all night.

"You all right?" she asked.

He shook his head, indicating he couldn't talk about it. He was in pain. She could see it in his eyes and the heaviness around his mouth. She wanted to press, to offer comfort. Being away from him these past days hadn't lessened the intensity of her feelings. If anything, they were even more intense.

She took one step into the doorway. "Okay, you win."

"I win?"

"You convinced me with that question about what I'd do to find out information about my mother. An underhanded tactic, to be sure. But I would do anything to know about her, to know why she abandoned me and my father." Her lower lip had trembled on those last words, betraying the anger she tried to tamp down. She'd never been allowed to talk about her mother; her father had dismissed her as though she'd never existed. But she had created Olivia, and she needed to find out what kind of woman could leave her baby. She cleared her throat, and the ball of fury lodged there. "I'll get you a copy of the folder." She stepped back out into the hallway, her voice back to business. "Darkwell wants to see everyone in his office in five minutes."

"Why?" The question was filled with suspicion.

"An announcement." She shrugged. "I don't know what it is."

She started to turn away, but he touched her arm. Just that touch, barely a touch, really, and her body stopped instantly, straining to do more than turn and face him.

"Thank you."

She didn't feel great about it, but she did feel right about it. She looked down at his fingers on her skin, not wanting to leave. With a nod, she forced herself to continue toward Fonda's room. The door popped open, as though Fonda had been standing there waiting for the knock. Even though she was barely over five feet, there was nothing little about her. Fluffy ash-blond hair that curled up where it reached past her shoulders set off enormous brown eyes made larger by charcoal eyeliner and shimmering shadow. Her teal shirt hung off one soft shoulder, and black leggings hugged her slim waist and legs. Incongruously, she wore black combat boots with stickers portraying a pink cat with x's over its eyes. She looked like she'd walked out of an eighties music video.

"What's up?" she asked. A small diamond glittered at her nose.

"Meeting in Darkwell's office."

"Be right there."

Olivia headed past Nicholas's suite to Jerryl's. He took the longest to answer. She told him about the meeting, then knocked on Robbins's door. No answer. Knocked again. A minute later she opened the door. It was dark.

She returned to Gerard's office. "Robbins isn't here."

"I know. He never came in."

"Should we call someone?"

"I sent someone to check his house. Car's gone, drawers are half-emptied. He's been acting strange. I have a feeling he's gone AWOL."

Her throat tightened. "Monday he was all worried, said he'd given you the wrong folder. He didn't want to anger you and asked if I'd let him in your office so he could replace it with the right folder. But I didn't leave him alone in here."

Oddly, he didn't seem upset. Her father could be quite paranoid. "I'm sure it was nothing. But never let anyone into my office if I'm not there."

Speaking of odd . . . "I saw Harry Peterson at Langley. He acted as though we'd never worked together. It was the strangest thing."

"Nothing strange about it. He was told to pretend his work here had never happened. Obviously, he's doing a good job of it."

"But he acted . . . different. Like he hardly knew me."

"He's a good actor. A good officer."

She shifted her weight from one leg to the other. "Why didn't he come back?"

"It was time for him to move on."

The answers didn't satisfy her. Now she knew why Nicholas was so frustrated. "I saw the director today. He asked about the two projects we're working on. He wants a report."

Irritation passed over her father's face. "I don't have time to deal with programs that aren't producing results. Talk to the two people heading them up."

She stepped closer to his desk. "Why can't the director know about DARK MATTER?"

"Because he would frown on my hiring outside help."

Nicholas knocked on the nearly closed door and stepped in. Gerard waved for him to take a seat, and she swore he looked happy that they'd been interrupted. Nicholas's hair was now combed, though she'd never seen it neat. Something about the choppy, thick locks was charming. *He* was charming in a quiet, understated way. But it was more than that. He treated her like a woman and not a girl. He saw something in her that no one, not even she, had seen. He was intriguing, daring, and sensitive. Just when she'd expected tension between them, he'd given her a cheese sandwich.

Fonda popped in next. "Are we in trouble or something?" She didn't look particularly worried, but she did look ready to defend herself. She had the gait of a cat as she slunk across the room and curled up in a chair.

Jerryl strode in as though the office was his. Olivia remained at the door, curious about the meeting but not part of it. She hoped Gerard wouldn't ask her to leave.

"I'm pleased to announce we have another victory. As you know, Jerryl found the terrorist cell. Recently, Nicholas found a contractor who had been taken hostage. He was rescued yesterday and is on his way home as we speak." He held up a photograph of a middle-aged man posed with his family during happier times. "He's tired, bruised, but otherwise in good shape. Nice work, Nicholas. This is what we can accomplish, people: saving lives, bringing hostages home. You can all take tremendous pride in your part of it. We won't get public credit, but sometimes doing the right thing is reward enough. That's all for now."

Olivia joined in the applause, still finding it hard to believe that anyone could find a hostage thousands of miles away. Wondering how Nicholas had done it. She'd seen maps, sketches the three of them had done, but what did they do in those mission rooms? Nicholas's questions had made her curious. If she gave him a copy of his father's file, she would insist on knowing more. But did she really want to know what her father was up to?

Fonda bent her knee and propped her chin on it. "When do I get a mission?"

"When you're ready. You've been practicing, getting better. I'll be giving you a new exercise tonight."

"Cool." She gave him a salute and hopped out of her chair. In a flash, she was out the door.

Gerard looked at Jerryl. "We'll begin our next mission in thirty minutes."

"Yes, sir." Jerryl gave him a sharp nod and left.

Nicholas got to his feet but halted when Gerard said,

"Nicholas, you had some questions . . . maybe some doubts earlier this week. I hope we've laid those to rest."

He hesitated, his mouth tightening. When she thought he might voice those doubts, he said, "Everything's fine, sir." He left, his eyes on hers as he passed.

Olivia shut the door behind him, walking over to her father's desk. "You look tired. You're overdoing it, getting up early and working here, going to Langley, then coming back and working more. It's taking a toll on you."

"Right now DARK MATTER is more important than rest and recreation."

She couldn't remember her father ever taking part in any recreation, having fun, or laughing. Had her mother's abandonment sapped his joy? Or had he been born like that?

She lowered her voice. "Look what happened to Uncle Leon. A heart attack in his fifties, and he overworked himself, too." The thought of losing her father . . . fear wrapped around her heart and stole her breath away. "Are you getting enough whole grains? Taking your vitamins?"

"Yes and yes." He opened one of his desk drawers and withdrew a syringe. "Give me my injection."

Her throat closed. "It's two days early."

"Give me the injection."

She hated this. Her father had been diagnosed with chronic fatigue syndrome, and a vitamin B deficiency that sometimes contributed to the condition. And he, tough man of the CIA, was squeamish about giving himself a shot. So Olivia, who was also squeamish about giving shots, had to buck up and inject him twice a week.

She couldn't even look away as the needle went into his skin. She discarded the needle in the sanitary container. "If that's all . . ."

"I've seen the way you and Braden look at each other."

How could an observant man like him miss it? She crossed her arms over her chest. "I've always respected the rules. Your rules, CIA's rules. Our family's rules. But I don't agree with the rule prohibiting me from socializ-

ing with the people in the program." Certainly she should
score some points for being assertive, honest, and straight-
forward, all Darkwell traits. Instead of being patted on the
head for exuding feminine qualities, for being obedient.

His mouth flattened into a hard line. "You mean
Nicholas Braden. Why can't you accept that marriage isn't
all those silly, useless feelings but a strategic partnership?
I've introduced you to several handsome men with lineages
and honors to stir any sensible woman's loins."

Hearing her father talking about a woman's loins . . . *ew.*
"Boring, not-my-type men." She hated the feeling she'd disappointed him by not finding his choices appealing.

He leaned back in his chair, regarding her with a raised
eyebrow. "What is your type of man, Olivia?"

"Someone who's not always a follower." Like she was.
"Someone who goes deeper, isn't into the material aspects
of life, like awards, medals, and possessions. Someone who
treats me with respect even though I see attraction in his
eyes."

"Again, Nicholas Braden."

Take a deep breath. And say it. "I want to see him.
Socially. And whatever else comes of it, if anything." If she
could convince him she could handle it. At least that would
be one secret she wouldn't have to keep. She hated keeping secrets. "I need a life outside this place." She gestured
to include the estate. Pride swelled in her chest. She was
standing up for herself. "I understand if you need to transfer me out of the program."

"You're not getting transferred. You're the only person I
completely trust."

That both warmed her and dumped a burden on her.

Despite his declaration, his expression was sober.
"There's something you should know about Braden."

"He's leaving. The way he says it, sounds like a dangerous mission he could die on. Are you sending him overseas?"

"It's very likely he's a traitor."

The word punched her in the gut. "No. You're just saying that—"

"I wish I were."

"Who is he betraying?"

He leaned back in his chair and steepled his fingers. "Us. The program. Our country. You know he's been asking questions. Doubting me. I think he had something to do with Robbins's going missing. It's why he looks so haggard. I didn't want to alarm you, but I think the Rogues have Robbins. Which means he's probably dead. And I have reason to believe Nicholas helped them find him. I can't get into details, but this you must understand: You cannot *see* Nicholas Braden socially. He's the potential enemy, and if he finds out you're my daughter, you will be vulnerable."

Olivia's hand went to her mouth. "I can't believe that. Not that I think you're lying," she added quickly. She'd heard this before, his insistence that her relationship to him could put her in jeopardy, particularly if she worked for the National Clandestine Service.

His expression softened to pity. "I'm sorry to say this, but his interest in you may well be only for what you can give him. And I mean information."

No. Maybe she was naïve when it came to things of a sexual nature. After what had happened with Liam . . . the pain was fresh again after reliving it for Nicholas. She'd lost the desire to date someone she knew her father wouldn't approve. Until now. But could she be that warped in her judgment? Nicholas *had* been snooping, though he hadn't been lying about its being his father's folder. She couldn't tell her father about that now. He'd be furious that she hadn't told him earlier.

"He said his father worked with you in a classified program twenty-four years ago but you hadn't disclosed your relationship. That's why he was asking questions."

"The reason he was asking questions was that somehow the Rogues got to him. But how?" He looked genuinely puzzled but hadn't addressed her comment.

"Did his father work with you?"

He stood. "I've got to meet with Jerryl. We'll talk about this later." Which usually meant they wouldn't. "But for now, I insist you not speak with Braden at all. Don't let him use you. Not only will he make a fool out of you, but he could cause some deadly problems. For now I want him unaware of our suspicions. Understand?"

She nodded and left, still unable to believe Nicholas might have allied with the Rogues. But he was suffering guilt over something . . .

She put her hand on Sam's office door, her chest hurting from the thought of his being dead. He was jumpy but considerate and pleasant. Now he was gone. Two other officers had disappeared. Now she feared the worst for them, too.

She'd seen the aftermath the Rogues had left behind at the asylum: five men shot, one beaten. None had died, her father had assured her. She believed him, but she hadn't seen any of them since, except for Harry, and that encounter had been plain odd.

She looked up to see Nicholas coming around the corner, a frosty glass of one of those funky protein shakes in his hand. He saw where she was standing, and guilt shadowed his eyes.

She turned before her expression could give away her fears, doubts, and what she suspected was a terrible truth: He *had* been part of Sam's disappearance.

CHAPTER 10

Saturday morning, Nicholas woke with a start, roused from a nightmare about Robbins's death. He blinked. Standing by his desk was Fonda. And yet . . . not quite Fonda. Maybe he wasn't awake or it was the early-morning light, but it looked like her ghost. Her body was translucent and shimmered with her movement. She turned, saw him, and disappeared.

He rubbed his eyes. His imagination. Still, given their abilities, maybe it *was* her.

Nicholas had asked once if, when they were remote-viewing, a person in the vicinity could see them. The answer was no. Their presence could be sensed by someone sensitive to such things, but not visually.

He pulled himself out of bed, an uneasy feeling pressing down on him. He had to be careful about Jerryl remote-viewing him. Darkwell had taught him to block an intrusion, but he wasn't sure how good he was at it.

Nicholas took a long, hot shower and emerged in time to hear his phone ringing. Olivia's voice wasn't sweet and cheerful as it usually was. "It's Olivia. Darkwell would like to see you in his office in twenty minutes."

The cool politeness matched the look she'd given him last night in the hallway. Granted, he was probably paranoid, but he'd seen accusation as she'd stood in front of

Robbins's door. Something had changed. She had said she was going to give him a copy of his dad's folder, but her demeanor had changed since then.

"Thanks, Livvie." What to say? "I—"

She hung up during his pause, probably thinking that was the end of the call. He knew she was the epitome of politeness. She'd never hang up on anyone midsentence. Well, it was for the best. He should be relieved there was now a wall between them. Problem was, he wasn't.

Nicholas had already decided that, no matter what, he couldn't continue in the program, not with the doubts he harbored. Oddly enough, the thought of not seeing Olivia again was what sent a sharp pang through his chest. He'd never let himself get close to a woman before, other than physically. Yet, he'd only kissed Olivia, and she'd touched him in a deeper place than any other woman. Hell, *he* had become emotionally involved.

Which meant leaving was a good idea.

Twenty minutes later, Nicholas paused in front of Darkwell's door. Maybe Darkwell was going to fire him. Nicholas wasn't ready for that yet. Before he left, he had to get hold of that folder. This time, not even Olivia would stop him.

He knocked. Darkwell called for him to come in, and he stepped inside, lingering by the door.

"Close the door and sit."

Uh-oh. Nicholas took a seat in front of Darkwell's imposing desk. The man had a pleasant expression on his face, not a *you're-fired* kind of look.

"Nicholas, you did a fine job with your first hostage." That was one good thing about Darkwell. He complimented his subordinates on their work.

"Thank you, sir. It was nice to finally help someone."

"You helped that man and his family, your country, and DARK MATTER." He held up a folder. "I've got another person for you to find. He's being targeted by the Rogues. We don't know where he is, not a clue. He's been living off the grid for over twenty years. His name is Richard Wallace." He set a picture of a man, perhaps in his thirties, on the table. "This is the last known picture of him. If you succeed, there will be a bonus."

Darkwell was making it harder to leave. On purpose? Did he suspect Nicholas was thinking of leaving? Probably. The man was intelligent and cunning. Even now he was studying Nicholas.

"I'll do my best." He stood.

"I'll see you in the mission room in twenty minutes."

"Yes, sir." He left.

Jerryl was out in the hallway. If Darkwell was suspicious of Nicholas, he hid it well. Jerryl did not. Nicholas shifted his gaze away from him, a knot tangling inside him. The flames from his nightmare licked at the edges of his mind. Time was running out.

Late Monday night Nicholas went down to the kitchen to see what he could scrounge up. He'd forgotten about dinner. Classical music drifted from the back, mostly unused portion of the kitchen, and the whole place smelled of baking cake and sugar. Olivia. Which brought to mind memories of their kiss, when she'd broken the rules, when he'd gotten a glimpse of the hunger inside her.

He stepped quietly, spotting her sitting on a stool at a long counter. The cake looked like a tower. Damn, she was beautiful, her long hair tied back with one of those white twist ties. Flour dusted her cheek and several strands of hair not captured in the ponytail. Her length of creamy neck pulled at him, physically pulled him, so he had to regain his balance to remain where he was.

She worked in such a state of concentration, she didn't even know he was there. He hoped she wasn't making that cake for him. No, no reason to do that. The dark blue shirt she wore was a little too large, slipping to the side and revealing a bare shoulder. The long, tight white pants she wore made her legs look long and slender. A gold anklet glinted in the light as she moved. She was worrying her lower lip, making it red and puffy. He could think of better ways to make her mouth look like that.

As he watched, though, he realized she wasn't enjoying the process. She made a window, then a face, then used yellow icing to make long tresses of hair falling to the base: Rapunzel. Her delicate features were tensed, her movements rigid, a furrow between her eyebrows. She grabbed a pastry bag, jabbing black lines to denote bricks.

She picked up something that looked like a hammer, held it over her head, and slammed it sideways into her creation. Pieces of cake and icing flew everywhere. She pounded it over and over, grunting in exertion.

Shock stuck his feet to their position. Finally, she stopped, staring at the rubble. Her chest rose and fell with her deep breathing, but the tension had left her features.

"Maybe you should call your bakery 'Angry Cakes.' "

She spun to face him, her hand to her heart, shooting out the words, "What are you doing in here?"

"I came to get something to eat, but this is much more interesting."

She scraped the mess into the garbage can sitting next to the counter. He walked over and saw the remnants of at least two other cakes in the can.

"A safe way to release your anger," he said, smiling to soften his words.

She nodded at the hammer, a meat tenderizer, he suspected. "Don't be so sure of that."

He reached out to wipe away a streak of gray icing on her bare shoulder. At her surprised look, he held up his finger and stuck it in his mouth. "You've got icing all over you."

And you want to lick off every bit of it, don't you?

Oh, yeah. He did a mental *thwap*. Maybe she'd gotten caught trying to get a copy of that folder for him. "Livvie, if you got into trouble because of me—"

"I didn't get into trouble." Her words came out clipped,

her mouth still in that compressed line. "But I sure got what I deserved for breaking the rules."

"What's that supposed to mean? Tell me."

When she ignored him by wiping down the counter, he said, "Are you angry with me? God knows the only reason I turned down your proposal was for your own good."

She turned to him. "Augh! For my own good! If everyone would stop making decisions for my own good, I could figure out what's good for me myself. But you're right, we shouldn't get involved. I am so over that. Now leave me alone."

"Ooh, you *are* mad at me. If not about that, then what?"

She gave him a smirk. "For reasons I can't explain. There seems to be a lot of that going on. And I'm just as mad at myself. I compromised the program. And my integrity."

"Sometimes having integrity means questioning the rules."

"Not in my family or my job. I'm the good girl. I'm loyal. I follow the rules."

He crossed his arms loosely in front of his chest. "Do you get medals for doing that? Or just a pat on the head?"

A growl sounded in her throat, and her hazel eyes narrowed in anger. She scooped up a glob of icing from the counter and hurled it at him. He was so surprised, he couldn't move in time. It hit him in the cheek.

A mix of horror and humor lit her face. He slowly swiped at it, looking at the cake and icing smeared on his fingers. He lifted one finger to his mouth and licked some of it off.

"I like it."

"It's butter cream," she said begrudgingly.

"No, I like this side of you."

Her expression changed to a serious one, as though he'd reprimanded her for acting up. "It's not a side of me. I simply lost my temper."

He moved closer. "Uh-uh. I see something inside you."

"What?"

"A feistiness, a streak of rebel." He smeared the frosting from one of his other fingers across her cheek like war paint. "I think this is the real you, not the well-bred, obedient Daddy's girl."

Before she could react, before he could think logically, he leaned forward and licked off that smear of icing. He loved the flare of indignation in her widened eyes and the way her mouth dropped open. All the invitation he needed.

He locked his mouth to hers, sweeping in and moving his tongue in and around. She held rigid for exactly one second before she responded, meeting his tongue move for move.

"Stop . . ." he managed to say.

"Stop? I didn't start—"

"Stop me. Just stop me, because I can't."

He couldn't. God help him, he really couldn't. No matter what he'd said to her, no matter the conviction he had about not getting involved with her.

Her hands went up to his chest, but they didn't push him away. Like a cat's claws when it's kneading in pleasure, her fingers flexed against him.

"Stop . . ." Her voice was breathless and not convincing at all. "Stop doing this to me. You're making me . . . crazy."

Crazy. That was all he heard. Yes, crazy, delirious, mindless. He wove his fingers through her long hair, and just as he'd fantasized, pulled her head back and ran his tongue down her neck. He tasted flecks of icing, making her all the more delicious.

He ground his hips against her pelvis, aching for her. Not only a physical ache, though. He wanted to take her, make love to her, hold her, protect her. All those feelings exploded like an emotional orgasm. His body, though, wanted more of her, to feel her, touch her. He slid his hands up her stomach, his thumbs grazing the edges of her breasts. It was all he could do to hold himself back, because once he touched her . . .

She moved into his hands, her breasts filling them, and he let out a groan, surrendering, squeezing, caressing, now wanting to feel them in the flesh. He kissed over the ridge of her collarbone, down to the top edge of her shirt. He saw the pink bra, lacy edge, the swell of her cleavage, ivory skin he knew would taste like heaven, icing or no. He undid the first button, then the second.

He wanted her so badly he could take her right there. He had such exquisite control over himself, but not with her. They were in the kitchen, where anyone could happen upon them, and he couldn't even begin to untangle himself to stop.

He unclasped the bra that thankfully hooked in the front and opened her shirt. "God, you're beautiful," he said, meaning all of her, but at that moment he saw only those pale, firm breasts. He covered her nipple with his mouth, and she exhaled in a quick breath. Her fingers kneaded his hair, the tips of her nails grazing his scalp as her breath came faster.

Before he moved to the other breast, he looked up at her. Her head was tilted back, her lips parted, her eyes closed. She had surrendered, too.

He was going to take her right there if she didn't stop him. She wasn't the sensible one anymore. He wasn't in control. They were going to make love right there in the kitchen, which wouldn't be right, not for the first time, not for anytime.

He needed to feel her skin against his, to bury his face between her legs and give her every bit of pleasure, and she couldn't scream out without bringing someone in response, and that would humiliate her, get her into trouble . . . and still, still he couldn't stop.

Yes, yes, yes . . .

"No."

Where had that word come from? Not him. No way.

"Nicholas, we can't do this."

"I know," he said on a gasp. "Need to find someplace private—"

She pushed him away and, with fumbling fingers, tried to clasp her bra. She was still breathing hard, her face flushed with heat.

So was he. He blinked, as though coming out of a trance. "You're right. Wrong place." Wrong time. Wrong man. He lifted his hands. "I'm sorry. I couldn't help myself. Mad, happy, frustrated, you're too damned tempting."

She kept missing the clasp and finally just buttoned her shirt. "You're the one who said we shouldn't—"

"I know, I know. And we shouldn't." He looked at her, running his hand back over his mussed hair. "And then I attack you in the kitchen. It's crazy; I'm crazy." Without thinking, he reached over to wipe away another fleck of icing on her arm. He caught himself, ripped a paper towel from the holder, and handed it to her. "Now I've given you something else to be angry about."

"I wasn't angry about that."

"And what I said about the medals, that was condescending. You've been brainwashed, manipulated. I'm not the guy who should break you out of that."

He'd apologized, then insulted her again. He had a problem being too honest sometimes, but he couldn't help it. It *was* brainwashing. The only thing that could save her was the rebel buried inside her.

She looked through the open shelves to make sure no one was within earshot. "I don't like what you do to me."

"I know; you do that to me, too."

"No." She rubbed her forehead in frustration. "Because of you, I'm keeping secrets from my father. I covered for you when you sneaked into his office, which I'm ashamed of. I was going to give you classified information until I came to my senses."

Which meant she'd changed her mind. But why?

She continued. "Why are you asking all these questions, doubting my father's integrity?"

He saw the agony on her expression. "It's making you doubt."

"No!"

"Don't you wonder what's really going on here? He hasn't told even *you* that much."

"I understand it's classified. I don't have that kind of clearance. Being his daughter doesn't give me special privileges."

"You blindly want to believe everything your father tells you because you're afraid not to, fine. I don't trust him. Not when I have questions he won't answer, questions that pertain to me, to my past. Like why the Rogues targeted me. I had to lie to the police, on his orders. I don't like lying. Scratch that. I *hate* lying. The world is black-and-white. You either tell the truth, or you lie."

He leaned against the counter. "And don't you think it's strange that with the shootout at the asylum, no one questioned us? People were *shot,* maybe killed. The CIA might not want anyone else involved, but they'd investigate. And what about that strange fire?" One of the garbage cans had ignited. Nicholas had frozen, seeing the flames, the smoke, choking before he could even inhale it. "Nobody could say how that fire started, only that somehow the Rogues had done it. Admit it, you have questions, too."

As he talked, her movements became more agitated as she wiped away the icing from her cheek, then the counter. "Maybe I do, but I trust his judgment."

"What are you afraid of? Finding out he's not what you've been trained to believe? Humor me for a second. Say you did find out he was up to something sinister. Then what?"

She was wiping the same spot over and over. "I'd have to confront him. I don't like confrontations."

Clearly. She wasn't even looking at him. But she was staying, not stalking out. That was something. "Why not?"

"Because I can't stand to see the look in his face that I've let him down when all these years he hasn't let me down."

Yeah, the man had her emotionally hog-tied. Bastard. "So he either denies it or admits it but won't stop. Then what?"

"Then I can't work with him anymore. I leave the CIA." Her voice quivered. "I lose my father, because he won't tolerate my disloyalty. I lose my family, because the Darkwells don't tolerate disloyalty."

"You're sure they would disown you?"

The fear of that tensed her mouth. "Then I have no identity, no roots."

Ah, he was getting somewhere.

The fear transformed to resolve. She looked at him. "I'm not brainwashed."

"That's what the brainwashed always say. Haven't you ever seen interviews with people in cults?"

She threw the paper towel into the garbage. "I trust my father. It's you I don't trust. And right now, I don't even trust myself." She walked toward the kitchen's entrance.

Nicholas called after her, "You're the only one you can trust, Olivia. Remember that."

Why did it bother him so much? Live and let live, right? She could spend the rest of her life playing daddy's good girl, and it shouldn't matter a bit to him.

But it did.

Get over it. You'll be gone before long and never see her again. The thought chipped away at him, but the sight of something on the end of the counter distracted him: her key ring.

Like with the kiss, he couldn't take time to think it through. This might be his only chance to get hold of that folder. He'd read the contents and decide what to do next. He grabbed her ring by the brass, etched heart and ran upstairs two treads at a time.

* * *

Olivia stalked around the grand rooms on the main floor, trying to push the kiss, and how it had made her feel, out of her mind. Her father was probably right about Nicholas trying to seduce her for information. She hardened her heart, because, dammit, her heart was all over that kiss. He pushed her, ridiculed her, and she should hate him for it.

She didn't.

He did push her . . . into thinking, questioning in uncomfortable ways, herself, her father, and what he was doing here. Nicholas insisted she face her doubts.

He was pushing her out of her Daddy's-little-girl role and into an independent grown-up role. Loyalty tore at her, but the thought of gaining her true self bloomed inside her, a perfect rose, with thorns ready to pop her bubble.

She returned to her suite of rooms in the east wing and reached into her pocket for her keys. They weren't there. She remembered setting them on the kitchen counter and headed back downstairs. Hopefully, Nicholas wouldn't be there. Damn him for throwing her loyalty in her face.

You just hate the part of yourself that's submissive. And that he's making you see it.

If he knew what it was like growing up Darkwell . . . if he knew how much her family was part of her life, of who she was.

Brainwashed!

Or was *he* brainwashing her, turning her against her father for his own cause? If she were going to look at this situation like a grown-up, she had to face that possibility, too.

She stepped into the kitchen and released a breath when she saw he wasn't there. She walked over to where she'd set the keys.

They were gone.

And Nicholas had been in here. He wanted that folder. He knew she had a key to her father's office on the ring.

She ran out of the kitchen.

CHAPTER 11

Nicholas's heart was banging in his chest as he sprinted up the stairs and around the corner. The hall was empty, but Darkwell was working with Jerryl in one of the mission rooms. He could come out at any time.

Nicholas stilled his heavy breaths and walked to Darkwell's office. He looked at the keys in his palm. She must have one for every room in the place. He knocked first. No answer. A check of the knob—locked. He picked a key and slid it in. It jammed immediately. He went to the next one.

He scanned the hallway again. All clear. Another key went in, stopped short. A fourth. The fifth slid in. *Click*. The knob turned, and he slipped in and closed the door. He went right to the credenza where he'd found the red folders. The others' files were there, too: Brandenburg, Vanderwyck, Aruda. He could take them all, but one or two missing folders wouldn't be as easily noticed. Grab Francesca Vanderwyck's. More information to study.

He closed the drawer and looked up to see Olivia in the open doorway, her face as white as a china doll's. The same betrayal he'd seen in her eyes before glowed even more so. She was shaking her head, but then she looked toward the end of the hallway. Her eyes widened. Darkwell had come out. She wasn't going to cover for him this time.

He'd never have the chance to see this folder again. He had only one choice: haul ass.

He ran to the French doors leading out to the balcony. Locked!

"Braden, put the folder down." Darkwell's voice.

Nicholas didn't turn. He unlocked the door, jerked it open, and covered the distance to the railing in seconds.

"Jerryl, stop him! Any way you can."

Olivia's voice: "What do you mean, 'any way you can'?"

He meant injure. Kill. Nicholas knew that in his gut. He braced his hands on the railing and launched himself over it. He braced for the landing one story down. The impact jarred his body. The folders flew from his hands, and he heard papers flutter to the floor. They blended into the concrete. No time to grab them all up. The two guards patrolling the property would be on him in no time. He put his hands on one of the folders and snatched it up a second before someone landed just feet from him.

Jerryl.

He shoved Jerryl backward while he was still off balance and tore out of the courtyard. The estate was huge, with a concrete wall all around. He'd never get his truck out of the compound. Lights snapped on throughout the grounds. Voices shouted. God, he was being hunted like a criminal. Like a Rogue.

Which meant he'd be treated like a Rogue. Imprisoned. Shot up with some strange substance.

No way.

Fog had started forming, and the lights cast it into ghoulish shapes. He ran to the west, where he knew he'd eventually come across a road. He had a lot of ground to cross before that. The landscaping gave him cover, though, and he raced from one unnaturally shaped tree to another, hiding in the shadows.

Footsteps pounded behind him. One of the guards came around a corner. Nicholas ducked into the maze. He ran to the right and took a corner.

"I saw him go this way," a man said.

"I'll check the maze." Jerryl's voice.

"You'll get lost in there." Darkwell.

"I can find my way around anywhere."

Lights were strategically tucked into the hedges, not bright but enough to guide a person along. Nicholas swore his feet made crunching sounds in the grass as he ran. Behind him, Jerryl's footsteps sounded quieter. Stealthier. The jerk was a Marine. Nicholas was a finder. Now he had to be a hider. He turned a corner and came upon a choice.

He chose right. Fog swirled around his feet, stirring with his movements, damp on his cheeks. He curled the folder like a tube and tucked it into his waistband. *You've run out of air one hundred feet underwater. You've come across a shark. You've been lost in a cave. You kept your cool. Do it now.*

Fear and exertion tightened his chest. Left went into the center. If Jerryl got lucky, he could trap him in one of the dead ends that spiraled out from it. He went to a path that led to the outer edge. It was like a house of mirrors sound-wise. He couldn't tell from which direction Jerryl's footsteps came. He ran to a dark corner and pushed himself into the hedge. The cut ends of branches scratched at him. He closed his eyes to protect them. Jerryl's steps came closer, but he wasn't coming into view.

Nicholas slowly pushed farther in, so as not to make noise. Each twig breaking sounded like a bat hitting a baseball.

"I can hear you, Braden."

Through the web of branches, Jerryl came into view, his eyes wild in the shadows. "Come out and face the consequences, traitor." Jerryl did a cursory scan of the area, then ran back around the corner.

Footsteps sounded on the other side of the hedge. Heavy breathing, whispers. Nicholas shifted his gaze to the outer edge without moving his head.

Darkwell walked across the expanse of lawn, as much bloodlust in his eyes as in Jerryl's. "Find him! If he's going to get away, take him out."

Those words shot fear through his chest as surely as what a gunshot would feel like. Another guard ran past, rifle at the ready.

Darkwell remained, within a few yards of Nicholas, his face cast in hard lines by the lights. He stared at the hedges, studying every section one foot at a time. Nicholas froze as the man's black gaze moved closer to his position. How much did the light expose? He couldn't move now. The slightest twitch would give him away.

"I may not be psychic, but I can feel you, Braden. There have been studies. Even ordinary people can feel when someone is watching them." Darkwell's gaze shifted, then moved on. He pulled his cell phone out of his jacket pocket. "I think he's in the maze. I want Jones on the south end, Canton on the north. Move in. Evrard's already in there."

Jerryl called out from several yards away. "Sir? I know he's in here somewhere, but . . . I seem to be lost."

Darkwell said, "Hold your position. Stay alert."

He walked out of view. Nicholas disentangled himself from the hedge and tore across the lawn.

"I see him!" a man called out.

Damn. Too soon.

A bullet zinged past him. They were going to shoot him in the back! He didn't even know in which direction he was running. All he knew was he'd eventually reach a fence or a gate, and he didn't have enough of a lead to climb over either without getting shot.

In the distance he saw the tennis courts at the edge of the property. He sprinted toward them. A tall chain-link fence, overgrown by trees, bordered the estate and the one next door. The trees would camouflage him, especially since they were in the shadows. He ran into the darkness behind the trees and darted to the right. His fingers grabbed on to the chain-link fence. His feet had a harder time getting a hold. Metal jangled as he climbed.

Behind him, footsteps thumped across the lawn.

"Spread out! I hear him climbing the fence."

And Darkwell: "Do *not* let him get away!"

The jagged edges of fence scratched him as he launched himself over and dropped to the ground. Dogs started barking and snarling. Their eyes glittered as two dark forms raced toward him.

Crap. No time for dogs.

He sidestepped them, arcing to the right. Behind him the fence jangled even louder as probably three men climbed over. That should keep the dogs busy.

Except he could hear one of them panting as it chased him.

The wall around this property was topped by sharp spikes. Not climbable. He spotted the lights at the entrance gate. He aimed for that, hoping it wasn't as enormous as Darkwell's gate.

Teeth grabbed at the leg of his jeans, accompanied by a growl. In the distance, he heard the other dog barking at the second set of intruders. He liked animals. He really did. So he whispered, "Sorry, pooch," before he kicked at the dog. "I can't let you get me killed."

The dog fell back, but it came at him again. Nicholas reached the gate, yes, every bit as tall as Darkwell's. It also had what was probably the family crest emblazoned in metal on the bars. With the dog tearing at his jeans, Nicholas grabbed on to part of the crest.

He heard the other dog in the distance whimper in pain. *Don't kill the dog!* His dog let go and ran back to help his comrade. Footsteps pounded across the ground toward him. He climbed up the crest and, careful of the spikes, began to pull himself over.

A bullet hit the metal next to his hand. He felt the heat as he dropped down on the other side.

Another bullet clanged.

He tore into the darkness flanking the driveway. Beyond was a road. He ran toward it, stepping into the oncoming lane and waving his arms at the next vehicle. The man's eyes widened as he slammed on the brakes. Thank God it was a man. He didn't want to put a woman through this.

"Sorry," Nicholas said, opening the passenger door and jumping in. "I'm being chased by muggers. Get out of here." When the man only stared, he added, "Now!"

He jammed his foot on the gas pedal and the car lurched forward. Jerryl and one of the guards ran into the road just as the car passed.

"I . . . I don't want to get involved in an-n-nything dangerous," the man said.

Neither did he. "Take me down the road a few minutes and let me out."

With relief, the man nodded and hit the gas even harder. Five minutes later, Nicholas said, "Stop here. And thanks. You saved my life."

He got out and ran across a field toward an angled building in the near distance. He hid in the alcove of a doorway and reached behind him. The folder was still there. He pulled out the tightly coiled tube. On aching legs, he limped over to a bit of light coming out of an office window and unfurled the folder.

It was empty.

CHAPTER 12

Olivia waited by the balcony in her father's office as he'd ordered, her insides knotted so tight, she was sure she'd snap at any second. Her father and three others were hunting down Nicholas. The man who'd just kissed her crazy, who'd seen a part of her she kept well hidden. Who'd not only betrayed her father and the government, but her. Used her. But she didn't want him hurt. The orders Jerryl had taken so eagerly weighed heavily on her chest: *Any way you can.*

She couldn't believe her father would kill someone for stealing. Arrest him, yes. Fire him, definitely. Not kill. Not hurt.

She had given Nicholas away. As soon as her father saw her expression, he knew something was up. If Nicholas got hurt, though, it would be her fault.

Liam. No, not again. She couldn't endure it a second time, two men she'd had feelings for, dead. One common denominator: her father. *And that I fell for men who were wrong.* Wrong according to her father. She paced, coiling a lock of hair around her finger, winding it as tight as she felt inside.

The cell phone she wore clipped to her belt rang. Gerard. She could barely squeeze out the words, "Did you find him?"

"No. He climbed over the fence and got away."

Relief engulfed her, guilt fast on its tail. She should be as angry as her father.

He continued. "Our men are still on his trail, though. We'll get him. I want you to go down to the courtyard and grab the papers that fell. I have to find out what he got. *Dammit to hell!*" He hung up.

She knew it was bad when her father lost his temper. At the top of the stairs, she thought of the fastest way to get downstairs. She'd often mused how fun it would be to slide down the curving banister, but she'd never had the guts to do so.

So what was wrong with following rules? Being a good girl?

You tell me.

She went out through the parlor and found one folder and papers scattered everywhere. He'd grabbed Lucas Vanderwyck's mother's folder for some reason. Next to a huge ceramic pot were several more papers. Nicholas's father. So he hadn't gotten them, or at least all of them. A small consolation for her father.

Her gaze went to words on the page. Dates. *Second administration of Booster . . . behavior erratic.*

She tucked the papers inside the folder. Whatever had happened in the first program was beyond the scope of her classification—and her father's trust.

Why didn't he trust her? For the first time she realized it bothered her. She hesitated, wondering what was in this folder that was so vitriolic? That Nicholas would risk everything to get, and Darkwell would kill him to make sure he didn't. She flipped it open, but the thought of betraying him more than she already had forced her to slap it closed.

She went back upstairs to find him in his office. He was even angrier than he'd been when the Rogues had broken out Rand Brandenburg. She saw the fire in his eyes, the rigid tension in his face.

He snatched the folder from her, poring over the contents. "His father's information. And . . . Vanderwyck's. Why?"

Words about finding Nicholas in here before pushed up her throat. *Honesty is virtuous. Lying is a betrayal of your name, your family, and yourself.* But what came out was, "He wanted to know about his father. It must have driven him over the edge."

"He got the folder, but it looks like that's all he got. How did he get in here?"

"He took my keys. I left them in the kitchen."

He found them on the desk and shoved them at her. "Never leave these out." He went to the credenza and opened the drawer, his fingers flipping through the folders. When he reached the end of them, his expression relaxed. "Nothing else is missing." He closed the drawer. "I should have let him go as soon as I saw his doubts. I was hoping he'd come around. I even offered him a bonus. But he'd been corrupted."

"Corrupted?"

"By the Rogues. They got to him somehow." He turned his hard gaze on her. "Didn't I tell you he was bad news? This is why you cannot socialize with the subjects."

She nodded, submissive, contrite Olivia.

To make sure she felt as bad as she could, he added, "He was only using you. You almost let your silly romantic notions override your common sense. Something else I hope you've learned today: I'm always right."

She wasn't quite going to agree to that. "What will happen if he's caught?"

"If he resists arrest, it may get ugly." His expression hardened. "Get that fretful look off your face. The man betrayed all of us."

He opened his desk drawer and pulled out a gun Olivia had never seen and set it on his desk. "Hopefully, they'll find him. Then he'll be dealt with."

Olivia shivered at the darkness in her father's eyes.

* * *

Nicholas took a breath, clearing his mind. His body ached, his skin burned from the scratches, and his chest hurt. His first thought was to go home. He couldn't go home. Not now. Not for a long time. He couldn't go to his mother's. No way could he explain this or involve her.

That left the Rogues. They weren't the good guys, either. He had seen their violence, and he knew they distrusted him. Damn, he hated gray. Now he was gray, neither black nor white. Could he trust the Rogues?

No. They had betrayed him.

Yes, you can. Think about it.

Lucas had killed a man after promising he wouldn't hurt him. That should be black-and-white, but something about it wasn't. He mentally took himself back to the car just before Robbins was shot.

Robbins was telling them about Darkwell's bringing another Offspring aboard. A dangerous Offspring. He was about to tell them something else, something important. Lucas shot him before he could say it.

That was it. Lucas shot him *before* he could give them a piece of vital information. If Lucas's intention had been to kill Robbins, why wouldn't he have waited until the man had spilled everything?

Hadn't Darkwell told Jerryl to get into Eric Aruda's head?

Hell.

He pulled out the cell phone he'd been keeping in his pocket in case they called. His finger hesitated on the button. If he called, he would be joining them. There was no going back.

Too late, buddy. You're already at the point of no return.

What he really hated was needing someone to bail him out. He'd always prided himself on his independence. But he knew when to ask for help.

One of the men answered, his voice wary. "Yeah?"

"It's Nicholas. I'm in a little trouble. I broke in to Darkwell's office. I had my father's file. And Lucas's mother's file. And he caught me."

"You had my mother's folder?"

"Had. I lost them both when I jumped from the balcony."

Lucas said, "Where are you?"

"In Potomac. I'm at Norwood School, off River Road near Harrington Drive."

"We'll call you right back."

The sound of a car engine snagged his attention. A car cruised into the parking lot.

CHAPTER 13

Nicholas ducked as a spotlight from the car played along the buildings. He couldn't see the driver's face, but he was sure it was one of Darkwell's men. The car turned around and began heading away. Then it stopped. A man got out, his body language that of a cop or someone who'd been in the military. He wasn't as built as Jerryl, so it had to be one of the guards.

The man disappeared into the darkness. Nicholas's heart thudded right up into his throat. He moved in the opposite direction, staying in the building's shadows. The lawn led down to a swale and woods. They'd provide good cover, but twigs and dried leaves could give away his footsteps.

His phone vibrated. He pressed the TALK button and blew into the phone to let them know he was there but couldn't talk.

"Nicholas, you there? This is Lucas."

One breath. Didn't that mean yes in Morse code?

"Okay, you can't talk. Listen. I'm looking at a satellite picture of where you are. Go past where the Dumpsters are and into the woods, going east. You're going to cross a street. You'll be in the woods from there on out. You'll come up on a creek. Follow that north. We'll meet you where Bradley Boulevard intersects with the creek. It's going to take us about an hour to get to you. We'll—"

Nicholas heard a *thump* and a woman's startled cry. He started to ask, *What happened?* but stopped the impulse.

"It's Rand. Lucas collapsed. He has these, well, we call them storms. He sees images of things that are either happening or about to happen. And I gotta tell you, dude, they're not good. Get out of there. We'll catch up to you soon."

Nicholas closed the phone, his throat tighter than ever. He scanned the surroundings. No movement. He ran into the woods between a fence and a line of evergreens. His footsteps sounded loud, every branch he broke a *crash*. When he was deep in the trees, he stopped and listened, trying to still his rapid breathing. He heard footsteps in the distance. He checked the compass on his diver's watch and headed east.

Jerryl could remote-view him, which was probably why the guard had stopped at the park. Jerryl obviously wasn't good at locating exact places, since Nicholas had been tasked with that.

It was Jerryl's other skill that worried him most.

He pushed that from his mind, staying tuned to any sensation out of the ordinary. Lucas's descriptions of the area were accurate enough to guide him. The sliver of moon didn't help much, but its reflection on the rippling water kept him from walking into the creek. It flowed quietly and blended in with the woods around him.

He double-checked his compass and walked north. The night chill clung to his skin and seeped through his clothes. The scent of pine trees and earth filled his nose. He jammed his hands in his jeans pockets and, for some reason, imagined Olivia back at the estate. Olivia, who thought he was a traitor. In her eyes he was. What did it matter? He'd never see her again. Unless he got caught and became a prisoner like Lucas had once been. She said she'd taken care of him, had obviously worried about him.

That was the kind of person she was.

So it's good you broke the bond between you. Broke it? More like tore it into a thousand pieces.

An eerie sensation prickled up the back of his neck, shooting the hairs to attention. He swung around, ready to face his opponent. No one there.

Not physically. But he felt someone. Pressure in his brain . . .

Nicholas, turn yourself in. You know it's the right thing to do.

The voice in his head . . . so compelling. Jerryl. He felt his body turning. Fought it.

Call out your location.

His mouth opened. He clamped it shut, his jaw cramping from the effort.

Fight, he thought. *No, fighting doesn't work. I'm sure Eric fought.*

Darkwell had taught him to shut out an enemy intrusion. Nicholas envisioned steel doors slamming shut, and Jerryl being thrown backward out of his mind. He put all of his energy, both physical and psychic, into it. The pressure lessened. Only his thoughts. It was little comfort. He had no idea how much Jerryl had seen. Or how close he was.

But he could find out. He closed his eyes and focused on the feral face he'd grown to despise. Tremors shook his body. Flashes of Jerryl came and went and then he homed in. His eyes snapped open, his heart jump-started again. He was close, too close.

He picked up his pace. His nightmare hadn't been about being shot in the woods. Why didn't he take some comfort in that? Because circumstances could change the future.

He kept looking behind him. He wouldn't see Jerryl, though. He would attack suddenly and swiftly. With a hard swallow, Nicholas walked faster.

He heard stealth footsteps and spun around, not sure which direction they were coming from. Two sets: one from behind, one several yards ahead. He wasn't going to outrun them. Time to go on the offensive.

The cold metal of a gun's barrel rammed into his back. "Gotcha." Jerryl's voice, low and sinister, filled with his smile.

Nicholas started to raise his arms in surrender but jerked his elbow back instead, hitting flesh and cartilage. The gun fell to the ground. He shoved his body backward, slamming Jerryl into a tree. They landed in a heap, Nicholas on top, faceup. Driven by instinct, he drove his elbow into Jerryl again, hitting what he thought was his chest. *Disable him, grab his gun, and get the hell out of there.*

Jerryl, however, had both training and instincts. Nicholas's fingers had just grabbed the cold metal when Jerryl shoved him forward. The gun flew out of his hands and landed in the darkness. Blood gushed from Jerryl's nose as he faced Nicholas, arms spread as though he were going to give him a bear hug. He was even growling.

Two sets of footsteps pounded toward them. Jerryl's comrades? *It's over.*

Except the big guy who materialized out of the shadows took aim at Jerryl, who raced off. Bullets hit the dirt with heavy thuds. The guy chased after him.

The second guy whispered, "Nicholas, it's Lucas. That was Eric."

Nicholas turned in time to see another man step up behind Lucas, gun pointed at his head. "Drop your weapon."

Nicholas didn't think, just acted. He slammed into the man, and both hit the ground. The gun went off, the bullet dinging a tree. Nicholas grabbed the man's wrist, pushing it, and the gun, away. The guy brought his knee up into Nicholas's stomach, driving the air out of his lungs. In that second, the guard brought the gun up to Nicholas's face. His finger tensed. The bullet exploded, ringing in Nicholas's ears.

Ringing. Which meant he wasn't dead. The man slumped across him, and Nicholas shoved him away and got to his feet. His frantic mind figured out what happened: Lucas had shot him.

Lucas looked at him. "Thanks for covering me."

"Yeah. You, too." But Nicholas couldn't help staring at the man's dark form. He was groaning, still alive.

"Let's find Eric."

They followed the sounds of bodies colliding, then a loud splash. Two men were slugging it out, waist high in the creek. Moonlight shimmered on the surface of the roiled water.

Jerryl's voice: "How the hell do you keep not dying? You *and* Lucas. He took a bullet in the chest. You shot yourself, hit an artery. You should have bled out."

Eric's voice: "I'm going to tear your head off."

Lucas aimed the gun. "Eric! Back away!"

"No way! He's mine."

Lucas let out a frustrated curse.

Nicholas started to move forward. "I'm going in. Eric needs help."

Jerryl had his hands around Eric's throat and was trying to throw him off balance. Lucas grabbed Nicholas's shoulder. "Wait. As soon as Jerryl steps back one inch, I'll have him."

Eric kicked at Jerryl's legs, making him step back and loosen his grip. He lunged for him again.

Lucas stood rigid. "Eric, move!"

"No!"

Lucas let out a sigh. "Stubborn son of a bitch. I ought to nick him." At Nicholas's horrified look, he said, "I'm kidding. Sort of."

Jerryl kicked Eric, sending him staggering back. Jerryl took advantage and came at him, trying to push him into the water. Eric resisted. The whole scene was surreal as the men struggled, their movements deteriorating into fatigued sluggishness. Eric slammed his fist into Jerryl's side. Jerryl kicked Eric's legs, buckling his knees and sending him down into the water. A shot startled Nicholas even though he'd been half expecting it.

Jerryl dove for the water as Eric fell backward in the other direction. He launched up and searched the water, but Jerryl left no clue to indicate his presence.

Eric turned to them. "What'd you do that for, bro? I almost had him!" He started slogging through the water, his gaze still searching the water.

"Didn't look that way to me," Lucas said.

Nicholas walked to the edge of the creek and held out his hand to help him out. Eric ignored that and struggled up the bank. Water sluiced off a body built like a truck. Anger radiated off him in waves.

"Let's get out of here. I disabled one guy back there." Lucas nodded behind him. He didn't sound too happy about it. "There could be others."

When they reached the road, an old, tricked-out car was waiting for them. He recognized the driver from the pictures Darkwell had given him when she was his target: Amy Shane. She was smaller in person and looked like a kid with the spray of faint freckles across her cheeks and nose.

Another man ran out from down the road: Rand. "I heard gunshots. Everyone all right?" He took in a wet, angry Eric. "Dude, what happened?"

Eric held his fingers an inch apart. "I was this close to drowning the bastard, and Lucas shot at him." He took off his shirt and wrung it out as he walked to the car. "He got away."

Lucas mimicked Eric's gesture. "He was *this* close to *getting* drowned."

They piled into the car, Nicholas and Lucas in the back, and took off down the road. Rand drove the motorcycle Nicholas had ridden on the back of in Baltimore.

Amy, in the passenger seat, made a quick call. "Everything went fine. We'll be back in an hour."

Nicholas felt all the energy drain out of his body. He

slumped back in the seat. "Thanks for coming." An understatement. They'd saved his life.

Lucas's expression shadowed. "I was surprised you called . . . after what happened to Robbins."

Nicholas told them why he'd decided they could be trusted.

Amy said, "We had a similar revelation. If you'd been part of the setup at your house, you wouldn't have left all of that neat stuff out. We could tell they were special."

Lucas ran his hand down his face. "The question for you is, now what? Unfortunately, you're a target. The way I see it, you have two choices: go into hiding until we can take out Darkwell, or . . ."

"You join us," Amy said. "You know what we're up against. It's going to be dangerous to get the truth, to conquer our enemies. It's all or nothing."

It wasn't a choice. No way was Nicholas going to hide out. Their enemies were now his enemies. Their truth, his truth. "I'm in."

Eric, who was driving, said, "You'd better not change your mind. You were an enemy once."

Lucas turned to Nicholas. "Have any of you ever seen our hideout or pinpointed its location?"

"No, it's got some kind of block around it. We—they only know it's in Annapolis."

Lucas said, "You said you had my mother's folder in your hand?"

Nicholas clenched his fist. "Yep. I've had my father's folder in my hand twice. Caught both times."

Eric twisted around. "You *are* going to tell us where Darkwell's place is, right? We need to get those folders. They have the answers to everything."

Nicholas remembered the two times the Rogues had broken into the asylum. "Is that all you want?"

"Well, that and to blow away anyone I happen upon," Eric said.

"Innocent people work there."

Eric's mouth twisted. "Like who?"

"Staff. They don't know what he's doing. Even the guards are just following orders. They think you're terrorists." And now they thought he was, too.

Eric shrugged. "Then we just take out Darkwell and his two stooges."

Nicholas winced. Until today he'd been one of those stooges. "I saw what you did to that guy at the asylum. You went nuts."

Eric glanced back. "You'd go nuts, too, if someone had your sister at gunpoint, and you had some asshole in your head taunting you. That's what your buddy over there can do, you know. That was the first time. The second time he tried to get me to shoot my friends at your house."

Amy's expression was sober. "He shot himself instead."

Nicholas cringed, remembering the conversation in the woods. "I felt him. He tried to get me to surrender. Instead of fighting him, I pushed him out." He turned to Lucas. "I can understand why you shot Robbins. Jerryl pulled the trigger, not you."

Lucas's expression was guilt-ridden. "It was different for me. Whoever was in my head took over." No way had he done it on purpose.

Eric was staring at Nicholas with narrowed eyes. "Are you protecting Darkwell? Is that why you're reluctant to tell us where this place is?"

"No."

"Who are you protecting?"

"All I've seen you do is barge in guns blazing." He remembered the scene at the hospital. No way could he put Olivia through that again. This time she might not be spared. Nicholas met Eric's surly expression. "Come up with a plan that's safe for the people who work for Darkwell, and I'll give you the location." He turned back to Lucas. "When you were giving me directions from the park, Rand said you got a storm."

Lucas nodded. "I saw you getting shot. The images come

so fast and violent I can hardly get a handle on the details. I saw the woods and Jerryl coming up behind you, and blood and . . . well, you get the idea. I knew we had to get you out of there."

"You get premonitions then."

Amy said, "Lucas is also a dreamweaver; he can get into other people's dreams."

"Are you also immortal? Jerryl said you wouldn't die."

They looked at each other, silently deciding what to tell him. Eric said, "I don't think we should—" at the same time as Amy said, "One of us can heal."

"Like miraculously heal?"

Eric held up his hand. "Don't tell him any more."

Amy said, "Darkwell already knows what some of our skills are. He knows I see glows, people's auras. Eric remote-views and—" She turned when he cut his hand across his throat.

"Wow. Wow." Nicholas scrubbed his fingers through his hair. *This is wild.*

Eric turned back. "What can you tell us about this other Offspring Robbins warned us about?"

"I heard nothing about someone else coming aboard. But Robbins was very nervous those last few days."

Lucas's face was still haunted. "He said the new Offspring was the last straw."

"A month ago we were all normal"—Amy looked at Eric—"well, mostly normal people going about our lives. We had our secrets, of course, but mostly they were just annoying or embarrassing and isolating. But we're here. And we're not isolated anymore. We have each other. That makes us more than a team; it makes us almost family. We expect your loyalty, and we'll give you ours. Unless you go off half-cocked"—Amy shot another look at Eric—"we have your back."

Nicholas said, "I'll have your back, too. But I'm not willing to put anyone who's innocent at risk of getting killed in the cross fire."

Lucas tilted his head. "None of us want to kill, but this is a war. Like tonight, we have to do things we never thought we'd do."

Nicholas shivered at those words and something that would forever be seared in his memory. "I saw you jump between a bullet and two women at the asylum."

"One of Darkwell's men was about to shoot her." He looked at Amy. "You do that kind of thing when you love someone. Petra's like a sister to me. And Amy . . . she's my life. I'd die for either one of them. I'd kill for them, too. You might end up in that same situation. You'd better think about what you're prepared to do."

"Killing someone goes against everything I believe in. Everything I am."

Lucas's words were low and ominous. "Everything you are, my friend, is about to change."

CHAPTER 14

Olivia waited for word in her father's office for what seemed like hours. She had the overpowering urge to nibble her thumbnail, an old habit her father had hammered out of her long ago. Fonda, the other independent contractor in the program, stood, worry for her lover's safety wracking her features. She could chew her nails all she wanted; she didn't have a father who'd slap her hand and tell her how undignified it was.

Gerard's phone rang, and he snapped it up. Olivia tensed as he listened to whoever was on the other end.

"All right." He huffed a long, disappointed breath she'd heard many times. "Come on back."

As soon as he hung up, Fonda asked, "Is Jerryl all right?"

"He's fine." He met Olivia's gaze. "The Rogues were there to rescue Nicholas. He was obviously in contact with them."

The betrayal cut so deep, she realized she'd been holding out hope for some other explanation. The pain engulfed her like a tsunami, stealing away her breath. He had chosen lawlessness over her, just as her mother had chosen freedom. Nicholas had used her, and the worst part was, she'd misjudged him terribly.

"The bad news: No one on their side was killed." Gerard

continued, "The good news is no one on our team was killed either, though Paul Emmert was shot in the upper chest."

Olivia's hand went to her mouth. "Is he going to be okay?"

"He's being taken for treatment now."

"Did . . . Nicholas shoot him?"

"No, it was one of the others. We're going to have to step up security around here. Nicholas has undoubtedly told them where we are. It's a good thing we didn't tell him much." He gave her a pointed look. *Like that you're my daughter.*

Her face blanched, a dead giveaway she'd been unable to tame. Luckily, he'd looked at the computer that contained views from their security cameras. "You both have to be very careful. Now that an insider has turned traitor, you're in danger."

Fonda jumped to her feet, her hands fisted at her sides. "I've been taking care of myself for a long time now. Instead of rapists and drug dealers, my enemies are terrorists. No big deal."

"Terrorists with weapons different than anything you've ever encountered," Gerard reminded her.

She gave him a smile. "But I've got a weapon, too. I'm going downstairs to wait for Jerryl."

For a small woman, Fonda packed more energy than anyone else Olivia knew. And passion. Subdued dignity had been drilled into Olivia. She could never display that kind of piss and vinegar in front of her father.

She *did* have that passion, though. Hadn't it roared out of her in the kitchen with Nicholas? And at other times.

"Nicholas wouldn't hurt me."

"Did you think he'd turn traitor on us?"

She paused, then shook her head.

"Exactly. I saw that romance novel you stashed in your desk drawer. Whatever you think love is, it's not what's in those books. That's fiction. Those insipid feelings that make you giddy and your eyes hazy also numb your brain and make you stupid. You're a Darkwell, and with that comes intelligence, cunning, and sensibility. While I've tried to instill in you feminine values, this is war, and you are now a soldier. Every time he talked to you, flirted with you, he had one goal in mind: find out what he could. Use you. If that hurts, good. Next time you'll listen to me."

She stood, every word like a dart aimed at her heart. "Thanks for setting me straight." She left, needing to release all of the anger and pain inside her. Damn, if it were only Thursday night. She desperately wanted to knock someone down.

She went down to the kitchen and poured a glass of wine. The hell with it. She grabbed the whole bottle and started up to her room. As she crossed the bridge that led to the east wing, she heard Jerryl's harsh voice.

"I'm going to *kill* him, him and Nicholas. I knew he was up to something the night Robbins got whacked. He was there, too, remote-viewing it. I could sense him. I could have had him tonight if Eric and Lucas hadn't showed up. I don't understand it. Those sons of bitches won't die. Nicholas went for me, and I lost my gun. Then Eric comes after me, and we end up in the creek slugging it out. I was too busy fighting to get into his head."

He paused when he saw Olivia standing on the bridge. His wet—and bloodstained—clothes were plastered to his muscular body. His eyes were swollen with bruises beneath them.

He'd said Robbins had gotten whacked. Killed. Her father said they only suspected he was dead, but Jerryl seemed to know for sure.

What did he mean by "remote-viewing"?

She locked herself in her room and cranked her stereo, choosing the classical channel. She took off her blouse and pants and put them in the hamper. She started moving to *Swan Lake,* trying to remember those ballet moves from years ago when her father had forced her to take ballet lessons. Neither the music nor the dancing was soothing her, so she changed the channel to Octane, Pure Hard Rock, and felt the drumbeat pulsing inside her. This she could move to, not to relax but to exorcise her anger.

She was stuck in the trap of pretending to be someone she wasn't and worrying about disappointing her father. But right now, while she was completely alone, she could be herself.

And who is that, a voice challenged. She ignored it and kept dancing.

Nicholas was about to learn what Darkwell most sought: the Rogues' hideout. They drove down a formerly residential street that was now galleries and stores. Shortly after, they pulled onto a gravel road, then into a stand-alone garage. Rand was already inside, waiting by his motorcycle.

Once the garage door went down, everyone got out. The air was fresh and cool, filled with the sound of rustling leaves and the distant hum of traffic. They walked across the yard to an old shed. Eric unlocked the door, and, when they were crammed inside, relocked it.

Lucas knelt and hoisted a trapdoor in the floor. "Follow me." He disappeared into a vertical tunnel.

Nicholas climbed the metal rungs and landed on the ground a minute later. Once they were all at the bottom of the ladder, they headed down a concrete tunnel. Footsteps echoed, and the air was damp and still. It was eerie, like being led to slaughter. His throat tightened at that thought. Lights dimly lit the long expanse. They walked for several minutes before reaching what looked like a blank wall at the end of the tunnel. Eric blocked Nicholas's view as he punched in a code on a keypad. The wall slid open with a beep.

Nicholas blinked, bombarded by both light, color, and two more faces looking expectantly at him. One was a tall beauty with long, straight, blond hair. She smiled with relief. "Back safe and sound." After a nervous laugh, she stepped forward. "I'm Petra."

"The one who told me the truth." He'd studied her picture often enough when he'd been ordered to target her. He turned to the looker with short, dark red hair and plump lips he'd met before. "Zoe." He shook her hand. She wasn't wearing as much makeup as the first time he'd seen her.

After hearing how vicious the Rogues were, he was relieved to see there weren't piles of guns and ammo on the long dining table near the kitchen. In fact, their hideout looked homey. He took in the space, one large room with a big pit group and artist's easel in the other half. A hallway led to more rooms. Each wall was a different vibrant color, and each was adorned with a painting of a different style. On one wall someone had painted a "window" looking out onto a mountainous scene so real he wanted to touch it just to make sure. They'd made this basement abode livable.

Petra looked at Eric. "What happened to you? You've got a big bruise on your cheek."

Eric touched his cheek where, indeed, a bruise marred it. He winced at the pressure and explained about the fight in the creek.

"And you're all scratched up." Petra, he realized, was studying him. "I'll get some ice for Eric and antiseptic for you."

"It's okay." But she was already heading off on her mission. He looked down and saw the scratches on his arms. His face, no doubt, looked as bad. "I had a run-in with some hedges."

Rand said, "We've all had run-ins, dude. My face was black-and-blue for a while."

Amy surveyed Nicholas. "They're not bad, but you do need them cleaned." She was shorter than the other two women, with a head of frizzy, dark blond hair. Not her natural color, if the pictures he'd seen were any indication. "Want something to drink? Water? Beer?"

"Water would be great." His throat was sand dry. "I can get it—"

"You sit." She walked into the kitchen.

It was odd being waited on. He was used to taking care of himself.

Petra handed Eric a bag of ice and went down the hallway, returning with some cotton balls and a bottle of hydrogen peroxide. She waved toward one of the dining chairs. "Sit. Hopefully it won't hurt much."

"You must be the healer."

Her eyebrows arched. "How did you know?"

"Because of what you're doing."

"I can't do the psychic kind of healing too much." She placed her hand over one of the scratches on his forearm, closed her eyes, and took several deep breaths. The others wandered over, except for Eric, who remained by the door, his body rigid.

When Petra removed her hand, the scratch was gone.

"That's amazing." Nicholas nodded to where she was rubbing her forearm in the place the scratch had been on his. "You take on the injury?"

"Yeah, something like that. I've never done a small wound before."

She started to place her hand over another one, but he stilled her. "It's okay. They're not worth your feeling my pain. But thanks, anyway."

She continued treating the rest of his scratches the conventional way.

These people were amazing. He could see why they had survived. As Lucas said, they looked out for each other. But he wasn't one of them yet. To be, he would have to give up the estate's location—and put Olivia at risk.

CHAPTER 15

Gerard sat in front of the grand fireplace in the parlor and tossed another red folder into the flames. He had suffered another loss tonight. The dark side was winning. The anger ate away at him just as the fire incinerated the cardboard. If only *he* had the ability to kill from a distance, to find someone no matter where they were. His mouth tightened in bitterness. He had to believe he would prevail. Jerryl was eager to begin targeting someone other than Eric. And then there was Andrus . . .

"Are you all right?"

Olivia's voice pulled him from his thoughts. Wearing silk pajamas beneath a robe, she looked beautiful but for the shadows in her eyes.

"You're up late. It's what, two in the morning?"

"Had a bad dream." She wrapped her arms around herself. He had seen her do that when she was a girl and had woken him in the night. He'd been woefully inadequate in consoling a child scared of something that wasn't real. He'd told her to toughen up and go back to bed.

She stepped closer and looked at the folder in his hand: Robert Braden's folder. "What are you doing?"

"Now that Nicholas is a traitor, the Rogues will know about these files. They'll do whatever it takes to get them.

I'm going to ensure their safety." He tossed the folder in the fire, and the flames flared.

He hated destroying the files. They contained the original notes from the first program and weren't on any computer. He didn't trust computers, not even encrypted ones. He knew there were ways to decipher anything. He had relented and put the basic information on the new program on the computer and backed it up to his home computer. But this data would only exist in his head.

She sat down on the wingback chair opposite him. "Did his father work with you twenty-five years ago?"

Gerard wanted to give her only enough information to sate her curiosity. "Yes. We had great success, as we're having now. Then someone sabotaged the program, and it fell apart." He gritted his teeth. "But not this time."

"Why did Nicholas want that file so badly?"

"Because the Rogues told him to get it, probably to get all of them." He tossed the next folder into the fire.

"What happened to Robbins? I overheard Jerryl telling Fonda he'd been . . . the word he used was *whacked*. How could he know that?"

His mouth tightened. "We know."

She paused for a moment, absorbing that. "He also said something about remote-viewing. What is that?"

She wasn't ready for the truth.

"There are things you mustn't see or know, things that would change everything forever, that would age you by decades and tarnish your golden light. I have spent my life protecting you from that and more."

He'd said this to her before, about other things, like her infatuation with the gardener's son. Usually she accepted it.

"What if I don't want to be protected?"

"You have no choice in the matter." He narrowed his eyes, studying what he thought was a shadow on her shoulder. "Is that a bruise?"

Her robe had slid off her shoulder, and she pulled it

up again. "I wasn't paying attention and rammed into the doorframe."

He'd seen other bruises on her. If she'd been dating someone, he would suspect abuse. "What was the point of signing you up for ballet and gymnastics, if not to teach you coordination?"

"Don't sidetrack me. I want the truth. You're going to have Nicholas killed, aren't you?"

"They all have to be terminated. They're a security and safety risk." He was annoyed to see her attachment to Braden on her expression.

She stood, hands fisted at her sides. "You can't kill him."

"Why not?"

Her mouth trembled. "I couldn't bear it. Have him arrested instead."

"Get it through your head: If I don't kill them, they'll kill me. Could you bear that?"

Her face blanched. It gratified him that the thought of his being killed seemed to terrify her.

"It's imperative you report anything out of the ordinary. It may seem odd or ridiculous, but if you notice it, there might be something more to it. Trust your instincts, just as I've taught you since you were a girl. Be on alert. And until they are eliminated, I want you to move into your suite of rooms here full-time."

"But—"

"No buts. I want you safe. I'll be here, too." He sent another folder into the fire. "I'm flying to Florida tomorrow. I'm appearing in court to take custody of a prisoner. He's going to be working with us for about four months."

"A prisoner? What kind of prisoner? What did he do?"

"He'll be under guard at all times. You will have no contact with him. In fact, I don't even want him to see you. He's quite charming, from what I've heard. Until he gets his hands around your neck. Don't be taken in by another one of our subjects. Especially this one."

Her mouth twitched in anger. "I'll heed your warning, Father. Good night."

Robbins also deserved his lesson. The search of his house had revealed that he, too, had gotten into these folders. He'd drafted a letter to Gerard, threatening to expose DARK MATTER if he disappeared. Fortunately, Robbins hadn't had time to set his plan into action. The copies were in an envelope with an attorney's name on it, and a note in Robbins's calendar indicated that his appointment was for the following day.

He threw the last folder into the flames. The past was over. All he cared about was the future. With Andrus aboard, the Rogues would finally be destroyed.

Fonda scowled at Petra Aruda's picture on the bulletin board above Jerryl's desk next to Eric's. "What's her picture doing in your room?"

Jerryl smiled at the jealousy in her voice. "I've always had a connection to her. She was the first one I could find. Then I tuned in to Eric and was able to mind-control him. So I focused on him. But I realized, what better way to get to Eric than taking her out?" He grinned wider. "I like the thought of him going berserk."

She was still looking at the picture. "She's beautiful."

He pinched her chin. "So are you."

"Not like her. Not like anyone, really."

He knew she'd had a hard childhood, but she hadn't talked much about it. She'd been drawn to him, and to his anger. He seemed to ignite it in her, allowing her to release it for the first time. Once she'd told him she was afraid to let it out, that it might consume her. She allowed those pent-up emotions out when they had sex, as though the act freed her somehow.

"What about the shield?" she asked.

"I've been thinking. You know how Gerard said Lucas and Amy had a psychic connection? That's how he knew when she was in trouble. What if I have that same kind of thing with Petra? Maybe I can get to her even if she's protected by the shield. I can't remote-view her, but maybe I can get under the shield to her head." He kissed her forehead. "Which means you'll have to sleep in your own room tonight. No distractions."

She never begged or whined. Despite her hurt expression, she simply left.

He settled into bed and looked at the picture of Petra. He filled his mind with her, so intensely his head hurt. For a second, he felt . . . something. Feminine energy. He could feel her, just like he could with Eric. He couldn't hold on to it, though. Maybe it was the shield or maybe it was that he'd already used his skills tonight and was too tired, but he lost the connection.

He would try again tomorrow.

Nicholas woke with a start, breath coming hard, other parts of him hard, too. He'd been dreaming of Olivia, kissing her, touching her, and just as he was about to slide into the warmth of her body, he'd woken. He sat up, rubbing his face.

She hates me now.

The thought hung in the dark, cool air of the room that was temporarily his. He was on the lower level of what he now knew was a bomb shelter. Zoe and Rand shared the room next door.

Forget about kissing Olivia or doing anything else. All he could do was keep her safe. She was the enemy to the Rogues, but he'd never see her that way. Her loyalty stood firmly with Darkwell, with her family; her self-worth was tied to her heritage. But he'd also seen the conflict on her face. She sure as hell hadn't wanted to alert her father to his presence in his office.

He dropped back in the bed, letting out a long sigh of frustration. They were a lost cause. So why was he dreaming about her?

The idea crept into his mind, as quietly and cleverly as

a snake. He could check on her. She'd be torn up, angry, probably lots of things. He'd just make sure she was sleeping tight.

He focused on her beautiful face, her delicate beauty, her smile, hell, she had such a gorgeous smile that started small, then bloomed, filling her hazel eyes. And the wonder that filled her eyes when he'd first kissed her. She was shy and sweet, so outrageously sweet. She had definitely been overprotected, and damn, but he wanted to show her what being made love to felt like.

There's no point in checking on her. What good is it going to do?

So he wasn't going there.

He shifted in bed, resettling on the soft mattress.

Yes, he was.

He sank into her, smelling her candy-sweet perfume, feeling the silk of her long hair, zoning in on her until he felt his body disappear. Then the *whoosh* in his stomach. A similar sensation to what he felt when he'd kissed her, he realized. His body twitched.

He expected to find her sleeping, so he was surprised to see her stalking angrily up the stairs.

I thought you were only going to check on her. You have. You've torn her up. There's nothing more to do but thrash yourself later.

He couldn't pull out. She walked into her room and let her robe drop to the floor, revealing white silk pajamas with thin straps over her shoulders. On one shoulder, he could see a shadow, dark as a bruise. She leaned against the French doors for a minute, pressing her forehead against the glass, her breath creating a foggy circle. She pushed away and started unbuttoning her top. Her fingers trailed inside the edge of her top, brushing against the curve of her cleavage as she continued undoing the buttons.

Time to get out. It's not right, spying on her like this.

She reached the last button and turned as she slipped out of it and tossed it to the chair. The moonlight shone through the part in the curtains, washing over her back and the dimples on either side of her spine. Her long hair fanned across her skin as she bent over and began to slide down her pajama bottoms. Black lace covered an ass so exquisitely shaped, so perfectly rounded, that his hard-on ached with throbbing.

She started to turn around.

Don't be a jerk.

He pulled out and threw himself out of bed. "Hell." He paced the small room, thinking of anything that would push those erotic images from his mind and punish him for lingering longer than he should have. He pressed his palms against the concrete wall and banged his forehead against it.

He could never have her, not now. All he could do was make sure she was safe until his death. It would come soon.

CHAPTER 16

Nicholas cooked everyone breakfast. Amy and Lucas had been in the office when he'd come up. They emerged, looking as though they had just read a funeral announcement.

"What's wrong?" Petra asked as she poured orange juice into glasses.

Amy took them all in. "Lucas and I had our DNA tested. There was a chance we were related, and we'd ordered the test before we found out we weren't. We just got the results."

Lucas held up the report he'd obviously printed. "There's an explanation of DNA, in simple terms. A strand of DNA is made up of building blocks, and there are only four of them: A, T, G, and C. The guy who wrote this says our samples were obviously contaminated, because they contain a fifth block. He's never seen anything like it." His gray-blue eyes were dark with fear.

"The Booster." Dread filled Amy's voice. "It changed our DNA."

The sizzling bacon, the others, everything else fell away for a moment. *Changed their DNA.* Nicholas lifted his hand, turned it palm up. It looked the same as before, but now he saw it differently. By the silence, the others were absorbing this truth, too. "What the hell could change our DNA?"

Amy's eyes were wide as she shook her head. "I don't know. But it can't be good."

"What do we do about it?" Petra asked.

Amy's shoulders stiffened. "We find Wallace and make him tell us what it is."

Nicholas set down a large plate of scrambled eggs in the middle of the table. "Richard Wallace?"

They all jerked their heads to Nicholas, who said, "Darkwell asked me to find him."

Amy put her hand to her throat. "Did you?"

"No. I was getting uncomfortable by then, so I pretended I'd encountered the same kind of block that protects this place."

"You had good instincts," Amy said. "He's the man who invented the Booster, the only one who might be able to tell us what's in it. How does Darkwell know Wallace is still alive?"

Eric shook his head. "No way can we approach him now that he's being targeted by Darkwell."

Lucas nodded in agreement.

Amy looked crestfallen.

Eric slumped in his chair, a surly look on his face. "So back to Darkwell. We go in, get those files, and kill everybody."

He had as much bloodlust as Nicholas had seen in Jerryl's eyes.

"And get yourself killed in the process," Nicholas said. "You think Darkwell hasn't upped the security suspecting I'll tell you where he is?"

Eric's mouth turned up in a snarl. "Which you haven't."

"The last time I gave you a location, a man was killed." He looked at Lucas. "I know you didn't intend for that to happen, but it did. I need to be sure you're not going to storm the place and kill innocents." Of course, Olivia's face flashed in his mind. "I agree we need to take out Jerryl and Darkwell. Get rid of them, and the program goes away."

If Darkwell was killed, Olivia would lose her father. She'd be devastated.

Amy had just stuffed a forkful of eggs into her mouth, and she talked around it. "He's right. The CIA doesn't know what's going on." She swallowed. "If they find out, they'll bury it, like they buried the first one."

Eric set his fork down on his plate with a loud tap. "They'll find out about *us,* though. They're sure as hell not going to want us out here knowing the truth."

Lucas said, "The only way they'll find out about us is if they look at Darkwell's files if they can even find them. They'll probably think he was nuts. Wouldn't you? Besides, they don't have the resources to investigate this kind of craziness."

Zoe's eyes widened. "Does that mean we'd be able to return to our lives? I could go back to my tattoo shop?" Her hopeful expression crumpled. "Except I'm wanted for dealing drugs." She looked at Nicholas. "Darkwell planted drugs in my apartment and tipped off the police. He figured they'd find me, then he'd swoop in and take me into custody. I've never even done drugs, and now everyone thinks I'm a dealer."

Rand rubbed her back. "The people who matter don't think that."

Amy turned to Lucas. "You can run your art gallery. I can be the Disc Angel who restores data from damaged hard drives." She rubbed her hands together at the thought. "Petra, you can—"

"I don't want to be a Hooters waitress anymore. I want to be a massage therapist. I want to heal people the normal way."

Eric picked up his fork. "I'm wanted for arson. Can't undo that, either."

Arson. *Fire.* Nicholas shivered. "The police think I'm involved in some kind of drug deal gone bad, but they don't have any proof. Yet."

Lucas sat back in his chair. "So it's agreed. We take out the enemy, no one else, unless necessary."

"And the Offspring chick." Eric looked at Nicholas. "Fonda, right? Didn't you say she's tight with Jerryl? And fierce?"

Nicholas reluctantly nodded. "But without Jerryl, she'll probably fade away."

Eric rolled his eyes before settling his gaze on him. "So, what, that's going to be another restriction before you tell us where this place is?"

He met his hard gaze. "Yes."

Petra said, "He's being chivalrous. You wouldn't know what that is, Eric, but it's a good thing. I don't think any of us likes killing people, except maybe you."

Rand pushed his plate away. "Even killing the badasses is hard. When I shot the assassin Darkwell sent after us, it made me sick. I was taking a life. I'd do it again to save any one of us, but it tore me up."

Zoe leaned her cheek against his arm. Just that simple gesture tugged at Nicholas. Images flashed through his mind, kissing Olivia, touching the scar on her temple. Which reminded him . . .

"Eric, you coldcocked a woman at the asylum when you broke in to rescue Lucas."

He didn't look the least bit remorseful. "Yeah."

Nicholas wanted to slam his nose for the scar he'd left on her and for his smugness. He pushed past that to something more important than caveman thinking. "She's one of those innocent people. I don't want her hurt, got it?" No way would he tell them she was Darkwell's daughter.

Eric gave him a smart-assed salute. "Yes, sir."

"I'll check out the estate to see what kind of security he's got in place. I don't want any of you to rush in and get killed, either."

After breakfast, Nicholas reclined on the couch and closed his eyes. He insisted that the lights be dimmed, ostensibly to focus. Even with people who were different, too, he wanted privacy.

He knew Jerryl could sense remote viewers, so he had to stay above the estate. He pulled out a few seconds later. "Just like I thought, he's got several guards outside now."

Eric turned up the lights, pushed up from the sofa, and stalked into the kitchen. "Remember what Robbins told us: Darkwell is bringing in the most dangerous Offspring yet. And Jerryl's bad enough. We can't afford to delay our offensive much longer."

Nicholas could understand Amy's comment about Eric going off half-cocked. "We're not going to accomplish anything if we get killed going in. Darkwell's expecting us. It's suicide."

Lucas sighed. "He's right. So we wait and see."

Petra nervously combed her fingers through her long hair. "The other night I thought I felt one of them—probably Jerryl, since he's always been able to view me easily. I didn't say anything because maybe it was nothing."

Nicholas saw the alarm on all of their faces. They simultaneously turned to him.

"I haven't heard anything about them getting through the shield, but they didn't tell me everything."

Petra started braiding her hair. "Cheveyo said his protection would only last so long. He said they would get stronger."

Nicholas asked, "Who is Cheveyo exactly?"

Petra's eyes glittered. "He's an Offspring, too, and he's the one who put the protective shield over the tomb. He helps us when we need it, but he stays at a distance."

Eric walked back into the living room with a glass of milk so cold there was a ring of ice around the edge. He leaned down into Nicholas's face. "Why don't you just tell us where he is?"

"When we're ready." Nicholas trusted them, but only up to a point. "What if I give you Darkwell's home address?" The man had to be eliminated. At least Olivia would be spared any direct violence.

"It's a start," Eric said.

The lights dimmed, and Nicholas sank into the ether again, picturing Darkwell's face. He sat up a minute later, shaking his head. "He's got some kind of block around him."

Eric narrowed his eyes. "Did you really try or did you pretend like you did with Wallace?"

Nicholas tilted his head, taking Lucas's cue not to let Eric ruffle him. "I tried."

Lucas said, "Remember, when we remote-viewed the asylum, Jerryl could bounce us out."

"Yeah, but there wasn't a shield."

Nicholas said, "What I felt was solid, like the shield that's over this place."

Lucas nodded toward the computer room. "We've already looked online and couldn't find anything about the Darkwells. Their properties are probably in some kind of trust. Let's check the estate in two days. Then we'll make a plan."

Nicholas sketched the estate's layout, and they threw some ideas around.

Zoe rubbed the back of her neck. A tattoo on the inside of her wrist speared Nicholas's attention. "What's that?" He walked closer and gestured for her to hold out her hand.

"It's our tattoo. We call it the Blue Eye." Lucas unbuttoned his shirt to show he had one over his heart. "Zoe came up with it. She's a tattoo artist. The eye is for BLUE EYES, the original project name. The O of the eye is for Offspring, and the R in the pupil is for Rogues. We all have one."

Nicholas turned to Zoe. "Where'd you get the idea for this?"

Her smile faded at the intensity of his question. "I dreamed it one night. I saw the eye and the slashes in the iris which I thought looked like an R. Why?"

"I've seen this before. Are you sure you haven't?"

"Not unless it was subconscious, but I'm pretty sure I'd remember it."

He told them how Pope had approached him about searching for classified items. He'd been sworn to secrecy, but now that Pope was affiliated with the enemy, Nicholas had no compunction about sharing the information. Not that he really knew much anyway. "Three missions were to find these bracelets made from some kind of strange gray metal with what I thought were gems embedded in them. I couldn't imagine why the government cared about them."

He shrugged. "But they were paying me, and it sounded like it was very important that he find them. One mission was to locate the wreckage of an experimental aircraft. I only found one piece, but he seemed pleased about it. He didn't ask me to find anything else, and we left." Nicholas nodded to the tattoo on Lucas's chest. "That was on the piece of metal I found."

No one spoke for several seconds.

Zoe rubbed the tattoo on the inside of her wrist. "Well, I sure as heck haven't seen any experimental aircraft."

Nicholas had a strange feeling about this. He couldn't tell if it was foreboding or if they were on the edge of something big. "Pope watched me as though he expected me to say something about it. The big question is, how did Zoe come to dream it?"

Eric looked at his tattoo, his brows furrowed. "You mean we might have some government insignia on us?"

Nicholas shook his head. "I don't know, but I'm going to find out."

Tuesday night Darkwell returned to the estate with Sayre Andrus and two armed men, both former prison guards. He'd beefed up security around the grounds, too, though that was mostly for the Rogues.

"Your quarters are this way."

"Ooh, *quarters*. Sounds impressive." Andrus's greedy gaze took in the luxurious surroundings as they walked from the kitchen to the winding staircase. Darkwell hadn't brought him in through the front entrance.

"They're in the attic." No need to let him think he was more than a prisoner. "But I think you'll find them comfortable, considering where you've been living."

"I'm here for four months," he said as they walked up the stairs. "Doing whatever it is you got me doing." He made quotes with his hands, the chains between his wrists jangling: "Top secret shit. And then you're going to work on extending my stay indefinitely."

"Right." But that would fall through, sadly enough. Gerard had a feeling four months would accomplish everything he needed, then he'd dump the guy back into the system. Or, if necessary, dump him permanently. He couldn't take the chance of Andrus's talking to anyone in prison about what he'd been doing.

Andrus's ankle chains had been removed. Gerard didn't think the guy would run now, if he was entertaining the thought at all. He was getting paid a lot of money in addition to relative freedom, but he wasn't getting a cent until he'd completed his work.

Andrus stopped at the top of the stairs and looked down. "Purdy place you got here. CIA must pay good."

Before anyone could react, he'd planted his hands on the banister, slung one leg over, and slid down, letting out, "Wheeeeeeee!" One guard ran down the stairs. The other jumped over the banister and, like a cat, landed on his feet at the same time Andrus reached the bottom. Andrus didn't sprint, though. He let out a joyful holler that was cut off when the guard tackled him. Both men landed on the marble floor, and the third guard took a stance, gun aimed at the scuffle.

Except Andrus wasn't fighting. In fact, he was laughing so hard his legs had pulled up into a fetal position. He let the guard jerk him to his feet.

"Hey, was just having some fun." He looked up at Gerard. "You ever done that when you was a kid?"

"No."

"Too bad. That was crazy, man. Crazy."

The guard pushed him back to the stairs.

Andrus gave him a broad smile that reminded Gerard of a kid's when they reached the top. "You don't know what you're missing."

"You could have been shot."

Andrus's smile mellowed to something smugger. "You wouldn't shoot me. You need me."

"I might not have shot you, but these men would. They have orders. You pull anything strange, and they take you out. Got it?"

The man's smile didn't waver a bit. "Maybe you'd better outline what, exactly, they consider strange. I don't want to get blown away 'cause I scratched my ass."

Gerard nodded for the men to lead Andrus forward.

Other than the rumors and insinuations, Andrus had been a model prisoner since his incarceration a year ago. The warden told Gerard that Andrus was polite and co-operated, though his streak of cockiness and an irreverent sense of humor grated. When one prisoner's body had been carried out, Andrus had been making a trumpet sound with his lips, doing "Taps."

When they reached the end of the hallway, Gerard opened the door and nodded for one guard to precede Andrus. The second guard would walk up behind them. Someone's footsteps—probably Andrus's—clunked up the wooden stairs.

In the past, these quarters had been used for the staff. He had, of course, secured them with bars on the small windows even though the drop would kill most men. Andrus wasn't most men, though, and Gerard was taking no chances. The door leading downstairs was replaced by a metal one, which would be guarded twenty-four/seven.

Once they reached the top of the stairs, Gerard stepped to the fore. "There are three rooms up here. You may use all of them as one space. One for your living area, in which I've installed a couch and television, one as a kitchen, which has been rudimentarily equipped, and one for your bedroom."

He was already exploring the room like an eager kid, opening doors and flopping on the couch, only to leap off again. "Windows! I get windows!" He ducked into the living room.

The guards reacted instantly, chasing him in, guns still at the ready. Gerard waved them back.

Andrus stood at the window and closed his eyes to the moonlight that was streaming in, a look of bliss on his face. He spun around, oblivious to the guards' alertness, and inspected the room. "I'll need cleaning supplies. A vacuum cleaner, duster." He swiped a finger across the coffee table and inspected it.

"Everything you need is already in the kitchen cabinets."

He knew about Andrus's obsession for cleanliness and order. His cell was impeccably kept, and he demanded stain-free uniforms.

Andrus walked down the hallway and into the next room, his makeshift kitchen. He opened cabinets as a child opens Christmas presents. When he found the cleansers, he pulled them all out, reading the labels. "Green. Good for the Earth. This one, no good. Pine-scented. Hate pine scent. No scent at all." He shoved it at Gerard, who had to take it lest it fall to the floor.

Andrus was already looking at the next product. "Acceptable. Good. Acceptable." One by one, he sorted them, so quickly his hands were a blur.

He shoved three more bottles to the end of the counter. "No good."

The guards watched, incredulous, but Gerard kept his expression passive.

"Do I get a computer?" Andrus asked.

"No. But if you tell me your reading tastes, I'll arrange for you to have books and movies to occupy your free time.

There's a phone. When you pick it up, you'll be put through to my phone. That's the only call you can make from here. If you wish to call anyone else—"

He stopped his perusal of the rest of the cabinets. "Got no one to call. My parents are dead."

"I know."

They had testified during his trial, and it hadn't been very complimentary. His mother claimed her adopted son had gotten into her dreams. Though she hated pickles, she would wake in the night choking on them. Then the next day he'd sniff the air. "I smell pickles. Isn't that odd?" Night after night she dreamed he was drowning her in her claw-foot tub. His father had told the police about a smart-assed comment Andrus made when he'd asked his son if he'd killed another woman who'd died in his apartment complex: "What would you do if I told you yes? Turn me in?"

That was a key piece of evidence, even if it didn't pertain to that trial, and probably what turned the jury against him.

Sometime after his conviction, his mother had drowned in her bathtub.

Gerard wasn't fooled by Andrus's childlike enthusiasm or his quirky tendencies. He had most likely killed a woman so viciously her neck was broken. From Andrus's files, one thing was clear: You didn't piss off Sayre Andrus.

CHAPTER 17

Nicholas woke at three in the morning. He didn't let himself think about Olivia, instead wracking his brain as to exactly where he'd seen the eye. Those four missions with Pope had been a whirlwind, hours spent tromping through the woods, more hours driving on rural roads and highways alike. He couldn't remember what he'd found at each location or exactly where he'd gone. He remote-viewed his house. Seeing the place and all his treasures made him homesick. His life had been so simple when he'd packed up and left.

He moved into his office and tried to focus on the map dotted with more than a hundred pins, some through his job at the salvage company, some with Bone Finders, and some on his own. He used red pins for government work. Which search had found the piece with the eye?

He took note of where the four red pins were and wrote them down when he pulled out. He went upstairs to find a map. When he stepped into the living area, he stopped at the sight of Lucas furiously sketching at his easel. Except that his eyes were blank, as though he were doing it in his sleep. Or being possessed. Amy watched him with a tense expression. She pressed her finger over her mouth and nodded for him to join her in the kitchen.

"One of the ways Lucas's premonitions come out is through sketches. He doesn't remember doing them." She looked over at him. "I've never seen him do one. It's a bit eerie, like he's not in there. Like when he shot Robbins. But I know this is different. He's saved people's lives, trying to figure out who's going to commit the crime and stopping him." Her eyes hadn't left Lucas. "If they come every night for four nights, whatever he's drawn comes true on the fifth day."

She returned to Lucas's side, hovering like a mother bird. Nicholas followed, looking at the sketch in a new way. It came to life under Lucas's jagged, hurried movements. A woman standing alone. A man behind her, and even as rough as the sketch was, Nicholas could see his menacing intent.

Lucas set down his pencil and slipped down from his chair to lie on the floor. Amy cradled his head in her lap, stroking his hair. Now her gaze was on the sketch, though, and her expression was even more concerned.

"He's seen one of us being murdered," she whispered. "But I can't tell which one."

The woman's hair was only a mess of lines and shadows, and she had no face.

"If he does another sketch tomorrow night, we'll find out more. And we'll be one day closer to its happening."

"What if we all stay here on the fifth day? Aren't we safe?"

She shook her head. "We don't know what this other Offspring Robbins was going to tell us about can do. Or how long we have until they can penetrate our shield. Once they do that, they can get to us anywhere."

A cold chill shivered down his spine.

Sayre woke from an erotic dream.

"Damn, my junk's all hard, and no one to use it on."

He'd taken care of himself in prison, but he was tired of handling it on his own.

It was about the woman again, the one he'd been dreaming of since he'd poked into Darkwell's head. She was connected to him in some way. He always had a connection to his dream victims.

He stood by the barred window, rubbing his hands together. "Come to me, baby."

In the dreams, he seduced her, slowly, sweetly, and then he slipped his hands around her throat and took her in the deepest way a man can take a woman. Far deeper than sex.

He'd only killed out of anger. His first victim he'd maimed. She was a lovely blonde he'd dated while in college. She'd dumped him, admitting she'd used him to get his help in biology. Pissed him off big-time. He wanted her to suffer like he was suffering every time he saw her with her new boyfriend, when she gave him a smug look. He'd been getting into his mother's dreams for a while, but he'd never tried to get into anyone else's dreams. Why not give it a shot?

He got in, all right, and saw her bedroom, her boyfriend lying beside her, everything through her eyes. He *was* her. He could feel the covers and the chill in the air.

She got up, naked as could be, and ran through the sliding glass door. He felt the glass pierce her skin, but not the pain. He felt her flip over the balcony's railing from the momentum and fall two stories to the ground. When she hit, he woke.

The news was all over campus the next morning, how that poor girl must have had a terrible nightmare. Yeah, she never did look quite as pretty. Shame, that.

Anyone who pissed him off got a visit from the Night Master.

His second girlfriend got it even worse. They'd met in one of their first-year veterinary courses. He told her not to go into the second bedroom, but did she listen? Noooooooo. She had to go in there anyway, nosy bitch. Yeah, he kept animal parts. From autopsies. No, he didn't go around slaughtering animals. He liked animals, thought they were a heck of a lot better than people.

Over the years of working for a veterinarian, he'd collected different animal parts that he preserved in jars. Kidneys, livers, eyeballs, even a dog penis. She looked at him in that belittling way his mother did sometimes when he explained his collection. She called him a weirdo and left. Then she told everyone on campus. He was getting roadkill left on his doorstep, and people looked at him like he was some kind of freak.

He realized he didn't want her hurt; he wanted her dead. He'd gotten into her dreams and made her walk down to the pool, which was dark in the wee hours. He joined her, but he wasn't willing to take a chance of leaving any DNA inside her. He felt her up instead, having the mind-blowing sensation of feeling him feeling her up. Then he pushed her beneath the surface and pulled out, giving her those few seconds of fear and panic when she woke to find herself underwater.

He'd fallen under suspicion as the ex-boyfriend, but they had no evidence.

That had given him the taste for murder. He'd waited a while. He didn't just kill to kill; he wasn't some crazy-ass serial killer. He needed a reason. It had to feel right.

A hot woman came into the veterinarian's office with her prissy dog, all worried about him. He helped her, was compassionate, all that shit, and she was grateful, so he asked her out. She went from friendly to condescending, looking at him as a lowly assistant. Yeah, he'd seen that look in his father's face enough times.

So he'd said, "What, you don't want to see my animal-parts collection? I got livers and eyeballs in jars of formaldehyde. I can show you my dog dick."

She got all out of sorts, complained to his boss, and nearly got him fired. So he'd looked up her address in the records and sat tight.

After toying with her dreams for a while, he lured her out of her nice and secure house to his car, where he took her to a nearby lake. In those dark depths, he strangled her. All of the hate he'd ever felt exploded out of him, and he took it out on her.

He'd sunk her body with two concrete blocks he'd discovered in the bushes earlier. She was found a day later by some boys who were fishing. Poor kids. Poor him, though, because the cops heard about his interest in her and her rebuff. They knew about the "accidental" drowning of his ex-girlfriend. The finger marks on the woman's neck roughly matched his fingers. Then they talked to his parents and cobbled enough together to make a circumstantial case against him. Despite his good looks and the nice suit he showed up in every day of the trial, the jury didn't like him. So they nailed him for life in prison, no chance of parole.

He'd paid some of them visits, too. They had nightmares about him, accusing them of sending an innocent man to prison.

Now he was going to pay this new woman a visit. He'd toy with her for a bit. Then he'd wrap his hands around her throat and kill her. In person.

He wandered the rooms, restless now. "I can't wait to find out who you are, pretty lady."

CHAPTER 18

Wednesday night, Jerryl finally made the connection with Petra. Triumph! Even through the shield that visually kept him out, he could feel her. He'd waited until he thought she'd be asleep. That made her more susceptible. He would finally get to take out one of the Rogues. The sweet part was that whacking Petra would get to Eric in a big way. It would weaken him, then Jerryl would use him to take the others out.

Darkwell had brought on some guy from prison. A convict, for God's sake. Jerryl couldn't let this guy best him. He had to make some progress, and quick.

"Petra . . . wake up."

Her energy changed.

"Wake up, Petra."

He felt her come fully awake.

"Good girl."

Cheveyo? Is that you?

That threw him off. Wait. He'd heard the name. Darkwell had mentioned him, the one who was protecting the Rogues. He'd rescued Zoe Stoker in Key West. She thought he was Cheveyo.

"Yeah, baby, it's me."

Are you in the garage?

Interesting. "Yes. I'm waiting for you."

I'll be right there.

How easy was this? She was coming willingly. So what could he use in a garage? Well, the car, of course.

"Bring the car keys. We'll go for a ride."

Mm, sounds interesting.

He waited a few minutes. "Where are you?"

Almost there.

She wasn't close to the garage apparently.

Where are you?

"I'll be right there. Why don't you start the car, get it warmed up? Don't open the garage door yet, though."

But . . .

"Start the car." This time more firmly.

All right.

"Now, stay there. I'll be there soon. If you get sleepy, close your eyes. I'll come to you like a dream."

Nicholas woke and looked at the clock: three again. Earlier, he'd refrained from checking on Olivia. But he would do it again. Not only because he wanted to make sure she was all right. As disciplined as he was, he couldn't stop himself from watching her, if only for a few moments.

You're a weak man. Maybe even some kind of pervert. A voyeur. Peeping Tom.

The recriminations didn't stop him. He closed his eyes and felt his body twitch as he sank into the ether. She was asleep, twisted in the sheets rumpled from restlessness. One bare leg stretched out of the sheets. He saw the creamy flesh of her waist and her arm. His conscience was glad he could see nothing more than that. Other parts of him, not so much.

He pulled farther back until he was in the hallway where his suite had been. Like a ghost, he floated through Darkwell's door. Nicholas couldn't read the papers on the desk clearly enough to make sense of them because of the lack of light. He backed up and headed down the hallway toward the mission rooms. He spotted an armed guard at the end of the hall. Another guard came around the corner. He listened to them for a minute, then tried to go downstairs. He encountered the block again and pulled out.

He got out of bed, threw on some pants and a shirt, and went upstairs. The tightness in his chest started again when he saw Lucas at the easel, Amy at his side. She met his gaze, even more worry on her expression than the night before. He wanted to put his hand on her shoulder for support but gave her a commiserative look instead.

He stood beside her, watching the sketch come together. Lucas had just finished the rough outline of the man, dark hair but no features. In that manic way, he started drawing the woman. She stood in front of the man, which was why his features weren't visible. He, in fact, was right behind her now. Lucas drew the man's arm around her shoulder, then his hand over her throat.

Amy's hand went to her throat, too, her gaze locked to the sketch.

When he looked at the sketch again, Lucas was drawing her hair. Long hair. Straight hair.

"Petra," Amy whispered. "She's the only one of us with that kind of hair. She's going to freak when we tell her they're targeting her."

The protective urge that swelled in him surprised him. Even though he didn't really know the female Rogues that well yet, the thought of any of them being killed—he shuddered and stopped the thought.

Lucas worked on the woman's facial features next. Movement behind them caught his attention, and he turned to find Eric walking out.

His expression sobered. "The second one," he whispered. It tensed when he looked at the details. "Shit. Petra. We've got to act now."

"I just checked and saw two guards inside. One said something about cruising the hall between Olivia's hallway and downstairs where Darkwell was staying. I hit the block, so he's definitely there."

Nicholas turned back to the sketch. Lucas finished the woman's mouth and nose. He worked on her eyes next. In another minute her face was finished. He dropped the pencil and lay on the floor, leaving the rest of them to study the picture.

Amy knelt next to Lucas and shook his arm. "Lucas. Wake up." She turned to the others. "He asked me to wake him if he did another sketch. Lucas!"

He roused, his eyes hazy. They came into focus when he saw them watching him. "I did another one?" His voice was slurred as he sat up with Amy's help.

"We think it's Petra," Eric said.

They studied the sketch in silence.

"It doesn't quite look like her," Amy said. "The eyes and mouth are different."

Once Nicholas put the assumption that it was Petra out of his mind, the features took on a different look. It sucked the breath out of him. He knew that face. His hand involuntarily twisted his shirt the same way fear twisted his chest. "It's Olivia."

Lucas stared at the drawing, nodding in agreement. "The woman at the asylum who cooled down my fever when I was being held there."

"But that doesn't make sense." Nicholas's knees got weak, and he knelt on the floor. "She's on their side." He turned to them, eyeing Eric in particular. "Unless her assailant is one of you guys."

"Sure as hell wouldn't be Lucas or Rand." Eric tilted his head. "I'd kill her if she was pointing a gun at me, yeah. But come up behind her and strangle her? Nah. Remember, I didn't kill her the last time I saw her."

Nicholas couldn't argue with that. He turned back to the sketch, his heart a chunk of ice. "Whoever this is, he's not killing her because he has to. It's because he wants to."

Amy wrapped her arms around herself. "You can see a smile on his face."

Lucas said, "Maybe it's Jerryl. Didn't you say he liked killing? Maybe she pissed Darkwell off, and he's targeting her."

Nicholas shook his head. "Not her."

"Don't underestimate his ruthlessness. If anyone gets in his way, he eliminates them. He killed his own brother."

"But he wouldn't kill his dau—" He stopped, wishing he could pull back the words.

Eric leaned closer. "His what?"

"His assistant."

Eric turned Nicholas's shoulder to face him. "That's not what you were going to say."

Amy's mouth opened. "She's his daughter. That's what you were going to say, isn't it?"

Nicholas reluctantly nodded. "He doesn't want anyone to know."

Eric said, "And you didn't want us to know."

"I didn't want you to target her because of that. She doesn't know what he's doing. She thinks he's this great man doing great things for the country. He raised her single-handedly, so she sees only the good in him. She's an innocent."

Eric stared at the sketch. "Maybe so, but she still works for the enemy. She's friggin' *related* to the enemy. So if a woman's going to be killed, at least it's not one of ours."

Nicholas looked at Lucas. "Does what you draw always happen?"

" 'Fraid so."

Amy slid her arm around Lucas's. "He intervened when he knew enough details. He saw me being attacked at a marina. He saved me from being raped and God knows what else."

Nicholas looked at the sketch again, that image searing painfully into his eyes, his chest. "I can't let this happen."

"She's not your problem anymore," Eric said.

"Yeah . . . she is."

Eric crossed his arms over his chest. "Crap. You're involved with her, aren't you?"

"We didn't get *involved*. There were rules against that, and she follows rules."

Amy tilted her head. "But you fell for her."

Had he? He'd never fallen in love. "I don't even know what falling for someone feels like. But the thought of her getting hurt tears out my guts in a way I've never experienced before."

She and Lucas looked at each other, and said at the same time, "He fell for her."

Lucas said, "Man, I know what you mean, believe me."

Eric shook his head. "No way are we risking our lives to save the enemy's daughter." He pointed his finger at Lucas. "And I will put my foot down on this one, so don't get all heroic on me again."

"He's right, Nicholas," Lucas said. "We can't do it."

Eric turned to the hallway. "I'm going to bed. This better not come up again." He disappeared into his bedroom, closing the door with a decisive *thud*.

Amy peered down the hallway. "I'm surprised Petra hasn't woken up."

Lucas stared at the drawing. "Soon after Eric, Petra, and I first learned about being Offspring, we found out Amy was one of us, too. I had been dreaming about her, connecting psychically to her, for years. I got a sketch of someone getting killed, and I knew it was connected to Amy and this Offspring business. I was afraid it was her. I didn't want to involve her, but I had to warn her to be careful, not to trust anyone. I recognize the fear and determination in your face, my friend. Nothing and no one could have stopped me from saving her."

She took his hand and kissed his palm. "He took the risk, and that's how Darkwell caught him."

Lucas closed his eyes for a moment before meeting Nicholas's gaze. "Immediately after the vision that compels me to do these sketches, sometimes I can go into the attacker's dreams and see his face. If I get another sketch tomorrow, I'll give it a try."

Amy put her hand on Lucas's arm. "Could you stop him?" At his darkening expression, she said, "To save this woman's life? She might have saved your life, you know."

"You can stop him in your dreams?" Nicholas asked.

"If I can get into his dreams and kill him, his body reacts as though it's really happening. Turns out the part of us that paralyzes our bodies during REM sleep is disabled when I'm in someone's dreams. I can't guarantee I'll be able to do that, though."

Nicholas nodded, though he could tell Lucas didn't like the prospect of it. Nicholas only felt a modicum of relief. "You warned Amy. How?"

"Scared me to death," she said, though she was smiling. "He broke into my apartment."

Nicholas shook his head. "That won't work. She's staying at the estate."

Amy asked, "Does she go anywhere at night?"

"She mentioned going to yoga class on Thursday nights, which is tonight. But I won't have any details."

"Take opportunity over details. At least she'll be on alert."

He had a plan. Sort of. "You just broke in and grabbed her?"

Lucas's grin was wry. "It wasn't what I wanted to do, but I didn't have time to earn her trust first."

Nicholas's laugh held not a speck of humor. "I sure don't have that with Olivia anymore. I'm the enemy in her eyes. So I'm going to have to do the same thing, grab her when she's not expecting it." He pulled his fingers through his hair. "I can't believe I'm even thinking this. *I'm* going to be an attacker."

"For good reason," Lucas said. "The key is, get in, tell her what she needs to know, and get out. She may not believe you right away, but hopefully she'll think about it. You took a big risk to warn her, and you didn't hurt her."

Amy said, "If you had any kind of relationship with her, she'll be able to tell that you care. I didn't know about our psychic connection, so I thought there was this mad rapist in my bedroom. Oddly enough, I could see he cared. Yeah, I thought I was crazy at the time, but that stuck with me. This guy took a big risk—and got caught—because he cared about me. If you and she had any kind of connection, you've at least got something to build on."

Again, an image of him kissing her taunted his mind. "Maybe." He looked at Lucas. "Amy said that whatever you're sketching comes true on the fifth day."

He nodded. "It's going to happen Saturday."

"There are only two days between when I'll get to warn her and the attack."

Lucas said, "Then you'd better do a damned good job of convincing her."

CHAPTER 19

In the dream, Petra found it harder to breathe. The air was foul and thick and heavy in her lungs. But every time she tried to open her eyes, his voice ordered her to stay asleep.

She trusted him, and so she obeyed. She felt her body slump onto the backseat.

Good girl.

She smiled at his words. He would be here soon. Until then, she would sleep.

Just a little while longer.

She tried to nod, but her head felt as light as a . . . she didn't know. Couldn't think anymore. Her thoughts floated away, leaving her head spinning.

Sleep. So much like death. Sleep. Die. Sleep. Die.

Die? No, not die. She tried to open her eyes again. Couldn't.

Panic fluttered in her stomach.

Not right. Head hurts. Can't breathe. The smell . . . can't breathe.

She imagined the smell like a snake, gliding across the seat. Up into her nostrils and down her throat. Into her lungs. Filling them.

Something touched her. Hands on her. Pulling at her. She couldn't fight. Couldn't move at all.

Didn't even care.

Sounds. A man's voice. Angry.

Her body moved on its own. Floating. No, someone lifting it. Carrying her.

The air changed. Air. Not that horrid smell. Cool, fresh air.

Her body being laid on the damp grass. Fingers tapping her face.

"Petra. Petra, come back to me."

Cheveyo. He'd come at last.

His mouth covered hers, breathing into her. Clean air into her lungs, chasing out the snake. His lips warm, hers so cold. He was breathing her.

"Petra, come back. Don't fall away, babe."

Another breath. His hand on her face, the other one cradling her head. His words coming on gasping breaths. "Petra. I'm sorry I'm late. But I'm here. Come back. You can't die, dammit."

The pressure in her chest was easing. He was drawing out that noxious air from her lungs. It burst out in harsh coughs, sending her body jerking upright. His arms came around her, pulling her against his hard body.

"It's all right. Cough it out, babe."

She had no choice. He held her tight as she coughed so harshly her throat felt raw. The movement sent her head spinning. Nausea came and went, replaced by tears that took her over.

He held her through that, too, stroking her hair and her back and murmuring, "You're okay, babe. You're okay."

"What . . . happened?"

"You were in the car in the garage. The engine was running."

Her head still felt fuzzy, but she knew what that meant. She turned to him, seeing the waves of his dark hair in the moonlight, the exotic slant of his eyes. "That's . . . what people do when they're trying to kill themselves."

He nodded.

"But I wasn't . . ." She tried to remember how she'd gotten to the garage. "I wasn't trying to kill myself."

He brushed a strand of hair from her face. "I know."

"It was you. Or at least I thought it was you. It's all kind of fuzzy now, but I remember you telling me to wait in the car, that you'd be there soon." Her eyes widened. "It was one of them. Jerryl."

He nodded again. "The one who can get into your heads. I had a premonition that woke me up. I saw you in the car dying." He rubbed his hand over his mouth. "I was almost too late."

"But you weren't." She tilted her head. "You live close by?"

"I'm staying close by for now." Before she could ask more, he said, "I'll be right back. I'm going to get you water from my bike." He disappeared around the corner of the garage and returned with a bottle. She gulped it.

"Slow," he said. "Your stomach might be touchy for a bit."

"He got to me. Even down in the shelter, he got to me."

"He's got a connection to you, like I do."

She wrapped her arms around him and hugged him tight. "Thank you."

"I didn't do you a *favor*." When she backed away to see what he meant, he touched her mouth. "If you died . . ." He couldn't even finish the sentence, but the fear of that thought was clear in his voice and expression.

She had been dreaming of him ever since he'd brought Zoe to them three and a half weeks ago. She'd felt the connection between them then. Now it engulfed her.

She saw his desire, as she'd seen it before, but also his conflict. "Stay with me."

"I wish I could." And he meant that. He stood, holding his hand out to her. "You don't know how hard it is to stay away from you."

"But why?"

He pulled her to her feet. "You'd better get underground again. He might be able to get into your head, but he still can't penetrate the shield. Not yet."

"Let's go." He led her to the shed. He knew where their shelter was, even knew where the secret entrance was. He was one of them though he seemed to have powers beyond those they possessed.

The strongest of those powers was the one to possess her heart.

He paused outside the shed. "If I call you, I'll say the word, *Yaponcha*. That is the wind god in Hopi Indian folk-lore."

"Who are you protecting, Cheveyo?"

"All of us." He rubbed his knuckles just above her heart. "I'll always be with you. Here." He raised her chin and kissed her gently on the lips. "Be safe. Now, go."

Reluctantly, she turned and opened the shed door, then made the long trek through the tunnel back to the shelter.

CHAPTER 20

Nicholas sat down to locate Olivia. He expected to see a class full of women in a quiet setting with their legs twisted around their necks. So the crowd of people screaming and the murmurings of an announcer in an auditorium almost knocked him out of the mission.

His brow furrowed as he tried to make sense of it. It was an indoor hockey rink. But no. The floor was concrete and lit in purple. And barreling at him was a group of women in helmets. Two teams, half wearing light blue tank tops, half in bright green. Garter belts, designer panty hose, makeup on some that reminded him of the rock group Kiss. They flew past on four-wheel skates.

What the . . . ?

He looked forward again. One woman careened toward him, aiming for the pack. Olivia! Olivia with a fierce expression, elbows stiff at her sides and chin down, a white star on her helmet. She wore a fluffy black skirt with cartoon characters from *The Flintstones* on it. Her legs were covered in fishnet stockings, and she had ribbons entwined in her two braids. She was on the light blue team: the DC Derby Divas he now saw on her tank top, which revealed an intriguing slice of her flat stomach.

She attempted to skate around the pack, and one of her opponents tried to bounce her out of bounds by knocking into her sideways. Olivia shoved back, knocking her down and pushing another opponent into one of her teammates, sending them both out of balance. A Diva grabbed Olivia by the hand and pulled her around, giving her momentum to fly ahead.

Just as she was about to break free, one of the green women bumped her, sending her flying forward. She tucked and rolled, then slid across the floor. His heart jumped, and he was about to run to her to see if she was all right when he realized he wasn't *there* to do that. One of her teammates helped pull her to her wheeled feet.

Olivia, none the worse for her fall, skated toward the pack again. He couldn't help the grin across his face. She kept on surprising him. He wasn't sure exactly what she was doing, but it intrigued the hell out of him.

She emerged from the front of the pack and tapped her hipbones with her hands. A whistle sounded, and the group headed toward the sidelines. Olivia bent one knee and slid in, trading hand slaps with the next group to get into position.

Wary of spending too much time and tiring himself out, he pulled back to pinpoint her location. He would be seeing her soon enough.

Olivia hated when the bout ended. She still hadn't expelled all her piss and vinegar. The locker room's energy was intense, since they'd won, and so was the smell of menthol. The girls compared bruises, but no one had broken anything, always a good thing.

They didn't have showers at the arena, and most of the girls went to a bar where they mingled with fans.

"Great jammin'," a teammate said as she stretched.

Because she was small and fast, she was one of the jammers, the player who scored the points by jamming through the pack. Blocking was more suited for the tougher, bigger women, like Candy Ripper, who was six feet tall and had Mohawk spikes that fit through the holes in her helmet.

Scornacopia was lying on the carpet, groaning. "Man, that's the second time I made love to my wheels." A term for wheels in the vagina, Olivia had learned but had been fortunate enough not to experience.

"Damn, Liv, you were a ball buster out there tonight." Angie, also known as Akill-eaze, laughed. "Someone piss you off?"

Olivia gave her a twisted smile. "You could say that."

"Must be a guy."

Two men, actually.

Olivia just laughed, unwilling to say anything more. She was new to the DC Divas Roller Derby team, though she knew she was going to continue with the team until her body couldn't take it anymore. The aggression, the camaraderie, the fun of being someone else, was an allure she would not give up anytime soon. She had told the girls on the team little about herself even as she longed to reach out. These women, from all walks of life, were a lot more fun than the few women she occasionally socialized with. What she wanted was a girl buddy, someone to share secrets and talk with about men.

Like a mom. Or a sister. Or her cousin. The women in her family weren't particularly interesting, all concerned with politics or shopping, things that didn't interest Olivia. Her aunt, Leon's wife, was the closest woman in her life to a mother. When Olivia was young, Eileen had taken an interest in her. She'd wanted a girl but couldn't have any more than her one son. Olivia had, for a time, become her surrogate child. But Eileen's constant reprise of, "If I had my own girl . . ." had finally made Olivia uncomfortable enough to put distance between them. She clearly had reminded Eileen of the daughter she'd never had, and over time her aunt's self-pity had taken on a bitter taste.

"You sure you don't want to go to Barnaby's?" one of her teammates called out as she headed to the door.

"I'd love to, but I can't tonight." She changed out of the "uniform" that let her be something outrageous for a few hours.

Like Nicholas had.

Stop!

But there was an annoying part of her that couldn't let him go. It didn't make sense that a guy who volunteered to find the remains of missing people would become a terrorist.

She had to get a cab to the yoga studio where her car was parked, where she'd pretended to go in, then slipped out the back way. A ridiculous but necessary detour to throw off the guard her father insisted follow her everywhere. If she stayed in class any longer, he might become suspicious.

Would it be so bad if her father found out? Maybe it was time to come out as a kick-ass roller-derby girl.

Once the cab dropped her behind the building, she entered from the rear entrance and out the main door. Her blue BMW was parked at the edge of the lot, the guard standing beside his car. She'd drawn the line at his riding with her. He was big and creepy, a former cop who'd lost his job because he'd been too violent. Yeah, that made her feel safe. She liked her driving time, cranking whatever satellite channel suited her mood and relaxing for about the only time she ever could. Now she needed something to wind her down.

She pulled into the shopping plaza that housed the coffee shop where she always stopped on the way home. The bulldog got out but leaned against his car and waited for her to go inside. Thank God.

She had a bad feeling her father was hoping Nicholas would make a move on her so the guard could take him out.

The scent of freshly brewed coffee filled the place, though she liked her flavored instant coffees best. She stepped up to the counter and ordered, then walked over to the restroom. She passed the tall silk tree next to the entrance and pushed open the door. Something rustled behind her. She started to turn to see what it was. A man pushed her into the bathroom and closed the door behind them. She inhaled to scream, and his hand went over her mouth. She heard the door lock click.

She did a hip check on him, turning slightly and nailing him. With him not being on skates, it wasn't as effective. He barely moved. She twisted and tried to jam her elbow into his stomach.

Then she saw her assailant. Nicholas! He was dressed in black, and he had scratches on his face. Her eyes widened in both shock and anger. He *was* a terrorist! His body was pressed against hers, his hand around the back of her head and over her mouth. His palm was damp and smelled of soap.

She kicked, tried to block with her head, illegal moves she couldn't use at roller derby. She managed to knock him off balance, but he was too strong to shove away.

"Livvie, I'm not going to hurt you. I'm sorry to scare you like this, but it was the only way I could talk to you. You've got a damned bodyguard. Is that because of *me*?"

He wasn't going to hurt her. She grabbed on to those words and the regret in his eyes.

"I've got to tell you something life-and-death important and then I'll leave. I can't afford for you to scream and alert your bodyguard, because if you do, he'll shoot me. You know that, don't you?"

She nodded, and as much as she hated Nicholas at that moment, the thought of him gunned down tore at her.

She felt his hold on her loosen, and she slammed him into the wall. Then she started beating on his chest, all of her pain and fury unfurling. "How could you turn traitor? You didn't just betray my father and our country, you betrayed me. You charmed me and made me feel something for you." Tears sprang to her eyes. "You used me to get information! And now you're one of them!"

He caught her wrists. "I never used you. I liked you before I ever talked to them." He took a ragged breath. "I liked you more than I wanted to."

How dare he look so damned sincere!

He continued. "I did betray your father, but only because he's not the good guy. He's using us to kill people. That's what his program is about, political assassination. The Rogues aren't terrorists. They only want the truth about their parents and the program they were in twenty-five years ago. Your father wants us dead because he doesn't want us to expose his program. He had Robbins killed for the same reason."

"Shut up."

"I'm not here to convince you of anything. I'm here to make sure you're safe. Listen to me. You remember Lucas? You helped him when your father held him prisoner. You asked about my special skills. His is getting premonitions that come out in drawings. He drew you . . . being strangled. It's going to happen this Saturday."

The emotion in his words, along with the words themselves, shivered through her. "Premonitions? You mean like . . . psychic premonitions?"

"Exactly."

She blinked. "I don't believe in that stuff."

"I need you to believe for just one day. Your life depends on it." As crazy as it sounded, he looked dead serious. "We can't see who it is, but it's not one of the Rogues. They don't kill unless they have to. This is a killing for pleasure. I want you to stay at the estate all day Saturday. You should be safe there."

"I'm already staying at the estate full-time now, because of you. My father thinks you're going to hurt me."

"I won't ever hurt you."

"Too late."

She saw a flash of pain in his eyes. It was quickly replaced by confusion. "I need to know what your plans are for Saturday."

"I don't really have any plans. I almost hate going out with a guard shadowing me. I probably would just stay around the estate."

His eyebrows furrowed. "I thought you'd be safe there . . . unless it's someone who's at the estate. Has anyone given you the creeps?" At her skeptical expression, he pressed further. "Humor me."

"Fine. I don't like any of the guards, but none have given me the willies. The guard assigned to me is a bit, well, he has some violence in his past. He used to be an overzealous cop."

"Hell. And you're alone with him. He could attack you and then blame it on one of us."

She shivered. "You're scaring me."

"Exactly what I want to do. The men your father hires are renegades by nature. Mercenaries."

"But their background checks revealed no records of violence against women."

"That just means none of them have been caught." He leaned closer, his nose touching the tip of hers. "The premonition is based on your current plans. Promise me you'll change them. Better yet, stay at your place, lock the doors. And get a different guard assigned to you. But still, be very careful. Don't put yourself in a position to be alone with any of those guys."

She didn't know what to make of his frantic warning. Damn him! And damn her, too, because her body was reacting to his, tingling where they were pressed together. Her heartbeat pounded inside her chest, but it wasn't all anger and fright.

He said, "You'd better get going before your bodyguard gets suspicious."

She opened the door, but he touched her shoulder, and she turned around.

"Don't trust anyone," he said.

"You taught me that lesson well."

He winced, and she turned and stalked out.

"Ma'am, your chai latte!" the barista called out to her.

She turned to grab it, spotting Nicholas standing next to the silk tree he'd obviously been hiding behind before, his expression bereft. She snatched up the cup and walked to the door.

The guard was walking in. "You all right? Saw some guy bothering you."

Her heart nearly stopped. She could tell him who that guy was. That's what her father would want her to do. What she should do. But that part of her that didn't believe Nicholas was a traitor, who knew what his fate might be, stopped her.

"Just some guy trying to pick me up."

She walked to her car and held her breath as the guard remained near the door looking in. Nicholas was just out of sight. The bulldog reached for the door.

"I've got to get back," she called out, but he walked inside.

She dropped the cup and followed, her throat tight with fear. He walked right toward the restroom. Nicholas wasn't there. The guard yanked open the door.

It was empty.

She looked around. Where was he?

The guard opened the door bearing a sign that read EMPLOYEES ONLY. One man, sitting at a small table eating dinner, jumped at the sight of him.

"Some guy come through here?" the guard asked.

"No."

Her gaze went to the exit door and then to the side window where an old car tore out of the parking lot. The guard returned and leaned down into her face. "Mr. Darkwell said some guy might try to contact you, and that you might cover for him."

"I wouldn't cover for that jerk." She turned and went back to her car. The bulldog would either keep looking or follow her. Either way, she was going back to the estate.

She slammed her car door shut. "Dammit, Nicholas. You really are one of them now. Go ahead and believe their lies. They're up to something. And I'm going to have to tell my father about it." Because as much as she couldn't stand the thought of something happening to Nicholas, she would lose much more if her father was killed, and she could have stopped it. She would wait, though, until Nicholas was able to get to safety.

When she returned to the estate, she checked her father's office. His door was closed, and she heard Jerryl's voice on the other side.

"I was so damned close. *Again.*"

The door opened suddenly, startling her. Jerryl stalked past her to his room.

Her father looked up, his face a mask of tension. "What can I do for you?"

So the guard hadn't reported the odd activity at the coffee shop to him, at least not yet. Good. She closed the door and sat down in the chair. "You look tired."

"I'm fine," he said in a weary voice.

The thought of losing her father made her stomach ache. "I ordered you some vitamins for stress. You have to take care of yourself, get enough sleep, eat right."

His face softened. "Thanks for your concern."

She lowered her voice. "You're all I have, Dad. I love you."

He actually smiled, something she hadn't seen in months. "It's been you and me for a long time. I did a good job, didn't I?"

He always reminded her of that. She nodded.

"And my job didn't end when you became an adult, even when you joined the CIA. It won't end until I'm in the grave, but hopefully everything I've worked hard to instill in you will continue on."

She wasn't sure which statement made her stomach tighten: the thought of his being in the grave or the obliga-

tion that went with his words. His devotion was her prison.
No, *her* devotion was her prison. She had to push out the
words. "I saw Nicholas today."

The paternal softness disappeared. "What?"

"He warned me that Lucas Vanderwyck had a premonition about my being strangled Saturday."

"Where was the guard? This is the kind of thing he was
supposed to prevent. Braden could have hurt you."

"But he didn't. The guard waited outside while I went
into a coffee shop."

"Olivia, I don't have to tell you how disappointed I am
that you didn't alert him. You're too soft. A Darkwell does
not protect the enemy."

"Would you rather have me destroyed by my responsibility for a man's being killed, haunted by the memory of
seeing it happen?"

He let out a sigh. "You need to watch more of the
History Channel. War is war. And make no mistake: This
is a war." His eyes narrowed as he studied her. "You have a
red mark on your arm. Did he do that?"

Now was not the right time to disclose her pastime. "I
toppled over in yoga class."

"Clumsy." He shook his head. "What exactly did
Nicholas tell you?"

She recounted it as best as she could remember, though
she didn't tell him about his accusations. *Did you have
Robbins killed?* She couldn't push out those words. The
mere thought was a betrayal.

"He wants you away from here. Why?" He tapped his
fingers on his desk. "Because they're planning something.
An attack on the estate. He doesn't want you here. Isn't that
sweet?" He gave her a bitter smile.

"He told me to stay here, until he realized that was my
plan."

"He's playing games with you, trying to figure out your
schedule. I appreciate that he wants you out of the fray.

Frankly, that works in my favor. Now I know what they're up to, and when they're coming." He looked out into the night. "We'll be ready for them."

She could see his mind working, plotting murder, growing a smile at the thought. It made her shudder. "I don't want Nicholas hurt."

He shifted his onyx gaze to her. "If he and his people come onto my property, I have the right to terminate them. Do you think they're going to spare my life?"

She shook her head, that question settling into the deepest recesses of her heart.

He asked, "Do you believe his warning?"

"I believe he's worried for my safety. And . . . I think you're right. He probably wants me out of the way knowing the Rogues will be coming."

He nodded. "And you will be away from here."

"I'll stay safely tucked in my condo. I don't need a bodyguard anymore. If Nicholas had intended me harm, he had the perfect opportunity. Besides, you'll need the guard here on Saturday." Did she believe Nicholas? Some part of her was anxious to get rid of her guard. "And I want you gone, too."

He raised his eyebrow at her assertions but didn't argue. "I don't like hiding, but I certainly don't want to give them what they want. The Rogues will be cut down as they enter the property, but should they penetrate the building, they won't find me."

She breathed out in relief. "Fonda shouldn't be here, either. She may be tough, but there's no point in exposing her to the risk." Fonda had talked about her skills. "The special skills Nicholas, Jerryl, and Fonda have . . . are they . . . supposed to be supernatural?"

"Is that what Braden said?"

"Not exactly, other than Lucas's supposed premonitions."

"Forget what he said. He's over the edge."

She stood, feeling agitated. "I'm going to bed now. Get some sleep."

Most of the time he was her father, but sometimes she was his mother.

As she reached the door, his words stopped her. "Olivia, you understand he's one of them now, don't you? He stalked you, accosted you. Whatever his intentions, he's now a Rogue."

She didn't turn, but nodded and continued to her suite. She took a shower, then tossed and turned in bed for the next hour. Her body had betrayed her. Was still betraying her. Because she could feel Nicholas against her and that electricity coursing through her veins. She still heard his emotional words about him liking her more than he wanted to. He'd woken up that sensual part of her she'd buried for so long, and her body wasn't going to let her forget it.

Nicholas couldn't sleep. He was charged up from seeing Olivia, from worry . . . from desire.

Get it out of your head. You're not going to see her again. You won't feel her against you, won't kiss her . . . nothing.

It wasn't working. He kept thinking about her on that roller-derby track, strong and tough, then later, holding her against his body, the hurt in her eyes, the betrayal . . .

He flopped onto his back. Maybe he'd check on her, a quick in and out and make sure she was all right. He closed his eyes. He didn't have to focus on her; she was already permeating every cell of his brain.

After the weightlessness, her room came into view. It was near dark but for the moonlight streaming through the gauzy curtains at the French doors. He turned toward her bed, expecting to find her asleep. The first thing he saw was a flash of movement. Then bare skin. His throat tightened. She was dancing across the floor, using all the space in the room. Wearing—he swallowed hard—only a black bra and matching panties edged in lace.

He couldn't hear much of the music, only a throbbing beat. Then it came in clearer, Alanis Morissette, "You Ought to Know." Her eyes were closed as she sank into the experience, singing along with the attitude song. Despite getting into the sentiment of the angry song (*Oh, that part about going down on him in a theater!*), he had never seen such grace, such beauty. She arched her body so that her stomach looked long and lean. Good God, she looked like a stripper, no, better than any stripper he'd ever seen. Her long hair slid over her shoulders, grazing her back, flowing with her movements.

He didn't care anymore if it was wrong to watch her. He was as caught up in it as she was. He wanted to put his hands on that waist, slide them down over her hips.

But you're not. Get that out of both of your heads.

The thought killed him. But the physical head wasn't the one he was worried about. The truth went deeper, and that was much worse.

CHAPTER 21

Lucas heard Amy's voice from what sounded like a long distance away.

"Lucas, go into the dream."

That was the cue they'd agreed upon if he had done another sketch. The third sketch, which meant this woman was probably going to die. If he connected with the attacker, he would go into his dreams, if the man was also asleep.

He saw Olivia's face, screwed up in panic and fear as the man's fingers tightened around her throat. She gasped, clawing at his hands, throwing her body against him to no avail, getting weaker and weaker, finally going limp. Lucas didn't want to be here. He could feel the man's evil pleasure as her naked body slumped to the ground.

He'd done more than just kill her.

The man's voice, a slight Southern drawl. "All right, sweetheart, now you gotta disappear. Can't let anyone find your body."

They were in the woods, in a small clearing, but the muted moonlight washed over the surface of what looked like a lake just yards away. The man's face was in shadow. He prowled the shore and hauled three rocks over to Olivia's body, where he re-dressed her, then stuffed the rocks into her clothing. He rolled her into the water, tripping and falling in, too. He let out a whispered expletive, shaking the water from his head.

Not enough to go on. Stay with it.

He groped down in the water, probably feeling for the body. Then he pulled her farther out.

The moon broke through the clouds as he walked to the shoreline. He stood. Turned around. Lucas readied himself to memorize his features.

He didn't have to.

His eyes looked back at him. His face.

The shock propelled him out of the vision.

Amy touched his shoulder. "Are you all right?"

He couldn't look at her. It didn't make sense. How could he kill Olivia? He'd never touch a woman in anger, much less kill her. The man he'd seen had enjoyed taking her life.

Me. Somehow, it's going to be me.

"Give me a minute." He rubbed his hands over his face, trying to figure it out.

Then it came together. He could kill through his dreams. And the Booster was making him crazy. He'd feared hurting his own people, like shooting them as Zoe's dad had done.

This was much worse. Something was changing in him. He was becoming a murderer. And he was going to enjoy it.

Fear vibrated through him like an electrical current. No way was he going to become a monster.

He took a deep, ragged breath and wiped the fear from his face. "It was pretty intense."

"I bet. Did you see the man's face?"

"No." He couldn't tell the Rogues, especially not Amy. "But it's going to happen Saturday night. I'm going to give Nicholas whatever I can to save her."

It was time to call in the promise he'd forced Eric to make.

Olivia saw the man in the shadows. He was coming at her, and she sensed the danger of him like a tiger stalking closer.

Where was she? How had she gotten there? The room felt like a large, concrete box, with only one shaft of light coming down from above. It was cold, dark everywhere but in the spotlight beam she was in. And she was naked.

"Hello, Olivia." His voice was low, seductive. He stood just outside the light, cloaked in darkness. "I've come for you."

He touched her throat with the tip of his finger, and she started to move away from him. But she couldn't.

Couldn't move!

"Please . . . go away."

"Not a chance." He moved into a shaft of light, illuminating his face. *Lucas Vanderwyck.* "You and me, we got a date."

He circled her, drawing his hand with his movements so that it trailed around her shoulders, her arms, then her hips. His touch repulsed her and left a burning path along her skin.

"What have you done to me?"

He came face-to-face with her, dipping his finger into the hollow of her throat, rubbing it up and down.

"You're in my prison, my little buttercup. Mine to do with as I wish."

"No." *Damn, why couldn't she fight? Move?*

"*No.*" He mirrored her panicked word, his eyes wide in mock horror. "No." The laugh that burst from him bounced off the hard walls and cut right through her. "Yes. Oh my, yes, when the time is right. Are you going to fight me, Olivia? Or are you going to let me do as I please? I like when they fight, you know. I like seeing the fear, hearing the choking sounds. Either way, it's going to be good."

His other hand had gone around her throat as he'd talked, and now it tightened. She was making those sounds. She couldn't breathe. He let up. Released her. "I'll be back, darlin'."

With a gasp, she sat up in bed, dizzy from the movement. Her hand had gone to her throat. She checked her room. Shafts of moonlight coming through the French doors. Not a concrete box. No Lucas.

She pushed out of bed, her knees weak, heart pounding. The dream clung to her like dark and sticky molasses. His voice still echoed in her head. She went into the bathroom and turned on the light.

She ran water and splashed it on her face, wanting to wash away that residue. Why would she have that kind of nightmare about Lucas? She had only seen him ravaged by fever, calling out for his girlfriend. Her mouth twisted in a frown.

Nicholas. His warning had tainted her dreams.

She dried her face and returned to bed.

Puppies. Babies giggling. Slamming Betty Ballbreaker at the bout the other night. Nice, pretty thoughts.

She curled up in a fetal position under her sheets. Only as she was about to drift back to sleep did something hit her: the icky way she felt tonight was how she felt after the unknown dream that woke her the night she found her father burning files.

Nicholas, along with the other Rogues, stood around the easel Friday morning, staring at a more detailed sketch of the man who was strangling Olivia. His face still wasn't clear.

His warning hadn't changed anything, at least so far.

No, she'll listen to you.

Sure, she will. Because you're the guy she can trust.

The thought knotted him up inside.

Petra chewed the tips of her fingernails as she studied the sketch. "That's scary."

Nicholas pointed to the edge of the sketch. "You can see part of the lake Lucas mentioned earlier."

Lucas was lost in thought, his expression dark. He only looked up when Nicholas said his name. "Yeah, some kind of water."

"I need to look at the satellite maps, see where a lake might be."

Nicholas checked online maps in the Potomac area but didn't find any lakes. The only real body of water was the Potomac River. Unfortunately, it was miles long.

He walked back to the living area. "It's probably the Potomac Riv—"

A small fire erupted in the garbage can next to the desk.

"Eric!" Petra ran to the kitchen sink. Amy picked up the can and met her halfway as she ran back with a glass of water.

Nicholas froze, his chest seizing up. The water doused some of the flames with a sizzle, but fire still licked at the air. Images from his nightmares pounded through his head. The heat, suffocating, his skin burning . . .

"I've got it back!" Eric shouted as though from a distance.

Amy turned on the faucet to extinguish the rest of the flames. "You could have warned us!"

He shrugged. "I didn't know it would work. I've been staring at that damned garbage can every day."

"What's wrong with Nicholas?"

Everyone's voices were tinny.

A hand waved in front of him. Someone called his name.

A shove to the shoulder finally jarred him out of his stupor. Rand stood next to him. "What happened to you?"

The fire was out, smoke curling out of the can and stinging his nostrils. "How . . . how did that fire happen?"

Eric's shoulders puffed in pride. "I did it."

"You . . ."

"I set fires. I have pyrokinesis. Pretty cool, huh? I lost my abilities when Petra healed me after I shot myself. They finally came back."

"Nicholas, are you all right?" Amy asked. "You were frozen."

He turned to Eric. "You're going to kill me."

"Not unless you piss me off." He tilted his head. "Kidding."

Nicholas shook off the last of the haze. He didn't want to get into his premonition. Eric wouldn't do it on purpose, but somehow Nicholas knew, that was how the fire was going to start.

Eric rubbed his hands together, an anticipatory smile on his face. "I need to take care of some unfinished business." He looked at Nicholas. "I'm not a finder. I need a location, at least the vicinity, before I can remote-view someone. Where is Darkwell?"

"Only Darkwell?"

"And Jerryl."

"No one else."

Eric huffed out a breath. "No one else."

Nicholas showed him on the map.

"Finally." Eric lay on the couch, crossing his arms over his chest as though he were in a coffin, and closed his eyes.

Nicholas still hadn't shaken the residue of fear from seeing the fire and discovering Eric's ability. He looked at the others, all spellbound, watching Eric. His jaw tensed, his eyes squeezed shut, hands curled into fists. Sweat broke out on his face. Several long minutes passed.

Eric's light blue eyes snapped open. He took a deep breath, as though he'd been holding it the whole time, and he looked at the group. "I couldn't get to Darkwell. That block Nicholas encountered. But I got someone else."

"Who?"

"We don't have to worry about Jerryl coming in anymore."

Everyone went silent for a moment, looking at each other, the statement sinking in.

Nicholas could hardly push out the words, "You set him . . . on fire?" Burned alive. His nightmare, burning flesh, screams of pain . . .

Eric nodded. "If he survives, he won't be much use to

anyone. He and his girlfriend were getting it on. He was distracted."

Petra put her hand to her heart. "I hate to be glad someone died . . . especially that way, but after what he's done to us, I am. Does that make me a terrible person?"

Amy put her arm around her shoulder. "No."

There wasn't a celebration, but the relief was palpable.

Eric collapsed back on the couch. "*Nobody* messes with my family. He tried to make me kill my own people. He tried to kill my sister." He took a ragged breath. "Fonda was on top. I started the fire beneath him to give her a chance to get away."

Nicholas's stomach heaved. "I need to go downstairs. Work off some nervous energy." He disappeared down the passageway.

Alarms woke Olivia. She threw on her robe before racing out into the hallway. The smell of smoke and an acrid odor hit her nose first. When she turned the corner, she saw smoke and heard shouting. Another sound cut right to the center of her chest—a woman's howling screams.

She turned the far corner to the hallway where the offices and the subjects' suites were. One of the guards was spraying waves of foam from a fire extinguisher into Jerryl's suite. Her father, wearing blue silk pajamas, tore past her. Something made a hissing sound, and water began spraying from the ceiling near the doorway. Smoke billowed out of the room, along with that terrible odor, making her eyes sting and her throat burn.

Fonda was the source of those horrible screams, punctuated by harsh coughs. Her naked body was folded into itself, her hands over her face. Olivia looked her over, expecting to find burns. Thankfully, she saw nothing but old scars. What she thought was a burn mark on her hip was a tattoo of a kitten. A guard raced past from behind, carrying another extinguisher.

Olivia hurried forward. Her father looked up at the movement. "Stay back! We've got it under control. You don't want to see this. Trust me."

The guard standing in the open doorway stared inside the room, horror-struck.

"What happened?" she asked.

Fonda screamed, "Erica Aruda burned him! While we were making love, they burned him!"

The Rogues . . . burned. The smell. Oh, God, it was burning flesh. "Is he . . . ?"

Her father was staring into the room, where smoke was still drifting out. "If he wasn't, he'd want to be."

Fonda started sobbing again.

Olivia stopped her imagination from filling in what Jerryl must look like. She sank to her knees and pulled Fonda into her arms. She shook so hard, Olivia could hardly hold on to her.

"How did he get in?" She looked around frantically, but no one was in a defensive posture, only dealing with the fire. She remembered when the fire had broken out at the asylum. Her father told her Eric Aruda had a special skill for setting fires but never explained how.

Fonda's voice chattered. "Pyrokinesis!"

"What?"

"He sets them psychically."

No. Impossible.

Fonda tried to talk between her sobs. "He did this out of . . . revenge, I know it."

"Revenge?" Olivia coughed. "For what?"

"Jerryl tried to kill Eric's sister."

Gerard said, "That's enough, Fonda. He did it because he wants to destroy us." He turned to Olivia. "You see what Nicholas is part of now?"

She couldn't deal with that thought. She pulled off her robe and helped Fonda into it. Everyone was coughing, jagged and raw.

A pounding noise on the door at the end of the hallway

got their attention, along with a panicked male voice: "Hey! What's going on out there? There's smoke coming through the floor!" The prisoner.

"We've got it under control. Just a small fire."

Just a small fire. To trivialize it like that. Not that Gerard should tell him what had happened.

To the guards, he said, "Check in with the others in case the Rogues are using this as a distraction like last time." He took a cell phone out of his pocket—did he sleep with it?—and made a call. "Pope, it's Gerard Darkwell. I've got another situation that needs to be handled . . . No, it wasn't Andrus. Eric Aruda just torched one of my people . . . Jerryl Evrard. I'll need a fire marshal's report. Accidental. Body disposal. . . . Thank you." He disconnected.

Pope again.

Gerard's expression was grim as he walked over and knelt in front of Fonda. "Did you get burned?"

She shook her head. "He . . . screamed, and I thought I'd hurt him and jumped off. A second later . . ."

He gently took her chin in his hand, forcing her to look at him. "Listen to me. This was an accidental fire. If anyone asks, if you talk to his family, a candle fell onto the bed and caught the sheets on fire. Do you understand?"

She nodded, her face wet from tears.

Olivia couldn't believe it. "You're covering it up?"

"I can't disclose the truth without exposing the program."

Fonda started crying again.

"What is the truth? Is it true, what she said? No, of course not. What is going on here?"

He took Fonda's wrists and pulled her to her feet. At first Olivia thought he might hug her, though he'd rarely done so to her. He put his hands on her shoulders. "Do you want to let them break you down? Or do you want to *take* them down?"

Anger transformed her grief. "I want them all to die. Especially Eric Aruda."

Olivia shivered at her hatred.

"Good. Use your anger as fuel. Keep working on your skills, and you'll be able to take him out."

Olivia asked, "What are her skills?"

"That's not important." She had never seen that mask of controlled anger on his face. He looked at Olivia. "Take her down to the kitchen and get her something to drink."

Olivia helped Fonda down the stairs. She led the girl to the table, where only days before she and Nicholas had shared a piece of cake—and more. She went to the sink and filled a teakettle. "You said Jerryl tried to kill Eric's sister. How?"

Fonda slumped in the chair, her gaze vacant. Her ears were pierced multiple times, each loop a different color. "He got into her head and tried to make her kill herself, but one of the Rogues saved her."

The water spilled out over the spout. Fonda said it so matter-of-factly. *She* believed it. Olivia shut off the water and set the kettle on the gas stove, remembering something she'd overheard Jerryl say to Fonda: *I was too busy fighting to get into his head.* Olivia thought he'd meant psyching out the enemy.

No, this was crazy. But how could the Rogues set two fires without being anywhere near? Special skills, that was all she knew, skills Fonda, Jerryl, and Nicholas used while closed away in those missions rooms.

What if it was real? What if her father *was* doing something much more sinister than just spying? Like what Nicholas had suggested? "Fonda, tell me more about how Eric set . . . how he did this?"

"I don't know *how* this stuff works, it just does. We were born this way."

Olivia's chest tightened. Impossible, her brain screamed, but she said, "Tell me about Jerryl, what he could do."

Fonda's wet eyes glittered. "He . . . was . . . *was* so talented. He could remote-view."

"What's that?"

"See other places without going there. Psychically spy."

No way. "And the thing about getting into someone's head?"

"That was his most amazing talent. He could mind-control." She looked at Olivia. "He could get into your head and make you do things."

Olivia shivered. "Like . . . ?"

"He tried to get Eric to kill the Rogues. But he was strong, too. He shot himself instead. He should have died! If he had, Jerryl would still be here!" A new wave of sobbing ensued.

Olivia tried to make sense of it, but it overwhelmed her.

"He was everything to me," Fonda said to no one in particular a few minutes later. "For the first time in my life I felt complete. Jerryl made me complete."

Olivia sat down at the table with her. "That's not true."

Fonda looked at her through teary eyes, her liner dripping down in black streaks that reminded Olivia of Akilleaze's makeup. "My mom died when I was a kid. She killed herself because I wasn't enough to live for. I was never enough, except with Jerryl. He loved me for who I was."

Olivia's heart squeezed into a hard, small ball. "I do understand, Fonda. My mom took off when I was a baby. I've never heard from her, don't know if she's even alive." Those words tightened her throat. She rarely spoke them aloud or let herself think them. That and Fonda's fear of never, ever being enough echoed in Olivia's soul.

It was hard to see Jerryl as someone who could care about someone, but maybe he had a different side that only Fonda had seen. Hadn't Nicholas made Olivia feel good about herself, before all his questions and doubts? He'd seen her as a person, not an expectation.

Fonda looked at her. "What about your dad?"

At first Olivia thought she knew Gerard was her father but realized the question was general. "I was lucky. He raised me. Loved me."

"Yeah, well, I didn't have anyone to love me. My dad

married the first bimbo who would put up with his drinking after she got a whiff of the money the Army gave him for my mom's death. Connie once told me the money was barely worth putting up with me, and back then I was a quiet, sad little girl who tried to be good because she desperately wanted to be loved."

Bitterness tightened Fonda's expression. "It didn't matter. She hated me whether I was cleaning the apartment or acting up. She screwed him in more ways than one, running up so much debt they went bankrupt and moved into a shit-hole apartment. She also introduced him to her circle of friends, druggies who got him hooked on heroin. He was worthless after that."

Olivia remembered hearing Fonda saying she'd had to deal with rapists and drug dealers, that she'd been taking care of herself for a long time. Now, with Fonda broken and vulnerable, Olivia saw beyond her cavalier façade. She saw the sad little girl who just wanted to be loved.

Then the little blonde Olivia was imagining morphed into a girl with long, brown hair and hazel eyes, trying ever so hard to be lovable.

"Can you top that?" Fonda said, covering pain with her bluster and need to have the worst story.

"No." Olivia didn't want to imagine what Fonda might have gone through, a pretty girl among people like that, no one to protect her.

The bluster faded, though, and Fonda pulled up her bent legs and hugged them to her chest. The robe fell away, revealing fine scars crisscrossing her calves. "Jerryl was the first person ever to protect me. For the first time in my life, I felt loved. Like I was worth being loved. And now . . . he's gone. And I'm nothing again. He's gone . . . gone!" She descended into tears, burying her face against her knees.

Olivia reached out to touch Fonda's shoulder but hesitated. She was a rose, beautiful, delicate, but prickly with thorns. Olivia dropped her hand. She wanted to point out that it seemed their relationship was more about sex than love, and that maybe Fonda was confusing the two, but she held her tongue. It wouldn't matter.

She sat in silence and watched the girl cry, her pain twining around Olivia's heart like a strangler vine. Olivia felt the same way. She hadn't attached her self-worth to a man's loving her. For her, it was her family. Without them, and their approval, she was nothing. So she toed the line, lived within their expectations out of fear, just as Nicholas had suggested. She only now understood why: *What were you worth if your own mother couldn't love you?*

CHAPTER 22

While Amy, Petra, and Zoe were out getting supplies, Lucas asked Eric to take a walk in the tunnel with him.

Eric's shoulders were puffed with victory. "It feels so good not to have to worry about that son of a bitch anymore. A big weight's been lifted off my shoulders." In the dim lights of the tunnel, he studied Lucas. "How come you look miserable?"

Lucas paused, jamming his fingers into his front pockets. "I've never been thrilled with the idea of your burning people alive. But I understand it with Jerryl. I'm relieved, too. That's not why I wanted to talk to you alone."

"So, shoot, bro. What's up?"

"I lied about not seeing the face of the man who's going to kill Olivia."

"You know I don't care if the enemy's daughter gets it. But Nicholas does, and that's a worry, too. I know how you guys are when you're in love. You go kind of crazy."

"Eric, listen to me." His voice echoed softly against the concrete walls. "I lied about seeing the guy's face."

Eric's face paled. "It wasn't me, was it? I consider her an enemy, but killing her like that . . . that's sick stuff."

"It was me. I saw my face."

For a rare moment, Eric was speechless.

"I felt the guy's pleasure at killing her. It wasn't because

she was in the way or the enemy's daughter. It was just . . .
pleasure. And then I saw his face. My face."

"No way, man. That's not you."

"I know. But with this stuff inside me, the blackouts, and
shooting Robbins—"

"That was Jerryl."

"I don't think it was. It was different than being mind-
controlled. You and Nicholas hear his voice in your head.
I lose control. I'm not even there. I doubt Zoe's dad was
the kind of guy who'd shoot people. But he did." Lucas
put his hands on Eric's shoulders. "Somehow, I'm going to
kill Olivia on Saturday. It's probably going to be psychically. That's how I killed those men who were going to hurt
people. I strangled them in their dreams."

"So we keep you awake Saturday. You don't leave the
tomb."

"It's not only Olivia. If I'm capable of doing that, of killing a man who was about to tell us something important,
I'm capable of . . . killing you guys. Remember the promise
you made."

"That you made me make. I'm not going to kill you,
Lucas. You're like my brother."

They *were* like brothers. When Lucas's mother died,
Petra and Eric's dad took him in. They'd just lost their
mother, when she'd burned to death in a supposed lab experiment gone wrong. Except they knew it was Darkwell's
experiment.

"I might kill you. Or Petra. Or Amy." Lucas shuddered
at the thought. "And if I did, I'd kill myself. I couldn't live
with that. It's hard enough living with the fact that I killed
Robbins. So if I'm going to end up dead anyway, take me
out before I hurt someone else. Spare us the pain."

"Does Amy know about any of this?"

"No. You can tell her afterward. I'll leave her a letter so
she won't blame you."

He slapped his hand to his chest. "Blame me? She'll
friggin' *kill* me!"

"Not when she understands. She knows about our pact, so it won't be a complete shock." He met Eric's gaze. "You can handle Amy. I'm calling in my promise. You and I will go down to the shooting range. The girls don't like being down there anyway, and if anyone else wants to tag along, we'll tell them we want to do some male bonding."

"Oh, great, they'll think we're gay lovers."

Lucas laughed despite himself. "You all like those sordid reality shows. It'll give them something to talk about."

Eric took a deep breath, planting his hand against the wall. "Until I tell them I shot you."

"You have to do it. It's getting worse. The other night I woke up in the storage room. *Where the guns are kept.* Amy didn't know, and I didn't tell her. I didn't want to worry her."

"And she *is* worried."

Lucas rubbed the bridge of his nose. "I know. It's going to hurt her."

"It's going to devastate her. That woman loves you like nothing I've ever seen."

The thought of leaving her, of hurting her, made his chest ache. "It would be even worse if I hurt one of you. Especially if I'm aiming a gun at her. This is no different from when Jerryl was in your head, trying to get you to shoot Zoe, Amy, and me. You shot yourself instead. That's what I'm doing here. You have to take me out first. Promise me."

Eric hesitated at that bit of logic.

"Dammit, promise me. I'd do it myself if I didn't think I'd either chicken out or just maim myself. Or that Amy or one of the girls would find me first."

"Okay, okay." He released a sigh. "I promise."

Lucas's shoulders relaxed. "Thank you. I know what I'm asking is hard."

"Hell, that's what it is. You're putting me in hell."

"No, Eric. For once, you're an angel."

* * *

It was afternoon before Olivia could go into the business wing to her office. All the windows had been opened, but the horrid smell lingered. The door to Jerryl's suite was closed, and construction and scrubbing sounds floated from within. Could you really clean away that kind of horror? Would she ever get it out of her mind or her nostrils?

She emerged from her office and came face-to-face with . . . Lucas.

The bizarreness of it stole away her breath. The armed guard who'd been stationed at the end of the hallway since Wednesday accompanied Lucas, who wore wrist and ankle chains. Had her father captured him again? Her stomach twisted at the thought.

Seeing him brought back the nightmare, especially when a smile broke out on his face. "Well, well, who do we have here?"

"Keep moving," the guard said, pushing him along, though Lucas kept looking at her.

"Wait." She caught up to them. "Lucas?"

"No, darlin'." He bowed, his chains clinking. "Sayre Andrus, at your service."

His Southern accent wrapped around those words, adding sensual undertones that were emphasized by the gleam in his blue-gray eyes. He took her in, not exactly leering, but with such intensity . . . it sounded crazy, but it made her feel like he was touching her. "Mm mm, you are like a dream."

She was dumbstruck. His hair was shorter than Lucas's, but he had the same lean build, same slightly exotic features.

"Olivia."

She turned to see her father standing in his doorway. She recognized the order in his tone and broke out of her spell to walk to his office.

He closed the door behind her. "He's not Lucas Vanderwyck."

"But it . . . he looks . . ."

"It's his identical twin. The prisoner I warned you about."

The one he'd told her not to get taken in by. She bristled at his suggestion that she'd fall for a prisoner. What had he said? He'd be charming until he got his hands around her neck.

"You didn't warn me that he looked like Lucas."

He narrowed his eyes. "You weren't even supposed to know about Lucas."

She'd wandered over to the east wing of the asylum and discovered the prisoner. It had bothered her that he'd been burning with fever, no plans to get him help other than some mysterious injection her father had ordered Harry Peterson to give him.

"Andrus is being temporarily moved into Nicholas's suite while his quarters are being repaired from the fire. It was so hot it burned up into the floorboards. He'll be back to his secured quarters soon."

"Is he dangerous?"

"He's got too much to lose to try anything. He'd go back to prison, and right now he's hoping to get transferred out of the country once his assignment here is finished. He's been a model prisoner. I expect nothing less here."

"He obviously has some . . . skill for you to go to the trouble and expense of bringing him here. Something you're going to use against the Rogues."

He smiled. "Yes. But the specifics aren't your concern."

"Yes, they are my concern."

His eyes widened. She hadn't allowed him to dismiss her this time.

She continued. "If I'm in danger, if what happened last night . . . if this touches me, my life, I'm entitled to know what's going on here. You said I was the only one you could trust. Prove it."

His eyes narrowed, and his voice was low. "What do you want to know?"

She couldn't believe she was asking, "Do Fonda, Nicholas . . . the Rogues, do they have . . . psychic powers?"

"Yes."

She sucked in a breath, hearing the word from her father, a man of logic.

He picked up a piece of paper. "If that's all—"

"It's not. I want to hear you confirm it. Jerryl could get into someone's head and control them? Eric Aruda can set fires with his mind?"

"Yes."

She put her hand to her chest. "You believe in this stuff?"

"I not only believe it, I've put everything on the line for it. And I'm not the only one. Our government has dabbled in psychic experiments for decades. During the Cold War, the U.S. thought the Russians were way ahead of us in using psychic powers to spy. We had to protect ourselves, or at least those who were in high positions. A program ultimately called STAR GATE was bandied from agency to agency through the 1970s and 1980s before being dismantled. I started my own program."

"The one Nicholas's father was in."

"Yes."

The secrecy, the reason the CIA director couldn't know, why her father was spending his own money . . . she could hardly wrap her head around it. "And Nicholas, what is his special skill?"

"Nothing deadly. He can find you anywhere. Are you wearing the crest pendant?"

"Always, just as you told me to." She automatically touched the pendant and felt the familiar grooves.

"It's not just a pendant. It has protective powers. A man who worked on the original project with me created it. Richard Wallace knew copper had protective properties against psychic energy.

"I gave Wallace pennies that were minted in your birth year and mine. He melted them down and took them to a special place out West. He charged the metal in one of the energy vortexes of the earth and, using his own spectacular powers, imbued the metal with super-protective properties. I had them molded into the family crest and added the quartz crystal, also for personal psychic protection. It's protected me over all the years I've worked with these people. It blocks them from remote-viewing me. Or you."

She squeezed the pendant in her hand. "What is DARK MATTER's purpose?"

"We find terrorists and we take them out."

"What about Sayre?"

"That's enough. I've got arrangements to make."

She walked to the door but stopped and turned back. If this stuff was real, Nicholas's warning took on a whole new meaning. "What about Lucas? Can he see the future?"

"That wasn't his skill. So no, the premonition was a hoax, just as we suspected."

She left. The sound of hammering filled the air. Back in her office, she did an Internet search on Sayre Andrus's name, trying two different spellings until she found news-paper articles on his trial.

He had been convicted of strangling a woman to death. Just like in the nightmare. She got the creepy-crawlies as she read. Her hand went to her throat. He'd been described as charming, pleasant, a psychopath, evil . . . even by his own parents. She found articles written after the trial about both their deaths. Their claim to fame was their murderous adopted son, something cited in both stories. His mother had drowned in the tub, his father died in a car accident, both in the middle of the night.

She closed the screen, unable to read any more. Yes, he was dangerous. Physically. But psychically as well?

She went down to the kitchen to pour a glass of wine. At a sound, she turned to find Arturo Esteban, one of the guards, walking in. He nodded and took out a frozen entrée from the freezer.

She nodded toward the box. "The Kashi ones are better."

He gave her a smile. "It's for the prisoner."

"Oh." She lingered long enough for the guard to set a bottle of Dr Pepper alongside the entrée on a tray and head out. She followed.

When they turned the corner, she saw that her father's office door was closed. This was the only chance she'd get to talk to Sayre Andrus before he was put back in the attic.

Pressure squeezed her chest. Dare she disobey her father? Risk his wrath? She thought of the realization that had hit her when she was talking to Fonda. What was she without Daddy's approval?

She was still Olivia Darkwell but not the meek, obedient girl Nicholas had taken to task in the kitchen. She took a fortifying breath and stepped forward.

Arturo paused when he saw her standing by the door. "No visitors."

"I'm not visiting. I need to ask him something. It's business."

His eyebrows screwed up. "The guy's weird. A woman shouldn't be talking to a guy like that."

"Right now I'm a CIA employee, not a woman." She gave him a forced smile. "You'll be there, with your big, bad gun."

He glanced at her father's door. She wasn't about to let him check with his boss. She stepped into the room. Arturo followed and set the tray on a desk. Sayre's gaze, however, was on her. He smiled broadly. "A visitor. Well, ain't that sweet?"

She walked up to him. "I wanted to meet the most dangerous man Darkwell's ever brought aboard."

His hand sprang out so fast, Arturo pulled his gun. Sayre wasn't the least bit bothered, giving the guard a recalcitrant look. "I was only being a gentleman." He jangled the chain. "Like I could do anything."

"Put your hand down."

Sayre gave her a sad look. "Sorry, can't show my manners." His frown morphed into a smile. "So, I'm the most dangerous, eh?"

She knew he'd like that. "And you're the one who's going to shut down those Rogues."

"Yes, ma'am. Bad dudes, they are. But you'll be safe soon enough."

Arturo was listening, but she was sure he had no idea about Sayre's special skills. Not that he'd believe it anyway. Olivia said, "I know what they can do. Get into people's heads, set fires. Are you up for all that?"

"You bet my balls, I am. Oh, sorry 'bout that. And in front of a lady yet. I am such a bad boy." He tapped his face, jangling the chain again. "I'm used to being around prison guys. We don't see beautiful ladies much."

She ignored his compliment. "I'm fascinated by all this stuff, especially what you can do." She hoped he did something unusual to warrant her bluff. He probably did, considering her father had gone to a lot of trouble to bring him on board.

He sat back and crossed his arms over his chest, his food untouched. He was much more interested in impressing her. "You wait and see, those Rogues will be history soon. I just found out I got a twin brother. He got to live with some nice guy in a nice house, and I got . . . well, I got pack rats with a house full of trash and cats and stuff."

"That must make you pretty angry."

He surprised her by waving it off. "I'll get even. I got a direct line into my dear brother's head. I'm going to get into his dreams and make him take out his friends. Ain't that some poetic justice?"

Get into his dreams.

Before she could ask more, he reached up and dipped his finger into the hollow of his throat, rubbing it up and down—just like in her nightmare.

Her nightmare about Lucas. But not Lucas. Someone who looked like Lucas.

"I'd better go." She stood so fast the chair tipped over. She went right to her father's office and knocked.

"Yes?"

"Do you have a minute?" She was already walking in and closing the door behind her.

"What's the matter?" Obviously she looked upset.

"I spoke to Sayre Andrus."

"You what?"

"I know, I broke your rules."

"It's not some arbitrary rule. The man is a psychopath."

"Yes, he is. But as you said, he won't hurt me, not physically. He said he can get into Lucas's dreams and make him do things." She stood, bracing herself on the desk. "Can he?"

"Yes." Again, that simple yet astounding answer.

She sank down in the chair, her legs weak. "Can he . . . get into my dreams?"

That took him back for a second. "I suppose he could, in theory. But he wouldn't."

"I think he did. I had a disturbing dream that woke me up the night I came downstairs and saw you burning the files. Though I couldn't remember much, it gave me the creepiest feeling I've ever had. Last night I had another one. Lucas had me captive somewhere and was going to strangle me. I thought it was Lucas because I didn't know about Sayre."

"He won't do anything to risk his relative freedom here. Or, I suspect, what he thinks is his chance at escape once I've paid him. You're letting all of this get to your imagination. Nicholas scared you with his warning and now, along with Jerryl's death, it's getting to you. I need you to be strong. For your country. For me."

He was pulling the "father" card again. For the first time, she actually saw it, clearly saw the way he manipulated her.

"The man in my nightmare did this." She mimicked what Sayre had done at the base of his throat. "Sayre did that, too, just now, like he was taunting me. He strangled a woman, like he was going to do to me in the dream. That man was in my dream."

"Sayre has never seen you until today. Has he?"

She shook her head.

"Then how would he know about you?"

That stopped her cold. Good point.

He set his pen down, a dark expression on his face. "Lucas is also a dreamweaver. That's what I call those with the ability to get into dreams. But why would he start targeting you now? Unless . . ." His eyes narrowed. "Does Nicholas know you're my daughter?"

She couldn't hide her response.

"Hell."

"He guessed and, as you can see, I'm not good at hiding the truth."

"Lucas is targeting you because they're trying to get to me through you. I hope all he wants is to taunt me." He slammed his fist down on the desk. Then he looked at her throat. "Do you wear the pendant at night?"

"I take it off before I go to bed. The chain broke once because I thrash around in my sleep."

"Don't *ever* take off the pendant."

Her fingers stilled at the vehemence of his voice and the snarl of his mouth. "Will it keep someone from getting into my dreams?"

"I hope so. I've only tested it on remote-viewing." His eyes narrowed. "Dammit, you've made yourself vulnerable by revealing the truth."

"Vulnerable?" Panic fluttered in her stomach. "Can he make me do things while I'm asleep?"

"As far as I know, and Lucas didn't exactly tell me all about his skills, he couldn't make someone do something. He could, however, kill someone in their dreams."

Her hand went to her throat. "How do I get him out?"

"Wear the pendant."

"And if that doesn't work?"

Fear sharpened his gaze. "Then the only way to keep him out is to kill him. And we're working on that right now."

She came to her feet and walked to the door.

Her father was right, as always: How would Sayre know about her before they'd met in the hall the day before?

She walked out and went into her office, pacing in front of the French doors. So it was Lucas getting into her dreams. But that didn't feel right. He didn't seem vicious. Well, what did she really know about human nature, especially where the Rogues were concerned? Look how she'd misjudged Nicholas.

Her father's voice echoed in her thoughts:

You know I'm always right, don't you?

I know what's best, you know that.

Always right . . .

Trust yourself. That was what Nicholas had told her. She sat down and closed her eyes.

"Who is coming into my dreams?"

Her father's voice: *Lucas.*

"I can only trust myself. Who is coming into my dreams?"

Sayre.

She knew it, felt it in her gut. Somehow, he had found out about her. *Oh my God. When we met that first time, he said I was like a dream!* Like when he'd stroked the hollow of his throat, he was taunting her. She was going to go tell her father but stopped. He was blind to the possibility. He believed in psychic abilities but not his daughter's suspicions.

If he was blind to that in his quest for justice, what else would he be blind to? More disturbingly, what was he willing to risk to preserve his program? *My safety?*

She had seen him burning those files and not questioned it. She had seen him not doing anything to help when Lucas was at death's door and not questioned it. She had seen her father cover up Jerryl's death and not questioned it.

She was as blind as he.

She banged her fist against the glass. For as long as she could remember, she had been holding back her truth. Her questions, doubts. Because, as Nicholas had forced her into admitting, she didn't want to lose her family or her identity. So who was she, then? A shadow of her father?

What do I believe?

If she believed Sayre was coming into her dreams . . .

She swallowed, and that belief was a hard lump in her throat. She did believe.

If she believed that, then she believed psychic abilities were real. Then it *was* possible Lucas had seen her getting strangled. As her father had said, it wasn't as though Lucas was in a state of mind to share what his abilities were.

Sayre Andrus had strangled one woman, maybe two.

She was dreaming about Sayre strangling her.

She shivered. The pieces were too much to ignore, not when she could clearly remember the fear on Nicholas's face. He believed she was in danger. Now she did, too. The best thing to do was stay away from the estate, not only on Saturday, but until Sayre was gone.

CHAPTER 23

Like an animal senses an oncoming storm, Sayre picked up on a different energy in the air Friday evening. He watched from his window back in his room, where, in the shadows of dusk, men wearing black got into position. Since the fire alarm and the woman's screams that morning, the house had been filled with the sound of reconstruction. Not to mention the stench of smoke and, he suspected, burnt flesh.

Something big had happened, and it annoyed him not to know what it was.

His mind was on other things tonight, though. Like Olivia. Damn, seeing her in person was a jolt to the balls. Then when she came in to talk to him . . . oh, yeah. He must have overwhelmed her, 'cause she hightailed it out of there real quick-like. He'd seen her when he'd probed Mr. Darkwell's head. Interesting that the man was thinking of her.

Sayre was going to have some mind-blowing sex with her, then he was going to kill her, right under Mr. Darkwell's nose. His gaze went to the shadows where he couldn't see the men in black now. They were a complication, sure. Not a deterrent.

He studied the landscaping below his window. Odd-shaped bushes led a zigzag path to the hedges along the wall. At the front corner were bars, and he was good at getting through small spaces. He had the cunning of an animal, too. The trick was to move very, very slowly, like a sloth. Those guys were looking for movement, sound.

He waited until midnight and drifted into the darkness of his mind. *First, pay a visit to my favorite gal.*

He slipped right into her dream about some guy and cakes. He changed the dream. Now they were in the woods, and she was kissing on the guy, only the guy became him. She opened her eyes and yelped, jumping back.

He pulled her back. "You love kissing me. Don't you?" he said between kisses.

She helplessly nodded.

He pushed back the straps of her dress and it fell to the ground. "It's been a long time since I've had some good sex. You're going to give it to me, aren't you?"

Again she nodded, her eyes filled with terror.

He looked in her eyes, leaning closer, closer, and then merging with her. He opened his eyes—her eyes—and saw a sleigh bed. He made her look down. She was wearing silky pajamas. He made her bring her hand up to one of her breasts. He was hard, throbbing with anticipation.

Oh, the things we'll do.

He'd toyed enough, though. He didn't want to use up his energy. He made her get up and walk out to the living room. It was a nice place, earth colors, statues in various niches, including Rodin's *The Kiss*.

Look for mail.

She walked to a small desk and pulled out a square basket filled with envelopes. She picked one up, and he looked at a Woodbridge, Virginia, address. He walked her back to bed and pulled out.

He stripped, folded the dirty clothes into neat squares, and set them in his hamper. He watched television (he loved crime television) and ate nuked popcorn. At exactly four o'clock, he settled back on the couch and probed the mind of the guard posted outside his door. Just as he thought, the guy was asleep.

He entered the man's dream and merged with him, opening his eyes to see the dimly lit hallway downstairs.

The guy stood and checked the second door. Earlier it had been slightly open, and he'd been able to see that it was an office. No light shone beneath the door. No sounds from within. The guy twisted the knob and pushed the door open. Dark. He walked in and found the computer in the light from the clock. He turned it on and sat down to wait for it to boot up. A minute later, he went to the online maps and searched for the address of the estate. He needed to find the perfect place for his date with Olivia, near water. It destroyed evidence, hid bodies, and bought time.

The guard scanned the area and found what he was looking for: a river, with a park. He zoomed in, and Sayre memorized the direction and roads leading to it. Next he had the guy look for Woodbridge. It was forty-five minutes to an hour and twenty minutes away, depending on traffic.

"My work here is complete." He laughed. "For now."

Olivia woke in her bed Saturday morning, sunshine streaming through her sheer curtains and spilling onto her bed. She usually loved waking up on the weekends, not having to go into work quite as early.

She rubbed her hands down her arms, feeling a chill that wasn't in the air. Vague but creepy memories of another nightmare filtered into her mind. She wanted to push it away, but she couldn't do that anymore. The dream . . . it wouldn't come to the surface, but she knew *he* had been in it. The question was, had it been a normal nightmare, or one that he had produced? She pressed her fingers against the pendant. Could this protect her?

She grabbed the phone on her nightstand and dialed her father at home. He answered, and she said, "Is there any chance Sayre could get out?"

"Escape? None. Not while he's in the attic quarters. The door and windows are impenetrable, plus there's always a guard at the door, not to mention the guards outside."

She heard the patronizing tone in his voice. He used to chide her about her nightmare terrors. Why be afraid of something not real? But this was real.

She would tell him about her decision not to sleep at the estate tomorrow. "I hope you're right."

"I'm always right. The guards will be checking in through the day and night. I want you to check in with me, too. I wish you'd let me assign a guard to you. Maybe Nicholas won't hurt you, but he doesn't run the Rogues."

"You're wrong about that. I don't think the Rogues will attempt an attack on the mansion. Nicholas's warning was exactly what he said: to protect me." But she wasn't at the estate now, wasn't physically anywhere near Sayre. "The only person I'm worried about is Sayre. And possibly the guards."

"Olivia—"

"You won't convince me otherwise, so don't even try."

After a pause, he said, "You don't sound like yourself. Is something wrong?"

She wasn't his compliant little girl anymore, but she wasn't going to tell him that on the phone. "Everything is fine. Goodbye."

In the shower, as the water sluiced down her body, it wasn't her safety on her mind; it was Nicholas's. What if Sayre really could get Lucas to kill his comrades? That included Nicholas.

Deep down she knew he wasn't a bad guy.

If he's not, then what does that make your father?

It was a question she couldn't answer.

She turned off the water, her chest tightening. She had no way to contact Nicholas, to warn him that Sayre was going to use Lucas to kill them.

"Nicholas, if you can hear thoughts, please hear this: You're all in danger."

In the kitchen, she heated water and scooped coffee

powder into her cup. Her stomach was too tense for food. She picked up the piece of paper lying on the table and looked at the three names and addresses on it:

Carl Merrimack. The last time she'd seen him, almost a month ago, Eric had just smashed his head into the floor. He was still unconscious when the medics arrived.

John Hanson, whom Lucas shot, also when the Rogues broke into the asylum to rescue Rand Brandenburg.

Mark Jackson, guard at the asylum, shot in the shoulder.

Her encounter with Harry haunted her. Maybe he *was* good at pretending. He was CIA, after all. Not so, these other guys. She was going to check on a hunch, one she wasn't even sure she could explain.

She poured hot water into her mug and stirred, breathing in the scent of French vanilla. She managed to down a piece of toast, then headed to her bedroom to get dressed. On the way, some envelopes on her desk caught her eye. She always kept her bills in the basket, so why was her electric bill perched on the edge of her desk? She put it back in the basket and continued on.

An hour later, she stood outside Carl's apartment door, the television blaring inside. She hoped to find a family member who could give her an update on his condition.

He answered the door, a pleasant but curious expression on his face. "Yeah? Can I help you?" Not a hint of recognition.

"Carl, it's me. Olivia. Don't you remember me?"

He raised his eyebrows. "Crap, did we go out or something? Look, if I didn't call—"

"No, we worked together up until a month ago."

He took her in again. "You and me worked together? I don't think so."

She saw no sign of injury on his head. "Can I see your right hand? Humor me."

Warily, he held out his hand. Eric Aruda had shot him in the hand. She turned it back and forth. No sign of any kind of wound.

"This can't be," she whispered.

"I think you're a little mixed up."

"Don't you remember working for Gerard Darkwell? At an old insane asylum? You were shot in the hand, beaten . . ."

He was shaking his head. "I just finished an assignment guarding some warehouse for a few months, and I've been working at a bank for the last three weeks. I took a bullet when I was a cop, but that was twelve years ago. You've got the wrong guy."

Maybe the men had been debriefed to keep their assignments quiet, but where were his injuries?

"I've got the wrong something. Sorry to have bothered you."

Next she went to John Hanson's house. His gunshot wound had been pretty serious. She'd heard Jerryl say Lucas had thrown himself between Hanson's bullet and Amy Shane. Hanson had taken a serious hit and was likely dead.

She knocked on Hanson's door, and a woman answered, her expression becoming wary when she spotted Olivia. "Yes?"

"I'm looking for John Hanson. I worked with him when he was shot, and I wanted to see how he was doing."

Her blank look wasn't a surprise. Bizarre, but not a surprise. "John wasn't shot."

"He was working on a classified assignment until recently, right?"

She nodded. "He came home a few weeks ago and said the assignment had abruptly ended. It was disappointing, what with our son's birthday coming up, but we managed."

"I must be mistaken."

Mark Jackson was a handsome man who'd worked the perimeter of the asylum. He'd been shot in the shoulder and hit in the face with a gun. He, of course, showed no sign of either injury as he walked to his car in an apartment complex parking lot. She walked within his range of sight and smiled at him. He smiled back in a polite, stranger kind of way and got into his car. No spark of recognition, despite the fact that he'd joked with her every week about being clandestine when she gave him his pay envelope full of cash.

These men weren't pretending they'd forgotten the assignment. They truly did not know her. And they'd miraculously healed from their injuries.

She leaned against a car, not one possible explanation coming to mind. She remembered something Jerryl had said to Fonda: The Rogues wouldn't die.

But these men were normal people. So what had happened to them? Or more precisely, what had her father done to them?

Lucas's whispered words woke Nicholas: "It's still going to happen."

He woke instantly. Amy was coming awake, too, and Eric sat in the chair, his eyes glazed.

Lucas had done the last sketch.

Panic shot through Nicholas. "Even though I warned her."

Lucas nodded.

"You intervened when Amy was going to be attacked. You stopped it. So can I. I'll watch over her all day from a distance."

"Too dangerous," Eric said. "Darkwell's men could be watching her."

"I'm not letting her die. I'm going to check on her."

Nicholas turned down the lights and reclined on the couch. His eyebrows furrowed, his body twitched. His mouth tightened. He tuned his focus in, putting all of his attention on Olivia. This time, as fear throbbed inside him, he felt the darkness of the abyss. It pulsed, like a living thing, threatening to swallow him. He had once been in the vicinity of a tornado, and the pressure in the air, or perhaps lack of it, felt the same as the abyss. He couldn't breathe. It pressed closer, forcing him back.

This is where he usually had to retreat. Not now. Not when Olivia's life was at stake. He tried to suck in a breath. *No oxygen. Must push past it.* He gritted his teeth and stepped into the miasma of what looked like . . . smoke. Thick, vile smoke, stealing away the oxygen. He stopped. That's why the abyss terrified him. Smoke. Fire.

His chest felt crushed from lack of air. The black mass had no smell, but the wall that stood before him was thick and oily. Not even fire could stop him from saving Olivia. He took a step. The vile blackness surrounded him, pressing tight against him. He took another step. Another. Like slogging through water, but it didn't stop him. And finally he stepped out on the other side, into a different kind of darkness. He'd been here before. The ether. Now he could find her.

He focused on her face, trying to keep the fear from interfering. Other than the times he'd tried to find a missing child, he'd never had a deadline. Now, time was running out.

He felt his spirit glide toward her. *Come on, bring me to her.* Just as he was getting nearer, he hit an invisible wall. It bounced him right out. He held on to his connection and went to the estate. He looked in her office, roamed the hallways, then checked her suite. He didn't see Darkwell or Olivia.

He pulled out and sat up. "I can't find her or see her. It feels like the same kind of block I got when I tried to remote-view Darkwell. I've got to check her condo. I know the city, but not the address. I need a touchstone to find a place. Sometimes that's a person. If I can't find her, I need something of hers that would be at her apartment. Then I can find that, at least." He tapped his fingers against his mouth in thought. "She wore some silver spiral earrings once. As long as she isn't wearing them, I could find them."

He zoned in on those earrings, coming down into her condo, looking around at the cozy and cluttered living room, kitchen, then her bedroom. He saw the jewelry box the earrings were in, but he was more interested in checking for Olivia.

A few minutes later, he opened his eyes. "She's not there, either. How am I going to find her?" Nicholas ran his hand through his hair and started pacing. "I've got to do something. I can't let"—he looked at the sketch—"that happen." He implored them with his eyes. "Don't any of you have some skill, anything . . . ?"

Amy shook her head. "I'm sorry. Seeing auras and talking to dead people isn't going to help. Rand can see ten seconds ahead, but that only helps in the moment. Zoe's got telekinesis, but moving things . . ." She shrugged.

Nicholas came to stop at the sketches, which were all laid out in a row. "Lucas, didn't you say you got images of things that were going to happen?"

"Sometimes, but I can't control them."

Nicholas studied the sketches, then the map. "He's going to take her to the water. There are two lakes near her condo. And there's the Potomac River . . . miles of it. But you saw a lake."

"It definitely looks like a lake."

"I'm going to search Woodbridge, see if either of the lakes matches the sketches."

"That's what I did when I saw Amy being attacked. I had a few details, and I was a man mad to find the marina that matched those details."

Nicholas could see the fear in Lucas's eyes at the memory.

"I can't let that psycho get her. If he touches her—" Nicholas stopped, his eyes widening, his cheeks flushing.

He turned to them. "I couldn't imagine having the urge to kill someone, for any reason other than self-defense. But now I know why you shot that guard, Lucas. And Eric, why you beat the guy who had Amy and Petra at gunpoint."

"When you love a woman, you'll do anything for her," Lucas said softly, looking at Amy.

"I don't know if I love her, but there's this feeling I've never felt before of . . . of doing anything to protect her. And I will."

CHAPTER 24

Nicholas drove toward Woodbridge, his head a jumble of frantic thoughts. Rand had offered to go with him. Nicholas's first reaction was to refuse; he did things on his own. He could see, though, the value of having a team like these people behind him. Two things ultimately pushed him to refuse: Olivia was, in their minds, the enemy, and if something happened to Rand because of her, the Rogues would never forgive Nicholas. The second: the fear in Zoe's face at the thought of losing someone she was obviously crazy in love with.

It still stunned him, the intensity of his feelings for Olivia. He'd never thought he could feel anything like that. Like what his mother had felt for his father, which had then destroyed her when he was killed.

It was easier to admit his feelings for Olivia because he could never be with her. He'd save her from whoever it was that had the nerve to think he could touch her, then they'd be adversaries again.

What if you can't save her?

No, don't think that.

And what was he going to do if he *could* find her? Lucas had given him a knife, which was tucked beneath the seat. He'd offered him one of their guns, but Nicholas had declined. It would be too dangerous without his having had any training.

So this was what it was like to care about someone so deeply he'd forsake his beliefs . . . his identity.

They were right. Love was a bitch.

Lucas pulled Amy close for a kiss. His last one, but he couldn't let the emotions washing over him give that away. "Eric and I are going to do a little male bonding down in the range. Don't wait up for me."

"Male bonding, huh?" She raised an eyebrow. "What are you two up to?"

He leaned close, inhaling the strawberry scent of her hair. "I'm going to get him to try remote-viewing Olivia. I'll have a better chance if he's not doing it in front of everyone else. He's got to keep up that blustery façade, you know."

"That's not a façade."

She looked at him with those green eyes, so innocent, so full of love. Her hair was sticking up, wild in a charming kind of way. *God, how I love her. God, how I hate to hurt her.* Hadn't he always known he would? She was strong. She'd survive, and she had a family here to protect and comfort her. At least they'd be safe from him.

His chest felt heavy as he and Eric went down two flights to the large room in the lowest level. They'd set up the storage area as a makeshift range, with white buckets as targets. They'd drawn faces on them, including one with Darkwell's thick eyebrows and moustache.

Eric closed the door and leaned against it, his arms over his chest. "You're sure about this?"

"Yes." Lucas laid out a tarp on the floor. "Eric, you look like hell. I thought you were going to take a nap."

He ground the heels of his palms into his eyes. "My mind won't shut down. It's this . . . this thing you've got me doing tonight. It's got me wired."

"Then let's get it over with. It's almost seven." Oddly,

he felt calm. He'd heard that when people were about to drown, a sense of peace overcame them. This was what it must feel like. "You're going to need time to clean up and explain it to everyone. Then you can get some sleep."

"Oh, yeah, like that's going to happen. You were always the sensible, calm one. This shouldn't be you." He braced his hands on the concrete wall, lifting his face and closing his eyes. "I've always had this streak of anger. Dad—the man I thought was my father—told me I was an angry baby." He turned to face Lucas. "Why do you suppose that was?"

"You were always mad and distrustful, even as a kid. It's probably the Booster."

"I've done some stupid things. You're the only person I'll ever say this to. But yeah, I admit it. Rage takes me over. I can't control it. I know it worries all of you. Sometimes it worries me, too."

"You have to master it. When I'm gone, you'll be in charge, at least unofficially. You were the first one to figure out something was going on."

He laughed, though there was no humor in it. "Yeah, I was the paranoid one. I guess that's in my DNA, too."

"Something is. Amy's determined to find out what it is. Watch over her. She's going to get a bit crazy after . . . well, you know. Don't let her go find this scientist guy alone." He lay down in the middle of the tarp. "If you stand over me and shoot, the mess should be contained on the tarp. Wrap me up tight and put my body down in the mechanic's room before you tell Amy. Don't let her see me."

Eric hefted the gun in his hand. "You're the meanest son of a bitch I ever knew, asking me to do this. And I'm insulted that you think I'm ruthless enough to do it."

"Not ruthless, Eric. But you don't mind killing people."

His eyes took on a sheen. "The enemy, not the man I consider a brother. I love you, Lucas. You're asking me to take your life to save the life of an enemy."

"Not just her. You're saving yourselves. And me."

Eric aimed the gun, though it looked off by a couple of inches. He took in a deep breath. Released it and turned away. "There's no way in hell I'm shooting you. But I am going to keep you down here all night. And awake. You can't leave, you can't dreamweave, so you can't hurt that woman." He spun a chair around and sat down on it. "So . . . should Lulu Lalane pick Bonehead Mike or Tom the Tool? Petra and I got our money on Tom, since she chose him to wax her pube hairs a couple of episodes back. What do you think?"

Lucas shot to his feet. "Don't be a freaking coward, Eric. You go off and do stupid things that endanger our lives. You owe all of them this one way to keep them safe."

Eric tilted his head, a smile on his face. "You're just trying to rile me up. Ain't gonna work."

"Fine, I'll do it myself."

Eric pulled the gun away. "No, sirree."

Lucas sank back to the floor. He was physically no match for Eric, who, as Amy liked to say, was built like a Hummer. "Okay, so you keep me from killing Olivia. Then what? Are you going to watch over me every second?" He pressed his palms against his forehead. "What if I hurt Amy when we're alone, and there's no one else to stop me? My coming after her like that would destroy her a lot more than my being dead."

"Jerryl's gone now. He was the one who got into your head, only it worked differently with you. Let's wait and see."

"If I blank out, like I did with Robbins, you have to promise me—and keep it this time—that you'll take me out."

The flash of a woman walloped him so hard, he tilted sideways. The storm of images. He closed his eyes, ready for the onslaught. They ripped through his head like lightning, crackling across the crevices of his brain.

Olivia. A vacant stare on her face. Driving in a trance.

He felt his body fall back to the floor. Before he hit, Eric grabbed him and eased him down.

"What do you see, bro?"

Man's face. His face. How? How could he kill her with Eric holding him hostage? Unless it was when he was passed out after the storm.

"Me," he managed. "Taking off her clothes. Folding them." More lightning flashing through his head. More images. "Raping . . . oh, jeez. He's . . . I'm raping her."

The image was horrifying, so bizarre and against his nature.

"Keep me lucid." He tried to mentally sort through the images. *Go back to where they're driving.* He felt his brain shutting down as it always did.

No, not yet!

He saw headlights on a street sign. *Look. What does it say?*

"MacArthur . . . Street . . . call Nicholas."

He slumped, his brain grinding to a halt.

"All right, but I'm sending Amy down here, so don't try anything."

His last cognizant thought was, *As if I could.*

Sayre focused on Olivia, sensing her, feeling her essence, and sinking into her dreams. Hell, she was having some pretty nasty dreams even without his interfering.

He moved closer to her dream self, facing her, looking into her eyes. *Let me in, darlin'. Time for me and you to play.*

He merged with her, then made her get up and scan the bed to make sure she was alone. She looked down at herself. As much as he was looking forward to seeing her naked, he didn't want her driving naked in case she was stopped.

She was wearing bloodred silk jammies. She grabbed her keys, went to the door and down the stairs to her car. He hadn't had the pleasure of driving in some time, and even that small thing was a delight. Nothing compared to what would come, of course.

Just past the estate, there's a park, kind of a grassy, open area.

He'd searched the area online for the best rendezvous point. Having her park in the street might attract attention, and he certainly did not want that.

Traffic was light, and it didn't take long.

Kill your lights and sit tight, darlin'.

He pulled out and probed the guard outside his door. Asleep. He wondered what all those men outside hiding in the bushes were doing. Probably some of them were snoozing, too. Whatever Mr. Darkwell was preparing for—and he was sure it wasn't his escape—hadn't happened yet.

Now, some people might look at that as a bad thing, having heightened security on the one night he was planning to take a little R&R. Not Sayre. It upped the challenge, the risk. Yeah, the last risk he'd taken had bit him in the ass, but this was a whole different situation.

He sank into the guard's dreams and opened his eyes to the dimly lit hallway. The guy turned and unlocked the door.

You're going to walk me downstairs to the kitchen entrance. If anyone stops us, you'll say I'm sick, and you're taking me to get help.

Then you're going to come back up and take your position. You're going to stay in this deep state of sleep until I come a'calling again. And tomorrow, you're going to tell Mr. Darkwell I knocked on the door at about four in the morning and asked for an antacid. You said you couldn't leave your post to get me one, so I was out of luck.

He waited for the door to unlock. The man had a blank look on his face, and, interestingly, Sayre could see himself in a green sweatshirt with a hood through the guard's eyes. The man turned like a robot and walked him downstairs. Sayre took note of the mansion. He kept his orientation, just as he had when they'd brought him in. Too bad he couldn't zip down the banister again. He needed to stay low-key this time. The kitchen was enormous, bigger than his quarters. It was dimly lit by two small lights.

Go back to your post, keep that badass in his prison.

If, somehow, Sayre was discovered missing, it would be evident when he returned. They wouldn't expect him to come back, so the whole place would be lit like a circus. He'd be a fugitive much earlier than he'd anticipated, and without the funds he needed, but he was flexible. Free was free, after all. Otherwise, he'd use this as a test run.

He pulled an impressive knife from the butcher block. *Never know when you might need some additional persuasion.* He doused the lights and opened the door just enough to slip through. That was the good thing about being wiry. According to his mother, he'd been sick a lot as a child, and that had set his growth behind. He'd put up with a lot of teasing over the years. Prison food hadn't exactly beefed him up, though he did work out. Not to bulk up but to stay fast on his feet.

He closed the door without making more than a soft *click* and kept close to the house. Bushes and ornamental hedges were planted in beds around the outside edge. Hyperaware of any movement out in the yard, he slowly dropped to the ground. Inch by inch, he slithered across the grass next to the base of the hedges. The guards could have night binoculars. The key would be not to arouse their interest in the first place.

It took a painstakingly long time, but caution was worth it. He got to the place beneath his windows and aimed for the bush he knew was shaped like a bear. He curled around the bear's feet and took stock of his surroundings. A twig creaked in the distance. One of the men had shifted positions. By now, though, they would be sagging with boredom. He probed in the nearby area. Someone was drifting in and out of sleep, waking with a start, only to drift off again. Through the man's eyes, he could barely see himself in the shift in the shadows.

He continued, finally reaching the edge of the wall. He rose in imperceptible degrees. He'd been practicing in his room since he'd arrived. He could have waited for his time with Olivia when he broke out for good, but who knew what her circumstances would be that night? He would have to scram immediately, so he might lose his chance.

He couldn't risk that. Why was he so compelled to take her? She hadn't pissed him off, after all. No, she intrigued him. She had haunted his dreams as much as he was haunting hers.

He finally reached his full height and moved his shoulder into the tight space between bars. He exhaled deeply, turned to the side, and pushed his way through. His movements didn't quicken once he was outside. He followed in the shadows along the wall.

Once he reached the sidewalk at the far corner of the estate, he took off toward the road. It wasn't very far to the park, and his hours on the treadmill had upped his stamina. He saw a car waiting. His chest nearly burst, from both pleasure and exertion, at the sight of her in the front seat, her head slumped.

Come on back. I need you to do the driving.

If she was spotted, a witness would see her driving alone. Who knew what kind of trouble she was up to?

From his place low in the front seat, he instructed her toward the park he'd seen. Though it was closed, it was a simple matter of moving two cones to drive through.

He helped her out of the car. "Time for our date, sweetheart."

CHAPTER 25

Nicholas had been driving around Woodbridge all day, back and forth between the two lakes he'd found on the satellite map, feeling helplessness and frustration building to an explosion point. He had as much of a chance of finding her in the right place at the right time as hitting the lottery.

He kept trying to remote-view her but ran up against the same block. Why couldn't he see her now?

"Dammit!" He pounded the steering wheel. What good was having psychic abilities when he couldn't use them to help someone he cared about?

His phone rang. "Yeah?"

"It's Eric. Lucas got a storm. He saw a sign: MacArthur Street."

"Did he see anything else?"

"It's not good. He saw her getting raped. He's passed out now. He usually comes around in about fifteen minutes, and I can ask him for more, but that's what we've got now."

Nicholas focused only on the street, not Olivia. Thank God, something to go on. Except . . . there was no MacArthur anything in Woodbridge. He expanded his search and found it in Potomac. "MacArthur Boulevard runs along the Potomac River for miles, terminating down near Washington." The north end was up near the estate.

"Yeah, but remember, Lucas said it was a lake."

"I know, but I didn't see any lakes in that area. I'm going with the river. It's all I've got. Thanks, man." He was especially grateful since Eric made it clear he saw Olivia as the enemy.

He threw the car into gear and tore out onto the road.

Olivia was in the middle of a nightmare. She recognized this. The man had his arm clamped around hers as he led her over a bridge that crossed a canal and down a wide path washed white in the moonlight.

Wake up.

"No, stay in the dream, Olivia."

The voice lured her back to the depths of the dream. Just a dream. But something was very, very wrong. Why couldn't she wake up?

They walked for a couple of minutes, then he led her down a narrow path into the woods. She stumbled, but he never loosened his grip. He pulled her to a small clearing next to what looked like a lake, its surface glittering in the moonlight. She felt the cool air against her cheeks and the cracked ground beneath her bare feet. This felt so real. Real and . . . not. Just a dream.

He set down a duffel bag and pulled out several strips of material from his pocket.

"We're going to play a game called tie-up-and-tickle."

He took her wrists and bound them together. She pulled away, or thought she had. Her body wasn't moving to her will, only to his.

"Good girl," he said, as she held out her wrists.

The seductive way the accent wrapped around his words, the way it compelled her to obey, wound a tendril of panic through her.

He guided her to the ground and knelt over her, pinning her down. His hand cupped her breasts, and he let out a ragged sigh. Somewhere deep inside, repulsion rippled through her.

"We're going to make love, darlin', and you're going to touch me and suck me and let me do whatever I want with that beautiful body of yours. And then when we can't take anymore, we're going to go for a little swim." His hand crept across her stomach. "You *can* swim, can't you?" He chuckled.

This isn't right. I need to wake up.

His mouth came down on hers, and his tongue probed inside. "Kiss me back."

Her mouth moved robotically, even as something inside her shriveled in disgust. He stopped, and she saw his face hovering over her, his eyes narrowed. "Olivia, sink down into the dream. Sink deeper, deeper . . ."

She held on to a thread of resistance.

He pulled more material out of his pocket and stuffed it into her mouth. Then he wrapped a long piece around her head and tied it tight.

"On the just in case. Now, where were we? Oh, yeah." He ran his hand along her inner thigh, moving closer to . . .

Wake . . . up . . . now!

She'd been unable to come out of the nightmare before, but she was stronger now. She fought her way out, clawing to consciousness. Her eyes blinked open. No bedroom! She was still in the nightmare, but awake. Not a dream. Sayre! He was on top of her, and beyond him was a canopy of leaves. Trees. The smell of earth and pines. The moon, barely visible. How had he gotten her to the woods? Oh, God, he was out. She gasped.

"Aw, man, now you've gone and spoiled it."

She started fighting, wriggling, trying to push and finding her hands tied together. Her scream came out muffled.

He shook his head. "And we were about to have us some fun in a cooperative kind of way. Tsk, tsk." He reached behind her and started tugging down her pajama bottoms. She kicked, but he patiently kept working on them. "Now it's gonna have to be wham-bam, kill you, ma'am." He shook his head in disappointment. "And I was really look-ing forward to spending some quality time with you."

She pushed, kneed him in the groin. He rolled away, spitting out expletives. She jumped to her feet, fight-ing to gain her balance with her hands tied. He came up behind her, his hands around her throat and threw her to the ground. He leaned close, his breath warm against her cheek. His fingers tightened against her throat. Like the nightmare. "Once you lose consciousness the first time, I bet you'll cooperate."

And he pressed.

The only person you can trust is yourself. Nicholas pulled off the road and looked at the map again. What did his instincts say?

Look.

Well, that's what he was doing.

He could keep driving MacArthur Boulevard and look for . . . what? He didn't even know what the psychopath who had her drove. From what he could see of the map, the entire road was bordered by woods and then the river.

No, *look.*

Remote-view. But he'd tried that. He shoved the map onto the seat. *Stay calm. Getting upset only hampers your skills.* He felt anything but calm. His chest hurt, every muscle was rock hard, and his hands were clenched into fists.

He took a deep breath and tried to zero in on her. He hit the block again. As he rocked his head back and forth in frustration, a thought shook loose: *remote-view the area, not her.*

He had done that for Darkwell, learned how to remote-view from above, where the Rogues weren't able to sense him. Even in the dark, he could see details.

He yanked the map in front of him and stared at the path the road traveled. The map shook in his hands. He took sev-eral calming breaths, aware of every second ticking away.

Aware of those sketches in the backseat, of what might be happening to Olivia right now.

Focus.

He closed his eyes and imagined the road as his target. In a few moments he hovered above it. As though he were flying, he started moving north from where he was, looking down. The trees, though, hid anyone who might be in the woods.

Find a car, then, parked in some odd place, maybe tucked in to the woods off the side of the road.

Traffic was light. Was she in any of those cars? He kept searching for anything out of the ordinary.

What he found was a lake.

Not exactly a lake. A small creek spun off from the main river and spilled into what looked like a lake. It then became small again as it remerged with the river.

It looked like a lake. That was what mattered. He pulled back onto the road, punched the gas pedal, and raced to the end.

He found a park entrance. The cones blocking traffic were thrown to the side. He tore into the parking area, empty except for a blue BMW parked next to the closed concession stand. He threw his car into park, jumped out, and as he was about to close the door, saw the knife.

Anger and fear raged inside him. He closed the door and followed the path, listening for any sound that didn't belong there. Soon he came to a bridge that crossed a narrow canal. His heart picked up its pace even more, and he turned to the right. *Please don't let me be too late.*

He ran to a platform that looked out over a larger body of dark water—the lake. He searched it and the perimeter for movement. Was she already at the bottom? *No, don't even think it.*

He wanted to shout her name but couldn't give himself away. The element of surprise would be crucial.

He spun around at a sound to his right, senses alert. Quiet now. He stared into the variable shadows of the woods. The sound came again, like an animal digging in the dirt. A grunt.

He gripped the knife in his hand and raced toward it. A path led into the woods. Next to the water's edge, in a small opening, he saw two people on the ground. He might scare the hell out of two lovers. Small price to pay.

The woman made a sound again as he approached. A sound of terror. Desperation. The man was straddling her, pinning her to the ground. Nicholas raised the knife. He couldn't tell if it was Olivia, but his heart boomed in his ears and felt like it would explode.

A twig broke beneath his shoe. The man's head snapped up. The woman tried to scream, but her voice was muffled. In the shafts of moonlight, Nicholas saw something tied over her mouth.

The man sprang to his feet, and in that second Nicholas saw his face. *Lucas.* "You're gonna regret being a hero." Lucas's face. Not his voice.

In that second of hesitation, the man rushed him. He saw the flash of a knife. He pushed the man away and felt the knife slice his arm.

Get to Olivia, make sure she's all right.

The man came at him again, and this time Nicholas was ready. He rammed his elbow into his face. The man's knee came up and slammed into Nicholas's balls. Pain wracked him, forcing him to bend forward. He dropped his knife.

Push past it.

The other guy's knife came down. Nicholas grabbed his wrists. They were face-to-face, force against force. He couldn't lose. Olivia's life depended on it. She was still alive. Her quick, panting breaths were filled with fear.

The man tried to knee him again, but Nicholas twisted out of the way. Blood trickled down his arm, and the pain seared down the line of the cut. Both men grunted with exertion.

The guy spun around, nearly snapping Nicholas's arm until he had to let go. He lifted the knife. Nicholas spun out of the way. But he wasn't aiming at Nicholas; he plunged the knife down where Olivia was.

"Noooo!" The word tore from his throat.

Still bent, he rammed the guy, sending him to the ground on the other side of Olivia. He landed on him, their bodies colliding. Nicholas tried to get in a punch, but the guy rolled them over and threw his fist into Nicholas's chin. Stunned, he couldn't gather his wits to respond fast enough. The guy pounded him again and again, quick as a striking rattlesnake. Nicholas lifted his hands to ward off the blows. Darkness throbbed in and out of his vision.

The guy leapt up, reached down next to Olivia, and ran off into the night. *Olivia.* Nicholas couldn't speak. A wall as black as the abyss swept in. *Need to get to her. To help . . .*

The physical agony was nothing compared to what he felt inside. He had come so close and failed.

CHAPTER 26

The sound pulled Nicholas from the depths of darkness into pain and consciousness. Sobbing. He was crying. . . . because Olivia was dead. Oh, God . . . dead. How long had he been out? He tried to pull his thoughts together under the onslaught of vicious memories.

He winced from the pain that ripped through him. Pain beyond his aching balls and the slice down his arm and bruises on his face. Emotional pain tore him to shreds from the inside out.

Except *he* wasn't crying.

His eyes snapped open. It was a woman's cries. *Olivia!* He rolled to his side, the movement excruciating. She was trying to crawl to him, her hands still bound. Her tears glittered in the silvery light.

"Don't move," he said.

He couldn't believe she was moving at all. Where had the son of a bitch stabbed her? She mumbled something. He crawled over to her, shoving the gag from her mouth. She spit out more material, and he pulled it out. He held her face. "Don't move. I'm sorry I didn't get here sooner."

"You got here soon enough. Get my hands free."

He patted the ground, looking for his knife. He felt the cold metal and found the handle. He gently took her arms and held them in the shaft of moonlight so he could see better. Damn, he wished she'd stop shaking for a second. He didn't want to cut her. He clamped her arms in his hand and pulled the knife up to cut the material.

"I've got to get you to the hospital," he said.

"No, he didn't . . . he didn't rape me."

"But he stabbed you."

She shook her head, running her hand over her body. Her dark pajamas were askew, the bottoms pulled low on her hips. Without thinking, he ran his hands over her, too. "I can't tell if there's blood."

"These are dark red. But I'd feel it."

His hand felt her bare stomach, the smooth skin free of sticky blood, and connected with hers. He looked at her. "He missed. Must have."

Her body was trembling. She nodded, laughing, then crying.

"Olivia." He pulled her into his arms. She trembled as she cried. "Are you sure you don't want to go to the hospital?"

"Yes. I just want to go . . . no, I can't go home." Her voice pitched higher. "He came into my *home* and brought me here."

"He broke in?"

"Broke in . . ." She looked at him. "It sounds crazy, even though I experienced it. He broke into my dreams." Her whole body convulsed. "Did you know someone could do that?"

"Lucas can. He looked like Lucas Vanderwyck."

"It's his twin brother. My father brought him into the program right after you left. He told me he could get into dreams and possess people. I was having these nightmares, and I thought it was because of your warning. I didn't believe in *special skills*, not this special! But it was *him*." He could hear her disgust and anger. "And my father, he knew, he brought these people, you, together, he . . ." She trembled violently.

He held her tighter, feeling everything inside him open up and pour out like a waterfall. Lucas's twin. He could barely get his head around that. All he really cared about right then was that she was all right.

She put her hands on his face and pressed his bruised flesh. He held back the gasp of pain. "I thought he'd . . . killed *you*. I saw him . . . beating you." Now her tears were for him. Her teeth were chattering, cutting up her sentences. "You found me, out here. My father said you were a finder, and well, there's no *normal* way you could have found me." Her words were a rush, her adrenaline, and he knew she was still trying to work it out.

"I had help this time. Lucas not only sees the future through drawings; he also gets flashes of images. He saw enough to get me here. I couldn't find you for some reason. I kept getting a block, but I found this place by going above. Lucas and even Eric Aruda had as much to do with saving you as I did."

She curled into him, her hands tightening in the folds of his shirt. "Get me out of here."

He helped her to her feet. "Do you want me to carry you?"

"No, I can walk."

He led the way to the parking lot, watching their surroundings, hyperalert the whole way. "Your car is gone. He must have taken it."

"Can you find him?"

"I want to get out of here first. He's going to take off, escape. I'll be able to alert the police." His mouth tightened. "Or find him myself."

He opened the Camry's passenger door, helped her in, and jumped in on the driver's side. She sat sideways, facing him, leaning against the seat. She looked small and vulnerable, another side to this unfathomable woman. Wasn't that what he loved about exploring, plunging into the depths of underwater caves? He touched her chin, wanting so much to take all this away. He forced himself to start the car and leave.

"You should call your father, tell him what kind of monster he's got working for him."

She nodded, her hazel eyes wide and slightly glazed.

"I can't let you use my phone. I don't want him to see the number. We'll find a phone booth."

He drove for twenty minutes, wanting to get out of the area. He stopped at a gas station and pulled around back where it was dark. "I'm going to find him." He sat back and went into the ether. A minute later he shook his head. "As soon as I got close, he kicked me back."

"We have to find him!"

"Your father will be motivated to find him, too. Are you up for talking to him?"

She nodded again, and he ran around to open the door and help her out. He had to lean back in and dig around in the ashtray for change. When was the last time he'd used a pay phone? He walked her to the booth, his arm around her waist. She looked up and gasped.

"What?"

"Oh, Nicholas." She reached up to his face but faltered. "You're a mess. Maybe *you* should go to the hospital."

"Too many questions. I'm fine. You're the one I'm worried about."

A man walking to his car did a double take when he passed them; he hurried on.

Nicholas saw his reflection in the laminated metal on the booth's wall. Its distortions made him look worse. He dropped the coins in the slot.

She punched in the numbers with trembling fingers. She stared out the glass, fear in her expression. After a moment, she said, "It's Olivia . . ." Her voice broke. "Sayre Andrus tried to rape me! He lured me out of my condo, *in my dreams,* he controlled me!" She took a breath. "And now he's out there . . . No, it wasn't Lucas. He had that Southern accent. . . . check the estate . . . All right, call me back at this number. I'm at a phone booth . . . no, check first. I'm safe here." Her gaze met his.

She didn't say she was with him. That was good. "He's calling the guard posted outside Sayre's door."

He pulled her against him, stroking her hair. Her arms went around his waist, and she settled against him, a perfect fit. God, what he felt for her. The thought of losing her, of nearly losing her . . . he could admit it now. Soon he'd be delivering her to her father, to safety, and he'd be out of her life forever.

The phone rang. He picked it up and handed it to her.

"Yes?"

Nicholas leaned close so he could hear.

"Olivia, Andrus is there. Moreover, the guard said he asked for an antacid an hour ago."

"No way, he was with me."

"I asked the guard to check, and he woke up Andrus. The man is there, Olivia. The man who had you was Lucas. You put yourself in danger by telling Nicholas who you are. Now they're targeting you. Where are you? I'm coming to get you."

She hung up, tears streaming down her face. "He's convinced himself of his truth. He's blinded with righteousness the same way I've been blind to his darkness."

He wiped the tears, but they were coming too fast.

"I don't know where to go," she whispered, more to herself.

"You're coming with me."

He wouldn't leave her alone, not now.

Not ever.

No, he didn't have *ever*. "We'd better get out of here in case he traces the call."

With his arms around her, he led her back to the car. She was like a little girl who'd lost everything, and he felt the need to find, to fix, to complete. What she'd lost he could never find. Like his father, hers was gone too, but in a way even more devastating. He pulled her into his arms once again and kissed her temple. "It's going to be all right."

She shook her head. "It's never going to be all right again."

Olivia thought they'd been driving for days, but it had only been an hour. She tried to push away thoughts of the previous hours, of the violation. It all seemed like a nightmare, and for now, she wanted to believe it was. She closed her eyes, but images played like a movie on the screen of her eyelids. She stared into the darkness down where her feet were.

Nicholas's hand rested on her thigh as he drove. When a streetlight lit the interior of the car, she felt his gaze on her. She looked up and cringed at the bruises on his face. He'd saved her life but almost lost his own.

She reached out to touch his arm and gasped. "You're bleeding!"

He glanced down. His sleeve was dark with blood, and a fierce slash went down to his elbow.

"It's not bleeding anymore."

"How . . . ? He cut you, didn't he?"

"It's not that bad."

"It needs to be cleaned, probably stitched. You should see a doctor."

"I'll take care of it when we get back."

It couldn't be too bad if he was driving. Still, it worried her. Then she realized she had no idea where they were headed. "Are we going to your house?"

His mouth tightened. "I can't go home." She knew he was too nice to tell her the reason: her father. "I'm taking you to the Rogues' hideout. You'll be safe there."

Her pulse jumped in her throat. "We can't go there. You didn't see what they did to Jerryl. They *burned* him. I can't be with those people."

"Jerryl was dangerous. I didn't like how he was killed, but it was the only way." He turned off the main road into a residential area. Her expression was still set in a stubborn frown. "Livvie, it's the only place I can take you."

No, not to those savages. Nicholas is one of them. One of them, but not.

"If I take you somewhere else, like a hotel, your father will find us. He'll grab you, and he'll kill me. Neither of those possibilities works for me. And I'm not leaving you alone. The hideout has a protective psychic shield over it, so he won't get to you there. It'll give you a couple of days to catch your breath."

She couldn't endanger him. And, dammit, she wasn't ready to be alone, either. "All right."

"But," he continued in a tone of voice that told her she wasn't going to like what he was going to say, "I can't let you see where the hideout is. I trust you, but they won't, and I can't disregard their need to keep it safe. When we get closer to where it is, you're going to have to look down or close your eyes. And . . . I'm going to have to blindfold you when we get there, just for a few minutes. Bringing you to the one place they feel safe without protecting them would be a huge violation of their trust in me. Your father's hunting them. I hope you understand."

She looked at him. He was serious. "No way."

He let out a long breath. "I know it's a lot to ask after what you just went through. I wouldn't if it wasn't so important."

"No, Nicholas. I can't." She twined her fingers. "Do they know I'm Darkwell's daughter?"

"Unfortunately, yes. I kind of freaked when I realized you were in danger and slipped. Now you understand why I have to assure them that you can't lead anyone to the only safe place they—we have." *We.*

"All right. I don't like it, but all right." Because she had nowhere else to go. No one to go to but this man who'd saved her life. "How did you come to join them? I don't understand how that happened. You're not a guy who storms buildings with guns or kills people. You weren't even comfortable finding the Rogues for my father."

"The Rogues don't kill indiscriminately. When Cheveyo

rescued Zoe Stoker in Key West as an assassin was about to take her out, he could have killed the guy. He incapacitated him instead. Rand Brandenburg had to shoot the guy when he caught them by surprise, and I could see it tore him up. It was kill or be killed." His voice got soft. "I didn't think I could ever kill another human being, but seeing that guy with you . . ." He looked at her. "If I'd had the upper hand, I would have killed him."

His words thudded heavy in her chest. She saw what it would have cost him to do that. The emotion underlying the statement scuttled through her body.

He told her what Petra had said and everything else that had happened since. "Do you understand now why I wanted my father's folder badly enough to sneak into Darkwell's office twice?"

"Now I wish I hadn't stopped you."

He nodded in agreement but didn't rub it in or even reveal any anger over it.

She could hardly process it all. "A few days ago I would have thought you were completely crazy."

"And now?"

"This is all so . . . insane, but I believe you." She pinched the bridge of her nose. "It must be real because there is no other way you could have found me."

"I felt the same way before working for your father. I thought I was just really good at finding stuff, though I knew there was something odd about it. With Bone Finders, or my former boss, I had to downplay my preciseness and the speed in which I could locate. Once my boss asked, 'What, you psychic or something?' in such a derisive way, I knew I could never reveal just how I find things. I had this conception about psychics. You know, crystal balls and tea leaves, all that hokey stuff. What I did was different. It blew my mind when Darkwell told me my ability is a psychic skill."

Nicholas jerked his head to look behind him.

"What? Is someone following us?"

"I thought I saw something . . . never mind." He settled his hand on the bottom of the steering wheel. "Yes, Eric attacked Jerryl—"

"While he was making love with his girlfriend!"

"It was unprovoked in that moment, but he had to take him out when he was vulnerable. Eric and Jerryl had a personal vendetta."

"I heard Jerryl talking about that. He *was* after Eric, hated him. And he tried to kill Eric's sister. But Eric doesn't sound like a good guy, either."

He let out a breath. "I have a hard time with him, too. I'm a black-and-white kind of guy. Either you're good or bad. The Rogues . . . I'm sorry, Livvie, but they're the better side. Your father is hunting them down because they're a threat to his program. He's crossed the line, now and twenty-five years ago, and he'll do anything to keep his program secret. He had our parents killed, the ones in the first program. He had me finding the women so an assassin could take them out. These women aren't cold-hearted terrorists. They heal, they love, they're scared, and they're angry."

She couldn't believe her father would kill innocent people. There was more to it, maybe a misunderstanding. Now Nicholas was taking her to the enemy's den.

She shivered. "Where are we?"

"Annapolis."

"Is it really safe there? Sayre can't get in?"

"Jerryl got in once, when he tried to get Petra to kill herself, but he had a psychic connection with her. I don't think Sayre will be able to get to you."

"I hope not." The words came out so soft and high-pitched, the fear so audible, Nicholas gave her thigh a squeeze of comfort.

A few minutes later, he said, "I'm going to have to ask you to look down, Livvie."

She lay down, her head on his thigh, and closed her

eyes. Dread tightened her chest. She could hear the tires crunch on gravel, then the sound of a garage door open and close.

"Stay there for a second. I've got to find something to use as a blindfold."

His regret at doing so was clear. She sat up in the seat but remained in a bowed position, remembering when he had donned a blindfold and jumped from the balcony. Now she knew he'd been using his psychic ability to find that ball.

He opened her door a minute later. "I found a clean rag in the tool chest."

Flashbacks of when Sayre had tied the bonds around her shot panic into her stomach. But this was Nicholas. He wouldn't hurt her.

The fabric was soft over her eyes. He knotted it at the back of her head and braced his hands on her face. "Are you okay?" Her nod was noncommittal.

Her legs were still wobbly when he helped her to her feet.

"Trust me," he whispered, the words vibrating into her chest.

"Right now, you're the only person I do trust."

He pulled her against him and smoothed her hair from her face. It was a tender action that softened her fear a little. "I know you'd never tell your father where the Rogues are, but they don't. I just want you to be prepared. They'll be angry at me, but they won't hurt you."

"I hope you're right." It hit her then. "Because . . . to them, I'm the enemy. If I told my father where they were . . ."

His voice sounded grave. "We would be dead."

He held her hand to his mouth and kissed her knuckles. "I wouldn't have brought you here if I wasn't sure."

He led her outside and across an expanse of grass. They stopped, and she heard him doing something.

He pulled her into what felt like a closed-in place that smelled of gasoline. He closed a door, she guessed, and opened another one. "You're going to step down a ladder. I'll be right below you if you lose your footing."

Had he noticed her shaky legs? He placed her feet on the top rung, and she felt her way down. She wasn't quite relieved when they reached the bottom. She was closer to seeing the Rogues. He led her down what felt like a damp, cool, underground tunnel. She wondered if they were in some bunker or hidden tunnels from an old war. To help the unease, she brought a song to mind that they'd played at the roller derby bout: "Headlong" by Queen.

Their footsteps echoed on concrete walls, and she saw faint light down by her feet in the gap beneath the blindfold.

He stopped a couple of minutes later. "We're here. Stay back for a few seconds. Let me tell them before they see you."

She heard beeping sounds, like a keypad being punched. Then a sliding sound.

"Nicholas!" a woman said. "Did you find Olivia?"

"Why didn't you call and let us know what happened?" a man asked.

Nicholas said, "I'm sorry. I was distracted."

"Oh, my God, what happened?" Yet another female. "Someone beat the hell out of you."

These people, they were concerned about Nicholas. And about, apparently, his quest to save her. Hadn't he said Lucas and Eric had helped?

"I'm all right. And so is Livvie. And . . . she's here." He tugged her forward. She heard the door slide closed behind her, making her throat tighten in panic. He removed her blindfold.

Six people stood in a large room, and instantly their looks of concern morphed to shock.

One man wasn't just shocked; he was pissed. He was big, with light blue eyes and bright blond hair. He stalked up to

Nicholas, his mouth in a snarl. "You brought her *here*?" He pointed to her but kept his fiery gaze on Nicholas. "You brought *her* here? Are you shittin' me? Are you *frigging shittin'* me?"

Nicholas pulled her close. Was he worried they'd hurt her?

"Eric, calm down. She can be trusted. She's been in the dark since we hit Annapolis."

So that was Eric Aruda. He was good-looking in a fierce way, with a square, muscular build and a face to match. "You just brought the enemy into the one safe place we have!"

"I have to agree." This from the man she recognized as Lucas—who gave her a shudder because he looked like Sayre. Except his eyes were beautiful, not flat. "Bringing her here was a bad idea. Even with the blindfold, she now knows enough to give him clues."

Eric kept jabbing his finger at Nicholas. "This is what I keep telling you all about letting your emotions get in the way of logic. I don't even know if *you* can be trusted yet, and you bring *her* here. Well, guess what? The only way to keep our location safe is to keep her here."

Everyone looked at Eric in surprise.

Nicholas's shoulders tensed. "What do you mean by that?"

His voice lowered, along with his chin, as he leveled a hard stare at Nicholas. "She's not leaving."

CHAPTER 27

Gerard Darkwell punched in the number from which Olivia had called. Then he called her condo and her cell phone. No answer anywhere. She'd hung up on him. Was he losing control over everyone? She was his daughter!

Nicholas's warning and her feelings for him were messing with her mind. Had she really been nearly raped by Lucas? She'd sounded scared, and she was calling at five in the morning from a location other than her home. Something had happened.

Wait a minute. Maybe she hadn't hung up on him. Maybe someone else had.

He tried her cell phone again. "Dammit!"

He threw it on the bedroom floor, where it bounced off the plush carpet. He had to find her. Jerryl and Nicholas, his remote viewers, were gone. But he had Fonda. She wasn't as good as they were, but she was learning. And besides Sayre, she was all he had. He didn't want Sayre to know about Olivia, so he called Fonda at home.

"Did something happen?" she asked in a hoarse voice.

"Olivia is missing. I think the Rogues have her. She was able to call me, but we got cut off. I need you to astral project to her."

"I'll call you back."

Fonda could project her soul to another location by focusing on an object or person known to be there. The only drawback was that she could be seen. She'd been practicing and popped into his office by mistake. It had been eerie; she looked like a ghost. But she couldn't stay anywhere long, not yet, anyway. He hadn't really worked with her much because he'd been too involved with Jerryl. And, he had to admit, he saw her as weaker because she was a woman, and a small one at that.

Fonda, though, possessed the same kind of fierceness Jerryl had. When she mastered her skills, she would be an amazing weapon. Especially now that anger had set her ablaze as much as Eric had set her lover ablaze. He hoped she would make Eric her blood feud.

Fifteen agonizing minutes dragged by before his phone rang. His first hope was that it was Olivia. It was Fonda, the next best thing.

"I was able to find her." She sounded breathless.

"Is she all right?"

"She's in a car with Nicholas. I projected into the backseat."

Fear paralyzed him. "I knew it. When he pretended to warn her about someone hurting her, it was a ploy to get her out of here. She was so sure he wouldn't hurt her. Now he has her, and he's probably taking her to the Rogues." Would they kill her to spite him? Or try to ransom her for . . . what? His daughter's life for his? For the files that no longer existed?

"I had to be careful; I didn't want him to see me like he did when I projected into his room. His arm was pointed in her direction, like he was holding a gun on her. I leaned around the seat to make sure she was all right. She looked scared. But not of Nicholas. His hand was on her leg, in an affectionate way. A protective way." Her voice caught. "Like Jerryl used to touch me." She grew silent for a moment. "She's with him voluntarily."

He was so shocked he actually stuttered. "I . . . d-don't believe it." Not his daughter. "How could she . . . ?" He couldn't wrap his head around it. If Lucas had just tried to rape her . . . but no, she didn't think it was Lucas. Now she would be going to their lair, and no one would protect her. Frustration and helplessness swamped him. "Report to the estate first thing tomorrow morning. We've got work to do." He would have her try to get into their hideout, though he wasn't overly hopeful she'd succeed. No one else had.

"Sure thing."

He hung up. His knees buckled, and he slumped to the floor. Nicholas had obviously brainwashed Olivia in a much stronger way than he ever could have. She was lonely, susceptible.

Or . . . she had simply betrayed him. The thought of it stabbed him like a sword through his heart. He would get his daughter back. Then he would deal with her as she deserved.

Olivia moved closer to Nicholas, pressing her body against his. Hadn't she known this was a bad idea? She had escaped one dangerous situation only to be thrust into another.

One of the women turned off a news story about a cult's mass suicide.

Nicholas tightened his arm around her waist. "Once we tell you what happened, you'll understand why there was no other place I could take her. If you don't . . . you'll have to fight me to keep her prisoner."

She swung around to face him. He would do that to protect her? Yes, she could see he would. If he would have killed Sayre, he'd probably do anything. For her. Like he'd described the female Rogues, she was scared. She was angry. And . . . she looked at Nicholas. She didn't want to, but she loved. Loved him? *Great time to realize that.*

She faced the group. "I'm not going to tell my father about this place. I don't want people killed, not even you."

Eric crossed his arms in front of his chest, making him look even bigger. "Not even the vicious bad guys. That's what you think we are, don't you?"

Lucas held out his hand. "She's here, so we might as well listen to what they have to say."

"Wait." Olivia stepped forward. "Nicholas was cut pretty badly. He needs it cleaned and dressed."

Nicholas had been standing so close to her, no one had seen the bloody sleeve. When she stepped away, she heard two of the women gasp.

A tall woman with long, straight blond hair walked over and took his hand so she could see the cut better. Nicholas grimaced at the movement. She winced at the sight of it. Then she closed her eyes and waved her hand over it. The wound just . . . disappeared. *Vanished!* The woman lifted her hand to his face and did the same to the bruises. She opened her eyes and smiled.

Olivia's mouth gaped, her eyes wide. She reached out and ran her fingers over Nicholas's unmarred face. "I can't . . ." She was too stunned to finish.

Nicholas looked at his arm, dirty but no sign of the cut. "That's amazing. Thank you, Petra."

Petra turned to the others. "I discovered I can heal smaller wounds without taking a hit."

Petra heals wounds. That's how Lucas and Eric didn't die.

Eric threw up his hands. "Great, now she knows something else about us."

The shorter woman with frizzy dark blond hair waved her arm toward the other side of the big space that Olivia could now see was divided into dining room and living area. "Let's sit down and talk. You both look like you're going to fall over."

Somehow, this basement dwelling looked cozy. It was decorated with bright, vivid paintings, the walls done in different colors. There was a pseudowindow on one wall that was so real she could almost smell the fresh air.

Eric might be angry, but the rest of them looked worried—because of her. To them, her father was the big, bad wolf. And so was she.

A screeching sound came from a hallway leading off the main room. "What's that?"

The dark blonde waved her hand in dismissal. "It's my parrot, Orn'ry. He hates being left out."

Eric narrowed his eyes at her. "Don't you even think about bringing it in here."

She met his gaze with equal hostility. "Fine."

"Popcorn!" it called in its parrot voice.

"Dead bird!" Eric called back.

"Kill the bird, kill the bird!"

Eric rolled his eyes in an *I'd love to* way.

Nicholas drew her to the end of a big pit group, tucking her into the corner and sitting next to her. Feeling his body pressing against hers gave her strength to deal with those angry or worried faces.

Nicholas asked her, "What do you know about the Rogues?"

"Not much. I work—worked in the administrative side, mostly dealing with the contract employees. My father kept me out of the program itself." Her voice got softer. "Now I see why."

Lucas sank onto a chair in front of an easel in the corner, and the dark blonde-haired woman settled on his lap. His expression was rigid.

Olivia met his gaze. "I'm sorry for what my father did to you."

"I appreciate what you did."

Her gaze moved to the woman with him. "You must be Amy. I never forgot Lucas calling out for you in his delirium." Amy, too, looked haunted by that thought.

Eric remained standing. "Speaking of prisoners . . . do you know what your dear father was doing to Lucas? Shooting him up with some substance that's tearing his mind apart. Rand here was also a prisoner, but he got off a little easier. Your dad only gave him hallucinogenic drugs to see if they would enhance his psychic abilities."

She wanted to deny that her father would do such a heinous thing. Before she could even finish the thought, a memory jumped to mind. Her hand went to her mouth. The injection Harry was supposed to give Lucas the night the Rogues broke him out.

Eric gave her a smug smile. "What's wrong? Can't stand the thought of Daddy playing mad scientist with someone's life?"

She ignored Eric's bitter question and looked at Lucas. "When you had those fevers . . ."

He nodded, his face shadowed. "From the injections."

"Harry was so insistent on giving you that shot the night they broke you out. He was evasive as to what it was, but you were shaking too hard for him to administer it. I told him I'd take care of it for him, so he could eat. But something about that shot bothered me, and I was more concerned with getting your temperature down. After you were gone, Harry was worried about my father finding out you hadn't gotten the shot." She stuck her thumb in her mouth and started chewing the nail. Had her father done all this? Was he the bad guy and these people innocent? The thought ripped at her.

"He got three of those shots." The anger in Amy's green eyes softened. "The fourth one would have killed him. You probably saved his life. But we've got to find out what was in those injections. Have you ever heard your father talk about the Booster?"

Olivia shook her head. "I wish I could help you."

Amy got to her feet and walked closer. "What about this Harry? Would he know?"

Olivia laughed without humor, shaking her head. "He doesn't even know *me*." She told them about the former employees who were miraculously healed, too.

Rand's face relaxed. "None of those guys died?"

"Their injuries were gone. And so were their memories of working at the asylum. But they did have memories of working other assignments, so it wasn't as though there was a gap."

Eric perched on the coffee table in front of her. "What the hell is going on over there?"

"I wish I knew." She remembered the guy who'd knocked her out that night. Big guy. Big, like Eric. "You're the one who hit me with your gun."

He shrugged. "It was nothing personal. You were in the way. Yeah, we hurt people. Shot people. Your father destroyed our families. Twenty-five years ago, he gave our parents the same stuff he put into Lucas. Within a few years, they were dead. All we wanted was the truth. Darkwell would rather kill us. So if I sound harsh, so be it. My mother burned herself to death, I'm a freak of nature, and now I'm a hunted animal. All because of your father."

Pieces began to click into place, little suspicions she'd ignored, questions he wouldn't answer. She remembered the coldness on his face when she'd talked to him about Sayre. "I'm sorry. Sorry for what he's done." She took a breath. "The man who attacked me tonight . . ." She looked at Lucas, and his face paled.

"Go ahead. Tell us," he said.

"His name is Sayre Andrus. My father brought him into the program from prison. He's a murderer, a psychopath . . . and he's your twin brother."

Lucas went perfectly still. She wasn't sure he'd heard her.

"Your identical twin. He said you were raised in a nice family and he was raised by pack rats. He was pretty bitter about it. But he's not your average psychopath. He can get into people's dreams and . . . make them do things."

Lucas asked, "Like possess them?"

"That's what he did to Olivia," Nicholas said, his hand tightening on hers.

She looked at Lucas. "My father thinks it's you, but I knew it wasn't. The way you called out for Amy, you weren't the kind of guy who could do this."

Trust yourself.

She had, and she'd been right. With Nicholas, too.

Lucas looked as though he was still trying to wrap his head around it.

Eric's eyes glittered with interest. "This guy *possesses* people? Not just gets in their head and mind-controls them with commands?"

"I didn't hear him talking to me. I have vague memories of things, like driving to pick him up, but nothing concrete until I started to wake up."

Eric gave Lucas a cryptic look. "Like what happened with Robbins. Your twin, who could have a strong connection to you."

Lucas had a skeptical look she didn't understand. "But I wasn't asleep."

Olivia looked at them. "What happened to Robbins?"

"I shot him," Lucas said, his voice low.

Eric leaned closer. "I'll bet your father had Sayre get into Lucas's head and make him shoot Robbins."

Rand shot to his feet. "He must be the Offspring Robbins was warning us about. Remember the word he said right before it happened? We thought he said 'scared.' He said Sayre."

Eric looked at Lucas. "See, bro, it wasn't you. Think about that. *It wasn't you.*"

Olivia said, "I talked to him, because I wanted to find out more about him." She turned to Lucas. "He said he had a direct line into your head, and he was going to get into your dreams and make you take out your friends." And her father had brought him in. She clutched her head. "I can't stand any more." It crashed in on her like a tidal wave, crushing her beneath its strength, drowning her.

Nicholas took her hand and stood, pulling her with him. "She's been through enough. I'm taking her downstairs. We can talk more tomorrow."

She expected Eric to object, but he didn't. Nicholas drew her toward a small doorway that went downstairs to another level. They walked through an open area with a gym on one side and couches on the other, and down a hall that mirrored the one above.

"I want to take a shower."

"Of course." He led her into the first room and opened a door to the bathroom. "It connects to Zoe and Rand's room. Make sure you lock their door." He did so for her. "There are towels and washcloths in here." He opened the cabinet beneath the sink and pulled one of each out for her. "I'll see if any of the girls have some extra pajamas or something you can sleep in."

She stood in the bathroom, feeling so lost, so alone.

"Are you all right?" he asked. "No, of course you're not."

"For the first time in my life, I'm afraid to be alone." She turned to Nicholas. "Take a shower with me. Please."

CHAPTER 28

Eric paced the length of the room. "I don't like it. He brought the friggin' enemy into our home."

Lucas pulled Amy closer. "There's nothing we can do about it now, and that includes keeping her prisoner. Just like she knew it wasn't me crawling into her dreams, I have a feeling she isn't going to betray us. Nicholas obviously trusts her."

Eric scowled. "Nicholas is thinking with other parts of his body."

Lucas shook his head. "I don't think so. He's in love with her, not just lust. And she was pretty shook up about what her father had done. She didn't deny it or argue. It was like she was accepting something she's suspected for a while."

Amy leaned her head against Lucas's arm. "She was devastated."

"How's this going to affect our goal? Will Nicholas be able to participate when we move in to kill Darkwell? It is her father, after all."

"We'll evaluate both of them in the next day or so." Eric gave Lucas a pointed look. "Maybe we better discuss this, because I'm thinking of killing them both right about now."

Lucas and Eric went two flights down to the shooting range. The place where he was supposed to die.

As soon as the door was closed, Lucas said, "You don't want to kill them."

"Not entirely. I just said that to give us a reason to talk. Good thing I didn't kill you. Look happy. It wasn't you."

Lucas shook his head, a humorless laugh erupting. "I have an evil twin. Great. Okay, it's a relief, but I still don't think it was him who made me shoot Robbins. I wasn't asleep. I blanked out, like I've been doing. I want you to keep an eye on me. At the first sign of—"

"Yeah, yeah, I'll kill you."

Lucas wasn't so sure he would, though, not after what happened earlier or the cavalier way he'd said it. Once again, he wasn't sure he could depend on him. That worried him most of all.

Olivia hadn't meant to say the words. The fear flooding through her was nothing she'd ever felt before. She was at a loss to deal with it. Right now she didn't want to deal with it alone. Physically, she was safe, at least for these moments. But knowing that man could get into her soul was the worst kind of violation. She couldn't sell her soul and move somewhere else.

"I'll do anything you want." Nicholas moved closer, his hands on her arms.

Anything. The words were like warm honey flowing over her.

She started unbuttoning her pajama top, wanting the filthy clothes off her body. They piled bloodred on the tile floor.

He turned on the shower and stripped out of his clothes. He stuffed the whole pile into the trash can. He had a swimmer's body, long, lean, with narrow hips and muscular legs. Even tired and scared and numb, she recognized his beauty.

Steam billowed out of the shower. She looked away when he stood to face her. She was trying not to look at his body, and he was trying not to look at hers. He helped her step into the tub and moved her beneath the flow of hot water. She closed her eyes and leaned her head into it. Despite the heat, she began shivering again and wrapped her arms around herself.

He folded his arms around her, pulled her close, and kissed the top of her head. "It's okay to cry or scream or whatever you need to do."

No, it was never okay to display her emotions. They were a sign of weakness. She pressed her cheek against him, losing herself in his comfort. Pain and anger and fear radiated through her, but his body buffered that somehow.

"I apologize for the hard-on," he said. "This isn't about that, but my body didn't get the message."

She actually laughed, and it felt good. "It's all right."

He squeezed some liquid soap on a washcloth, then washed her arm, her hand, even between her fingers. He moved the cloth across the back of her neck to start on the other side. He was so tender, careful not to touch her too intimately. He washed her back, then her stomach and down her legs, as though it was the most important job he'd ever done.

"You have a lot of bruises," he said in a soft voice.

"From roller derby."

When he rose, he came face-to-face with her. She took the cloth and washed her intimate areas. Then she washed the cloth, lathered it, and turned to him.

He said, "You don't have to . . ."

She started washing him the same way. She gently traced the remnants of scratches on his chest. "How did you get these?"

"Escaping the estate. I had to push myself into the hedges in the maze."

She couldn't stand the thought of his being hunted like an animal, especially at the direction of her father. While she stood and obeyed her father's command to stay in his office.

Don't go there, not now.

A wall of emotion hovered at the edge of her consciousness, like a tidal wave frozen in place.

She focused on washing his shoulders, chest, the ridges of his stomach, the firmness of his biceps, down his back, and over his small, firm buttocks. He had bruises, too. She washed his legs as he'd washed hers and couldn't help but notice the rigid length of him at full attention. She'd only touched one man, their lovemaking fired by teenaged lust. Since then, her dates had never inspired her to go much further than a kiss.

When she turned to hang the cloth over the shower rod, he was pouring shampoo into the palm of his hand. He rubbed it on her hair, scrubbing her scalp and running his fingers through her long hair. She closed her eyes, his touch relaxing her. Several minutes later she stepped into the flow of water and rinsed out the shampoo.

She took the same bottle and poured some out and then reached up to his head. "You have the most interesting hair I've ever seen." He bent to accommodate her, and running her fingers through his hair was as nice as feeling it on her head. "I mean, in a good way. It's thick and choppy and has that just-woke-up look."

"My cowlicks are a barber's nightmare. I started cutting it myself rather than frustrate them. It comes out about the same."

After rinsing, he cut the shower and stepped out, handing her a towel. She tried not to watch him drying his body. *Like he said, this is so not the time for those thoughts.*

She caught her reflection in the mirror, her hair as messy as his, her face pale, her eyes haunted. Everything seemed unreal, as though it were happening to someone else.

She touched her copper pendant. "My father said this pendant was supposed to protect me from people with psychic abilities. He had it made for me when I was young and told me to wear it every day. I thought it was because of the family crest, honor . . . all that crap. When I told him my fears about Sayre, he said it should keep him—he thought it was Lucas—out. But it didn't."

He touched the pendant, their fingers brushing. "This was why I couldn't remote-view you. It was making me crazy."

She looked at him. "Have you ever remote-viewed me before?"

Something crossed his expression, like a boy caught with his hand in the candy box. "Yes, after I left the estate. I was worried about you."

"During the day or night?"

"Only at night."

"I took off the pendant at night. I didn't know I was supposed to wear it at all times. What . . . did you see?"

"Once you were sleeping. The other time . . ." He took her hand and led her into the bedroom. She dropped her towel as he tugged her into his embrace. Then he started dancing with her. His gaze was on hers, one hand on her waist, the other entwined with hers. He spun her in slow circles.

"You saw me dance?"

"I know, I shouldn't have. After what you just went through, it must seem like another violation. You were so graceful, sensuous, and there wasn't a chance in hell I could tear away, even if my conscience was screaming at me."

How embarrassing. "I dance to release pent-up energy."

He grinned. "I could tell."

Could she die right there? "I didn't know anyone was watching! Did I look stupid?"

"No way. But I can tell you also release anger." His smile dimmed. "I assumed it was aimed at me, especially the Alanis Morissette song."

"I remember that night, after you'd grabbed me and warned me about Sayre. I *was* mad at you. And myself."

"Why?"

Shoot, she'd said too much. "Because I should have hated you . . . but I didn't." Her mouth twisted in a grimace, but she changed the subject. "You're a pretty good dancer yourself."

"My sister and I used to dance with our mom. She talked about how she and Dad danced, and we wanted to fill that need, give her that glow, like kids think they can because they don't know any better." His eyes shadowed for a moment. "And I wanted to be like my father." He focused on her. "You like dancing. You're good at it, though I'm glad you didn't use that skill to make a living at strip clubs." His eyebrow quirked. "Unless there's another secret side of you?"

She laughed. "No, roller derby is it. I do love dancing. When I was a child, I wanted to be a CIA agent, a dancer, and own a cake shop. But even then, my father was luring me in. I see it now. He set up these treasure hunts, secret missions. He made it sound so enticing to do what he did. And I idolized him. I wanted to be like him, too." She shuddered, thinking of what she knew of him now.

His laugh was a sweet sound, lifting her out of her gloomy thought. "Roller derby! Here I thought I was going to find you at a serene yoga class." His eyes sparkled with delight.

"My secret alter ego: Pebbles Bamm-Bamm."

"I love it."

He really saw her. In his eyes, she was a desirable woman, a fascinating woman. She'd never been fascinating to anyone before.

She leaned up and kissed him. He kissed her back, gently, his hand cradling her cheek. It was she who deepened the kiss, sweeping her tongue across his teeth as they'd done in the kitchen.

"Livvie, you don't want to do this," he said between kisses.

"But I do."

He cradled her face with both his hands. "You need time to wrap your head around everything. And you must be exhausted."

"I just want to feel. To feel alive. Safe."

"This isn't the right time."

"Yes, it is," she bit out.

"I'll do whatever you want, as long as you really want it."

She kissed him again, and he responded, but he was trying hard to restrain himself. He pulled back, gentling the kiss.

"Don't . . ." she whispered.

"Don't what?"

"Don't . . . don't . . . stop."

He chuckled, remembering the exchanges they'd had. She felt him surrender, plunging into the kiss. She was hyperaware of every physical sensation, everywhere their bodies touched. She ran her hands down his back, over the curve of his buttocks, and he groaned with desire.

She took his hands and placed them on her breasts. "Touch me."

She knew what he was thinking: *Are you sure, after what almost happened tonight?*

"I want to erase what Sayre was going to do to me. I want to forget where he touched me."

He ran his hands over her breasts, watching her as though she would shatter at any moment. She sensed he was holding back, treating her like fragile glass.

"Where else . . . did he touch you?" he asked.

"Here." She slid his hand across her stomach and then down to her inner thighs. "But no farther." Even that was too much.

She didn't realize he was lowering her to the bed until she felt it beneath her. His brown eyes didn't blaze with desire, though. He was concerned about her mental well-being.

She wanted him inside her, filling her, and the need was overpowering and scary. She pulled him close and kissed him. He kissed her back, deeply and passionately, as though he couldn't get enough of her.

She was shocked to feel his fingers slide across her wet cheeks.

"Let it out, babe," he whispered.

He knew she was going to break down. Somehow he knew, and that was why he'd put her first when his body wanted to give in to her demands. She held on tight and sobbed. He held her just as tight.

"Oh, God . . ." The words squeaked out like a little girl's. Everything crashed in on her. What almost happened. What was happening now. She was hiding with the Rogues, alone, nobody, nothing.

Not alone, not right now. Tomorrow she would face all that threatened to drown her. Tonight, right this minute, she let the fear and anger and grief drag her down with its undertow while she was safe in Nicholas's arms.

CHAPTER 29

Olivia climbed from a terrifying nightmare to terrifying reality. Not her bedroom. Gray walls, no windows. Nicholas lying beside her, breathing evenly. Not terrifying, but scary in its own way. The light on the nightstand was still on. The green glow of the digital clock read 11:30. Night? Morning?

She looked down and saw she was naked. The sheet rode low on Nicholas's waist, angling down to reveal a bare hip. So he was, too. Because she'd wanted him to make love to her, to erase what Sayre had tried to do.

She squeezed her eyes closed, wishing she could go back to sleep and have another chance of waking up in her own room, her normal life.

The mewl that escaped her lips woke him.

His hand wrapped around hers as he jerked himself to a sitting position. "What happened?" He looked around, expecting a threat. When he saw none, he asked, "Bad dream?"

She wanted to grip his hand and push him away at the same time. Instead, she let her hand remain limp. "Bad reality. I'm here, in this place. And everything . . . it happened, didn't it?"

"Yes. I'm sorry."

She shoved out of bed, dragging the sheet with her.

"You're the one who started all this. You had to go digging. You had to make me question my father. And now
I'm with the enemy, and *I'm* the enemy, to both your
group and my father." Her voice grew hoarse. "I have no
one. Nothing. I'm no one. I need clothes. I need to get out
of here."

He came up behind her. "Calm down. Where are you
going?"

"I need to find my family." When the words came
out, she realized that was the dark entity pushing at the
edge of her consciousness the night before. "My mother's
family."

"Livvie, you've just been through hell. Give yourself a
few days to absorb, decompress. You can't run off and—"

She spun around. "And you can't tell me what to do. I
hate to admit it, but now it's clear. Painfully clear. My
father manipulated me my whole life, and I let him. I was
his obedient little girl. You gave me a hard time about that,
and it pissed me off. Because you were right. I was the good
Darkwell daughter because I didn't want him to reject me
like my mother did. But maybe she didn't reject me. Maybe
she . . . she . . ." Could she say the words, even think them?

He brushed a lock of hair from her cheek, tucking it
behind her ear. "Your mother's leaving had nothing to do
with you."

She pressed her hand over her eyes, knowing he was
right and yet, not really believing it. "I always felt it did.
And now . . . now that I'm starting to see the truth about
my father, I remembered something that happened when I
was three. Her family came to the house. They wanted to
see me, but he wouldn't let them. I heard them accuse him
of having something to do with her disappearance. I never
asked him about that, of course. In fact, I shoved it into the
darkest recesses of my mind. It was easy. He told me they
were greedy white trash, and he was protecting me from
them."

She tightened the sheet around her. "If my father is the awful person, maybe her family isn't so awful. And maybe . . . maybe he did have something to do with her disappearance." The thought cut through her like a razor blade, but she wouldn't let herself deny the possibility. She would not hide from the truth anymore. "I don't know which would be worse."

"I get your need for family, but you're going to overwhelm yourself."

"I'm not staying here another day. I'm not welcome, not that I blame them. It's bizarre to be hated and distrusted by people who don't even know you."

"How about finding your aunt and cousin?"

"I need to find my mom's family first."

"Do you want me to—?"

"No, I want to find them the normal way." She pinched the bridge of her nose. "No offense. I just need normal." She looked down and realized she had the sheets, and Nicholas was naked.

"Fine, I'm coming with you."

"I don't want you to."

"Why?"

She looked at the question in his brown eyes. His world had also been cracked. He couldn't go home, either. At least he had the Rogues. They were like a family, the way they interacted, looked out for each other.

"Nicholas, you're one of them now. I'm not."

"You are when you're with me."

She shook her head. "You see the world in black and white. I saw my father as white, but I was wrong. But what does that make you? I don't even know. There's so much going on inside me right now." She rubbed her forehead, hoping to smooth away the ache forming there. "I need time alone to sort it out. I don't know who I am anymore."

He touched her chin, tilting her head to look at him.

"You were raised to believe that being part of your family, obeying the rules, was who you are. But you're so much more than that. You're still Olivia Darkwell. You're a dancer, a baker, a creative woman . . . a sensual woman."

Her eyes teared up. "I'm so confused. I'm angry at my father, but I still love him. And . . . I have these crazy feelings for you, and anger is one of them. Why? *You saved my life.*"

He ducked his head and ran his fingers through his mussed hair. "I'm the person who made you see your father in the harsh light of reality. And you'll probably never forgive me for that. I'm sorry as hell, but I didn't make him the bad guy. He was already that. As for anything you feel for me, anger is the safest. Leaving is probably the best thing you can do. But we've still got Sayre to deal with."

Her stomach churned at the thought of him. "He can only get me in my dreams. I'll leave my car keys at the hotel desk where I'm staying and I'll take sleeping pills. They interfere with my dream state." Her eyes widened. "The Rogues will let me go, won't they?"

"I won't let them keep you prisoner." He looked as though he was going to argue further, but he let out a breath instead. "I don't like it."

"I need access to a computer to find their address. I know where the key to one of my grandfather's cars is. He doesn't drive much anymore, and the car is just sitting there."

"What about money? Your father could be monitoring your accounts, your credit cards."

"I'm a fugitive." That hit her. A fugitive from her father. Would he hunt her as he'd been hunting the Rogues? Use the government's power to freeze her accounts? "I need to make him think I'm coming to talk to him, so he won't do anything yet. I'll withdraw money from my account, get the car, and leave."

"I'm with you until you're ready to go on your own. I won't take no for an answer on that. And if you change your mind about my coming with you, I'm there. Got it?"

She nodded. "But if my father or his men find me, they'll hurt you."

His brown eyes gleamed with determination and something she dared not identify. "That's the chance I'm willing to take."

"Why is it better if I'm angry at you?"

He gave her mixed messages, further muddling her emotions. He was devoted, but he wanted to keep her at an emotional distance.

"Don't you think it's better, given our situation?" He went to his dresser and pulled out clothes. "I'll go ask one of the girls if she has some clothes you can borrow."

She nodded, hating to need anything from them. He opened the door and stopped, then knelt to pick up something on the floor. He turned and held up a stack of folded clothing.

"They're ahead of me. Here's a note: *We figured she'd need something to wear. Not sure of the sizes. Olivia's about Amy's size, so this should work.*" He closed the door and walked over, holding the clothing out like an offering. "That's the way these people are."

She chewed her lower lip, touched despite herself. "Well, I suppose they don't want me running around naked." She went into the bathroom and changed, reluctantly reliving the moments she and Nicholas had shared in that shower. She used a washcloth to wash her face and toothpaste to brush her teeth the best she could. She returned to the room, where Nicholas was waiting for her.

She was grateful he hadn't gone up without her. The thought of going upstairs was intimidating enough.

She walked to the door. "Let's get this over with."

He paused before turning the knob. "I wish I could take all this away from you."

She nodded, thinking, *So do I*, but unable to voice it.

Eric and Lucas were working out in the gym. She avoided their gazes. When Eric let out a loud groan, she stiffened, prepared for a verbal onslaught. The weights clanged down, but he said nothing.

Zoe and Rand, on the couch looking over a notepad, glanced up and gave them a civil nod but nothing more.

When Olivia and Nicholas were in the middle of the stairs, she stopped, forcing him to stop, too. In a quiet voice she said, "I've made you their enemy because you brought me here."

"They'll get over it. I don't regret my decision."

A ghost of a smile lit her face, and her heart. She moved on, walking out into the main living room, glad she didn't have to deal with all of them at once. Amy and Petra were talking in the kitchen, and by the low tones, Olivia guessed she was the topic. A cockatoo was standing on a PVC perch. His crown feathers flattened at the sight of her, and he bent low and let out a growling sound as he rocked back and forth. Great, even the parrot didn't like her.

"Orn'ry! Stop that."

Must be Amy's parrot, because it stopped and stood upright, but it still eyed Olivia with as much suspicion as Eric did.

Olivia walked over to the counter that opened into the kitchen. "Thanks for the clothes."

"Yeah, that was nice." Nicholas walked to the refrigerator. "What do you want to eat?"

Olivia put her hand on her stomach. "Oh, the thought of food doesn't sit well."

"You've got to eat. I'll fix you some toast with peanut butter."

He was taking control again. But he wasn't fighting her on the bigger issue of leaving on her own, so she acquiesced.

She looked at the two women, who were both compulsively stirring their coffee. "Can I use your computer?"

They gave each other a questioning look that clearly said, *Dare we trust her? She might send an e-mail to her father.*

"You can stay in the room with me if you're worried," Olivia added.

"I guess," Amy said, nodding for her to follow. The parrot rushed to the end of its perch as though it were going to attack Olivia as she walked past.

Amy shook her finger at it. "Stop it, brat."

It leaned away and made clucking noises.

Amy waved all that away. "It's nothing personal. He doesn't like strangers. Or, really, anyone but me." She led Olivia down the hall to a small room with a desk, computer, and a rack of car batteries. Aiming for the power button with her bare toe, Amy booted up the PC, dropped into the seat, and a few seconds later opened an Internet page.

True to Olivia's offer, she remained standing nearby. Olivia typed in the few facts she knew about her mother, Mary Thompkins Darkwell. Her family came from Spartan, West Virginia, a wretched town, according to her father. If he could be believed.

She wrote down several addresses and phone numbers and closed the page. "Thank—"

Amy was gone. Nicholas walked in bearing a plate with peanut butter toast topped with banana slices. It actually smelled good. He was right; she would need her strength. It was going to be a rough day.

Nicholas left Olivia alone for a few minutes to eat her toast while he went downstairs. Eric and Lucas were working out with a fevered intensity that spoke to their fear of needing to be in shape if Olivia gave her father clues as to their whereabouts.

Nicholas sat on one of the unused benches and leaned against the preacher curl piece. "Olivia and I are heading out this morning. Family's important to her. Now that she's lost the only family she ever had, she's got this idea about connecting with her mother's side of the family. She wants to go alone, but I'm going to get her to her grandfather's car. I'm blindfolding her all the way out."

Eric threw his towel on the floor. "I don't like it."

Lucas tilted his head. "What are we going to do, hold her hostage?"

Nicholas looked at both men. "She's not going to tell her father anything. She understands what kind of monster he is."

Eric scowled. "And we're supposed to believe that?"

"Yes." He shifted his gaze to Lucas. "I've tried to locate the eye piece, but it's as though it disappeared. I'm going to three of the crash sites I worked on, see if I can find anything that might have been left behind. I figure they probably scoured it pretty good, but you never know. I need a car for a few days."

Lucas said, "I'll get you the keys to the Camry and some cash." He nodded toward Olivia, who was standing in the stairwell opening. "You going alone?"

"Yeah. That's the way I like it." Normally he did. As he looked at her, though, the last thing he wanted was to be alone. Or even more importantly, for her to be alone. "I'll keep in touch. Do you have an extra phone? I want her to have one in case she needs to get hold of me."

Eric rolled his eyes, but Lucas said, "We've got a few extras."

"Just make sure she only has your number." Eric turned back to his machine and continued to work out.

Lucas went upstairs to the desk, programmed Nicholas's number into the extra phone, and handed it to Olivia. He held on to it for a second as she took hold of it. "Our lives are in your hands. You understand?"

She nodded. "You won't see my father or his thugs because of me. I want nothing to do with this war." She walked to the door, her anxiousness to get out of there clear in the tension of her body.

Nicholas knew she also meant she wanted nothing to do with them. And probably him. She wanted to escape the whole mess, her father, everything that reminded her of the betrayal she'd suffered. Unfortunately, he was afraid it wasn't going to be that easy.

CHAPTER 30

Once they were on the road, and Olivia could remove her blindfold, she said, "I need to call my father. This is going to be the hardest call I've ever made. I've lied to him a few times, covered for you. But this is different."

He reached over and squeezed her hand but quickly let it go. She was amazed he was there, taking care of her. It made it easier, and harder.

See how confused you are.

He pulled into a service station and parked near the pay phone. He got out with her and handed her some change. "Do you want me there?"

"I'll do it alone, thanks."

She waited through three agonizing rings. He answered with a gruff, "Darkwell."

"It's me."

"Olivia, where the hell are you? Have you gone mad?"

She felt herself shrink at his ire. Then she stiffened her shoulders. "I'm thinking more clearly than I ever have."

"Obviously not. You're with them."

"Them?"

"Don't play coy with me. The Rogues, dammit. You're with the Rogues."

"I am not *with* the Rogues."

"You're with Nicholas, and he's one of them."

She pressed her hand against the glass. "How did you know?"

"I still have someone who can check on things."

Her body stiffened. "Sayre? Don't you dare—"

"Fonda saw you in a car with Nicholas."

"Fonda *saw* me?" Would she ever get used to this? "I thought this pendant was supposed to protect me from remote viewing."

"Yes, but that's not what Fonda can do. Olivia, you're letting this infatuation get the best of your common sense."

"This has nothing to do with infatuation." She glanced at Nicholas, who was leaning against the car watching her. "It's about you not believing me. Have you asked Sayre about last night?"

"He would laugh his head off. He was here, Olivia. It was Lucas, plain and simple."

She knew Lucas wasn't the type to attack her, but she couldn't tell her father that. Or that she'd talked to them, much less been to their hideaway. "I want to talk to you about all this. Meet me at my condo in an hour."

He paused for a moment. "I'll see you there."

She hung up and walked to the car.

Nicholas met her halfway. "How did it go?"

"I think he bought it. He knows I'm with you."

"How?"

"Fonda saw us in the car." Her fingers curled around her pendant. "Which means this thing doesn't do a damned bit of good protecting me from spying eyes. Or creeps who can get into dreams." She twisted the chain and flung it into the trash can. "Take me to a bank, please."

Nicholas walked her back to the car. "I thought I saw something in the backseat, but when I glanced back, nothing was there." His eyes widened. "When I was at the estate, I saw Fonda in my room. But . . . not Fonda. She was like a ghost. Somehow she can project her consciousness to other places. Technically not remote viewing."

She slouched in her seat. "That's what my father said."

An hour later, while her father was waiting at the condo for her, she pulled her grandfather's old Cadillac out of the garage near the back of his property. She'd left a note in case he noticed it gone.

"This was my grandmother's car. When she died, he couldn't bear to drive it or sell it. He had his staff drive it periodically."

Nicholas sat in the passenger seat, ducked down in case anyone saw them driving out. "My mother was so heart-broken when my father was killed that she became a hermit for years."

She pulled out of the driveway but glanced over at him. "My father was responsible for your father's death, wasn't he?"

He slowly nodded. "But that has nothing to do with you. Did you know your father had our blood taken when we started working for him? Mine, Fonda's, and Jerryl's."

Alarm shot through her. "He wasn't giving you any-thing? Like what Amy was asking me about?"

Nicholas sat up and snapped on his seat belt. "No. But now I wonder why he was doing it."

"You said the substance the original subjects got was passed down to their Offspring. Maybe my father was checking to see if it was in your blood."

"He could have isolated it and given it to Lucas when he was a prisoner at the asylum."

Her head spun momentarily. What was her father really capable of? She pulled into the shopping center's parking lot where they'd left the Camry.

She nodded toward the store. "I'm going to buy maps and clothes and toiletries. Then I'm going to Spartan, West Virginia."

"You're sure—"

"Yes." She didn't want him to offer again and weaken her. She wanted him with her. "But tell me something: You said it was better to be angry with you, you've warned me before that you don't get involved, that you're leaving. Why do you want to come with me?"

"To make sure you're all right. I care about you . . . too much. I don't want you to make the same mistake."

Too late.

He continued. "If your family is decent people, stay with them. Stay away from your father."

"And you?"

"Yes, and me. But if you need me—"

She put her finger on his mouth. "You're making me crazy. I'm going to do this by myself. I'll stay a couple of days, then I'll figure out my next step."

He pressed a piece of paper into her hand. "This is your cousin's address. Go there next."

"How . . . ?"

"I looked up Audrey Darkwell on the Internet and found her MySpace page. With her picture, I could find her location."

She wasn't sure how she felt about that. "What are you going to do?"

"I'll be doing some investigating on my own for a few days." He leaned down and kissed her, softly and quickly, before moving back. "Bye."

She leaned forward and hugged him.

"Bye," she whispered, and hurried into the store. She felt his gaze on her the whole time, but she never looked back.

Amy woke up, immediately sensing Lucas wasn't in bed. It was four in the morning. She didn't see the bathroom light. She hated worrying, but she didn't like the feeling she'd had lately that something was going on, and that, as usual, he was protecting her by not telling her.

She walked out into the hallway. The light under Eric's door illuminated the floor. She was about to walk into the living area, hoping she'd find Lucas getting something to drink, when she came face-to-face with him.

He was holding one of the rifles.

"Lucas! What's going on?"

She turned on the light, and her heart plunged. His eyes were vacant. Eric flew out of his room. Petra's door opened, too. Lucas began to lift the gun.

"He's sleepwalking!" Amy held his arm with one hand and tapped his cheek with the other.

Eric grabbed the gun and tugged, but Lucas wasn't letting go or waking up.

"Lucas!" Eric shook him, and only then did he blink and look at them in confusion.

Then he looked down and his face paled in horror. "It's happening again, isn't it?"

Eric pulled away the gun without resistance. "No."

"Denial is dangerous." Lucas took them in, his gaze zipping from one to the other and finally settling on her. "It's not Jerryl. I'm going crazy."

Petra said, "It could be Sayre. Olivia said he can possess people."

Amy rubbed her arms. "And you looked possessed."

Lucas looked at Eric. "Either way, I can't take that chance."

Amy took in the look they exchanged. "You are not killing Lucas."

Petra waved her hands in anxious little movements. "Kill Lucas? My God, that's crazy."

Lucas took Amy's hands in his. "I will not let myself hurt you, whether it's Sayre or me."

Fear bloomed inside Amy. Lucas would do anything, anything, to keep her and the others safe. And Eric, well, she couldn't be sure what he'd do. He looked haggard, as though he hadn't slept in days.

She knew it was no use arguing. "Let's get back to bed. We'll talk more in the morning."

An hour later, as Lucas breathed evenly, she was wide-awake. She crept out to the living area, glad to find it empty. The light was still on beneath Eric's door, though; she had to be quiet. She took her cell phone and went into the storage area. This was one time she had to risk making a call from the shelter.

Nicholas's sleepy voice answered. "Livvie?"

"No, it's Amy. We agreed to find Richard Wallace. Find him. Please. He holds the key to whatever is tearing Lucas apart."

"Give me a few minutes."

"I'll call you back." She waited the longest minutes of her life. "Any luck?"

"I think so. There was a block, so I couldn't get close. He's in an area south of Annapolis. It's wooded, miles from civilization. I saw a sign that said, BIOLOGICAL RESEARCH AREA, PRIVATE PROPERTY, NO TRESPASSING hanging across a gravel road." He gave her some road signs he'd seen.

"Thanks. And, if you talk to anyone else, don't tell them what you told me, okay?"

He hesitated. "Why?"

"I lied. We didn't agree." She hung up and walked to the end of the hall to Petra's room. She opened the door, stepped inside, and closed the door behind her. In the night-light coming from her bathroom, she could see a form swaddled in blankets. "Petra?" She came close. "It's me, Amy."

She came awake fast, her eyes wide. "Is everything all right?"

"It's fine. Well, sort of. I'm going to see Richard Wallace. He created the Booster. He's got to have some idea of how to counteract it." She met Petra's gaze. "I'm going alone. I know Lucas won't let me go, and Eric would probably torch the guy. Honestly, I'm afraid Lucas might hurt him, too."

Petra said, "I'll go with you . . . if you want."

Amy shook her head. "I'm not endangering anyone else. I have to go without anyone knowing. You can tell them after I'm gone."

"You'd do that for Lucas? Risk your life?"

Amy nodded without hesitation.

"He's going to be really mad."

She nodded again. "It's the chance I've got to take."

CHAPTER 31

The sleeping pill left Olivia groggy. Because of her low-quality sleep, she woke at ten, far later than normal. She remembered no strange dreams, no dreams at all. She'd woke twice, her thoughts on Nicholas, on their good-bye. He wanted her away from him and close to him. He'd been doing that since the beginning, when she'd dared to propose an affair, and he'd, rightly, decided she would be hurt when he left. The thought of not seeing him again tore her up.

She picked at the breakfast in front of her, at the diner, hearing Nicholas's voice urging her to eat. Her emotions and nerves were wreaking havoc. She focused on what was ahead. What would she find?

That her father was a liar? That he was hiding much more than the depths of his darkness in regard to his program? Maybe she wanted to shatter the last remnants of love and respect she held for him.

"Nice and optimistic, there, Livvie." *Livvie.* Like Nicholas called her. "Maybe I'll find out Father was right about these people, and that he had nothing to do with my mother's disappearance."

Her grandmother's old car didn't have a GPS in it, and Spartan's detail wasn't on the Virginia map, so once she reached town, she resorted to asking for directions at a gas station.

"Oh, that there's Goofy Ridge."

She raised her eyebrows. "Goofy Ridge?"

"That's what it's been called for 'bout forty years," the old guy said. "You're gonna take that road up thataway for about ten minutes, and turn right at the old shoe factory. It's not open anymore, but you'll see the shoe sign. Go down that road for ten more minutes, and you'll see an old fridge sittin' on the corner, and that there's Goofy Ridge. The road goes in a loop, and all the houses are right on the road, so you can't miss the one you're looking for."

"Uh, thanks." The accent reminded her of Sayre's, even though his wasn't as strong as this man's. A cold chill left a trail of goose bumps across her skin.

She paid for the gas and, with a dry throat, continued down the road. She saw why the man had used landmarks; street signs were either missing or knocked down. The whole town had a sad, vaguely abandoned air to it, like the shoe factory itself.

She drove past the refrigerator, its doors removed, thank goodness, and down a gravel road. Most of the houses were mobile homes in various states of decay. Yards were filled with toys and lawn equipment, partially hidden by weeds. The vehicles she saw were in similar states, up on blocks. A few children played around one truck, pretending to shoot at each other. They stopped and stared at her as she passed, and she realized she was doing the same. She smiled at them, hoping her pity and unease didn't show.

She had never seen such poverty, and the despair seemed to seep into the sunshine, tinting it with an odd yellow cast. She saw the numbers on the mailbox that matched the ones on her paper and turned into the dirt driveway. A putty-covered Buick that looked drivable indicated someone was home.

Someone. Her family. She stared at the door of the house. Giggling brought her attention to the children she'd seen earlier, who were now at the edge of the property, watching her with open curiosity.

A barefoot boy of about ten stepped forward as Olivia opened her car door. "You must be lost, ma'am."

She sighed. *In so many ways.* "Do the Thompkins live here?"

"Yes'm."

"Then I'm not lost."

"Come on." He took her hand and led her around planting pots bursting with flowers and the scent of mint from an herb garden. He pushed open the door, and hollered, "Mama, we got company!"

The interior wasn't as bad as she might have imagined. The carpet was wrinkled but looked clean. She couldn't say the same about the two well-worn recliners. An étagère was filled with pictures and knickknacks, and the place smelled like bacon and cigarette smoke. The living room was smaller than the second bedroom at her condo.

A woman in her late thirties came out of the kitchen, drying her hands on a towel, a questioning expression on her face. She came to a dead stop at the sight of Olivia. "Who are you?" The words came like bullets out of a mouth with the starburst wrinkles of a smoker.

"My name is Olivia Darkwell. My mother's last name was Thompkins. I think her family lived here."

She stared for another few seconds, until the boy tugged her shirt. "Mama? You're being rude."

She turned toward the hallway. "Mama! Daddy! Get out here!"

Olivia winced at the sharpness of her words. But the woman's expression softened as she walked closer, still kneading the towel in her rough hands. "Oh, my Lord up in Heaven." She took in Olivia with eyes now full of amazement. "You look just like her."

An older man and woman emerged from the hallway, and their expressions seemed to confirm what the woman had said. The older woman's hand came up to her mouth. *"Mary."*

"No, Mama, it's her daughter, Olivia. She's finally come home."

Olivia wasn't sure how she felt about that assumption, but she had no time to ponder it. The couple rushed forward, taking her in the same way the younger woman had.

The woman took her hands, and either life or cigarettes had made her look older, too. A long, gray braid swung past her derriere. "I'm your grandmamma, Fanny. I jis' can't believe it. We never thought we'd see you." Her expression darkened. "Your daddy, he wouldn't never let us call or see you. How did you find us?"

"It's a long story."

Fanny pulled her into her arms, and Olivia felt every bone in her skinny body. "We got you back! It's a miracle."

The younger woman hugged her next, a long, cloying hug. Olivia wasn't used to a lot of affection, but this felt uncomfortable in a different way.

Finally, the woman let her go though she kept clutching Olivia's arms. "I'm your aunt Lulu, your mama's little sister. I was fourteen when she went off to Washington, D.C., all gonna make something of herself. Then she married your daddy. She went on and on about this knight in shining armor who rescued her and a whole bunch'a stuff we later found out was a load of bull." She waved toward the sagging couch. "Sit, sit! Let me get you some lemonade." Lulu dashed into the kitchen.

Fanny nodded toward the older man. "This here's your granddaddy, Tommy."

He shook her hand, his expression more solemn. "So, why *are* you here?"

Fanny nudged him with her elbow. "Tommy, please give the girl some time to breathe. She came to find her family, ain't that right, honey?"

Olivia nodded. That was true. And it didn't matter if they were poor, really it didn't. They were just a little too much all at once.

"My father never told me much about you."

From the kitchen, Lulu said, "Yeah, I bet he didn't." She swept into the living room with a glass of lemonade for Olivia and one for her mother.

"That's 'cuz he killed our daughter," Tommy said.

"Daddy, we needn't go there yet." Lulu waved to her son. "Bobby Jr., go outside! This is grown-up talk." He grumbled but trudged outside. She turned back to Olivia. "He came here once, a year after they got married. He was the biggest snob, looking down at us because we don't have a big ole mansion. He came in one of those fancy cars like yours out there, and the moment he stepped out, you could see his disgust. That look never left his face the whole time he was here, which was, what, twenty minutes?"

Fanny was taking a sip of her lemonade. She nodded as she set it down on a wooden table covered in water rings. She lit a cigarette. "He said Mary lied about where she come from and that he just found out. We could see he'd turned her against us. He called us white trash and made her admit she was, too." The betrayal still hurt. "He stomped back to that car of his, and she went running after him. They had a fight, in front of God and everybody, then told him she was pregnant. They got into the car, and we didn't hear from her until she sent a picture of you."

Fanny walked over to the collection of pictures on the étagère and pulled a small plastic frame from the back: Olivia's baby picture. "We wrote saying we wanted to visit, but she called and said it wasn't a good idea. She had to forget about her past and become what he wanted her to be. We could tell she was afraid of him. She hung up real quick, like he'd walked in, and she didn't want him catching her talking to her family. Her own family! We heard from her a few months later, and she said she was coming to visit, maybe for a while. She had to get away. Those were her exact words, 'get away.'"

Tommy waved away the trail of smoke that drifted past him. "And then she was gone. He called and asked if she was here."

"Where else would she go, except here? And we couldn't believe she would have left her baby," Lulu said. "He said she couldn't handle being a mother."

Tommy's mouth tightened into a line. "We drove up there, but he wouldn't talk to us. Or let us see you."

"I saw you," Olivia said, setting down her half glass of lemonade and walking over to the étagère.

Fanny handed her a picture of a woman in her late teens that did, indeed, look like Olivia.

"I'm sure he told you terrible things about us." Fanny lit her own cigarette. She nodded when Olivia's expression confirmed that. Her voice stretched tight. "Your daddy did something to your mama."

Fanny's eyes watered. "The police said there wasn't any proof of wrongdoing."

Tommy waved his hand in anger. "The guy's a Fed. Of course they won't find anything!"

The anger and tension was fresh. Olivia returned to the couch, feeling too fatigued to stand. She reached for her lemonade again, drawing in a long gulp of the supersweet drink. Had her father killed her mother? *Isn't that what you came here to learn?*

Fanny's expression softened. "I'm sorry to say this about your daddy, but he's an awful, awful person."

Lulu scooted closer, edging into Olivia's personal space, along with her cigarette smoke. "Tell us about your life, Olivia. It must have been nice, with all that money. You probably went to fancy boarding schools. I read about them in novels."

Fanny asked, "Did he ship you off? What kind of father was he?"

Tommy said, "What kind of father could he be, the murderin' son of a bitch?"

Lulu said, "You're going to stay a few days, of course.

We'll get the couch all ready for you. It's real comfy. Can't have you staying at a hotel."

Olivia's head began to spin. What was happening? They'd drugged her! Her whole body began to shake as their voices became a hum.

She slumped back on the couch.

Nicholas woke, his body trembling and slick with sweat. It wasn't even light out yet. He sat up and shook the dream from his head.

The fire nightmare. Something about it, though, nagged at him, beckoning him to go back in. He pulled up the pieces: fire; heat; smoke. The funeral. Crying. His mother with an eye patch, sister, heart-wrenching sobs. He saw some of the other people there, uncles, an aunt he hadn't seen in ten years . . . and Olivia.

She was sitting alone, crying, and he realized he'd seen her before. He hadn't known who she was then. Good thing they'd parted ways. Too bad he didn't feel good about losing her.

Losing her . . .

He shook the need away, got up, and looked out the window. Dawn was breaking. He took a shower and ate breakfast in the small town nestled in the mountains of southern Pennsylvania. After driving to the place he remembered, he stepped out of the car and breathed in the cool, fresh air. This was the most relaxed he'd been in months, in his element, in the woods, alone.

Lonely.

Wasn't this what he wanted? To be alone, on his own?

Lonely.

He'd convinced himself for so long, and Olivia had shattered his illusion. There wasn't a damned thing he could do about it.

He'd used his location ability to go to the same spot where he'd found one of the pieces. Just like the eye, he couldn't find the bracelets, either. He pulled himself into the memory: rings made of a metal he'd never seen before, as though the government had taken what was available and stepped it up a notch. He turned in circles, seeing it clearly. No eye there.

He looked up through the trees and into the bits of sky he could see. The forest spun around him with his movements. He could spend all day there, listening to the birds calling, inhaling the scent of pine and earth.

He had two other sites to check out, and those were farther from Spartan, West Virginia. Olivia had thrown away the pendant, he'd realized during the restless night. No way could he not check on her. A scene came into focus: living room, people hovering over something on the couch. No, someone: Olivia. She was lying there, as though asleep, and a woman was fanning her with a pillow. Another woman was looking at her ring as she tapped Olivia's hand.

His heart clenched. Was she sick? Dead?

He pulled out of the vision. He started walking, then running, out of the forest. She was roughly an hour and a half away. He reached the car and jumped in, breathless. "I'm coming, Livvie. Hang in there."

CHAPTER 32

Voices and people touching her pulled Olivia from her sleep.

Sleep?

She opened her eyes, the pieces coming together. Three faces hovered over her. Fanny was waving a pillow in front of her, Lulu was admiring her emerald ring, and Tommy returned to the room with a blanket.

Olivia tried to sit up, but her head spun. "I think I'm going to be sick."

"Get the bucket!" Lulu hollered.

Olivia sat very still and quieted her stomach's heaving.

Fanny's hand went to her mouth. "Did you give her some of the lemonade from the yellow pitcher?" She took a sip of her own glass. "Oh, no. That one's loaded with vodka. I spiked it last night."

"Mama, you're supposed to put the liquor in the clear pitcher!"

Olivia could barely swing her eyes toward the woman. "There's liquor in it?"

"'Fraid so. I didn't even think about it." Fanny gave her a sheepish smile. "It blends in with the lemonade, so I didn't notice. Lulu, get her some crackers."

"I probably should go back to the motel." Olivia tried to push up from the couch.

Tommy put his hand on her shoulder. "You can't drive like this."

Panic curled around her throat. He was right; she couldn't drive. Couldn't escape. Trapped.

Lulu returned with a box of saltines.

Olivia tried to focus in on them. "But I don't want to get crumbs on the couch."

Fanny waved that concern away with a laugh. "God knows what's living in the cracks of this thing. A few crumbs sure won't hurt."

Olivia wanted to pop off the couch, but her body wouldn't move.

Fanny studied her. "Not much of a drinker, are you?"

Olivia began to shake her head but stopped when the whole room rocked. "I haven't eaten much today." She started nibbling on the crackers, watching to see if anything crawled out of the cracks to grab the crumbs.

Lulu tucked a blanket around her. "You'll be back to your old self in no time. We'll get out the photo albums, and when you're feeling better, you can tell us all about yourself."

"And your daddy," Tommy added.

Fanny returned a few minutes later and settled in next to Olivia with the album. Lulu pressed up against her on the other side, making Olivia feel like the filling of a sandwich.

For the next hour and a half, she nibbled crackers and listened to story after story about her mother. More than she wanted to know, like how she'd gotten stabbed in the butt by a pitchfork's tine while fooling around in the hay. Bobby Jr. wandered into the kitchen, taking a few moments to stare at her on the way. They kept asking her if she was ready to eat, but her stomach rebelled at the thought.

Everyone looked up when someone knocked on the door.

"Don't know who that could be." Fanny sprang up and opened it.

The sight of Nicholas injected Olivia with relief and longing and such a mix of emotions, her eyes welled up. Concern and determination filled his brown eyes, as though he'd come to rescue her. His hair looked messier than ever, like he'd been worrying it on the way there.

She smiled. "Nicholas."

He came in without invitation and walked over to her. "Are you all right? You look . . . not well."

"We got her drunk, by accident," Lulu offered, taking in the stranger with interest. "Who are you?"

Olivia waved toward him with a floppy arm. "This is my"—what was he?—"friend, Nicholas. And this is my mother's family."

Lulu tugged her T-shirt down over her jeans. "You didn't tell us you had a friend coming." She held out her hand. "I'm Lulu, Olivia's aunt."

He shook her hand but his gaze was on Olivia. She gave him a subtle nod as he turned to meet the others. "I'm taking Olivia back to her motel."

Fanny said, "But we still got a lot of catching up to do. Join us."

Nicholas was already holding out his hand to her, and Olivia clutched it. He pulled her to her feet, even as the three of them pushed in closer and objected. She had been listening to them for hours, and their voices, their stories, and their accusations about her father pounded into her head as hard as the headache. Even now the women held on to her arms as though they were going to engage in a tug-of-war with Nicholas.

"We've hardly gotten a chance to get to know her yet," Fanny said.

Nicholas pulled her out of their grasp and against his chest, his arm around her collarbone. "She's had enough for now." His voice, deep and strong, carried authority. "She'll come back when she's ready." He steered her to the door.

She waved. "I'll be in touch."

"Wait," he said. "Can I see a picture of your mother?"

Olivia led him to a shelving unit and pointed to several of the pictures.

"Yes, you definitely look like her." He nodded and led her out the front door.

She saw his car parked behind hers in the drive. "I can drive back to the motel. I'm not woozy anymore, just tired. Overwhelmed. Brain boggled. But not drunk. I think I ate a whole package of crackers."

He studied her. "Are you sure?"

"Yes. Besides, if I leave my car here, I'll have to come back for it."

"Understood. I'll follow you."

The dim coolness of the motel room was welcoming, though she could still smell the smoke on her. She turned to him. "Thank you for coming. But how did you know I needed—you remote-viewed me, didn't you?"

He nodded, no regret on his face. "I saw you lying on the couch looking as though you'd passed out."

"I fell asleep." She covered her mouth. "At least I didn't get sick. They were happy to see me but unloaded years of both anger at my father and history on me at once. They think my father killed my mother. And the worst part is, I couldn't say he wasn't that kind of person."

He pulled her into his arms and kissed the top of her head.

She said, "I think they're good people who have had all these emotions and questions stuffed inside for so long. But I need a breather before I go back." She gave him a wry smile. "You were right; it was too much." Fatigue permeated her voice. "I'm not ready to rush out to California and see my cousin."

Nicholas led her to the bed, then curled up behind her spoon style. Just comfort. "Sleep for a while. Then you're coming with me for a few days."

She nodded, too tired even to be annoyed that he was

taking control. For the moment, that was okay. She had no-where to go.

Just before she drifted off to sleep, he said, "I hope you like camping in the woods."

Richard Wallace grabbed hold of the black mouse with his gloved hand. He tried to be gentle . . . as gentle as one could be whilst inserting a needle into its body. He set the mouse down, and it scrambled toward its den.

"Sorry, fellow."

He froze as a spidery sensation crawled over him. He looked around the white glare of his lab but saw nothing. He knew better than to discount it.

He picked up his satellite phone and made a call. "I need you here. We may have trouble."

CHAPTER 33

Gerard Darkwell stepped out of the hotel where Nicholas Braden had spent the night and slid on his sunglasses. The room was empty, but he was getting closer to finding him, and with him, Olivia. Though Sayre hadn't seen a woman with Nicholas last night when he'd possessed him in his sleep, Gerard knew she must be with him.

The small town wasn't far from Spartan, West Virginia. He had an idea why they were in the area. He drove to the horrid place where his wife had come from, the past she had hidden from him until it was too late. He hoped to catch Olivia there, and he hoped she'd never go there. When he got out, he leveled a hard glare at the children to keep them away from his car. The alarm chirped.

He knocked on the door, and the woman he remembered being Mary's sister answered. Her eyes went wide, and her mouth dropped open. The stench of bacon and cigarettes assailed him.

"I want to know if you've had any visitors lately." No need for pleasantries. These people disgusted him, and they weren't fond of him, either.

"Did Olivia come ba—?" Mary's mother came out of the hallway and stopped dead when she saw him.

"That answers my question, thank you. How long ago did she leave?"

Both sister and mother clamped their mouths shut. He glanced at his watch. It couldn't have been very long. That Olivia had come here boded very badly for her state of mind. He had to get her back into his hold. These women were standing in his way.

He gripped the sister's bony shoulder. "How long?"

She buckled, but he kept a hold on her. "'Bout an hour ago."

"Was she with a young man with dark hair?"

"Get your hand off her! Tommy!" The mother tried to pry his hand away.

"Answer the question, and I'll let go."

"Yes, yes, yes," the sister said, hatred in her eyes.

He let go and gave her his most pleasant smile. "Thank you for your assistance."

The father came barreling out of the house a minute later, but Gerard was already locked in his car. His crazy accusations were lost as Gerard turned up the opera music and backed out of the drive.

He made a call to Fonda. "Find Olivia."

Amy gave the excuse of doing some girl shopping to head out by herself. She knew Lucas would be furious when she returned, and she wasn't about to do so until she had something of value.

Not that he hasn't hidden things from me.

Her chest was tight as she continued her drive. Galesville, where Wallace's supposed research facility was located, was about thirty minutes from the tomb.

She called Nicholas. "It's Amy. Everything all right?"

"So far. But I'm glad you called. We figured out what Fonda's ability is. She can project her consciousness to other places. She looks like a ghost."

"Astral projection?"

"I guess. So if you see a young woman who's there but not there, you're busted."

"Good to know. I need to tell you something, too. When

Sayre is coming in, you'll feel a cold prick at the back of your neck. At least that's what Lucas felt when he came in the night we were with Robbins. I'm not sure if you'll feel it when he comes in while you're asleep, though."

"Damn, this stuff is crazy."

"I know. But there are only two Offspring on their side now. Dangerous ones, perhaps, but only two."

"Amy, what's going on with this Wallace thing?"

"I'm going to find out what's in our bodies. I'm sorry I lied to you, but I didn't want to put you in the middle. I've got to go. Be careful."

"You, too."

She signed off, made a quick call to Petra's phone to pass on Nicholas's information, and concentrated on her driving as she reached Galesville. The roads Nicholas had seen were in the rural area, and she nearly missed the turnoff. Several minutes later she came up on a gravel road leading into the woods with no signs or mailbox.

Once she pulled down the drive she saw the NO TRESPASSING sign hanging from the chain going across the road. Posted to a nearby tree was the sign BIOLOGICAL RESEARCH AREA, PRIVATE PROPERTY, NO TRESPASSING. She got out and walked up to the chain. It was triple locked, with a ditch cut down the sides of the road to discourage anyone from driving around it.

Something in the thick pine forest caught her eye. It was shiny, about three feet high, but she couldn't tell what it was. She stepped over the chain. The woods were filled with sound: birds, the rustle of a breeze through the trees, and the crunch of gravel as she walked down the road. Oh, and her heartbeat crashing against her ribs.

Down the rabbit hole I go . . . again.

And again, for Lucas. For all of them.

Scattered all over the property were more of those shiny things. She walked through the grass to inspect one. It looked like a yard ornament, made of copper and crystals, in the shape of a butterfly. A man who had pretty orna-ments all over couldn't be so bad. Right?

A scream made her jerk her head around. It sounded like a woman, but not quite. She shivered. She'd come to a stop, and every muscle in her body strained to turn around and run back to her car.

Keep going.

She heard another sound: footsteps. She swiveled around. Nothing.

An arm jerked her against a hard, male body. Where had he come from? She'd just checked all around and seen no one. But he was real. She struggled to see her captor, but he wasn't budging.

From behind and above her, he said, "Gotcha, mate."

"Did you say something about camping in the woods, or was I dreaming?"

Olivia threw her toiletries into the little bag and walked to the door of the motel room. She felt wretched, even with a shower and the two bottles of water Nicholas had forced her to drink when she'd woken up. No matter what, she felt better now that she was with him.

"You weren't dreaming," he said, hoisting her bag. "You can't take all this stuff into the woods. Just the basics."

"How long are we going to stay there?"

He opened the door and nodded for her to precede him. "Maybe a night or two. If Fonda or Sayre sees us, there won't be any landmarks for them to find us by when we're in the woods. I don't know exactly what Sayre can do, but Darkwell said I was the only one who could pinpoint a lo-cation without using a landmark."

Just as she was about to step outside, she caught sight of her father's car. She pushed back, knocking into Nicholas and closing the door. "My father's here!" She stepped to the curtain and peered out. "His car is slowing down. Do you think he saw me?"

He came up behind her. "No. He'd be slamming into the parking lot. He's curious about something."

"My grandfather's car. You don't see a lot of Cadillacs around here."

The black Mercedes cruised into the parking lot, and the driver's window slid down as it pulled up behind the Cadillac. His eyebrows furrowed as he no doubt saw the distinctive MRS. MAJOR plate. He pulled into the parking space next to it and hurried to the office, cell phone to his ear.

"He's alone," she said. "But probably calling for backup."

"We've got to make a run for it."

"My father's inside. Let's go!"

They slid out and, ducking down, ran toward the Camry. She got into the passenger side and lay down.

Nicholas pulled out of the lot, watching the rearview mirror. "He's walking out of the office with a short guy, heading to our room."

Tremors shook her body. "We almost got caught. What would he have done?"

He looked over at her. "He would have taken you back to the estate. Once he has you back, he'll keep you there."

"He wouldn't do that."

He flashed her a doubtful look.

"And what about you?" she asked.

"He would have killed me."

He stomped on the gas pedal as soon as they were out of sight of the motel.

She sat up and put her hand on his arm. "If I'm going to put you in danger, please don't take me along."

He glanced at her. "Livvie, if he gets the chance, he'll kill me either way. You being with me, well, that only pisses him off more."

His words sent a chill spiking through her. "I think I know what the Rogues feel like. Maybe a little, anyway. Being chased, hiding . . . hunted. So in a way, I am one of them. Whether I like it or not."

CHAPTER 34

Sayre's phone rang. He was lounging on the couch watching *Judge Judy*. He waited for the fourth ring before answering. "'Lo, Pete's Pizza, where our sausages are the longest and spiciest."

Silence for a moment. "Sayre?"

"Yes, sir." Man had no sense of humor.

"Keep working on finding Braden. We were close, but he was already gone."

"That early? Man, the guy must'a been up at the crack of dawn."

Darkwell had tasked him with finding Braden, who, as it turned out, was the son of a bitch who'd broken up his little date with Olivia. He'd gotten into Braden's dreams and had the guy walk outside and identify the motel. He might have had the guy do himself in if Darkwell hadn't told him to hold off for now. Darkwell gave him free rein on these Rogue people, but most of them were in a protected place. Lucas, though, he could get into because of their twin connection, or that was Sayre's best guess. Unfortunately, his girlfriend woke him up before he could finish his task. Lucas was going to have to take her out first, then blow away the rest of them.

"I want you to find him again tonight. He'll be with a woman. Don't hurt her."

Don't hurt the woman. Hm, intriguing. "And Braden?"

"I'll take care of him myself."

He hung up without so much as a bye or thank-you or howdy do. Fine manners for a guy who lived in a big house.

Now if Sayre only knew what was really going on. He figured Olivia had snitched on him because the guard checked to make sure he was in residence. Darkwell must think it was Lucas who attacked her. Sayre couldn't wait to see if the woman with Braden was Olivia.

Amy's heart pounded so hard she thought it might burst out of her chest. The man, whose iron-hard arms wrapped around her, actually lifted her off the ground. Her feet kicked at his shins but didn't budge her captor.

He leaned close to her ear. "Who are you and what do you want?"

"My name is Amy Shane. I'm an offspring of the people in an experiment Richard Wallace headed up twenty-five years ago, and I have some questions for him."

The man said, "Did you hear that? . . . All right, will find out and advise."

Another man stepped out from the cover of woods, a rifle aimed in their direction. He was tall and wiry, with a prominent Adam's apple. Maybe it was his longish, wavy brown hair, but he reminded her of a British rock and roller. And, most shockingly, he had the Offspring glow. It was jagged, matching his dark, fierce expression as he approached.

"You armed?"

"No." Coming in armed didn't seem like a good idea. Not that it would have done her a lot of good, as it turned out.

The man holding her, who felt as big as Eric, set her down. "No fast moves. Lachlan's been practicing his shot since he was five."

He patted her down while Lachlan held the rifle on her. He wore a headpiece like the cell phones that reminded her of *Star Trek*. He said, "She's not armed."

"But are you alone?" said the man behind her. He stepped around and took a good look at her.

"Yes."

Her captor *was* as big as Eric and just as muscular. He was probably six-two, with a boyish face and a Cupid's bow mouth. He also had an Offspring glow.

"We're bringing her in," he said.

He clamped his hand on her arm and led her down the road.

She tugged to free herself. "There's no need to manhandle me."

His mouth quirked, but he didn't release her.

They came around a corner and upon an earthen-colored wall with an ornate gate in the center. Beyond were a lush garden, then the house. Copper scrollwork, now turned verde, adorned the top of the wall. The gate opened as they approached, and she saw a camera pointing at them.

This garden was different than anything else she'd seen. Mixed among the flowers were oddly shaped and colored specimens that were neatly labeled with scientific names. A network of copper webbing covered the courtyard like a dome, and the roof as well. They followed a curving path to a stained-glass door, and the walls on either side were glass.

A man was waiting for them: Richard Wallace with . . . an Offspring glow? But he couldn't be an Offspring. She stared at his calm halo of colors.

Richard's light green eyes were sharp with both interest and a hint of wariness. His hair was short and bright white. He tucked his earpiece into his lab coat pocket. "Amy Shane, daughter of Henry Shane?"

Hearing her dad's name from this man's lips shot anger

through her. "Well, at least you remember your victims' names."

His white eyebrows rose, and he almost looked amused. "You've come to accuse me?" He had a languorous, almost theatrical way of speaking. "Well, I suppose I was, in part, to blame. But I was a victim as much as anyone else. Magnus, you can release her."

Yeah, like she was going to believe *he* was a victim. The guy holding on to her finally released her. She crossed her arms in front of her. "I've come to find out what you put in our parents that made them crazy. Because it's in us, too."

He smiled. "Funny you should come here. I was about to go looking for you. All of you."

"Why?"

"Because I've been working on the antidote."

Could it be that easy? No, nothing was that easy.

He stepped aside, gesturing for her to go in. She did, taking in the narrow hallway that stretched left and right, with an exterior wall comprised mostly of glass that looked out into yet another courtyard. A black pond was the centerpiece, with junglelike growth around it.

He led her to the right, where a small sitting area was intimately lit by small, silver lights that dangled from long cords. He pressed his hands together and bowed toward her, then gestured for her to take a seat. "May I get you something? I have lychee tea shipped in from China. Or perhaps a soda?"

"Nothing for me." She sank down onto the modular chair. Tea from a botanist with a predilection for fungi . . . no frickin' thank you. "You were—"

"Tut-tut." He lifted a finger to quiet her. "Must never talk while making tea. The vibrations permeate the tea and ruin the taste."

He walked into a gourmet kitchen just beyond and went through a meticulous process of getting out an exotic teapot and preparing tea. She turned to the two men, who were still standing and watching her. There was a slight resemblance between them, at least in eye and hair color and the sensuous shapes of their mouths. Both men had brown hair, though Magnus's was rich with curls and Lachlan's was merely wavy. Neither looked a thing like the man in the kitchen.

Richard returned, setting the tray down on the coffee table. "I brought you a cup in case the aroma changes your mind." He sat down and gingerly dropped two pink sugar cubes into his tiny teacup. "How did you find me?"

Amy stuffed her annoyance that he had stopped her from asking questions but then had launched into his own. Shades of those first few encounters with Petra and Eric. That didn't mean she had to answer him, though. "Darkwell is looking for you, too."

He stopped stirring. "You're here on his behalf?"

Amy had to stifle a horrified laugh. "God, no. You were in the program, too, weren't you? You took the Booster."

"The Booster." He shook his head. "Terrible name for it. No romance, no resonance. Darkwell's name. Yes, I took it. How did you know?" He especially drew out his *yes*es.

"Because I can see your glow, your aura." She turned to the two men. "Your sons?"

He smiled with pride. "Lachlan and Magnus."

That was a good sign, that he was introducing them, wasn't it? "You passed it on to them."

"Passed . . . *it*?"

"The Booster."

His expression darkened for a second. "Yes. Tell me about this glow you see."

"They usually indicate moods, but Offspring—that's what the children of the people in BLUE EYES are called—have a mixed glow, like static on a television."

He took a sip of tea and set down the cup. "I see. Well, I *don't* see the glow, but I see what you mean. Your father had the same ability. And many more."

Her throat tightened at the mention of him. "Like what? I know he could remote-view."

"The best I've ever seen. He could read documents, hear everything." He raised a brow at her. "Can you do that?"

"No. Could he channel the dead?"

"Yes." He'd drawn out the word again. He took another sip, his pinky extended. "And you?"

She nodded.

He set his cup down and sat back in his chair. "How did you find me?" His expression remained merely curious, but she saw a spark of fear in his eyes.

"One of us can locate."

His face got even paler than it already was. "The copper didn't keep him out."

"Copper?"

"Copper has protective qualities, especially when it's charged in energy vortexes. It keeps out psychic eyes. It has been protecting us for many years. Until now. I felt one of you here." He looked at his sons. "I told you someday our protection might not be enough."

Lachlan hoisted his gun in an automatic gesture. "We'll be ready."

Richard's face was like a mask, stiff and calm. "We don't know what they have."

"We do." Amy planted her hands on her knees. "Darkwell has two Offspring working for him, trying to hunt us down. But I'm not telling you any more until I have what I came here for. We inherited our parents' boosted psychic ability. And some of us have inherited the mental instability, too. My boyfriend is . . . he's breaking down. Darkwell captured him and put more of that stuff into him. I'm afraid Lucas is going to die if I don't get him help." *Dammit.* Her voice had broken. "You said something about an antidote."

"He injected Lucas with more of the Booster? But . . . how? It was destroyed. I made sure of that." He stood. "Come with me, daughter of Henry Shane."

She swallowed hard, wishing now she'd taken some of that liquid. She accompanied him out a glass door that went into the courtyard behind the house. His sons followed.

"I knew Darkwell two years, four months, and ten days before BLUE EYES started. He was fascinated by psychic abilities. He wanted to use them to help our country, but his vision grew out of hand. I admit to being narrowly focused, but he far surpassed me."

The house was a large square that encircled the back courtyard, which was covered like a greenhouse. It was warm and humid, steaming the Plexiglas panels that made the roof. Huge koi swam in the dark pond, ducking from sight as the four of them came near. Tiny birds flitted from branch to branch, chirping in alarm.

"I heard a scream," she said.

"Peacocks. Years ago this was an animal sanctuary. It's mating season."

More of those odd-shaped growths filled this area. He paused, tilting his head and gazing at one particular grouping. Amy wanted to push him for more answers, but she intuitively sensed pushing would get her nowhere.

So she would engage him, gain his trust, whatever it took, because she wasn't leaving until she got the antidote. And answers. "I understand you're a biologist and mycologist. And that you're very talented."

His smile deepened momentarily and then faded. "Yes, I was."

"Was?"

His focus, though, was on some small, pink balls growing on a fern. "Did you ever see such beauty?" He waved his hand over the centerpiece island. "Such variety? These are myxomycetes. Slime molds, my favorite type of fungus. I have always been fascinated by the odd, especially when it comes to nature. Especially that of the psychic nature." He bent down and bounced his finger gently on top of some spongy red growths that reminded her of something from a Dr. Seuss book. "But these I could see, touch. Others could see and touch them, too, though most people were repulsed."

He picked up a rotted branch and held it up to her. "This one is named after me." The wood was covered by something that looked like a lacy red sea fern. "People walk past these every day and don't even notice them. But these are life-forms, as lovely as any flower. Just because we classify them as fungus does not make them less valuable."

His voice became impassioned on those last words, and his gaze was on the specimen in his hand. He gently set it down, giving it a look of fatherly love.

What did this have to do with—? "Was the Booster one of these?"

He gave her an odd smile. "You think I'm some mad scientist who sampled one of my specimens?" He laughed, shaking his head. "I did, but by accident."

"How could that have happened?"

"It moved onto my plate."

Her mouth dropped open. "Moved?" She looked at the specimens with trepidation now. "These things can *move*?"

"Some can. Afterward, my abilities increased tenfold. Darkwell wanted to know what had made the difference. He wanted a sample, and to my everlasting regret, I brought one in. I suffered no side effects, for a while, anyway. It took time for them to manifest. Darkwell thought it was safe, and I . . . I'm afraid I didn't object enough. Before I knew it, he was giving the subjects the so-called Booster, though they didn't know exactly what it was. We were getting amazing results."

She followed him down the path, wondering if one of these specimens had been in the Booster. Some were amazing and so odd she would have definitely stopped to check them out. They were in such an array of colors and shapes, some stalks, others round balls or clusters, white and blue and yellow and red, and for a moment she could understand his being smitten by them.

He walked to a door in the far right corner of the house. She followed him into what appeared to be a lab, with glass cages filled with mice, refrigerators with containers of substances, and beautifully framed pictures of more fungi. These looked more like gelatinous blobs in fluorescent blue, purple, and bright yellow.

He walked over to an aquarium and petted a black mouse that was reaching toward the top of the tank. "Astrid 4222 is doing well so far."

"Astrid 4222?"

"I name them all after my late wife." When Amy gave him a questioning look, he said, "She adored the mice. She made their food from scratch and apologized for what we were doing to them. I don't like to hurt any creature. If I could do this without them, I would. I've been working on the antidote for many years, using mice as subjects like Darkwell once used people. I feel sorry for the mice. I felt sorry for the people. He never did. I gave Astrid 4222 the latest version just before you arrived. I'll have to see how she fares through the night."

"Lucas and I, we sent off for a test to make sure we weren't related. When it came back, there was a note about our DNA having an extra marker. *This stuff changed our DNA.*"

The mouse trotted to its wheel and furiously ran.

Richard's gaze was on the mouse. "We have twelve strands of DNA, but ten of those are considered junk DNA or shadow DNA by scientists. The *stuff*, as you put it, activates some of those other DNA strands. But, unfortunately, it overactivates them for us who have psychic abilities. Thus, the exaggeration of our powers, and also the mental deterioration. You said your boyfriend is breaking down. What are his symptoms?"

"Storms of precognitive images so painful he passes out. We know what happened to Jack Stoker, how he killed people. Lucas is afraid he's on his way to doing that . . . to us."

Richard closed his eyes and took a deep breath. "Jack Stoker. That was when we couldn't deny what was happening. I felt the side effects, too. And when I saw the subjects dying, I went into hiding. I didn't want to end up like them."

"But how could you stop it? You would eventually end up like them anyway."

He looked at her, his gaze so hard it gave her a chill. "Some of those deaths were a result of the insanity. Those Jack Stoker killed, Camilla Aruda, who accidentally set herself on fire. But the rest . . . they weren't accidents. That was Darkwell covering his tracks. Those people were murdered."

CHAPTER 35

Later that afternoon, Nicholas and Olivia reached Arcadia, the small town between the Shenandoah Mountains and the Blue Ridge Mountains. She loved the rural countryside, which was flanked by mountains on either side.

Nicholas sat in studied silence as he looked for landmarks. "I remember that farm with all the painted horses."

He turned onto a dirt road and left a trail of dust behind them as they drove for about a mile. He pulled into a small alcove and turned off the car.

"So how does this work?" She nodded into the forest. "You just think about the item and go right to it?"

"Usually. It's not as precise this time because I'm trying to zone in on a memory of something that's no longer there." He started to walk away. "Give me a couple of minutes."

"Where are you going?"

"When I go into find mode, my eyes look . . . different. It freaked out the first girl I ever had a crush on. She thought I was possessed by the devil."

"How long ago was this?"

"I was twelve."

"Hm, so the last and only time you let someone see you was over ten years ago. And it still bothers you that much? That is serious."

He narrowed his eyes, obviously realizing she was mirroring the conversation they'd had about Liam and her feelings for him. "What shattered my young, tender self then would only bother me now, but the echo of that humiliation is still there."

She smiled at the thought of him as that young, tender boy. "You were trying to find something she'd lost?"

"A sweater. I loved being her hero when I found her missing ring." He stared off into the woods. "There's something compelling about finding something that's lost. I see now that it goes back to thinking I could find my father, because my mom always said we lost him. But it didn't end there. Finding something that's lost makes me feel complete. It's hard to explain."

She tilted her head. "And do you, Nicholas? Do you feel complete?"

He considered it for a moment, finally looking at her. "No."

Her heart opened for him. She could so clearly see him looking for his father, and still looking, always looking.

Probably sensing the gravity of her thoughts, he said, "Be right back."

She grabbed his arm. "Oh, no you don't. I want to see you. And it's only fair. You've watched me."

He hesitated, then bowed his head in defeat. "Touché."

He sat down and leaned back against a tree trunk. "It's weird, but I can't close my eyes. They have to be open to see." He was quiet for a moment. "I don't think I can do this with you watching."

She was crouching next to him. "Yes, you can. I'll back up a bit." She sat down a few feet away.

He released a sigh, and his body relaxed. His eyes went completely black, and she did have to admit it looked a bit like an evil movie she'd seen once. It was more intriguing than scary, though. She could see black swirls in his enlarged pupils. Tremors moved across his body. A minute later, his eyes shrank back to normal, and he took a quick breath.

"You don't look as odd as you think. Or scary."

"I just didn't want to freak you out."

"Oh, I'm long past that." She gave him a wry grin. "Did you find it?"

He got to his feet. "I found where it was. Let's go."

He had a look of intense concentration, and she held her comments so as not to distract him as they walked into the woods. He wore a backpack, and she carried a bag with some food and supplies. He'd warned her they'd be roughing it, at least in her terms. Sleeping outside with bugs and animals and the like wouldn't be as bad as the last few days, though.

"Wait up," she said breathlessly, as his pace picked up.

They'd been walking for twenty minutes now. The silence, apart from their footsteps, was nice. The late-afternoon sun slanted down between the trees in streams of light. Dust motes danced in those streams like fairies, and the sun felt good whenever she walked through one.

After another twenty minutes, he came to a sudden stop. He dropped his backpack and started turning in a circle. She remained several feet away. His eyes went dark, his expression tense.

A moment later they returned to normal. "It was here, the eye, the piece of aircraft." He took a deep breath. "Being at the site brings it all back." He walked several yards away and dropped to his knees, pushing at the layer of leaves on the ground.

She watched over his shoulder. "Did this search have anything to do with my father?"

"I don't know. I'd never heard of him at that time. I only dealt with Pope, but seeing him at the estate makes me wonder if they were working together all along. I'm baffled as to why they're acting as though they weren't. Pope didn't indicate we knew each other, not a hello or anything.

In fact, I could have sworn he gave me this look, almost hypnotizing, that clearly told me not to acknowledge him." He went back to digging. "I'm sure they did a search of the entire area, but I want to look anyway. Maybe we'll find something."

They spent the next two hours digging around in the leaves with a trowel and hand rake and searching in the crevices of trees. As the sun began to cast long shadows across the ground, she sat down and saw he'd given up, too.

"If this thing is so important, why can't you find where the piece is now?"

He dropped to the ground next to a tree. "I tried it. I got nothing, as if it didn't exist. But it wouldn't hurt to try again."

He went into that unknown place again. He had thick, nicely arched eyebrows, and his mouth had a bit of a pout. Maybe that was what made him such a great kisser.

His eyes returned to normal. "I found it." He scrambled over to the backpack and pulled out a map, unfolding and leaning over it. "I'm seeing a spot south of here, a white building in the woods. No signs."

It still amazed her that he could *see* anything. She stifled her scream as a black beetle ambled across her hand. "Being captured or bugs? Bugs are good. Nice bugs."

He smiled. "That's my girl." His smile faltered. "Not *my* girl . . ."

She cat-walked over to him on her hands and knees. "Why not, Nicholas? Why not your girl? You do like me, don't you?" She gave him a teasing smile, but she wasn't going to back down this time.

He didn't smile back. "If you get too close to me, I'll hurt you."

"Hurt me how?"

He released a breath. "I'm going to die."

Those words thudded like stones in her chest. The word "Why?" came out as a squeak. "Because of my father?"

"It's fate. I've had the same nightmare since I was a kid. I die in a fire, then I see my funeral, my mother and sister crying."

Of all the crazy things she'd seen, this was one she couldn't accept. "How do you know for sure?"

"My father had the same kind of nightmares about being shot. His came true. So will mine. You're in the dream, Livvie, one of the mourners at my funeral. You were sobbing, and God, I could hear your heartbreak. I don't want you to hurt like that."

Fire. Like Jerryl died. She shivered, but the heaviness settled into her bones. She remembered his reaction when he saw the candles on his birthday cake. "That's why you only got involved with women who didn't want anything permanent?"

He nodded. "I saw how your first boyfriend's death still hurt. I tried so damned hard not to get involved with you." He gave her a sad smile. "I'm still trying. When my father died, my mother was devastated. She never married again, never even dated. Every day she aches from the loss of her one true love. I don't want to do that to someone. I keep my distance, even with her and my sister.

"It was easy not to get involved with anyone, not on a deep level. Like you said, I'd never met anyone who made me want to. Then I met you. It should have been easy not to get involved with you. There were the rules, and you are— were a rule follower. Our paths are totally different. We're different."

"But you kissed me anyway."

He nodded, a soft smile on that lush mouth of his. "Kissed you and completely fell in love with you. I realized how much when I was trying to find you that night."

Fell in love? Her heart stopped beating. She felt the answering pull of her heart. But he wasn't smiling or making a declaration. "Don't look so grim. You saved me, after all."

"Go to your cousin's house. Stay away from here until it's over."

"Stay away from you?"

He nodded.

Anger bubbled to the surface. "Don't you dare to try protect me. I've spent my whole life being protected and controlled." She stood. "I'm not that manipulated Daddy's little girl anymore."

He looked up at her. "You need time to figure out who you are."

"You're right, and what better way than to dive right in." She stripped off her shirt.

That sent him to his feet, grabbing her shirt and trying to put it over her. "Livvie, you don't know what you're doing."

"Hm, let me see. I'm taking off my clothes." She slid her pants down her legs and stepped out of them. She unclasped her bra and flung it aside, then slid her panties down. "Does that about sum it up?" She jabbed her finger into his hard chest. "You woke up this tiger inside me, and now you're going to make her purr." She started unbuttoning his shirt.

"Livvie . . ."

She pushed his shirt back. "Do not tell me you won't touch me because you want to protect little ole me from making some big ole mistake because I'm not in my right mind. Maybe I'm not. But you're going to put me in my right body."

She reached down and unsnapped his jeans, feeling a surge of her feminine power and such heat radiating through her, she had to fight to keep from ripping off his clothes. She loved that he looked shell-shocked but that his body was right on track. She pushed both his pants and briefs down in one action, and he stepped out of them. She kissed her way up his legs, feeling his coarse hairs pressing against her lips, loving the feel of them and his hard muscles.

Face-to-face, she said, "Stop fighting what we both want. You've done the honorable thing—now give in." She kissed the soft, pale skin on his hip, traced her tongue around his belly button, and kissed her way up his smooth chest. When she reached his collarbone, she slid her fingers around his penis, and he groaned.

She kissed him, pushing him against a nearby tree, devouring him with her mouth as she continued to stroke his penis. He slid his hands behind her head and plunged into the kiss. She pulled him down to the ground but twisted so that he was lying down. Crouching over him, she felt like a tiger as she prowled over his body, taking her ever-loving time, teasing, loving on him with her lips, and finally taking him into her mouth.

All day she'd been bouncing between different emotions: anger, confusion, and lust. She'd spent enough time with the first two. Now it was time for lust.

Except you feel more than lust for this man.
Shhh.

She loved running her hands over his body, loved hearing his labored breathing, feeling his body tense in pleasure. But she didn't want him to go too far. She kissed back up to his throat. With a growl, he turned her over and nuzzled her neck, then nibbled her ear. All the while, his hands roamed her skin. She shivered in pleasure.

That was nothing compared to when he went lower, putting his mouth where his hands had just been, loving on her breasts, every inch. She plunged her fingers into his hair as her body arched. His hand slid down over her stomach and teased at the edge of pubic hair and the ridge that led to her inner thigh. He feathered his fingers across her soft skin there, inching closer to where she throbbed with wanting. Her breath came in soft pants as he trailed his tongue across her stomach, following the path of his hand.

His fingers slid between her legs, where she was already wet, and spread them so he could slide between her folds. His mouth followed. The delicious build of her orgasm thrummed through her when his tongue dipped and swirled. Just as she was about to fall over the edge, he kissed her inner thigh, only to make her gasp with a flick of his tongue on her swollen nub. Her body tightened so much it hurt.

He was teasing her, knowing she was about to go off and not letting her. She moved into his mouth, and he slyly evaded her. She was nearly pulling his hair now, her breath in staccato bursts, and finally he gave her what she wanted, needed, desperately needed.

Her orgasm shuddered through her body, and she knew what the phrase *rock her world* meant now. Then he dipped his tongue in again and sent her rocketing off once more. *Holy . . . holy . . .* She didn't even know she could go twice.

He worked his way up to her neck again. "Livvie, we can't go all the way. I don't have a condom."

He really was trying to protect her, in more ways than one. "I do." She twisted around and grabbed the box she'd bought at the store earlier that day. Seeing the display had revved her up, and on impulse, a very non-Olivia thing to do, she threw the box into the basket.

His eyes filled with both surprise and pleasure. She opened the foil package and slid the condom down his shaft. She batted her eyes, looking up through her lashes at him. "My, what a big, bad boy you are."

He grinned. "And what a bad girl you are."

She put her arms around his shoulders. "Mm, you bet. I kinda like this Olivia."

"Me, too."

While he was still sitting, she sat on his lap facing him. She eased onto him, and he fit perfectly, tight and snug. Her breasts brushed against his chest as they kissed, and even the slight movement sent shock waves through her. With his hand bracing her lower back, he tilted her back, and she felt him push even farther into her. She began to rock, slowly, then faster.

Little gasps escaped her, almost like high-pitched yelps. Just as she felt that growing sensation, she held off by slowing down. He kissed her breasts and dipped his tongue in the hollow between them. She was amazed he held on to his orgasm so long. She knew he'd been on the edge when she'd gone down on him.

His breathing, though, became more labored, deeper and shorter. Those waves of pleasure rocketing through her stole away her breath, too. The orgasm hit her like an explosion, sending her screaming in pleasure. His fingers dug into her back as she felt him throbbing inside her, heard him let out a long groan.

She pulled her head back, her face flushed, her mouth in a smile she couldn't even begin to tame. He had that same kind of smile on his face. Warm aftershocks pulsed through her, and she could feel his heartbeat.

"You were incredible," he said at the same time that she said, "You were awesome."

She laughed, hugging him close, loving the feeling of being in his arms. Loving feeling him still inside her, and amazingly enough, still hard. Loving . . . him? He'd fallen in love with her. He hadn't professed it in a, *I want to be with you forever* way, but that's because he believed he was going to die soon.

She held his face in her hands. "Don't try to protect me. It's already too late. I've fallen for you, too. If you leave my life now, it'll hurt as much as if I lost you in any other way. I'm already in up to my eyebrows. Let me make the choice. Whatever heartache might come, it'll be worth it."

He looked at her, his gaze intense. "I am so lost."

She put her palm against his cheek. "Little boy lost. All those missions, that need you feel. For a man who's good at finding things, you never realized you were missing a piece of yourself."

His voice was barely audible when he said, "You're that missing piece." His gaze darkened. "But—"

She pressed her finger against his mouth. "Let's just be, no buts." No way could she let him go now. She sure as hell wasn't going to let him die.

The sound of a twig snapping shot through the air. They both jumped to their feet, and he pushed her clothes at her, his gaze on where the sound had come. The sun was almost gone, leaving only wisps of light in the woods.

They both dressed wordlessly. He palmed his keys and took hold of her hand. He squeezed it and, leaning close to her ear, whispered, "Get ready to run."

CHAPTER 36

Lucas spent the evening jumping down everyone's throats. He finally put them out of their misery and went to his room. As agreed upon, Eric moved the desk in front of the door so Lucas couldn't come out during his sleep. He sank onto the bed and tried to calm himself enough to go to Amy's dreams.

He didn't bother to take any nice scenery with him, as he'd done before. He pulled her from a dream about a talking black mouse.

"I want you home *now*."

She turned around, her expression chagrined. "I didn't think about your coming to my dreams."

"Either you get home, or I'm coming to get you."

"No, let me do this. We're waiting to see how the test mouse did with the newest version of the antidote. Lucas, this may be your salvation."

"Have you found out what it is yet?"

"Not exactly, but it may be a myto . . . myxo . . . a slime mold. He's obsessed with them. He said one of them moved—*moved* onto his plate! That's how he accidentally ingested it."

She did sound excited, but he couldn't get past her deception. Especially since that deception could put her in danger. "I'm giving you one last chance to either come home or tell me where you are."

Her expression fell. "Lucas, I can't take the chance you'll come here and kill Wallace. Not on purpose, like Eric might. But through Sayre. I'll be back tomorrow." She put her arms around his shoulders and gave him a look that threatened to melt him. "I love you."

"I love you, too." But he was going to have a hard time forgiving her for sneaking off.

He pulled out before he said something he'd regret. Besides, he didn't want to tire himself. He had something else to do.

He pictured his twin brother, focused on him with every cell of his body. The process was faster this time, and he felt his soul fly into the other man's dreams. A dream of violence, Sayre pinning a woman to the floor with his body. He looked up. The woman disappeared, and he came to his feet with a feral smile.

"Hey, there, brother. Nice of you to drop in."

Lucas had nothing to say to him. He'd read about him on the Internet and knew what kind of monster he was. There would be no reasoning with him.

He wrapped his hands around Sayre's throat. They struggled, Sayre with his hands around Lucas's throat as well.

"Aw, brother, you don't have to give me a hug," he said in a strained voice. "I know you love me."

"Leave me and my people alone."

"But I love my little visits. And your girlfriend, she's cute."

Lucas brought up his knee and shoved it into his gut. Sayre doubled over, looked up with a snarl, and sent him hurtling right out of the dream.

Lucas woke with a start, his body soaked with sweat. *Hell.* Of course Sayre had seen Amy when he'd possessed Lucas. The crazy part was, she might be safer where she was—away from him.

* * *

Nicholas pulled the knife out of the backpack, gripping it so hard his knuckles hurt. He knew, somehow, that the sound was either Darkwell or his men. Probably both. Darkwell wouldn't hurt his daughter, but she could get caught in the cross fire. And if he forced her back to the estate, Sayre could get to her.

He did a location on the car. Straight out to the west. With Olivia's hand gripped in his, he led her in that direction. Two figures moved out of the shadows up ahead. He stopped, hoping they wouldn't see their movement.

"Over there!" a man shouted.

Damn. They probably had night goggles or heat-sensing ones. There was barely enough light to see by.

"Sir, they're heading west."

Sir. Darkwell.

He led Olivia in a different direction. The two figures separated and disappeared among the tree trunks. He wanted to call a time-out and get her out of there. Footsteps sounded in the distance. He could hear her fearful breathing, see the whites of her eyes as she searched around them. He gave her hand a squeeze of reassurance.

A gun pressed against his side. "Don't move."

He jammed the knife into the man's arm. The gunman screamed and dropped the gun.

Olivia gasped. Another man grabbed her from behind and pointed his gun in Nicholas's direction. "Drop the weapon."

Nicholas kept his grip on the knife.

"Look, buddy, our orders are just to bring you in. Unless you cause trouble. Then we take you out. Your choice."

No way was he going to be a guinea pig like Lucas.

The first guy tore his shirt and wrapped it around his gushing arm.

"You all right, Dan?" the second man asked.

Olivia took advantage of his momentary shift of attention, grabbed the hand holding her, and bit down hard. He jerked his hand away, and she grabbed his gun. He wouldn't let go, and they struggled.

Nicholas felt around on the ground until his fingers touched the cold metal of Dan's gun. He pointed it at the second guy as he wrested his gun from Olivia's grasp.

"Don't move. I will shoot." He meant it. Something inside him changed, grew harder, stronger. He really felt like a Rogue.

Olivia took the gun from the guy.

Nicholas jabbed his gun into the uninjured man's back. "Move, both of you."

His heart thudded as they walked toward the edge of the woods. "Be ready," he told Olivia. "Your father's probably going to be waiting there."

Her body stiffened, but she nodded. He saw something change in her, too, in the way her shoulders broadened and her chin jutted out.

The second man looked back at Olivia. She narrowed her eyes, holding her gun just inches from his shoulder. "I'm a CIA officer. I know how to shoot." She winked at Nicholas to indicate she was bluffing. It had worked. The men walked even faster.

They broke out of the forest, the two men first. Darkwell was behind his car, gun aimed at them. His headlights were on, illuminating the area and nearly blinding Nicholas.

"Try anything, and I'll shoot them," Nicholas said. He'd never shot a gun before, but he'd do it if he had to.

"Go ahead."

He went cold. The man meant it.

"Father!"

"Olivia, get over here. You're a Darkwell, not a fugitive or a traitor. I don't want you hurt."

She stepped in front of Nicholas. "You're right, I'm not cut out for this stuff. But I won't let you shoot him. Let us leave, and I'll come back and talk to you."

"Livvie . . ." God, that she would shield him from her father's bullet. That she would risk her safety.

"It's okay," she whispered.

"Olivia, you're acting like a foolish teenager. Get over here *now*."

"Tomorrow. You'll have to trust me, just as you asked me to trust you all these years. Promise you'll let us leave, and I promise to meet you tomorrow."

He hesitated.

One of the men began to slowly reach back, and Nicholas jammed the gun into his back. "That son of a bitch doesn't care if you die. Why should I?"

The man relaxed his arm, his mouth tightening.

Darkwell's mouth was pinched, his eyes hard and cold. "All right."

"I'm trusting you, Father. Don't shoot this man in front of me. I would never, ever forgive you for that." His stance faltered at that, and he laid the gun on the roof of his car. She stayed close to Nicholas as they walked to the Camry.

"Don't let me down, either, Olivia."

"I won't."

She took the guns from Nicholas once he was in the car. They tore down the road, both looking behind them. No headlights followed.

"You could have been hurt, putting yourself in front of me like that."

She wrapped her fingers around his arm. "I had no choice. I knew he'd kill you, and that scared me beyond words."

"You can't go back to him. Remember what I said."

"I have to. I gave my word. A Darkwell always lives up to her word."

He looked at her, seeing the seriousness of her expression.

"I'm not going to stay." She turned toward the back again. "I need to confront my father about my mother. I need the truth from him. If he did something to her, I'll have some leverage. I'm going to use it for you. I can find out the truth about BLUE EYES. He owes me that. And I'm going to reason with him about his mission to kill the Rogues. I'm the only hope in convincing him to leave them alone." She looked at him. "To leave you alone."

"He's got a history of manipulating you."

"That *is* history. I'm not that Olivia anymore. You can't stop me, Nicholas, so don't try."

His expression hardened, but he relented. He reached over. "If you can't convince him, stay away from the Rogues, from me. I don't want you in another situation like this one."

"There you go again, trying to protect me. I'm a big girl. I can take care of myself." She gave him a strong, beautiful smile. "But first we go to this place where the eye is. I want to see it, too." Her smile faltered. "Then I go to my father."

It hit him. "You're trying to save me from dying."

Her expression was even more serious. "I know that fire is going to happen because of my father. I'm going to do whatever I can to stop it."

CHAPTER 37

Amy woke the next morning in the guest suite, anxious to see how Astrid 4222 had fared through the night.

She followed the aroma of coffee to the kitchen, where she found Magnus looking at the courtyard, a dark expression on his face.

He turned when she stepped up beside him. "You'd like some coffee."

Though he hadn't actually asked more than stated, she said, "I'd love some. It smells wonderful."

"Comes from the rain forest." He pulled down a dark brown mug and poured her coffee from a French press. "And yes, it's fair trade."

She narrowed her eyes. "How did you know I was going to ask that?"

His mouth quirked in a smile. "I'm a mind reader."

"Seriously?" With anyone else, she would have thought he was kidding.

"Yes, but everyone else isn't like us."

Point made. "Okay, seriously. How does it work?"

"I just get words here and there. I can't read every thought. Most people's thoughts are noise, repetitive thoughts of worry, running conversations, to-do lists. From you I got: *Mmm, coffee. Fair trade?*"

She started to think it would be quite annoying to live with someone who could read minds but stopped. "That could come in handy with the women."

His mouth twisted in a sardonic smile. "It's not like I've had much of a chance to try it."

"Your father has been in hiding for probably your whole life."

He took a sip of coffee. "Yeah. We've lived here for the last ten years. Home-schooled by Mom, socialized by television. When Lachlan and I were young, we imitated canned laughter whenever someone told a joke or fumbled something.

"Our father arranged for us to get false identities showing that we got our education in Japan to explain why we weren't in the American school system. I had just gotten a job at a record store and hooked up with a band. I was actually beginning to live a normal life . . . until my father phoned yesterday. Now we're in hiding again."

He glanced away for a second, then looked at her again. "I saw you roaming around last night, mate."

"Me? I don't think so."

"You were heading back to the guest room. What were you doing?"

"Getting a drink of water." The words came out, but she didn't actually remember doing so.

He studied her, probably reading her thoughts to see if she was lying. "Hope you found it all right."

"I think so." She took another sip of coffee. "What do you know about BLUE EYES?"

"Dad told us about the program, what they accomplished."

She stepped in front of him and tried not to sound too desperate. "What's in the Booster?"

"He says it's best if we don't know. The antidote is the important thing."

She followed his gaze to the courtyard. Lachlan was sitting on the stone floor, wearing only shorts, his legs crossed. "Is he meditating?"

"He's punishing himself. Come on, I'll take you to the lab."

They walked through the courtyard, and Lachlan didn't seem to notice them. The goose bumps on his body made her wonder how long he'd been out there. The mornings started out cool.

When they reached the lab, Amy asked, "What's he punishing himself for?"

"Killing our mother." He opened the door, letting her hang on those horrible words.

It's not nice to drop a bomb like that and walk away, you know.

He gave her an unapologetic look and walked inside.

She followed him to where Richard was leaning over Astrid 4222's cage. She had decided not to tell Lucas about Richard's accusation of murder. That needed to be told to all of them in person.

She leaned close to the cage. "How is she doing?" The mouse was sniffing up at them, bobbing her head.

"Not bad. I've examined the video of her through the night. No seizures, normal sleep patterns." He looked at her. "Tell me, how many Offspring are with you?"

It was hard to trust anyone, especially someone involved in the program. "A few of us."

He nodded, as though he understood her reluctance. "You said Lucas was experiencing blackouts and painful storms of images. Does anyone else have odd symptoms?"

"Eric's always been on the edge. One of us can heal, but she's been warned if she heals too many mortal wounds, it could psychically break her down."

Richard nodded. "It isn't so much what she's doing but the frequency and intensity. That's true for all of you." He looked at Magnus, who was watching other Astrids in an adjacent cage. "My sons started showing their abilities when they reached puberty. They had each inherited some of my abilities. I'd told them about BLUE EYES years earlier; I had to explain why we were living the way we were . . . and what was going on inside them."

"That sure beats the birds-and-bees talk for complexity."

Magnus laughed but Richard didn't. "It would have been easier to explain string theory."

Magnus looked at the clock and left.

Richard picked up Astrid 4222, but not by the tail like she'd seen in the movies. He let her sit in the palm of his hand. "Both boys embraced their skills. Lachlan is the oldest one, by eleven months, two days. He's twenty and one year, two months, four days. Thirteen months, one week, three days ago he had mastered many of his skills. But he was also showing signs I had seen in myself: agitation, no impulse control, blackouts, and sleeplessness."

"Sleeplessness?" Eric hadn't been able to sleep since he'd burned Jerryl.

"It was maddening. I had been working on the antidote, giving it to myself in various doses over the years, but it proved to be unstable. It decreased my symptoms but also my abilities. I was afraid to use it on my sons. Because I knew the more we used our powers, the faster the insanity came, I warned the two not to use them, at least on purpose. The way you see glows and Magnus's ability to hear thoughts can't be controlled."

Amy shook her head.

"I can astral project, have since I was fourteen years, four months, and twelve days. The first time, it seemed so natural. I quickly discovered it wasn't natural at all, that, in fact, no one even believed me. I validated my sons when they began showing the signs. I prepared them. Magnus can move things, as I can, at his target location. Lachlan and I could astral project to not only other places but other time periods as well."

"You can go to the past?"

"It made teaching him history quite fascinating." He was still focused on Astrid, stroking her back. "We've gone to the Wild West, Victorian England, and even the Civil War period."

"That's incredible!"

A reminiscent smile crept onto his face. "It was. I have an affinity for time. I can tell you what day it was on any date you give me." Thus his way of breaking down measurements of time. He sank into his thoughts for a moment.

Amy leaned against the counter. "What's the difference between remote viewing and astral projecting?"

"When we project, we have an astral body. We can interact with people or objects at the target location. And we can be seen as an apparition."

"An Offspring who's working with Darkwell can astral project, too."

His head whipped up. "Who?"

"Fonda Raine."

He got very pale.

It didn't take her long to figure out the timing his mind was calculating. Offspring inherited their parents' abilities. The Booster had made the recipients amorous.

"She's your daughter, isn't she?"

"Possibly. Her mother said the child couldn't be mine, because the timing of ovulation didn't work for our single assignation. She was married, you see. But she couldn't astral project."

"Which makes Fonda an Ultra. That's what Darkwell calls the Offspring who come from two of the program's subjects. They're even stronger, and more susceptible to all of the side effects." Which explained why Nicholas heard her and Jerryl having crazy-monkey sex.

Richard put his hand over his mouth, his thoughts deep and dark.

She was thinking, too. "What could her mother do? Fonda may have inherited that skill as well. We need to know, because right now, she's our enemy. Your enemy, too. Darkwell no doubt has her trying to locate you."

"She could freeze time for a period. Really, it's a matter of changing the perception of time. Time freezes for the other person. So even if a target was being guarded, our assassin went in, shot him, then got out. When time resumed, the target was mysteriously dead."

"That's wild. And scary as hell. Did Darkwell suspect you'd gotten her pregnant?"

"No. We kept it quiet."

She was startled to see Magnus walking across the courtyard wearing a kilt and carrying a sword. He walked purposefully over to Lachlan, swung the sword up and then down in an arc to press against his throat.

"Oh, my God. Am I seeing that? Or did I just slip to another time period, too?"

"It's time for practice. Lachlan will stay out there all morning unless Magnus prods him. They've been practicing swordsmanship since Magnus was ten years, two months, and two days and Lachlan eleven years, four months, one week, and two days. I thought they should be prepared."

Lachlan didn't seem bothered or afraid. He stood, slowly and painfully, with resolve on his face and followed Magnus.

"Magnus said he was punishing himself."

"Yes, though in a way it was my fault."

Astrid 4222 squeaked as she ran up Richard's arm and hid under his lab-coat collar. "Lachlan wanted to go to the battlefield of Culloden because of our family history. My wife's history. I didn't think it was a good idea, given his symptoms, but he was twenty and three weeks. Who listens to his father when he thinks he's an adult? I didn't realize he was addicted to astral projection. He had been covertly doing it every day. It finally caught up to him.

"Lachlan took that trip to Scotland and became mentally trapped there. Magnus came running up the basement stairs yelling that Lachlan was going crazy, slashing his sword as though he were in battle. We all ran down . . . including my dear Astrid. Lachlan saw not us, but the enemy: English soldiers. And he came at us. He nearly lanced Magnus as he was trying to put his body between Lachlan's and ours. Lachlan turned and stabbed Astrid in the stomach. I would have risked anything, even our safety, to save her, but she didn't want that. She knew she was dying. So much blood. She died within five minutes."

Astrid darted down his arm and jumped into the cage. She leapt onto the wheel and began running furiously. Richard's eyebrows furrowed, but he continued with his story.

"By then Magnus had brought Lachlan back. He was devastated, still is. I can't hate him, though I know he hates himself."

He was studying Astrid 4222 with a concerned expression. "Lachlan insisted I give him the latest version of the antidote. He was in a desperate state, and I complied. He slept for twenty-four hours straight. Over the next week, he had no blank-outs, no episodes, slept normally. But he'd lost his ability. He still hasn't regained it.

"I gave the antidote to Magnus, too. I couldn't take the chance. He, however, did not lose his ability. I don't like the instability of the antidote, but seeing what Lachlan went through—what we all went through—I decided I must find the children of the subjects. If my sons were experiencing this, you might be, too. But will your people take it?"

She shook her head. "I don't know."

Astrid 4222 had worn herself out. She was panting

on the cedar chips. Amy looked at Richard. "You said Darkwell killed our parents. How do you know?"

"Because I projected into their final moments. I saw a man pull the trigger on your father. I saw Francesca Vanderwyck's car get nudged off the highway by another vehicle. I saw a sniper take out Jack Stoker, even though he'd been brought under control after the shooting spree. And I saw two men hanging Wayne Blackhawk Kee."

Amy's hand went to her mouth. Her heart tore as she imagined her father, a gun the last thing he ever saw. So he hadn't killed himself, hadn't failed to think about his daughter finding his body. She tucked that away to think about later. "Darkwell covered it up."

Richard continued. "If we went crazy, families would investigate, demand answers. It was easier to take us out. I knew I was next."

"What about Rand Brandenburg's father? He supposedly embezzled money and killed himself when he was caught."

"Another cover-up. I doubt he took a dime." He nodded to a fridge filled with jars of liquid. "I will prepare the antidote for your people. Each syringe will hold the exact amount I gave Lachlan and Magnus."

"I'll need eight of them." She was including Cheveyo, though she didn't know if they would see him again.

He walked out of the lab, leaving a soft light on for the mice. Amy heard metal clanging together. Behind one of the glass walls, Magnus and Lachlan engaged in a swordfight, both wearing Scottish regalia. Magnus had his curls tied back in a queue. Lachlan's hair was loose and wild.

She wandered over to watch them, caught up in the magnificence of their moves, the fierceness of their expressions. Magnus was everything she imagined a Highlander would look like, with his bare, broad shoulders and combination of strength and grace. Lachlan was no less handsome, but his moves were stiffer, angrier. His glow was jagged, even when he'd been meditating.

She could also see Richard in the glass's reflection as he knelt and took in the beauty of his slime molds. At the same moment, he sprang up and Magnus dropped his sword. Both men looked at each other, their expressions stark with fear. All three men walked toward each other.

Magnus opened the door. "You felt it, too."

"Yes. Trouble. Not Amy Shane trouble."

"Darker, dangerous," Magnus said. "We need to get her out of here."

"Not without the antidotes." If something happened to Richard . . . she couldn't chance losing the only way she knew to save Lucas. "I need at least two of them." One for Eric, too.

"I'll prepare them now. Then you must leave. I don't want anything connecting you to us, even a phone number. But I will give you ours so you can contact us later. Then I'll give you the rest of the antidotes." He sprinted to the lab.

Lachlan stepped up, his mouth in a bitter snarl. "She brought them here. They probably tracked her."

Amy wasn't about to be cowed by his bitterness. "If one of our people found you, one of Darkwell's can, too."

Magnus held his brother back, his hand on his upper chest. "Don't blame her. We knew it was inevitable. It's why Dad has prepared us all of these years." He looked at Amy. "We have a safe room. Even if Darkwell finds our house, he won't find us."

Richard burst out of the lab and handed her a box. "There are two syringes and my phone number. Check with me in a few days." He looked at his sons. "Magnus, walk her to her car. Lachlan, help me prepare the lab. I can't let Darkwell find my notes." He turned to her. "I never told him about my wife's pregnancies. They happened at the end of the program, when things were falling apart. The boys took my wife's maiden name, MacLeod, to add an extra layer of protection. Darkwell must not know about them." He waved for Lachlan to follow him to the lab.

Box clutched in her arms, Amy ran back into the house, Magnus shadowing her. She gathered her things and left. She still hadn't found out what the substance in the Booster was. And she might not ever if Richard didn't survive.

CHAPTER 38

Gerard was hunched over a map with three of his hired mercenaries when Pope walked in. The men stared at the six-foot-five man with shaved head and eyes an unusual shade of violet-blue.

"Excuse us for a minute," Gerard told the men, who got up and left.

When the door closed, Pope said, "Andrus is here."

"How did you know?"

"I know, just as I know that his being here will bring much trouble. But I have a proposition for you. You can change what will happen if you send him back to prison now and cease all contact with him."

"You know? You can see the future?"

Pope had always been evasive as to who he was and what he could do. He had never alluded to the fact that he had any psychic abilities, and yet, somehow the men who'd been injured had miraculously healed without any memory of the ordeal, or of working for him. Gerard could hardly push for answers when Pope was helping him.

"Yes, and yours is very bleak indeed. But it can be changed, as I said."

Gerard felt that twitch he got whenever Pope tried to take control of his program. His supposed prediction was meant to scare him into complying. Gerard wouldn't be cowed.

Pope continued, "I found another Offspring, one you will never find. I will give you his name if you comply."

A new Offspring: Gerard's mouth salivated at the prospect. He wasn't going to ask questions. He knew Pope wouldn't offer any more information until he *complied*. He was already planning to find Nicholas's sister, though Darkwell wasn't too hopeful in bringing her over, at least voluntarily.

"I'll consider it."

Pope's eyes narrowed, and Gerard saw an expression he'd never seen before: a childlike smile.

"I must go."

Pope stepped out without even a good-bye, which was fine with Gerard. Sayre Andrus had found Richard Wallace when he'd gotten into Amy's dreams and had her roam the house for clues. Andrus was going to be his salvation. And when nothing terrible happened, and Andrus either returned to prison or was killed in an accident, Pope would admit he'd been wrong. Maybe not in so many words, but in giving him that name.

Soon his daughter would be back. All he had to do was get her under his control, and she would return to her senses. If she didn't come on her own, Braden's death would shatter the spell she was under. Gerard would treat this like a hormonal rage and let her grovel for forgiveness.

He smiled. Soon all the Rogues would be dead, and he could finally move ahead on his plans to save the country.

"This is too easy," Olivia whispered, as they stepped into the clearing surrounding a white, windowless building in the woods. It wasn't large, but it was tall, and flecks shimmered in the paint. It bore no identification of any kind. There was no gate or imposing signs about trespassers being shot at the road's entrance. No security cameras were visible, no sign of an alarm system. "What if it's a trap?"

"We shoot our way out of it."

Nicholas had remote-viewed it from above and even looked inside the building. There was no sign of anyone, as though the place had been abandoned, but no weeds had sprung up through cracks in the asphalt.

He tightened his hand on the gun he'd taken from the men in the woods. He looked at Olivia, her beautiful face creased with worry. "You should go back to the car."

"No way. I'm part of this."

Now that she had taken control of her life, she was stubborn. He wasn't going to argue with her. "We go in, take a look, and get out. No more than five minutes."

He looked at his watch and nodded toward the door. It wasn't locked. The place had an eerie feel, as though someone was expecting them.

He snapped on the lights and suppressed a whistle, seeing clearly what he'd glimpsed psychically: shelf upon shelf lined the walls with no visible way to reach them. The shelves he could see were covered in pieces of what he could only guess were recovered experimental aircraft. Each had a tag identifying a location and a code. Some pieces were large, more than forty feet long. The piece he remembered seeing the eye on was about two feet in length. He set his mind to find it, no longer worried about Olivia seeing his eyes.

She picked up a piece of broken metal. "You're right. I've never seen steel like this. What is our government working on?"

"Stuff they don't want the enemy to know about. Or the public."

She set one shard down and picked up another. "That's why I always suppressed my curiosity about what my father was up to. I respect that there are things that can't be made public."

He climbed up one of the shelves to reach the third one up. "I found it." He reached over and pulled at it. "Damn, it's heavy. I can't imagine what this metal is being used for in an aircraft."

She climbed up the center of the shelves and came up right in front of it. "Is that the same eye Zoe tattooed on everyone?"

His heart thrummed. "Exactly the same, even the color blue. The slashes could be interpreted as an R, but they could be something else, too. So how does a tattoo artist know about the symbol used on a top secret experimental aircraft?"

A vibration rippled through his body, and he instinctively turned toward the door. The sight of the man standing there sent his heart racing. Pope.

"Did you find what you were looking for, Nicholas Braden?" he asked in a calm, deep voice.

Olivia gasped and slipped down the two shelves to the floor, landing on her feet.

Nicholas jumped down, not wanting her more than an inch away from him. He drew the gun but kept it pointing down. "We didn't take anything."

The man's expression didn't hint at anger, curiosity, or, oddly, anything. "I know."

Nicholas took Olivia's hand, wanting her out of there. "We're leaving." He gave the man a wide berth, ready for him to try to stop them. *Stupid, bringing her in here.*

Pope never moved, even when they passed within a few feet of him. The vibration, however, got stronger. They cleared the door and broke out into a run. He looked back once. Pope remained by the open doorway watching them.

They didn't slow down until they reached the car. He threw it into gear and tore out onto the highway. They were both panting with fear.

She was watching behind them, her eyes wide. "No one's coming out. Nicholas, that was weird. Beyond weird. He didn't try to stop us from leaving or even ask what we were doing."

"Did you feel him?"

"Feel him?"

"That was how I knew he was there. I felt this vibration go through me, like maybe what you'd feel if you touched a live wire but not painful. I felt it when I was around him before, but not so intense."

She shook her head. "I didn't feel anything like that."

He glanced in the rearview mirror, seeing no suspicious vehicles behind them. "How did he know we were there? For that matter, I didn't see a vehicle anywhere."

"It was like he appeared out of thin air." She shivered. "The man always gave me the creeps. Oh, there was one thing I didn't tell you when you asked about him at the estate. I walked into my father's office and saw Pope reading files on you and Jerryl. I couldn't believe he would allow anyone to read those files."

Nicholas took that in with a grim expression. "I'm confused. The question is, why did he let us go?"

"I don't know, but I'm glad he did. I wonder if he'll tell my father I was there."

Nicholas was going to go back without Olivia. He wanted more answers. "I hope you've changed your mind about going to your father. I called your cousin. She's very excited to see you."

"You shouldn't have."

"You can't stop me from trying to protect you, Livvie. It's what I am." He looked away for a moment, preparing himself. "I found your mother."

Her expression changed from irritated to stunned. "Is she . . . ?"

"Dead. I'm sorry. I know where her remains are. I searched after I saw her picture. They're not far from here."

She swallowed, sadness marring her face now. "I want to go."

"We can't touch them, or dig them up if they're not vis-

ible. I doubt there's much there, after all these years. The
police will have to be notified."

She put her hand to her mouth. "She was murdered,
wasn't she?"

"Probably. Unless she often went hiking out in the
woods alone."

"I doubt it."

They drove in silence, she deep in thought. He pulled off
a dirt road forty minutes later, then parked. He tuned in,
allowing his instincts to lead him. She followed, and for an
hour they trudged through the forest with only the bottles
of water they'd bought at a gas station.

He came to a stop and circled, trying to get a feel for the
exact location. "She's here." His soft words were swallowed
in the rustle of leaves and birdcalls of the forest.

She was turning in circles, too, as though she were
trying to sense her mother's presence.

He walked three yards away and dropped to his knees.
His hands waved over the ground. "Here. Down about four
feet."

She knelt beside him, placing her hands on the rich dirt
and loam. They were trembling. He gave her time to absorb,
to mourn the loss of the shred of hope of finding her alive.
He knew that hope, and he knew how it left a gaping hole
inside when it was torn away. When a tear dropped to the
soil, he pulled her into his arms.

"I wish she'd been alive."

"Me, too." Her voice was thick with emotion. "But
I had a feeling . . ." She wiped at her eyes and looked
at him. "Thank you. Ever since you asked me how far
I'd go to find the truth about my mother, I've felt that
hunger to know. How are you going to explain finding
her remains?"

"I'll make it a Bone Finder investigation." He turned to
her. "Your father will be implicated."

"I know." Her face was rigid now.

"If he could do this . . . do you really want to go back?"

"More than ever I need to convince him to let the Rogues go." She braced her hands on his face. "I'm your only hope. The Rogues' only hope. I know my father. If he has a goal, he'll achieve it. His goal right now is to kill all of you. I'm going to change it."

Olivia returned to the estate only after making sure Sayre was locked in his quarters. She wasn't going to stay the night there.

Nicholas dropped her off at the estate, but she waited thirty minutes before ringing the buzzer at the front gate to give him time to get far away. She went to her suite first and showered, dressed in clean clothes, and was finally ready to face her father. She knocked on his office door and opened it without waiting for his invitation. He was on the phone. "That sounds good. Keep me informed." He hung up and leaned back in his chair. "I hope this means you've come to your senses."

She walked up to his desk, bracing her hands on the edge. "Yes, I have definitely come to my senses."

"I have put my life into raising you. I took care of you, loved you, and taught you what you needed to know. You broke my heart when you ran off with Braden." He rubbed his chest. "I hope you can live with the fact that you shaved ten years off my life."

The old fear of losing her father reared itself. "Have you had chest pains?"

"I'm sure they're only heartbreak pains."

She ignored the jab. "Seriously, Father, are you having chest pains?"

He released a breath. "Just some tightness. It's hard to sleep or eat when your daughter's gone AWOL."

Was he playing her? Damn, she could see he was and yet, she still felt the panic. "I'm sorry I worried you."

"Worried me? You made me crazy, Olivia! You didn't just dally with the gardener's son. You ran off with the enemy, for God's sake. You betrayed me, your family, and your country. You made off-the-wall accusations about a man who is under guard. You got in the way of my eliminating a problem."

"You mean Nicholas."

"If he isn't stopped, he'll destroy me. You were with people who want your father dead."

She couldn't deny that.

"You are my daughter. I love you more than anything."

Those words softened her, but she had to ask, "More than DARK MATTER?"

He hesitated. "Those are two totally different things. The program is going to save our country. You would want me to choose between that and you?"

She sank into the chair in front of his desk. He really did believe that. Was it true?

He walked around the desk and leaned against the edge in front of her. "I need you. I need the woman who held this place together, who took care of me, the woman who used to be that little girl I devoted my life to."

He was using the past to manipulate her, and she saw so clearly that he'd been doing it since she could remember. How much did she owe him for being her father? "I'll come back and be your trusted assistant on three conditions: I know everything. Get rid of Sayre Andrus, call him off. I won't work with him in the house. And—"

"You're being irrational. Besides, he's only going to be here for another month or so." Until the Rogues were dead. "I'm prepared to forget everything you've done. Going AWOL from the CIA, consorting with the enemy, all of it. No one need know, not even our family. On *one* condition: Tell me everything you learned about them."

The unspoken threat was clear. If she didn't cooperate, he would tell the family. Her betrayal would be unforgivable. She could not let him keep the upper hand.

"So, I can earn your forgiveness by telling you where they are so you can kill them." Which opposed her third condition. *Like hell.*

He continued. "If you help me do that, Andrus goes, and I tell you everything."

They were at an impasse. She needed to get what she could before he forced her to refuse. "I saw the warehouse. The eye."

"The what?" So Pope hadn't mentioned it. "What's the eye?"

She backpedaled. "Tell me what DARK MATTER is and let me decide who's right and who's wrong."

He studied her. "I can't trust you." His anguished words cut right into her. "You will have to earn it. By telling me everything."

Her words were just as tightly strung as his. "I can't trust you, either."

He let out a disappointed sigh. "You're going to make this hard, aren't you? What if I promise not to kill Nicholas?"

"No, all of them. You destroyed their families. You were responsible for the deaths of their parents. They only want the truth. And so do I."

"I can see you haven't returned to your senses at all. Time will take care of that. I've sheltered you for too long in my misguided attempt to protect and love you. So when the first man who fires your interest comes along, you're willing to throw away everything—your family, your career—to be with him."

Olivia stood. "This isn't about lust. Or even love. This is about the truth. Where is my car? Last I saw it, Sayre had me drive it to the park, then he took it somewhere when Nicholas showed up to save me."

"Lucas, you mean. Your car was found in a parking lot near here."

"Of course. So Sayre could get back before you checked on him."

He shook his head. "You give him way too much credit."

She stood. "And you don't give me enough. You can't manipulate me anymore."

The phone rang. He held up a finger and answered it. "Yes? . . . Excellent. Was he alone? . . . Too bad. Bring him in and down to the basement. Good work." He hung up, a smile on his face.

Her heart was about to implode. "Who?"

"Not your precious Braden. Yet."

"I'm leaving." She opened the door and came face to chest with one of the guards. "Excuse me."

He didn't budge. She turned around. "Make him move."

"Take her to her quarters."

"What?"

The man took hold of her arm in a boa-constrictor grip. "Yes, sir."

She spun around. "You are not—"

"Olivia, you need to spend some time thinking about what you've done. Soon the Rogues will be no more. You'll have to let go of your infatuation and come back to reality. For now you're on administrative leave because of mental illness. I'll have a doctor attest to your unstable behavior. Your suite has been, shall I say, safeguarded. You cannot leave, you cannot make any calls." He looked at the guard. "Check her for weapons or phones. With respect, please."

She tried to hip-check the man, but he wouldn't let up. She glared at her father. "You bastard!" She feared, most of all, that he would win—and the Rogues would die. She had to think.

The man patted her down, finding her cell phone. He tossed it to her father. "Nothing else." He walked her down the hall, past the curving staircase, and to the east wing. Her prison.

She continued to struggle, knowing it was futile. She

spotted his cell phone clipped to his waistband. Just as they reached her door, she put up a bigger fight, kicking, screaming, and, in the melee, grabbing his cell phone.

"Don't make me hurt you," he said as he shoved her into her room.

The door closed with a resounding thud. What was Nicholas's number? It was programmed into her phone. *Come on, remember! That thug is going to realize his phone is gone before long.*

The number came in pieces. She punched the buttons, fumbling and missing the third one. She had to clear and start over. Her fingers were trembling.

She dialed the number. It rang.

The key slid into the lock.

She ran into the bathroom. Ring three. "Answer, dammit!"

The door opened just as she slammed the bathroom door closed and locked it.

"Livvie?"

"Yes, it's me."

"I went back to the building to explore it more, but it's gone. I'm at the exact spot where the gate was, but there's no gate, no road. No nothing."

"I don't have time to talk. My dad captured someone. I don't know who it is, but he's going to be put in the basement. You were right. He's locking me in my suite."

"He's keeping you prisoner?"

"Yes."

"He's mad, Livvie."

The man started pounding at the door.

"What's that?"

"I borrowed the guard's phone, and he wants it back. I'm all right, but I wanted you to know because I won't be able to talk to you until I figure a way out of here. And he has the phone you gave me."

"I'm getting you out of there."

"No! That's what he wants. At least Sayre can't get me to go anywhere. I'm locked in."

She heard his frustrated expletive just as the door cracked open.

CHAPTER 39

As soon as Nicholas walked into the tomb, he scanned the group sitting around the living area. They looked tense but not upset like they would if someone was missing.

"Is everything all right?" he asked.

Lucas and Amy were faced off, clearly not in a loving moment.

Petra said, "Amy just got back from Wallace's."

Lucas's hard gaze was on Amy, ignoring everyone else. "What you did was stupid. He could have killed you."

"But he didn't." She crossed her arms over her chest. "Now you know how I felt when you were hurting and didn't tell me."

His face was a taut mask of anger. "I didn't run off and put myself in danger against your wishes."

"I did it for you. And your making Eric promise to kill you *is* putting yourself in danger against my wishes." She pointed to a box. "This is better than you dying, either from the storm of images or Eric."

Nicholas jerked his gaze to Eric, who waved away the insane comment.

"And you trust this?" Lucas pulled out a syringe and pointed it at her. "The last time someone injected something into me, it screwed me up. You don't know what's in this. We don't know what Wallace is up to. Throw them away, because I'm not taking it. Who's the second one for? Not you, I hope."

"He was going to make enough for everyone, but they sensed danger coming."

Lucas shook his head. "More than ever I need my ability. I tried to kill Sayre in his dreams. He kicked me out, but I'm going to try again."

"The antidote might not take away your abilities. Magnus still has his."

She touched his arm, but he shrugged her off. "I'll never forget how I felt when I found out you were gone. It was like I didn't even know you."

She swiped at her tears. "I'm going to do whatever I can to save you, Lucas. You should know that much about me by now."

Nicholas's heart broke for her. Hadn't he seen that kind of devotion on Olivia's face? These women who would risk their lives for their men. The men who would risk their lives for their women.

Lucas leaned into her face. "You can't save me. I warned you that the Booster had messed me up, and we shouldn't get emotionally involved. You said you could handle it. Running off to some wacko scientist is not handling it. Eric's right; we shouldn't let our emotions get the best of us. Having him take me out is the safest thing for everyone. If I hurt you, I would never forgive myself. And right now, I don't know if I can forgive *you*."

It looked as though his words had lanced her with a knife.

Nicholas couldn't listen anymore. "No one is taking anyone out."

Lucas and Amy looked at him as though they'd just now realized he was there, that anyone else was there.

Lucas's voice was low when he said to Amy, "We'll discuss this later."

Nicholas addressed all of them. "Livvie went back to her father's estate."

Eric shot up from the couch. "I knew she was a traitor! We've got to get out of here. How long ago?"

"She went back to plead our case, but her father's keeping her prisoner there." He'd never forget the cracking sound, her gasp, then the phone going dead. Fear pulsed through him like a drumbeat. "She was able to call me. She said he'd captured someone."

Amy's hand went to her mouth. "Richard Wallace. Did she say one man or three? He has two sons."

"She said *he's* going to be put in the basement."

Eric said, "It's a setup. She knows you'll come rescue her."

"She told me not to come." But how could he leave her there, vulnerable to the madness that was her father. He wasn't sure Darkwell would stop at killing her now that she was a traitor, too. Those bones in the ground were probably proof of his anger.

Amy said, "Regardless of whether she's on her father's side or not, Darkwell could be expecting us. He might think Nicholas will rescue her and, since he knows I was with Wallace, that we could go in to rescue him. I'm calling the number he gave me."

She went into the computer room and dialed a number. Everyone followed, crowding into the small room.

A man answered, and she said, "It's Amy. Who's this?"

"Magnus."

"Did Darkwell—"

"His men came in and grabbed my dad. We were in the safe room. He knew Darkwell would have his men focus on the lab. Dad was worried about the Astrids. He ran over to put all the mice in a cage and bring them down. That was when it happened." His voice broke when he said, "We watched it, but we couldn't get out to help him. He'd locked us in."

A man was screaming in the background, but his words were unintelligible. Amy clicked on the MUTE button. "That's Wallace's other son, Lachlan."

"What's he saying?" Petra asked.

"Probably blaming me for bringing Darkwell there, and he may be right. I was thinking about it on the drive back. Sayre might have come into my dreams and had me look for something that told them where his place was."

Lucas's face reddened with rage, but he said nothing.

She clicked the button again. "Are you still locked in?"

"No, the timer allowed us to unlock it. The lab's a mess, but the rest of the house is all right. It's Dad we're worried about."

"We know where he's being held." She looked at Nicholas. "But it's dangerous to go in."

Nicholas walked closer. "When I go in for Olivia, I'll find the basement. Maybe I can get him out of there, too."

To the computer microphone, Amy said, "Magnus, did you hear that?"

"Yeah, but what if he doesn't succeed? We may not have a lot of time. Darkwell only has one reason for taking Dad: to kill him. Dad has no skills for Darkwell to use, and he sure isn't going to cooperate. We need to know where the place is and get him out."

Amy said, "We should coordinate our efforts."

Eric pinched her shoulder. "Don't start volunteering us. I'm not willing to risk my ass for the enemy's daughter. Why should I do it for the guy who invented the Booster?"

"Give us a minute, Magnus." She muted the microphone and faced Eric. "Because he's the only one who knows what's in it and how to make the antidote. If he dies, we'll never find out. And with Wallace's sons, we've got a bigger force to go in with. You can find Darkwell."

Eric turned to the others. "Who here is going to take this antidote? I'm sure as hell not."

Lucas shook his head, and slowly the others did, too.

Amy turned to Eric. "Sleeplessness is one of the symptoms of the Booster psychosis. Wallace said his son was having the same problem. And then he killed his mother."

"There's just a lot going on. I'm not having any thoughts of killing people, other than the bad guys."

Lucas said, "Forget the antidote, Amy. Even Wallace admits it's unstable. For all we know, it could make us worse."

Eric leaned down in Amy's face. "I want Darkwell, but you're not going to use that to get me to do something stupid, and going in with that son of a bitch waiting for us is just plain stupid."

Amy tilted her head. "*Now* you get sensible."

"And you're the one so narrow-minded with your idea to save Lucas that you're going over the edge. You're not seeing the whole picture. He's not going to take that stuff. And maybe we don't ever find out what's in the Booster, but knowing may not help anyway."

Nicholas stepped between Eric and Amy. "I'll get Olivia out tonight. We can decide what to do next."

Lucas put his hand on Nicholas's shoulder. "What makes you think you can slip in there unnoticed when he's expecting you?"

"Sayre did. I'll find the guards' positions and circumvent them. I know where she'll be. I'll climb up her balcony."

"Go in armed, Romeo. Those guys will take you down in a heartbeat."

Nicholas nodded. "I have two guns. I took them from Darkwell's men when they found us."

Amy turned back to the computer. "Magnus, give us tonight to see what Nicholas can find out."

Once she'd hung up, they filtered out to the living area.

Eric faced the group. "Maybe lover-boy here believes in Darkwell's daughter, but I don't. We don't hear from him, we get out of here and watch the tomb, see if

Olivia's told her father where we are. If Nicholas manages to bring her back, we've got leverage. He touches us, and his daughter gets it." He looked at Nicholas. "It's a bluff."

Lucas pushed a lock of Amy's gelled hair from her cheek. "I'm going to work with Nicholas in the shooting range. We'll get some sleep tonight and be ready for whatever happens tomorrow."

Zoe stepped closer to Nicholas. "Did you find the eye?"

He told them about the disappearing building, the piece of odd metal, and Pope.

Petra smacked her forehead. "Oh, no, another enemy!"

"I don't know. He didn't try to stop us. The question is, who is he?"

Zoe turned her right wrist and stared at the eye. "And how the hell did I know about this?"

Gerard looked up at the knock on his door. "Come in."

The guard who'd escorted Olivia to her suite stepped in. "She put up a fight, but she's secured now. She grabbed my cell phone. I didn't realize it until a minute later. She made a call before I could get it back."

He handed the phone to Gerard, who looked at the Annapolis area code on the screen. He knew exactly whom she'd called.

"I'm sorry, sir. If—"

"It's all right. What it means is that we'll have to be ready for a visitor tonight."

He knew Nicholas would rush in to rescue Olivia though he wasn't sure the Rogues would help. He would at least take care of Nicholas, who had done more damage than any of the other Rogues combined. He had turned Gerard's daughter against him.

Another knock sounded at the door, and a guard brought in Andrus. Gerard wanted to meet with him before going down to speak with his new guest. Now that he had Olivia back, he could move ahead on his plans to destroy the Rogues once and for all.

The guard led Andrus, in handcuffs and leg chains, into his office and left them alone.

Gerard sat back in his chair. "We can now proceed with the plan."

Andrus's eyes glittered with anticipation. "What about the woman who was with the Rogues?"

"She's back here, so you take out anyone you—or Lucas—sees."

His smile never faltered. "Yessirree. I'll have Lucas take out Amy as soon as I come in. Then he'll pound on the door, all scared 'cause something's wrong with her. They're on to me. They locked him in the room last night. I'll just play him along, she ain't breathing, everyone'll be in a panic, and while they figure out what's wrong with her, he'll get a gun and take 'em all out."

"Maybe you should go in now while he's not locked in his room."

"I tried to poke in the other day, and he kicked me out. He needs to be asleep and vulnerable. You know, that son of a bitch tried to come into my dream last night, just like you warned me he might. I kicked him out, too."

"It won't be a problem after tonight." Finally, things were coming together. He could focus on the future. He would target terrorists in Iraq, Israel . . . the world was his to clean up.

Andrus rubbed his hands together, clanging the cuffs. "As soon as they go to sleep, all your problems will be over. But you did promise me some girls to kill. If I have Lucas take them out, well, that ain't no fun."

"Save one, then. You'll have to do it through Lucas, but you've got all the time in the world. No one is ever going to find them."

That made Andrus smile again.

"If Nicholas is there, make him suffer. And Eric Aruda, too."

"Gladly."

Gerard stood. "Let me know when it's done."

He went down to the basement to talk to Richard Wallace. He wanted to know only two things: If he had any of the Booster; and if he had any Offspring of his own.

CHAPTER 40

Olivia had been demanding to see her father for hours. Finally, after her dinner had been delivered and the sun had set, he agreed. The guard escorted her, his hand gripped around her arm again.

"Do you have to manhandle me?"

"It's either that or cuffs. Darkwell said he didn't want you to be cuffed unless it became necessary."

"Wasn't that sweet of him."

He knocked on the door, and Gerard called for him to enter.

She flung the guard's arm away but looked at her father. "You're having me guarded like a prisoner!"

He swiveled in his chair. "Because you're acting like an outlaw. Since you made a phone call, presumably to Braden, we have to be ready when he comes barging in to rescue the fair maiden." He smiled. "Like the fairy tales I used to read you. The harsh father out to save his lovely daughter by locking her in a tower."

"Nicholas is not the bad guy."

"And I suppose I am." When she didn't answer, his expression hardened. "I will not discuss Braden or the Rogues with you."

She walked to the front edge of his desk. "Then talk to me about my mother."

He took a deep breath, as though he were losing his patience with his recalcitrant little girl. "And they also told you what a bad guy I am."

"Did you kill her?"

He stood and walked around the desk. "I suppose I shall have to tell you the sordid truth now that you've got something even worse in your head. Your mother was a lying, manipulative woman. I'm sorry to say that, but you want the truth, and the truth you shall have. She lied about who she was and where she came from. When I warn you about falling in love and letting your emotions rule your mind, I speak from experience. I admit she swept me away, and I ignored the signs. When I discovered the truth, she announced she was pregnant. The news softened me. I thought maybe, when I saw her being a good mother, I could forgive her.

"But she wasn't a good mother. She complained, even though I provided her with a nanny. She resented that she couldn't party or socialize. Then one day I walked in and caught her screaming and shaking you. When I saw her harming my beautiful baby girl, I went crazy. I tried to take you out of her arms, but she fought me. I wrapped my hands around her throat and squeezed, my only thought to save you. She collapsed to the floor, and I grabbed you before you fell. When I checked her pulse, she was dead."

She thought her chest would be crushed under the pressure of her shock. "You strangled her."

He nodded, not a shred of remorse on his face. "I am willing to do what is necessary to protect my own, and that includes you, my program, and our country."

She didn't know if she could believe his story, but she did know he was telling the truth on that last statement. He would kill without a second thought. Maybe even kill her. She saw that now, saw everything she'd been blind to all these years.

"Where did you leave her body?"

"Where no one will find her."

She wasn't about to tell him someone had found her. "You're no better than Sayre."

"I'm nothing like that man."

Shouting floated from outside. A gunshot pierced the air. With a fearful gasp, she ran to the French doors, but her father grabbed her by the shoulders. "Don't go near the windows!"

The guard stepped into the room and closed the door. "They've spotted an intruder."

Please don't let Nicholas have come!

The guard listened to the earpiece. All she could hear was the buzzing sound of someone's voice.

"They've got him."

Him.

"Who?" she couldn't help but ask.

Her father ignored her question. "Watch her." He walked out.

She raced to the door.

The guard lifted his jacket to reveal handcuffs and his taunting expression: *Make me use them, honey.*

It had to be Nicholas. No one else would come to rescue her.

"Don't you dare hurt him!" she screamed after her father.

Agonizing minutes dragged by after everything went quiet outside. The guard shadowed her as she walked as close to the French doors as he allowed and tried to look out. She heard voices, saw the landscaping lights on. She tried to make a run for it, but the guard grabbed her arm and yanked her back.

"I want to see what's going on!"

Everything inside her was tight and brittle. She heard sounds in the hallway and rushed to the door, but again, the guard stepped in front of her.

She strained to listen but couldn't hear anything definitive.

A few minutes later her father returned, a triumphant smile on his face. "As it turned out, your involvement with Braden worked in my favor. He came for you. Now he's dead."

He dropped those last words like bombs, and each one exploded in her chest. She slid to the floor, sobs tearing from her chest.

"How?" The word tore from her.

"Shot by one of the outside guards."

Through her tears she saw the guard leave, and her father sat in the chair next to her. "Cry it out, sweetheart. When it's over, you'll see that it had to be. Your vision will clear, and you'll understand. And I'll be here, just as I've always been."

Nicholas tried to pull out of the grip of the three men dragging him down the hall where he'd once worked and lived. Darkwell stepped out of his office. Behind him, he heard Olivia's voice: "I want to see what's going on!"

He tried to call out to her, but all he could get out from behind the gag they'd tied on him was a muffled cry. His hands were cuffed.

Darkwell smiled. "Nice of you to come back." To the guards he said, "Bring him this way."

A guard stationed at the end of the hallway unlocked the door, and Darkwell preceded the guards. "I have a gift for you," he said to someone upstairs. "Take care of him any way you'd like."

Nicholas was pushed up the stairs, and when he reached the top, he came face-to-face with Lucas's twin: the son of a bitch who'd tried to rape and kill Olivia.

"Keep the gag on him," Darkwell said as he turned to go back down the stairs. "We don't want anyone to hear screaming."

Darkwell was giving him to Sayre as a *gift*? Sayre's eyes flared in recognition, and his mouth broke out into a broad smile. His face twitched. When the door downstairs closed, he said, "You really pissed me off, you know that?"

Nicholas rammed him, sending Sayre to the floor. He spit out an expletive as his head hit the wood floor and Nicholas landed on top of him. He had one chance, the advantage of surprise, to put the son of a bitch out. For Olivia.

He rolled off and kicked Sayre in the gut. Sayre sprang to his feet, out of Nicholas's range, and jumped over him. Before Nicholas could spin around, Sayre had kicked him in the back. Pain flashed through his body. Nicholas rammed his foot into Sayre's knee, sending him stumbling back with a grunt. It didn't keep him from striking again with his other leg, nailing Nicholas in the kidneys. Black spots floated in front of his eyes. Nicholas punched, cracking Sayre's nose. Blood spurted everywhere. Nicholas aimed again, but the punch wasn't as powerful. The pain sapped his strength. Sayre dodged it and caught the blow to his cheek.

Sayre spun around and slammed another kick into Nicholas's stomach. Nicholas tried to strike out, but the blows kept coming. The spots pooled together, becoming one large dark mass, obliterating his vision.

"I'm gonna take care of your friends tonight," Sayre said. He aimed at Nicholas's solar plexus.

Nicholas couldn't hold on. He dropped to the floor.

Sayre kept beating him. "Soon as they go to sleep, Lucas is gonna take 'em out." He knelt, and whispered, "Then I'm gonna take care of your girlfriend. I'm gonna torment her dreams until she can't stand it no more, then I'm gonna find her and rape her until she begs me to kill her."

Nicholas tried to move, spurred on by rage, but even a slight motion sent spasms of pain through him. No one would save her. Not the Rogues, if they survived. Not her father, who wouldn't believe her. Not him, unless he could get out of here alive. Even his desperation couldn't overcome the pain immobilizing him.

"I'm not done with you yet," Sayre said in a gravelly, low voice next to his ear. Blood dripped down his face and neck. "Before long, you'll be begging me to kill you, too."

"Hell." Eric, lying on the floor, remote-viewed Nicholas. "Sayre's beating the bejeezus out of him. He isn't going to take that much longer."

"Sayre?" Lucas asked. "How the hell did that happen?"

"I can't watch." As mad as he was at Nicholas, his stomach clenched at the sight of him getting pummeled. "I'm getting the block in Darkwell's office, but I can see the hallway and hear a woman sobbing. Has to be Olivia. She's giving him hell for killing Nicholas." He came out of the vision. "She thinks he's already dead."

Lucas rubbed his temples, still recovering from the storm that had revealed Nicholas's capture. "Dammit, we shouldn't have let him go alone."

Eric continued to troll the estate. "I see three guards outside." He pulled himself off the couch, shaking his head. "I can't do any more remote viewing and risk losing my strength, not if we're going in tonight." And they would go in. No way could he leave Nicholas to die like that, not if he could help it.

He joined the others gathered around the table and studied the surroundings of the estate they'd printed from the Internet maps. With a red marker, he designated positions. "I saw outside guards here. We come in over the wall here, between these two guys, and take them by surprise. We have to take them out, understand? If we have any hope of doing this, we've got to eliminate as many as we can. And quietly."

Amy jumped to her feet. "I'll contact Magnus."

Lucas said, "One of the guns Nicholas took from Darkwell's men has a silencer. And we've got Steele's gun and the one Rand nabbed from the guy at Nicholas's house."

Eric clenched his fist. "I'll take a knife."

Zoe said, "Remember, these are just hired men who don't know what's really going on. Only kill when necessary."

Eric rolled his eyes. "Yes, Mother. You and Rand can handle your guard as you see fit. Just make sure he's incapacitated."

Amy returned to the living room. "We meet them in Bowie as fast as we can get there."

"Do Wallace's sons have guns?" Eric asked.

"I don't know, but they have swords." She gave them a crooked smile. "And they're damned good with them."

CHAPTER 41

Olivia's voice was hoarse, her face wet with tears. She had avoided looking at the man responsible for Nicholas's death. Now her anguish turned to anger.

"You're as bad as the terrorists."

It amazed her, his calm expression. "You will change your mind once you come to your senses."

"You think I'm going to *come to my senses*? Forget that you killed the man I love?" She stood in front of that damned massive desk, her fingers pressed against the top, her voice pitched in anger. "You think that's going to just go away? Is that what happened with my mother? You killed her, dumped her body, then went on with your life as if nothing had happened? Only a sociopath could do that."

He seemed unmoved by her tirade and accusations. No, not unmoved completely. His eyes darkened, hard as onyx. "I want you to see that you have twice gone against my wishes to fall for a man who was wrong. Twice you have caused his death. Have you learned yet? Nicholas was already a target because of his betrayal, but his feelings for you brought him here. I wouldn't have had to send your boyfriend and his father out into the storm that night if it weren't for your disobedience."

Her mouth dropped open. "You sent them? You said they left . . . don't you dare lay this on me! Coward! Take responsibility for what you've done. *You* are the murderer! The cold-blooded murderer. You destroyed our family, and so many other families. But you won't destroy me."

She stalked to the door and opened it. The guard stood there, blocking the way. She body-checked him. He knocked her to the floor.

Her father was standing now, his face a cold mask. "Don't be afraid to hurt her if necessary. She's tougher than she looks."

She got to her feet, facing him. Did he know her secret? "What are you going to do, keep me here forever? Lock me in a tower like Rapunzel? Because I'm never going to change my mind about Nicholas, or about you."

"I'm afraid you can't leave here." Only then did she see a flicker of emotion on his face. Regret. She had seen the same thing when he'd talked about her mother . . . about having to kill her.

The Rogues met Lachlan and Magnus in an empty parking lot. The brothers stepped out, wearing their Scottish regalia, though thankfully they'd left the swords in their truck. Both men had their hair bound in leather-covered ponytails. Amy had to admit, they looked freaking hot, like something right off the cover of one of those historical romances.

"What the hell?" Eric said, taking them in with disbelief.

Amy gave him a quelling look. "Guess I forgot to mention the attire."

Lachlan was the first to march over, pointing at her. "You brought this."

Lucas stepped between them. "Get your finger out of her face."

Amy held up her hands as the rest of the Rogues took

defensive positions around her. "Hold it. Right now we're on the same team. We have one goal: We get in, cover each other's backs, and carry out our tasks." She met both of the MacLeod gazes. "We have to work together."

Lachlan didn't exactly agree, but he stopped accusing her, at least. They went over the estate's layout, making their plan.

Lucas marked four points between the guards on the estate's layout. "We go in two by two."

Magnus said, "I'll go in first, assess the guards' movement. They won't see me." That got all of their attention. "I can make myself invisible."

"Not really invisible," Lachlan added, his jealousy clear.

"I just change the way people see me. The energy around me changes."

Amy said, "That's how you snuck up on me."

Magnus nodded and pointed to a far corner of the property. "I'll go in and recon here."

They synced their phones so each person had another's number on speed dial. Eric pointed to the sketch of the mansion. "Darkwell's office is here. I'm going there first to take him out. Lucas, find Nicholas, take care of Sayre. When I'm done, I'll meet you."

Petra said, "I'll go with you, Lucas. It doesn't sound like Nicholas is going to walk out on his own."

Amy put her arm around her. "But you've got to be careful."

"I know. But what's the use of having this ability if I can't use it? I like Nicholas."

Lucas looked at all of them. "If I drop, don't risk your lives trying to get me out."

Eric gave him a sardonic smile. "Yeah, right, bro."

Magnus said, "Let's move, mates. We're running out of time."

They drove separately, Zoe and Rand on the bike, the rest of the Rogues in the 'Cuda with the MacLeod brothers following. As they neared Potomac, evil-looking clouds raced right to where they were going.

"What the hell?" Eric said from the driver's seat. "I checked the radar. There wasn't so much as a cloud."

Lightning shattered the sky up ahead.

"Actually, it might help." Lucas leaned forward for a better look from the passenger seat. "Rain could cover us, both visually and sound-wise." He looked at Eric. "What, you afraid you're going to melt?"

"Yeah, 'cause I'm made of sugar." He rolled his eyes. "I hate having to do this in the rain."

"Probably not as much as Rand and Zoe will," Lucas said, glancing to the right, where they rode on their bike.

Petra giggled from next to Amy. "No, I'm not laughing at them getting wet. I just got a message from Cheveyo. He sent the storm to do what Lucas said, help cover us."

"He can manipulate the weather?" they all asked in some variation at the same time.

She shrugged. "I guess so. You said it, Eric. There wasn't a cloud on the radar."

When they reached the estate twenty minutes later, rain drove down in diagonal sheets. They parked their vehicles in different places.

Eric held out his hand for them to wait before getting out. "I want to check on Nicholas, see if he's still alive." He sat back in the seat and closed his eyes. A minute later he turned around. "He is, but only because Sayre is having fun taunting him. But he sure doesn't look good."

They met up to orient themselves. They had to talk over the rain and thunder. Magnus went over the wall, or at least she thought he did. As soon as he approached it, he disappeared.

They waited for his word. Several minutes later, Lachlan lifted his phone to his ear, shielding it from the rain. He called Amy. "The guards only walk a few yards in each direction."

"Let's move," Lucas said.

They got into their positions, and in the rain, they all seemed to disappear into the night. Lucas scaled the wall using the decorative light fixtures, then reached down and helped her up. They dropped, splashing down on the wet earth, and crept out from under the trees, scanning for the guards. They came up behind the man they were to drop. Lucas knocked him in the head with the butt of his gun, and Amy gagged him and tied his feet while Lucas tied his hands. The worst thing that might happen to him, other than a humongous headache, was he might drown in a puddle.

They ran to the front of the mansion, where they met Eric and Petra. They each gave a thumbs-up and went to the front entrance. Through the massive glass door they saw a guard. They needed to get his attention without his signaling to anyone that something might be up.

When he started to look in their direction, Petra leaned into his view and then out again. Just a glimpse of a beautiful blonde, enough to catch his eye but hopefully not create more than curiosity.

The man opened the door and leaned out. Petra stepped out of the bushes, her arms wrapped around herself. "Thank God someone's home."

Before he could put together that the woman shouldn't be there, Eric came up from the side and knocked him in the back of the head. They pulled him into the bushes and tied him up. Eric gave them a derisive look, but he complied. Amy wasn't sure if he was really as bloodthirsty as he acted, at least most of the time.

They crept inside and closed the door, leaving puddles as they went up the stairs. Eric kept his gun aimed down in case someone walked in from below. Lucas kept his gun aimed up.

The most dangerous part was turning the corner to go down the hall where Darkwell's office was. Eric closed his eyes and remote-viewed it. He held up a finger: one guard. This one they would have to incapacitate immediately. She hated this part. Petra did, too, by the nervous way she wrung her hands.

The men mouthed *one, two, three* and stepped into the hallway, guns aimed. She heard the *thwump* of the silenced guns and a *thump* as a body hit the floor. Lucas and Eric dashed down the hallway, Petra and Amy on their heels. They burst into the second door on the right and found Darkwell and Olivia.

"Freeze, you son of a bitch!" Eric aimed the gun at him. "Where's Nicholas?"

Darkwell's eyes were wide in shock as he stood. Lightning flashed into the room, followed by thunder.

Olivia shot to her feet, feeling both relief and fear that they'd come. "He's *dead*." She could hardly utter the words.

Her father remained calm, his mind calculating behind his dark eyes. "How did you get in here?" He was buying time. Olivia saw Amy watching his hands.

"Where is Nicholas?" Lucas asked again. "He's not dead. You put him in with Sayre."

Not dead. Had she heard that right? Then the other words hit her. She looked at her father. "*You put him in with Sayre?*"

Amy's mouth tightened. "He's as much a monster as Sayre Andrus is. He killed our parents. Yes, we know you had them killed. I haven't had the chance to tell you yet." She turned to Lucas. "Wallace told me not all the subjects' deaths were suicide or accident. Your father and mother were murdered, just like my dad."

Darkwell took a step back, surprise on his expression. "I didn't have them killed. They held the keys to the future of our country." His eyes shone with the truth of that. "Do you think I would destroy what I created?"

His hand slipped down behind the desk and came up with a gun. A flame erupted on his sleeve, and he released the gun with a scream. Another flame started on the other sleeve and in seconds his arms were engulfed. Olivia couldn't believe what she was seeing. Flames, out of nowhere.

The smell of burning hair, then flesh filled the room. Darkwell threw off his jacket, sending it toward the French doors. The heavy drapes instantly caught fire. The flames on the drapes caught the carpet, and a trail moved across the room. The smoke alarm went off, pealing in ear-shattering waves. Round discs fell from the ceiling over the fire and sprinkler heads popped out. What looked like soap bubbles sprayed the fire and spit everywhere.

The foam stung Olivia's eyes, and she covered them. She looked when the sound of the sprinklers ceased a minute later. Her father was gone. The foam hadn't covered every surface, though. The fire still raged along the credenza behind the desk and the top of the drapes.

Eric wiped the foam from his eyes. "Where is he?"

Lucas looked around. "He must have stood beneath one of the sprinklers."

Eric dashed after him. The flames raced across the desk and surrounded it.

Olivia shouted, "We have to find Nicholas! I know where Sayre is!"

She closed the door behind them to keep the flames in the room. A second later, though, it raced beneath the door, across the hall, and set that door aflame. They heard a *whoosh* inside as flame caught to fabric. Outside Darkwell's office, the sprinklers only sprayed water. It wasn't enough to quell the superhot flames Eric had created.

"Oh, my God." Olivia looked to the ceiling, her heart imploding. "Sayre's above that room. And Nicholas . . . his nightmare. He's going to die in the fire."

Nicholas could barely breathe. Sayre leaned over him, his breath washing over him. Rain pelted the window in waves, and thunder made it rattle. The lightning made Sayre look more sinister, almost surreal, in the dimly lit room. He was thoroughly enjoying himself if his smile was any indication.

He lifted a knife. "This is my souvenir from my little foray with Olivia. How fitting that I get to use it on you."

Between the gag and what he thought was a broken jaw, he couldn't talk.

A *thump* got his attention. "Don't know what they're doing down there."

Blood poured out of Nicholas's nose, and his eye was swollen shut. From the excruciating pain, he knew his insides were a bloody pulp. Every breath was tight; he was sure his lung had collapsed.

He wasn't supposed to die like this. Had his fate changed?

For a second he thought the smell of smoke was his imagination. Sayre sniffed the air.

An alarm went off downstairs.

"*Again.*"

Smoke drifted beneath the door to the stairs. Sayre went to the window and twisted to see down. "Holy shit! There's flames coming out the window below this room."

Nicholas didn't think he'd ever welcome the nightmare come to life, but now he did. Burning would be better than dying by Sayre's hand. He managed a smile, though he doubted it looked like one. Sayre would die, too.

They heard a sound below, like a door opening. Sayre turned. Darkwell stood there, gun pointed. With him came the sharp smell of smoke and . . . burnt flesh. His face was blackened on one side, his hair melted. The skin on his hands was blistered.

Sayre tucked the knife behind his back. "Hey, good thing you came to get me out of here!"

"You know too much. I'm afraid you're going to have to—"

Sayre didn't wait for him to finish. He tackled Darkwell, knife out. The gun fired, but the bullet went wild, hitting the wall. Sayre slashed Darkwell's leg, and the man screamed in agony. He kneed Sayre in the groin, and the knife dropped. The men struggled. Damn, if only Nicholas could get the hell out of there. He could hardly move, much less escape. But he could do something. The knife had dropped only a few inches away. He reached out, his fingers touching the handle. He couldn't get a grip on it without moving closer.

Sayre rammed his elbow into Darkwell's back. The men rolled over the knife, grinding Nicholas's fingers into the floor. He tried to pull his hand back but couldn't.

Sayre growled, "You were going to squash me all along, weren't you?"

Darkwell didn't answer. "Did you get into Olivia's dreams? Did you attack her?"

"Yeah, I did. I got out of here and would have had some fun with her if it wasn't for this jerk. And I came back without anyone ever seein' me. That's how smart I am."

Darkwell growled and pulled his hand back. Sayre hit him on the burnt side of his face, and Darkwell screamed again. He staggered to his feet. Sayre jumped up, the stronger of the two.

Nicholas's fingers throbbed, but he forced them toward the knife again. He scooted his body one agonizing inch, enough to wrap his fingers around the handle. Sayre's shoe stomped down toward his hand as the men continued to battle. Nicholas pulled the knife back just before he would have been crushed.

Kill or be killed.

Darkwell would kill him or leave him there to die.

The smoke tickled his throat and burned his eyes. Coughing would be hell. He tried to fight the instinct.

Sayre pushed Darkwell and tore down the stairs. Darkwell fell toward him, his arms wheeling. Nicholas braced himself for the weight of the man falling on top of him. The knife blade was pointing up. He tightened his hand around the handle.

Darkwell twisted around as he fell, facing Nicholas with hatred in his eyes as he landed. Then surprise. Pain.

"No more," Nicholas tried to utter, but the words came out garbled.

Darkwell's body slumped, lifeless, next to him. They would both die there.

He heard thumping on the stairs. Sayre?

"Nicholas!"

Olivia's voice. He struggled to look at her through his one good eye. He couldn't talk, couldn't tell her how her father had ended up there. She stopped cold, taking in the grisly scene.

She dropped down next to him. Petra and Eric came up, too, their hair and clothing covered in what looked like soap bubbles.

Eric took in the scene, too: "You took him out."

Olivia looked at her father and quickly looked away. She turned to Nicholas, her face filled with horror. "He did this to you. My father did this. We've got to get you out of here."

Eric pulled Darkwell's body away. "I can't wait to hear how this happened."

Petra sank to her knees beside Olivia and put her hands on his side. Even that gentle touch shot pain through him. "You're a mess."

Olivia coughed. "What are you doing? We have to get out of here."

"We'll make his injuries worse if we have to carry him out of here. Shh." Petra, eyes closed, leaned over him. Her expression was pained as she flung her head back.

Olivia obviously remembered that Petra could heal. She sat back, hope filling her expression as she watched. He felt the pain ease by degrees. Each breath came a little easier and less painfully. The ache in his ribs subsided. He could breathe. She passed her hands over his face and he felt, actually *felt*, his jaw slide back into place, the ache gone. His eye returned to normal. Petra slumped over, and Eric grabbed her.

Flames erupted through the floorboard as Nicholas got to his feet. "Is she all right?"

Eric hoisted her into his arms. "I don't know. But we better get out of here."

Nicholas grabbed her hand, feeling the heat envelop them. The panic returned. Fire. Flames. Smoke. He was living his nightmare, and now Olivia was in it, too.

Eric carried Petra down the stairs, then the hall.

"Do you need help?" Nicholas asked Eric.

"I've got her. Just go. Lead the way."

Nicholas held Olivia's hand as they raced down the hall toward the stairs. "Where are Amy and Lucas?" he called out to Eric.

"He saw Sayre coming out and went after him. Amy followed. Zoe and Rand are outside."

Smoke was filling the upper area of the foyer. There were no sprinklers there. Apparently Darkwell had only installed the foam ones in his office and a few water ones down the hallway.

Nicholas went first, watching Eric's blind steps, ready to catch Petra if necessary. "Almost there."

Just as they reached the bottom of the stairs, another guard stood, gun at the ready. "Hold it right there."

Eric didn't stop. "Are you friggin' kidding me? The house is on fire!"

Nicholas started to raise his arms in surrender and instead dove at the man. The gun went off, then flew out of the guard's hand. Nicholas heard the man's head hit the marble floor with a *crack*. Nicholas launched up, but the man remained on the floor, blood pooling from beneath his head.

"Move it!" Eric said, stepping over him.

Nicholas looked behind Eric at the flames climbing down the walls, eating their way down wallpaper and
the banister. Chasing them. He could hardly breathe, not
so much from the smoke but panic. Olivia screamed. He
grabbed her hand, and they ran toward the front door. She
opened it, and Eric walked through first and nodded. "Go
that way!"

The rain was letting up but still fell with a steady drone.
The smoke alarm pierced the air. They raced across the
lawn toward the far wall. Two people ran toward them.
Please, not more guards.

No, Lucas and Amy. "What happened to Petra?" Amy
asked, racing to her side.

"She healed Nicholas. What about Sayre?"

"I lost him in the smoke." Lucas looked into the night.

They helped Petra up and over the wall. Rand and Zoe,
as soaked as the rest of them, caught her on the other side.
She mumbled, coming awake.

Amy looked around. "I don't see Magnus and Lachlan."

Sirens wailed in the near distance.

Eric stared at the flames reaching out of every door and
window they could see. "Unfortunately, they're on their
own. We've got to get out of here before the cops and fire
trucks show up."

They carried Petra to the car, and six of them crammed
in. Rand and Zoe ran to the motorcycle and sped off.

As soon as they cleared the street, Nicholas looked at
Olivia, whose face was ashen as she watched the house.

He touched her face. "You're all right."

"I thought you were dead. He told me you were dead.
And you almost were, because of him."

"I'm fine. But . . . I'm sorry it was me who killed your
father."

"He escaped my wrath." Eric, who was driving, looked
at Nicholas. "At least you got the pleasure."

"I didn't want that *pleasure*. But I knew he'd kill me."

Nicholas squeezed her tight, feeling her body shake. He kissed her temple. "I'm sorry all of this had to happen."

"My father was an awful person." Her voice trembled. "I'm sorry for what he did to you. All of you."

Amy reached over and held Lucas's hand. "Do you believe what he said, that he didn't have our parents killed?"

"I . . . I think I do."

"Either way, he deserved to die." Eric turned onto the highway.

Amy's phone vibrated. She answered it. "Magnus! Are you and Lachlan all right? . . . Oh, God, I'm so sorry . . . What is it? . . . Okay, we'll come tonight." She hung up. "They found Richard, but he was locked in the wine cellar. They couldn't get him out before the fire and smoke spread down there. They . . . they had to leave him."

Amy's face was taut with both grief and excitement. "Magnus said we should come to the compound. Richard told him something about the Booster. He said it was going to change everything. And that he wasn't sure we were going to like it."

Amy looked at Olivia. "You, too. Even though you're not an Offspring . . . you are one of us now." She flicked her gaze to Nicholas and gave him a soft smile before turning it to Olivia.

No one objected, not even Eric. Olivia smiled back, relief on her expression.

Nicholas pulled her close. "We don't have to go. You've been through a lot tonight."

She sat back. "I want to know the truth, too."

With Nicholas's help, Petra pulled herself to a sitting position. "So, this is over, right? Darkwell's gone. There's no one else to come after us, no one to protect the program, because there is no program." Her gaze went from one person to another. "Right?"

Olivia nodded. "There's no one else. Fonda, the other Offspring, must have been sent away when my father knew Nicholas might come to rescue me." She sounded tired and sad. "Without my father to direct her, she'll probably go back to her life. The guards are just hired men. Without a paycheck, they have no reason to pursue us. They don't know anything about the program." She let out a soft sigh. "It's over. Except . . ."

"Pope," Nicholas said, finishing her thought, his expression as grave as hers.

"Augh," Petra said. "The new, unknown enemy."

"We don't know if he's the enemy or not. Remember, he let us go, even when we were in his weird building. But he's definitely someone to watch out for."

"And Sayre is still out there," Lucas said. "I bet he's not going away anytime soon."

Petra's eyes glittered with tears. "But mostly it's over. I can't believe it."

Amy reached over and clasped her hand. "We can go back to our lives. Oh, my God, we can really go back to our lives."

Rand looked at Zoe. "We can find a place in Baltimore. You can go back to tattooing."

"Oh, the thought of that." Her dreamy expression faded. "But I'm still a wanted felon. Just because Darkwell's gone doesn't mean those bogus charges he set up are. And the police sure aren't going to believe the truth."

He touched her cheek. "We'll get it figured out, doll. Maybe we'll go to Canada or something. Really start over."

"What about you? What will you do for a living?"

"I'm done with my Robin Hood thing. Maybe I'll use my art in different ways. I do happen to know an art gallery owner."

She let out a sigh and curled up against him. "At least I have you. That's all I care about."

Nicholas pulled Olivia closer again. It wouldn't be over for her, not for a long time.

CHAPTER 42

Olivia and Nicholas walked into his bedroom at the tomb. All she wanted to do at that moment was wash off the smoke and tears. She turned to him as soon as he closed the door. "Take a shower with me. Not because I need you or because I'm afraid to be alone." She took a halting breath. "Because I want you to."

He took her hand and led her into the bathroom. There was something healing about running water. Even the sound soothed the edges of her ragged nerves. A minute later steam billowed into the bathroom. Without words, he undressed her, then she undressed him. After they stepped into the shower, he pulled her close and held her as the warm water washed down her back.

She was trembling, and he bracketed her face with his hands and kissed her. Soft, sweet kisses on her mouth, nose, forehead, that said more than any words could. He stroked her face, his expression full of the same tornado of emotions that tore through her.

She cleared her throat. "If the storm of images Lucas suffers from is worse than what I feel now, I can't imagine how he survives. Thinking you were dead—that bastard told me you were dead—seeing you so beaten I hardly recognized you." She closed her eyes. "Seeing my father ignite, then dead, the tip of a knife sticking out of his back." Her tears were lost in the water raining down from the shower. "I know he was evil, that he was willing to sacrifice even me for his cause. But he was my father."

His eyes were filled with sympathy and pain. "Go ahead. Cry. Scream. Beat my chest."

"Everything is in a ball lodged here." She pointed to her solar plexus with her fist.

He put his hand flat against her stomach. "Let go, babe. You're safe with me."

Those last words did it. They released the dam, and she let it all out in great gushing sobs. He held her, rocking back and forth and whispering against her hair. She couldn't hear his words, but they didn't matter.

Finally, she leaned into the stream of water and washed away the tears. When she moved forward, he wiped away the drops from her forehead.

He looked contemplative, though he forced a smile. "Feel a little better?"

She nodded. "Thank you."

"Don't thank me." He seemed to be struggling with something. Finally he said, "Do you hate me for killing him?"

He had told her how it had happened. She shook her head. "I could never hate you, Nicholas. Never. You don't deserve that guilt. You didn't sign on for this. I'm sorry it was you who had to end it. You had every right to kill him with rage and hatred. But you didn't. It was self-defense, sweetheart."

He released a ragged breath. "Rand was right. Killing someone, no matter the reason, tears you up inside."

"Forgive yourself. My father said many times, people die in war. He would have been honored to die for what he believed in, whether it was right or wrong. Like . . . like any terrorist."

He brushed her long hair from her face, letting his fingers linger against her cheek. "I used to think in terms of black or white, nothing in between. But your father was shades of gray. He had good intentions. That's what you have to remember about him. That's what you got from him: strength; integrity; dedication. But you'll apply those to life far differently than he did."

Tears filled her eyes. "Thank you for that."

He shook his head. "I can't believe I said it myself."

She took his fingers and pressed them to her lips. "I thought I'd lost you. And then when I saw you, I thought I was still going to lose you. Witnessing the miracle of Petra's healing you, I'll never forget how I felt at that moment. When you got up. When you were whole." Her heart lifted even more. "You're not going to die in a fire now. It's done."

He blinked as her words seemed to sink in. "I haven't had time to think about that." He ran his hand over his face, his eyes widening. "For the first time in a long while, I have a future. I can make plans." He took her hands and squeezed them. "But right now, I'm worried about you."

"Don't be. I don't want anyone worried or protecting me again."

As though he hadn't heard a thing she'd said, he pulled her into his arms. "No deal, Livvie. I'm going to worry about you and protect you, for now and always." He leaned back enough to look at her. "But protection and love doesn't mean controlling. You've never had one without the other. Now you do. It's going to take time for you to get used to that, to figure out who you are, what you want. Take as much time as you need. If you want to make wild love every night or if you just want space, which would kill me, I'm your willing slave.

"Now I know how it feels to love someone like my mother and father loved each other, like I see between Lucas and Amy, and Rand and Zoe. But I don't fear losing that love like I used to. Feeling this outrageous love is worth whatever pain I may suffer in losing it someday."

He had said the word *love* before. As she looked in his eyes, she saw it. And felt it, glowing inside her like a warming fire. She touched his face, tracing his mouth. "I may not know who I am, but I have an idea: a little wild, a little sensible, not so much of a rule-follower anymore, not CIA. Definitely Pebbles Bamm-Bamm. I do know what I want: you. I love that you would give me time to figure it out, on my terms. I love that you would help me forgive a man who has done so much to hurt you. But mostly, I love you. And that's all I need to know right now."

"Don't," he said.

She raised her eyebrows. "Don't say I love you?"

He smiled. "Don't ever stop loving me."

"No chance of that."

"We'd better finish up here and find out what's going to change everything . . . again." He looked worried, and she knew that, whatever it was, her father was involved in it.

He paused. "This substance inside us—me—could make me crazy someday."

She wrapped her arms around his waist and looked up at him. "I know that what's inside you is stronger than that. And that we'll handle it together."

They all pulled up to Wallace's compound that evening. A chain that had once stretched across the gravel road was down. Lights intermittently lit the road that led to a square house. Nicholas and Olivia had driven separately, holding hands the entire way.

Everyone got out of the cars, and Rand and Zoe parked the motorcycle. The night was dark, filled with the sound of crickets, a chill in the air—or was it just Nicholas? They stood in front of the open gate that led to a courtyard. Colored lights sprayed the foliage, making it look like a piece of paradise.

A woman's scream pierced the air. Olivia stiffened, fear in her eyes. She'd been through so much.

"It's just a peacock," Amy said. She inhaled deeply, taking them all in. "Are we ready for the truth? He made it sound ominous."

Nicholas noticed they'd all carefully avoided specula-
tion. Or maybe, like him, they just couldn't imagine what
it could be. The chance to discover the truth was the only
thing that kept them from falling into an exhausted sleep.
He brushed his hand against Olivia's cheek, feeling an exquisite mix of joy, love, and protectiveness flow through
him. She closed her eyes and leaned into his touch. She
looked so delicate, so fragile, but he knew her strength.
That strength would get her through these next few hours,
days, and months.

"Nicholas? Olivia?"

He pressed Olivia's hand to his mouth, and they joined
the rest of the group. Amy led the way to the entrance and
pressed the doorbell. She had told him and Olivia about
Magnus and Lachlan and what had happened during the
rescue, so Nicholas assumed the big guy opening the door
in a kilt, his hair a mass of curls, was Magnus.

"Come to the lab," he said without preamble.

The foyer was a narrow hallway, with a door that led out
to another courtyard. Magnus walked through it, his shoulders drooping, his shirt bedraggled and dirty. The shadow
of defeat darkened his eyes. The lights were blazing in one
of the rooms of the square house.

He looked at them when he reached the door to that
room. "Lachlan is beyond himself. Be prepared."

They walked into what looked like a lab hit by a hur-
ricane. Lachlan was sitting among the debris, looking
through a box of pictures. He shot them a bloodshot glare.
"Who started the fire?"

"I did." Eric didn't look the least bit cowed. "I tried to
set the son of a bitch on fire."

Magnus asked, "Is he dead?"

"Yes." Thankfully Eric didn't elaborate.

Lachlan stood and stumbled toward them, stopping in
front of Eric. "So is my father. You could have killed us
all. What the hell were you thinking? Not of us, not of your
people."

Eric followed Lachlan's gaze, looking at Nicholas, at Lucas, then Amy. Something changed in Eric's eyes. The fire of revenge died.

Lachlan tilted his head. "You set people on fire? That's your ability?"

"Yes."

Nicholas didn't see that smug glow Eric had when he'd told Nicholas what he could do.

Lachlan leaned into Eric's face. "I'll bet you think you can control it, because you're so damned powerful. You have no idea what this power can do to you." He nodded to the group. "Or to them. And when you hurt one of your own, you will want to kill yourself every minute of every day, and nothing can take the pain away. But living with it is the best, most appropriate punishment. I don't wish that on you, but I predict it. Because I see in your face what I saw in my own not long ago. Now, when I look in the mirror, I see the hole I put into my mother, the blood, and the pain I have caused all of us. I don't have to be psychic to know you will be seeing the same thing someday." He turned and walked back to the box he'd been organizing.

Those who knew Eric best watched him, expecting a biting response, no doubt. To their surprise, he turned away, not meeting any of their gazes.

Magnus picked up one of the tapes neatly stacked in a box. "Before our father ordered us to leave him there, he told us what's in our bodies." The group fell silent, riveted now on Magnus, on his next words. "He called it Blue Moon. He told me to find this videotape. And he said, 'I hope you can handle the truth.'"

"We can," Amy said.

They nodded in agreement.

He stuck the tape into an old VCR and turned on the television. "We've seen it, but I will let you form your own conclusion."

A younger Richard filled the screen, along with flecks

of static. He was in a lab, but not this one. His expression was bright and shiny with excitement.

"It is October 30, 1984. I have found my most interesting slime mold yet. From the first time I witnessed a meteor shower when I was seven and trudged out in the snow at dawn hoping to find a piece of it, I have been fascinated with slime molds. On that day I found the most interesting blob of slime. I later discovered they're called *powdre ser,* Welsh for star rot. Some call it star jelly or star shoot, that last because it resembles sperm. I prefer *powdre ser.*

"The specimen I found that day disappeared the next morning. From then on, I made it my life's ambition to find more. I learned of stories of *powdre ser* found in backyards, given to NASA for examination, who supposedly found it to be industrial waste. These rare, gelatinous blobs have been found over the centuries and are usually associated with meteor showers. They dry up when the sun hits them.

"I have spent years following sightings of meteor showers and have found four specimens. None exhibit any of the normal characteristics of slime molds other than their jellylike quality. How this jelly survives its entrance into the Earth's atmosphere is a mystery, too."

Lachlan and Magnus watched their father's image with haunted expressions.

Richard walked over to a table and held up a large petri dish filled with an opaque jelly of a blue-violet hue. He lifted it with the gentleness and awe of a man holding his newborn baby for the first time. "I heard about a particularly interesting sighting in Arcadia, Virginia, and immediately dispatched myself there."

Nicholas and Olivia looked at each other. "That's where the aircraft with the eye went down."

Richard wore a conspiratorial expression. "I found this." He wiggled the dish. "The small specimen has grown by

30 percent in four days, something I've never observed in a slime mold before. I've heard what sounds like a heartbeat, faint as can be, though I know it can't be, because it has no heart. And it moves. Moves! I caught it trying to climb over the edge of the dish. I have cut portions away, to no apparent detriment of the entire piece, and studied its nature. Its cell structure compares to nothing in nature or other *powdre ser* I have seen. It is *fascinating*. I think I'm in love."

The screen went blank for a few seconds, then Richard returned. "The date is November 14, 1984. A most unusual thing has happened. I accidentally ingested Blue Moon. I have a bad habit, as my wife is wont to remind me, of eating while in my lab. I was studying Blue Moon whilst eating tuna salad on rye. I had gone for seven minutes, twenty-four seconds to get more to drink, then I returned, immersed in my notes as I ate. I noticed an odd taste after several bites. That was when I looked at my plate and saw that the mass had moved onto my sandwich. I wasn't worried, but I did make note of it, should I die. At least Astrid would know what had happened.

"I didn't die. I did notice that my ability to astral project had increased. Not only could I see my destination—I could touch things, move them." He wiggled his fingers. "And the process was much quicker. I'm sure it's Blue Moon. This has helped me immensely in my work on a classified research program. It is *amazing*. I wonder what would happen if I ingested more?"

Magnus turned off the tape. "Unfortunately, the tape gets warped from here. We've searched, but there's nothing more about BLUE EYES or the program. But you get the idea."

The Rogues looked at each other as the pieces came together.

Amy said, "Your father believed Blue Moon came from a meteorite."

Nicholas shook his head. "He followed a report about a meteor shower, but he never said anything about finding meteorites; just the slime. It wasn't a meteorite. It was the aircraft that crashed, the one I was commissioned to find over twenty years later." He told the MacLeod brothers about the eye.

Zoe's mouth dropped open. "That wasn't a government experimental aircraft, was it?"

Amy's hand came up to her throat. "Are you saying . . . ?"

Nicholas nodded. "What's inside us . . . I think it's extra-terrestrial."

EPILOGUE

He walked among the smoldering ruins of Darkwell's estate. Something was smoldering inside him, too. He had learned enough to figure out that the man had revived the program that had nearly ruined his career twenty-five years ago—and still could.

One of the officers came up to him. "We found three bodies. It'll take some time to identify them."

He hoped Darkwell was one of them.

The witnesses, men Darkwell had hired unbeknownst to the CIA, described a harrowing night. People they knew only as the Rogues had come in, attacking the building and setting it afire. One man had heard them referred to as Offspring.

The offspring of the original program. Darkwell couldn't let it go. He had been obsessed back then, endangering people, their country's reputation, and their careers. Apparently he was still obsessed.

Another officer walked over with a notepad. "I have a list of people who could have been here. There was a woman named Fonda Raine, but she was seen leaving early that day. She has been living here for the last month. Nicholas Braden also lived here until about a week ago, and there was some kind of skirmish involving him."

"Thank you." He spotted a tall man with a shaved head standing alone on the other side of the ruins. "Who's that?"

The officer turned, blocking his view for a moment. "Who?"

The man was gone. "Never mind." He walked back to his car, giving his driver Darkwell's home address. He would discover everything he could about these Offspring and what Darkwell had been up to. He would find the two who'd lived here and question them.

BLUE EYES could not come to light. Not now. Not ever. He would eliminate all evidence . . . including the Offspring.

ACKNOWLEDGMENTS

Antonio "Tony" Sanchez, MSM, CLET, Captain, Biscayne Park Police Department . . . you da best!

To critique buds Marty Ambrose, Diane O'Key, and Lynn Hallberg for all your great advice and input.

Thanks to the Blue Ridge Rollergirls, for letting me hang out and ask questions, especially Moong Chi, Mazel Tov Cocktail, Freckles Kaboom, Skelly Tor, and Candy Korn.

My everlasting thanks to my fans, friends, and all the cool people who love books!

Megan O'Hearn, Nicole Tedesco, Pat Hommel, Verna Johnston, Michael Joy, Josh Romm, ShaRee Parker, Shannon Emmel, Marilyn Campbell, Bernice Renkawek, Tabatha Holley, Diana Di Giacomo, Kandy Russell, Stephanie, Linda Henderson, Christina Greenawalt, Janae Wilson, Amie Hennigan, Cathleen Heredia, Joy Traversie, Nancy Viviani, Kristie Campbell, Lyndsee T, Denise Pallotta, Barbara Stewart, Charissa Butta, Beverly Maddox, Stacey Liptack, Monica Pulliam, Paula Mellody, Rebecca Seals, Jerri Rubio, Mariska Hadienns, Sheryl Brown, Sam Ballard, Heather Stuhler, Jackie Jenkins, Emily Kocevar, Ann Garber, Tristen Tharp, Sherry Mackintosh, Trudy Jones, Anastasia Maria Dawn Poole, Joanne Hering, Raeanne Ayers, Becky Thornton, Carmen Rexford, Tammie King, Carolyn Deaton, Sherry Strode, Beverly Gordon,

Amber Hall, Julie Fine, Suzette Finks, Tracey Dent, Jeanette Bowman, Carol Luciano, Dani Batth, Ericka Nile, Ashton Ross, Rhea Alder, Melissa Inez Ramirez, Frana Lokas, Amanda Ross, Aerynna, Joan Woods, Maggie Johnson, Kate Martin, Sarah Johnson, Joanne Mosher, Naomii Willis, Linda Beane, Teonda Tollison, Jessica, Amanda DeViese, April Strength, Sabrina, Linda Tremper, Betty Ivy, Timothy O'Berry, Suzie Shakespeare, Elena LaMotte, Jennie Hutchinson, Janet Kay Gallagher, Allyson Van Zandt-Cox, Tracey Britton, Diana Fike, Melissa Mulvihill, Amanda Toth, Anna Dougherty, Adeline Despinos, Lori Quest, Kandy Russell, Karen Witkowski, Deidre Durance, Sherrie Trick, Stephanie Trezza, Shelly Ash, Judy Jeanes, Aryssa Ivy, Brett McDavid, Patricia Harris, Kathy Turrell, Kara Gibson, Christy Hawkes, Shontell Henagan, Sandra Martin, Elizabeth Buckel, Roxanne Rhoads, Dawn White-Raymer, Diane Sadler, Margie Whitten, Lyndsey Leask, Rudolf Spoerer, Arlene Medder, Anna-Marie Highlander, Danielle Atwater, Dana Wade, Sandyra O'Meara, Sheila Corriveau, Cecilia Bedigrew Huddleston, Susan Galley, Marlee Abbott, Sharon Mostyn, Jason Budisic, Cindy Freitas, Leah Lohden, Mary Lynch, Alicia Hall, Amanda Schoeffler, Christine Jones, Leslie Brown, Nikole (Niko) Abrams, Robyn Fort, Angela MacRae, Sandy, Crystal Fulcher, Trina Chase, Julia Sciavolino, Taschima De Marco, Tami Bates, Isaac Hedrick, Virginia Cantrell, Christaline Crain, Cec Smith, Melanie Baxter, Amanda G., Vikki Parman, Krystal Wilson, Kimberly Stockman, Kerry Morgan, Angi, Roxanne Korpal, Martin Vidal, Rita Smith, Gina Gallo, Veronika Wright, Lisa Douglas, Dana Allison, Stacy Stewart, Beth Browne, Teresa, Kelly Steed, Karen Lawrence, Jeanette Hornby, Larissa Benoliel, Brook Dale, Jacqueline Tierney, Kimberly Lizan, Ali Flores, Kara Gajentan, Janice Murphy, Bella Franco, Shannon Daniels, Donna Locklin, Vanessa McQuaid, Krystal Merideth, Melissa Mason, Cara R. Fisher, Annetta Stolpmann, Marita Mondares, Elizabeth Parzino, Kristi Herbrand,

Dawn Detkowski, Kelli Jo Calvert, Kara Conrad, Cari
Emmel, Shanell Tanaka, Angel Tanaka, James Cook, Lori
Sears, Vanessa Hunter, Erin Magner, Whitney Reynolds,
Vanessa Alicea, Christina Baxter-Perry, Lorraine Larose,
Joshua Mello, Adrianne Gelatt, Kelly Crissy Nickerson,
Lacey Ferris, Caroline Allard, Zina Lynch, Gayla Gale,
Lisa Freitas, Marlene Planko, Shannon Clark, Michelle M.
Santiago, Dina Stornello, Nikki Hilton, Carlina Richardson,
Vasiliki McDonald, Rachael Grime, Beverly Bennett,
Guiomar Calvo, Karen O'Connor, Reynolds Bond, Ronin
Demarco, Katie Ankrom, Candy Manring, Dawn Rhoades,
Joshua Mc Neil, Kristin Sanders, Renee Marmolejo, Gavin
Bolling, Crystalyn Burns, Keith Dylan, Stacy Walker, Laura
McLaughlin, DeAnne Chappell, Jennifer Henry, Cassandra
Buziba, Rachael Dimond, Raymond Wahl, Linda Hinckley,
Scott Romanski, Kate Bourne, Ayliphelet Ramirez, Amy
Lynn Rhodes, Maria Olsen, Dana Nelson, Roberta Dixon,
Nicole Cruz, Sarah Mason, Jason Trimble, Cassandra
Billerman, Jennifer Baker, Kandace Scarsella, Dawn
Saunders, Lily Wirth, Barbara Shedlock, Tara Woods,
Jennifer & Matthew Roberts, Alexsis Atkinson, Jane Chase,
Tara Colletti, Nicola, Carin Forero, Barbara Ryan, Karen
Sopprani, Vernice Bates, Stephanie Dawe, Deanna Roy,
Abigail Rodriguez, Andrea, Eleni, Fiction Vixen, Rebecca
Taylor, Susan Lathen, Natasha Carty, Jenny Ng, Shannon
James, Amy Santos, Hilda Oquendo, Lisa Richards, Jessica
Fishman, Glowie Bruner, Lindsey Proper, Ivonne Suarez,
Cynthia Ziegler, Stephenia Disabella, Shannon Cooper,
Connie, Maya Jimshitashvili, Renee Jones, Maria Gonzalez,
Ralph Sharninghouse, Lea Ellen Borg, Jennifer Howard,
Lisa Jass, Alexa Nagasue, Kaitlin Adolf, Lyra Rose, Sarah
Richardson, Carolina Alejandra Delgado Valentin, Andre,
Misti Lancaster, Jobie Marshall, Wendy Cueto, Kimberly
Long, Caitlin Day, Pamala Burnsworth, Lea Johnson,
Corrine Leegstra, Danielle Jordan, Lisa Glidewell, Veda
Martin, Sarah-Lynn Giese, Jessica Richardson, Kimberly
Cockerill, Kelsie McKibben, Patricia Kasner, Michaelene

Werth, Cinquetta Allen, Juanita Stender, Nadia Davis,
Lakisha Spletzer, Holly Vanderhule, Isabella Lenora
Wilson, Michelle Rossignol, Loretta Wheeler, Patricia
Cochran, Carla Ribeiro, Jennifer Caillouet, Christina Groll,
Brittany Franklin, Charles Motin Jr., Amber Polo, Heather
Foster, Stephanie Martin, Stephanie Willis, Rebeca Garcia,
Lexie Davis, Elaine Pavlu, Christi Caudill, Theresa Ratliff,
Tina Protheroe, Rebecca Santa, Deva Perez, Ha'ani Perez,
Jeanne Miro, Shelly Itkin, Heather Harris, Joanne Hicks,
Lisa Philpot, Heather Burch, Rosemarrie Charles-Douglas,
Felicia Plastini, Kristen Gaul, Cherie Michalec, Montrell
White.

Here's a sneak peek at
BURNING DARKNESS
Book Four in the Offspring series!

Fonda Raine perched on the edge of her sofa and watched the morning news, riveted to the footage from the night before about a Potomac, Maryland, estate on fire. In the glow of the flames licking at the night sky, vile smoke spewed up and disappeared into the darkness. Her fingers curled into the orange velvet cushion, cramping the muscles. Not just any estate. She had lived there for the last month, worked there, loved and lost. Now the estate was gone, and investigators were speculating, so was Darkwell. She knew who had started the fire. The same son of a bitch responsible for Jerryl's death: Eric Aruda.

He had always been an enemy. First, because he was one of the Rogues. Then the battle became personal between Eric and Jerryl. When Eric set Jerryl on fire, while she and Jerryl were making love, for God's sake, Eric had become her personal enemy.

She hugged the cushion tight, wishing it were Jerryl. Watching the flames on television brought those horrible moments back: Jerryl's scream of pain, the eruption of flames, the ungodly smell of burning flesh. She had been right there and couldn't help him. She'd thrown a blanket over him to smother the flames, but it was too late. She still had nightmares, still heard his screams of agony, and worse, the silence of death.

She couldn't continue with her life, couldn't feel worthy of taking another breath if she didn't kill Eric. For revenge, yes. That was reason enough, but she had another, higher reason: for Darkwell, for her country, to complete the mission Jerryl never got the chance to.

Her eyes narrowed as hatred flowed through her veins. "Eric, if you weren't one of the three bodies they found in the rubble, you'll wish you had been." She doubted that he was dead. The man seemed to be immortal.

All she had left was revenge. It would fuel her, drive her, sustain her until Eric was dead.

She had only been able to use her powers in training sessions. Darkwell had given the important missions to Jerryl and Nicholas Braden. Maybe Darkwell had dismissed her because she was a woman, a petite woman at that. She would show them—no, there was no one but herself to show. That was okay. What had she accomplished in her twenty-two years? Survived growing up in a drug-infested neighborhood with a strung-out father. Fought off a rapist with a razor blade. Managed a vintage clothing store. She'd always told herself she could kill if another sleazy tweak-head tried to force himself on her. She was tough, more than tough. She could definitely kill Eric.

She walked to the kitchen and pulled out a piece of paper and pen from the drawer, then slid into the ice-cream parlor chairs at the table. She stared at the purple lava lamp she used as her centerpiece and brainstormed ways to accomplish her task.

With Darkwell gone, the Rogues no longer had to hide or keep the psychic shield. She should have access to Eric. She would astral project to wherever he was. The only drawback to her ability was that her ethereal form was visible at the target location. If he saw her pop in, he'd probably know who she was and that she was targeting him.

Someone knocked on her door. She rarely had visitors. Her open and charming personality, of course. She peered through the door's peephole to see a man she didn't recognize.

"What do you want?" she called out.

"Fonda Raine?"

"Yes."

"John Westerfield with the FBI. I'm here to ask you about your work with Gerard Darkwell."

She tried to get a better look at him. He wore a simple

suit, hair brushed back in a neat style, posture straight and businesslike, sort of Fox Mulder-ish, she supposed. She'd had a terrible crush on David Duchovny in the *X-Files* days. He wanted to believe in monsters and psychic abilities, and in oddities like her. The man at her door was handsome, but he was no Fox. She swiped the switchblade she kept in the red acrylic telephone stand by the door and pressed it behind her back as she opened the door.

"Yes?"

The man was probably in his late forties, his brown hair streaked with silver. He glanced in both directions before saying, "You may already know that Gerard Darkwell is—"

"Dead." She'd almost spit out the word. "Yes, I know." She heard the tremble in her voice. She had no feelings for the man, but hell, it still affected her.

"The FBI is studying the, shall we say, unusual project you were working on with him. With the fire, some of the data is lost. I need you to fill in the gaps."

"Will the FBI continue the project?"

"Possibly."

She liked doing important, top secret work. For the first time in her life, *she* had felt important. And the money had been great, enough to give her a cushion of security she'd never had.

"Your ID?"

He showed her a badge that certainly *looked* authentic.

"Come in."

For the next half hour they talked about DARK MATTER, the Rogues, and she even managed to tell him about what Eric had done to Jerryl without breaking down. Barely. She didn't, however, tell him her plans. He taped their conversation with a digital recorder. After she told him Darkwell had sent her home because he'd suspected there'd be trouble that night, the agent abruptly stood.

"Thank you, Ms. Blaine. I don't have to tell you that this remains a highly classified subject that should not be discussed with anyone. I trust you haven't."

"Who would believe me?"

"True."

"Do you believe me?"

"We'll be in touch."

She watched him walk to a black sedan parked out on the street and get in, though the car remained in its spot for several minutes. She backed away from the window. Tonight, she would pay a visit to Eric Aruda. And if she was lucky, tonight he would die.

The man posing as John Westerfield closed the car door and dialed his brother. He knew Malcolm would be in a private place awaiting his call.

"It's Neil. Darkwell was doing exactly what we suspected. He re-created the program with the offspring of the original program. Blaine seems to know nothing about that part."

He could feel Malcolm's fury pulsing in the silence but knew restraint would overcome it. After all, restraint had been bred into them from birth.

"Why didn't he come to me?" he said at last, a rhetorical question, but Neil answered anyway.

"Because he knew you would shut him down. You have a lot more to lose now if this gets out. There are seven offspring who are an immediate problem. Darkwell called them Rogues. Interestingly, his daughter ran off with one of them."

He chuckled. "I'll bet he loved that. First take out Blaine. We don't want her mouthing off to anyone about all this."

Neil's mouth watered. "Now? She's still in her apartment, so small, my fingers could go around her neck twice."

"You're salivating, aren't you?"

Neil swallowed the excess saliva. "It's been a long time since I've been able to kill someone."

"Not now. We have to be very careful. Everything we've worked for is at stake. Someone might have seen you. Wait.

Watch her. She's bound to go someplace where you can take her out neatly and quickly. Then you can work on finding the rest of them. You'll get to kill plenty."

Eric Aruda stared at his reflection in the bathroom mirror. He had alien DNA in him. That friggin' rocked. Yeah, it was freaky, but it opened up possibilities. What could he do? Who were his ancestors?

The Rogues had finally found out what substance their parents had been given while they were in the first classified program: meteorite slime. Something extraterrestrial had boosted their psychic powers, and the Offspring had inherited that as well as their abilities.

He flopped down in bed, but his eyes were open, his brain wired awake. Why couldn't he sleep?

Psychosis.

The warning he'd gotten echoed in his head. Another offspring had suffered from sleeplessness right before he went whacked and killed his mother. Eric hadn't slept since he'd burned Jerryl.

"Too much on your mind, that's all."

He opened his nightstand drawer and took out a Ho Ho. As his teeth sunk into the chocolate cake, his mind went to his next task: find Sayre Andrus, who'd been menacing the Rogues. Then Eric would stop using his pyromania, unless absolutely necessary. He no longer had the taste for watching the flames. Yes, he'd felt victory when he'd sent Jerryl to his fiery hell, but something had changed in him, erasing that sensuous pull of destruction. He wasn't even pissed that he hadn't been the one to kill Darkwell.

There was one other enemy Offspring out there. Fonda Raine could astral project, which was like remote-viewing; nothing deadly there. He didn't feel the need to hunt her down. There could be others, though, who should know about their heritage, their skills. He would find them.

But first, he had to sleep.

* * *

Fonda waited until four in the morning, when she thought Eric would likely be asleep. She stared at the bathroom mirror. During DARK MATTER, they had learned that she retained her overall appearance when she projected, though it was diaphanous in nature. Nicholas might have described her to the Rogues, and perhaps they'd even seen her. She had to change her look.

"It's wartime."

Her blond hair curled up just past her shoulders, giving her a soft look. Jerryl had said he liked it that way. Even the diamond stud in her nose and quadruple piercings on her right ear lent no toughness. Now she had to become a warrior. Like she had when she was thirteen and her father's drug buddies began to see that the sulky girl was becoming a woman. When one of them had gone too far. She'd chopped off her long hair and camouflaged her body in oversized clothing.

She'd been entranced by Helen Slater in the movie *The Legend of Billie Jean* who'd cut her blond hair as she prepared for war in a beachside town. Fonda grabbed the shears from the kitchen drawer and stared at the mirror. Her mouth in a tight line, her eyes narrowed in determination, she cut her hair. Hanks of light blond hair rained into the sink. When she was done, she gave her reflection the hard smile of someone with a hard task in front of her.

"Time to kick Aruda ass."

She dug into the cabinet beneath the sink and pulled out a box of hair dye. Thirty minutes later she had a dark pink streak on her right side. Her fingers sifted through her locks, still longish in front and short in back. She reclined on her bed and got into the meditative state she'd been getting into since she was twelve, when escaping her surroundings became imperative to her sanity.

The memory of the picture of Eric that used to be on Jerryl's bulletin board filled her mind. Her soul lifted out of her body. She loved the weightlessness of this state, the freedom. The humming sound started here, pleasant but pervasive.

All around her, clouds swirled like a gentle tornado, sweeping her through the ether. She had learned to go along for the ride, keeping her mind clear. The humming turned into a loud buzzing that hurt her ears and vibrated right through her. Just when she couldn't stand it anymore, the sound faded, the clouds cleared away, and she stood in a bedroom.

A light on the nightstand was on. She scanned her surroundings. Eric, not dead. He was lying on the bed, his head propped up slightly on the pillow. Her heart sprang to her throat. His eyes were open and staring right at her! She was about to return to her physical body but stopped. He hadn't reacted. His stare was . . . blank. Was he dead, after all?

She shifted her gaze down to his chest, which rose and fell evenly. Then lower. He was lying on top of the rumpled sheets naked. Where Jerryl had been wiry and lean, Eric was . . . well, he was just big. *Everywhere.* She forced her gaze farther down to his legs, then back up to his massive chest. If she had a twin sister, they could both recline on top of him without falling off. His body was absolutely magnificent.

Who cares? Who freaking cares! That body is going to be lifeless. Dead!

But *her* body wasn't lifeless. She felt her etheric body stir. Her self-hatred cut into her soul like jagged bits of glass.

You worthless bitch. This man killed the love of your life. And here you stand feeling . . . aroused. Slut! Whore!

She shoved her gaze back to Eric's face. Even slack, his expression retained a hardness. She knew he was deadly. She'd overheard Darkwell and Robbins talking about the two agents he'd torched and the one he'd shot. His icy blue eyes were glazed. Bloodshot. He was in some kind of catatonic state. Maybe drunk, though she didn't smell liquor. Couldn't miss that smell on someone who'd passed out. Drugs maybe.

His questionable state made it tricky. What if he was aware of her and pretending to be out of it until she made a move? Not that he could hurt her, but if he saw her, she would lose the element of surprise. Getting to him would be a lot harder.

She studied him, watching for the slightest twitch to give away his awareness. His face was slack, square mouth slightly open. His breathing didn't change.

With a groan, he shifted to his side. Okay, he definitely wasn't conscious. He wouldn't put himself in a more vulnerable position where he couldn't see her. She advanced on him and stopped beside his bed, tensed for any sudden movement. After several minutes, she relaxed.

Through Darkwell's training, she'd learned she had the ability to touch objects at the target location. She and Jerryl had had much fun with that. She would astral project into his bedroom and wake him in quite intimate ways. They had been working on achieving astral sex, and the practice had been delicious.

Again, her heart ached, and she pushed the thought away. *Focus. Grief will weaken you.*

Though she was good at projecting, she was like an astronaut in a space suit when it came to manipulating physical objects. Her movements were clumsy and unwieldy. She searched the small room for something she could use as a weapon. The walls were covered in original artwork, and every piece depicted either a couple in a provocative position or a naked woman in a sensual pose.

She reached for the lamp on the nightstand. It had sharp edges at the base. If she could manage to smash it down on his temple, she could render him unconscious. Then she could keep bashing him until he was dead.

She concentrated and grabbed at the lamp. She couldn't grip it. It tipped. *No, don't fall!* She swung her ghostlike hand to keep it from toppling over. She couldn't feel the cold brass, only a dense energy. She pushed it back, and it settled on the surface.

Damn. Now what?

She doubted she'd have the strength to strangle him in his sleep. Even if she were there physically, she probably couldn't do it. She'd tried working with a knife but couldn't get a strong enough grip on it. She might as well be wearing boxing gloves.

She looked at him. The light gilded the coarse hairs on legs as thick as pilings. His chest was deep, and she could just see his indent of ribs beneath his pale skin. Big, strong . . . cruel murderer.

And I can't do a damned thing about it.

Frustration swamped her. She would have to keep working on her skills. How long would it take?

Eric rolled onto his back and looked right at her. This time he saw her. He rubbed his eyes.

"Great. Now I'm friggin' hallucinating women." His voice was slurred.

He closed his eyes and opened them again. "Still there." He closed them for another few seconds and reopened them. "Maybe something good'll come of sleep deprivation." He reached out to her. "Come here, beautiful, and gimme some love. I'll take it any way I can get it, real or imagined."

Sleep deprivation. That was why he was acting out of it. So he wasn't totally awake but not asleep, either. Her gaze slid down to his penis, which was now rock hard. And he wanted her.

Again, her body stirred, and she chastised herself. That was Jerryl's fault, in a way. After years of associating sex with lewdness, fear, force, and just plain depravity, then a couple of safe but boring encounters, she'd stuffed her sexuality deep down inside her. Jerryl had awakened her. For the last month she'd had crazy, hard, wild sex at least once a day with him, and her body craved it now.

The last person on earth she wanted to have sex with was Eric Aruda. As delicious as his body looked, she only had one intention for him: murder.

His eyes had drifted shut, his hand lying on the bed

stretched out toward her. She had to get out of there, think of another way to get to him.

Wait. She could use this. She might not be able to kill him psychically. So she would have to do it physically. The plan clicked into place. Eric was obviously hungry for sex, and he thought she was a hallucination. Could she seduce her enemy? Did she have seductress in her? Well, she'd seduced Jerryl, she supposed. He hadn't wanted a distraction from his all-important work, but she'd kept working on him, drawn to him for many reasons.

Maybe she could plant an idea in Eric's mind to meet her somewhere for the real thing. When he showed up, she would obviously have to play dumb. She couldn't admit she was the one he was seeing in his sort-of dreams, after all. Then he'd suspect something. No, she'd pretend she was just at the same place, wanting the same thing he did. And once she got him alone, maybe in a cheap hotel room, she would drug him and tie him to the bed so he couldn't use his strength or his deadly ability.

But she wanted him to know why she was killing him. Oh, yes, he would know. So she'd wait until he started to come out of it and tell him who she was and why she was killing him. She had no doubt she could. The hard part would be pushing back her hatred enough to seduce him.

Use your own sexual hunger. You're only doing this for Jerryl. Spies have to do shit like this. Mata Hari or whatever her name was, I think she slept with the enemy. Forget who he is, what he's done. Focus on just the physical aspect of his body. He is beautiful physically. The hate can come when you're driving a knife into him.

She reached out and touched his arm, and he opened his eyes again. Her fingers slid around his elbow and down his forearm. Like when she'd touched Jerryl, Eric's energy was so thick and hot, it was almost like touching his skin. She forced a smile, slightly sly and coy. "Hi, sexy."

"Who are you?"

She leaned closer and pressed her lips against his neck, wishing instead she was strangling it.

"This isn't real." His words were a half groan.

Her hand slid over his chest and across his stomach. "But doesn't it feel good?"

His answer was another groan, and he tilted his head back and closed his eyes in ecstasy. She knew he could feel her, her touch as soft as cashmere, with the same heat she felt from him.

She closed her eyes for a moment, reliving how it felt with Jerryl, wishing it were him. She didn't think she would ever feel this again. The heat, the intensity, only came with touching another person like her. She'd experimented on Darkwell, no, not touching him like this, and she'd felt no heat. He couldn't hear her, either.

She teased all around Eric's erection, dipping her fingers between his thighs and then up to the pale skin of his pelvis. He was tense, making every muscle stand out, sculpting his body like one of those statues she'd seen in pictures.

He reached out again, and his hand went through her ethereal body. "My . . . imagination," he whispered, a shadow of agony on his expression.

"Maybe," she said, giving him her coy smile again.

"Who . . . are . . . you?"

She liked that he couldn't catch his breath as she moved her hands over his body. So far, she had him just where she wanted him. "Call me whatever you'd like."

He laughed, soft and husky. "This has got to be a dream, which means I'm finally asleep. Thank God." He looked up at her. "I'll call you Tawny. Come here, Tawny. I want you to sit on me. Since you're just a dream, I'm going to grind into you and suck you and eat you raw."

She leaned down, as though to do much more than just place a kiss on his stomach. That close, she could see a fine dusting of golden hairs over his stomach. She bet his skin was soft and that those hairs would tickle her lips, and if she impaled herself on his massive erection and drove her fingernails into his chest when she came . . .

Shock and disgust threw her out of her mission. She blinked to find herself in her bed, covered in a fine sheen of perspiration. Her breath came in shallow pants. The worst, the absolutely worst part was the throbbing between her legs.

She got to her knees and smacked her forehead against the wall. "Whore! Slut!" Her body had responded to her enemy's. She was weak, a traitor worse than Nicholas Braden. "Piece of trash."

Those were her stepmother's words, echoing in her brain as they often did. And now they were hers, and she deserved every one of them. Back then, no. Now . . . yes.

With her forehead pressed against the wall, she banged her fists on either side of her head. Big, gulping breaths kept away her fury and tears. The fatigue rushed in, and she sagged back onto the bed.

"Jerryl, I will do this for you, love. I'll kill him even if I have to die trying."

Eric blinked as the sexy nymph disappeared. He propped himself up on his elbows and looked around. Was he dreaming? He felt very much awake, just as he'd been for the last many days.

He even pinched himself and felt the pain of it. Damn. Awake. Bleary-eyed, rubber-brained, but awake. He dropped back on the bed.

"Hell. I *am* hallucinating."

This wasn't good. He was one step away from insanity. First visions of naked women because it had been way too long since he'd had sex. And then what? Would he see the enemy sneaking in with guns and kill them, only to discover he'd killed his friends?

He had rushed headlong into dangerous situations since Darkwell had entered their lives. He'd faced death. Never had he felt afraid. What the sleeplessness and hallucinations meant . . . the prospect scared the hell out of him.

Next month, don't miss these exciting new love stories only from Avon Books

Seven Secrets of Seduction by Anne Mallory
She might not be part of society, but Miranda Chase is just as captivated as everyone else by the salacious book that has the *ton* atwitter. When she writes an editorial about it that draws a debaucherous viscount to her uncle's bookshop, Miranda's quiet life will never again be the same.

Sugar Creek by Toni Blake
Rachel Farris returned to Destiny with one mission: protect her family's apple orchard from the grasping Romo clan. But hard-nosed, sexy Mike Romo is the law in town, and he won't back down until his family gets what's rightfully theirs. This longtime feud is about to heat up with electricity that neither anticipated.

Tempting a Proper Lady by Debra Mullins
Captain Samuel Breedlove needs to stop Annabelle Bailey's wedding. Priscilla Burke is desperate for it to go on. As the proper lady and questionable gentleman meet head to head, it seems a seduction—with unforeseen consequences—might be in order.

When Marrying a Scoundrel by Kathryn Smith
When her dashing husband left to seek his fortune, heartbroken Sadie Moon made a new start for herself. A successful businessman, Jack Friday has everything he ever wanted… except Sadie. But when their paths cross under most unexpected circumstances, will their undeniable attraction rekindle a love once lost?

Unforgettable, enthralling love stories,
sparkling with passion and adventure
from Romance's bestselling authors

At Avon Books, we know your passion for romance—once you finish one of our novels, you find yourself wanting more.

May we tempt you with . . .

- **Excerpts** from our upcoming releases.

- Entertaining **extras,** including authors' personal photo albums and book lists.

- Behind-the-scenes **scoop** on your favorite characters and series.

- **Sweepstakes** for the chance to win free books, romantic getaways, and other fun prizes.

- Writing **tips** from our authors and editors.

- **Blog** with our authors and find out why they love to write romance.

- **Exclusive content** that's not contained within the pages of our novels.

Join us at
www.avonbooks.com

AVON   *An Imprint of* HarperCollins*Publishers*
www.avonromance.com